ARLENE McFARLANE

A Valentine Beaumont Mystery

ISBN-13: 978-0-9953076-3-6

Published by ParadiseDeer Publishing
Canada

Cover Art by Janet Holmes
Formatting by Author E.M.S.

Acknowledgments

First, my warmest thank you to my dear readers for loving Valentine! Your enthusiasm for her adventures delights me.

My deepest respect and gratitude to these amazing people for giving so generously of their time and knowledge:

Chief Scott Silverii, Ph.D., for your friendship and insightful answers on police investigations. Any mistakes I've made are my own.

The nuns at Mount St. Mary's Abbey, for their kindness and for explaining monastic life.

Tracy Brody ~ the Ethel to my Lucy. You pushed me to tell the best story possible. You're a valued and trusted friend!

My sister, Rosemary, for helping me keep my Boston setting real. Any detours I made were strictly to entertain.

Friend and believer, Susan Pitcher, for your encouragement and for providing your maiden name to a character. You're an incredible lady, and your faith in me is a gift I cherish.

My extremely talented team: My editor ~ Karen Dale Harris, formatter ~ Amy Atwell, cover artist ~ Janet Holmes, and proofreader ~ Noël Kristan Higgins. Without you ladies, this book wouldn't be what it is.

New York Times Bestselling Authors Liliana Hart and

Denise Swanson, for your heartfelt endorsements. Knowing that writers of your caliber enjoyed my story gives me the inspiration and courage to sit down every day and do what I love most.

My dear husband and children ~ words will never express how much I treasure your love and support. You're my life, and I thank the Lord each day for you.

Lastly, thanks to God for Your love, for blessing me with a passion for creativity, and for reminding me all things are possible through You.

To my husband, John:
My rock and my own hero. I love you.

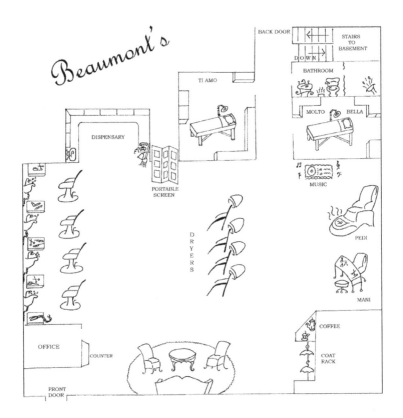

Beaumont's

Chapter 1

Max licked powder off a Friar Tuck's jelly donut, his gaze on the last stylist who'd traipsed out the door into the pouring rain. "What was wrong with this interviewee? You don't like stylists who wear leather shorts and are covered in body tattoos?"

I slashed a red mark through the latest applicant's name, then flung my pen on my desk. If I'd known owning a salon would be this much hassle, I would've made a career in music, or as a stand-in bridesmaid. "It was the harness and outer suede thong I had a problem with."

He stared me down like a Queen Bee. "You need to unleash your wild side, girl. Did you see the handcuffs that guy was toting? He made Marilyn Manson look like Justin Bieber."

And if I had a dollar for every one of Max's smartass comments, I'd be richer than Oprah. Truth was, Max was my sidekick, my Steady Eddie, my confidant. Although I was beginning to wonder about that, too. "I don't need to unleash my wild side. I'm perfectly happy running a dysfunctional salon with a nosy staff member questioning my every move."

"You know what your problem is, lovey? You're too fussy."

Oh boy. Here we go. Not only did I have an unstable

business since the second murder I'd gotten involved in this past June in my salon, but I needed a new employee. Plus, I had to get Max off my back.

"This one's too quiet. That one's too loud." He flapped one hand at me while he balanced his donut in the other. "For Pete's sake, you had Godzilla working here until a few months ago. What made you hire *her*?"

"I'm trying to enjoy my breakfast. Let's not talk about Phyllis." I felt my eyes cross simply thinking about my distant cousin on my mother's side. Distant meaning in the same league as horses being related to asses—I mean donkeys. Phyllis Murdoch couldn't find anyone who appreciated her lack of skill at beautifying others, and she was forced on me by my Grandma Maruska's dying wish. And disobeying a dying wish in a Ukrainian family was even worse than wearing white after Labor Day.

I could see Max debating the wisdom of pursuing this line of questioning. After all, why would a seemingly normal boss keep on such a failure for so long? With my heavy mortgage on the salon, employing someone without talent was professional suicide. But being related to Phyllis was my secret, and I intended to keep it that way.

He held my stare for a moment longer, then gave me his it's-your-life shrug and took a dainty bite of his donut.

I sighed, relieved by his withdrawal, yet still anxious I was having no luck finding a qualified replacement. Three days before it was officially fall, and I'd already wasted half my Monday morning in my eight-by-eight cubbyhole of an office, interviewing unsavory applicants. The rain pelting on the roof didn't help lighten my mood either.

I patted my temples with cotton pads splashed with peppermint essential oil, hoping it'd ease the low-grade headache I couldn't afford. I had rollers to wind at Rueland Retirement this afternoon. I preferred to go there in a cheerful mood.

I fixed my stare on the final candidate's name. "Hmm. J. de Marco." Maybe I'd saved the best for last. "I hope this one's an answer to my prayer. I don't think I can handle another fruitcake."

Max stopped squeezing red jelly into his mouth and gave me an accusatory glare. "Watch who you're calling a fruitcake. Anyway, I'm here to help, so the next one will be it. And if it means never seeing Phyllis's ugly mug again, I'd work with Attila the Hun."

"He's dead."

"See? Even the dead seem more appealing." He leaned his elbows on the sales counter beside my office door, eyeing the rainfall outside with the curiosity of a child.

Despite myself, I smiled at Max. His streaked hair wisped forward, and his cargo pants and red-and-white striped shirt made him look more like a gondolier than a thirty-one-year-old stylist. With Max, it was all about presentation.

I was reflecting on how beautifully he coordinated with the twinkling lights and grapevines in my Mediterranean-themed salon when suddenly the air shifted and the ground vibrated. I paused eating my Boston cream and waited for the pictures on the walls to stop rattling. Thankfully, the racket only came from the monstrous roar of a motorcycle, and its engine finally cut.

Seconds later, the front door swung open, and a damp breeze swept away the last sting of ammonia that had hung in the shop since Saturday. Max's legs buckled, and his jaw unhinged. Probably because someone had the nerve to park on the sidewalk out front when there was a perfectly rutted parking lot next door.

I wolfed down the last hunk of pastry and turned the corner from my office so I could see who had tied Max's tongue.

Standing at six three—or four—was a man dressed in black leather from his jacket down to his snakeskin boots. I gawked like I'd spotted Hercules in the flesh. I coughed out a few crumbs, the weight of my sparkly bracelet suddenly so heavy I absently clunked it on the sales counter. The man tore off his helmet and shook his streaked blond hair into a long windswept style that covered his ears. His roots, the color of a panther's coat, added to his ruggedness.

Water dripped from his jacket, his shoulders slightly hunched like big men did who were used to ducking through doorways. He looked from the twinkling lights on the walls to the four wood-framed mirrors at each station, his full mouth nearly grinning in his well-defined mocha face. Despite the grin, he looked menacing. If he'd worn an eye patch and brandished a sword, I'd have fainted instantly.

I feathered a stray bang behind my ear and licked custard off my lips. Max stood there dumbstruck, or rather, hunk-struck.

Well, one of us had to take control, and it looked like it was going to be all five-foot-four of me. I yanked up the shoulder on my green, loose-knit top, and elbowed Max aside. Most likely, the man wanted a haircut. "I'm sorry," I said, "Beaumont's is closed Mondays."

Holding back a smile, he set his helmet down, then zeroed in on my eyes. "I'm looking for Valentine Beaumont."

I have long burgundy hair, olive-toned skin, and eyes that in the right light glinted more amber than brown. As puny an asset as it was, having dark coloring meant I wasn't prone to showing it if I blushed. But I felt my face turn beet-red as his deep-set eyes shone into mine.

"I'm Valentine Beaumont."

He nodded and shook my hand. "I'm here for the job."

"Job?" I worked hard to restrain the tingles from his strong, warm grasp.

"Yes. J-O-B." He spelled it out like I was learning my alphabet. "I'm Jock de Marco," he added with a slight trill on the *r*.

I slid my hand out of his and examined my sheet. Yep. There it was. Ten-thirty. J. de Marco.

"Did you say *Jock*?" Max piped, Mr. Conversationalist all of a sudden.

"Yes." He was dead serious. "It's Latin."

Max uttered a girlish sigh, and before he got all giggly, I stared him down. I mean, *really*.

"I'm Maximilian Martell." He pushed past me. "Maximilian is also Latin, but my father was English, hence the Martell. You can call me Max. Should we call you Jocko?"

Jock's eyes steadied on Max. "Someone called me that once."

Max's Adam's apple bobbed up and down as if he'd swallowed a marble dipped in peroxide. "Jock, it is," he squeaked, sliding back beside me.

Jock shifted his gaze to me, and I immediately felt my temperature soar. Maybe because I was seeing him in a loincloth, wrestling a great white shark in his arms. Or maybe the tingles from his touch had gone to my head. This wasn't going to help during the interview process.

Jock removed his jacket and pulled a folded paper from an inner pocket. Then he tossed his jacket over a chair.

Gulp. Muscles upon muscles rippled beneath his thin black sweater, the weave so fine it outlined even his nipples. I looked up. Okay, Lord, this was a cruel joke, a bad romantic cliché. The big, strong cowboy struts into the saloon, and all the lady folk, taken aback, sweep up their skirts and fan themselves, all the while batting an eye at the newcomer in town.

Aptly, Max looked like he could use a fan in both hands.

Well, I was above petty flirtations. So, the guy had good looks and muscles. I'd dated his kind before and always ended up with a wounded heart. Most recently, this summer when I'd fallen for Detective Michael Romero, formerly of the NYPD. He'd been assigned the murder case in my salon, which I'd helped solve, and we'd immediately developed a love-hate relationship. He was macho, New York City tough, and didn't appreciate my interference in police matters. I didn't appreciate his arrogance. The more we sparred, the more irresistible he became.

I'd last seen Romero on a yacht at his sister's wedding in July. We'd gotten over the hate part of the relationship and were working on the love—or so I thought—until he disappeared. That was two months ago. But the hurt felt like yesterday.

No more. I'd eliminated dating from my diet. And I'd find a suitable stylist. I'd look over Jock's work history, then give him the kiss-off. Nicely, of course. My headache subsided with my take-action attitude. I ushered Jock into my office and slammed the door in Max's face, almost catching his tongue in the doorframe.

Jock handed me his résumé and took a seat. The smell of leather spiced with citrus and the rainy outdoors wafted by my nose.

I stroked the warm paper that moments ago was pressed inside his jacket. Then I looked into his eyes. I was so taken in by the warmth of dark caramel and a splash of cognac flecked around his pupils, I was almost dizzy. I slid behind my desk and composed myself. "You didn't mention what you did before hairstyling."

The steady stare suggested he wasn't going to either. This raised my antennae, but what did it matter? I wasn't hiring him. "You're from Argentina." I was going through the motions.

"Originally. I'm a U.S. citizen."

I scanned the sheet. "Says here you trained in Rome. Worked in Los Angeles under Mr. Armand and two years in Chicago running one of José's salons."

He pushed up his long sleeves and shrugged like it was no big deal.

"Why come here? Boston's fifteen minutes away. Why not there or New York?"

He leaned his toned arms on his knees. "I've heard about you and your awards. Seen your creations at hair conventions. Thought this would be a good opportunity to work with you."

I straightened in my chair, totally not affected by his praise or arresting presence.

He gave a slight sideways nod. "Plus, I have other business here."

I deflated. "Then you're just passing through."

"I'm not planning on going anywhere." His voice was self-confident.

"Look"—I refolded the paper—"you're obviously used to working in high-end salons, which Beaumont's isn't."

"I'm willing to give it a try."

"I can only pay you on a commission basis."

"That's what I'm used to."

"And," I continued, trying to convince someone here, "I'd have to run an ad. Since you're from out of town, you probably don't have any clientele in the area."

"Maybe. A few have heard of my hands."

My gaze traveled to his ordinary…strong…sensual… hands. Next thing I knew, I was giving him the rundown, ignoring the fact that he reeked of the forbidden apple. His work experience *was* impressive. And he couldn't be as bad as the Marilyn Manson look-alike or the others I'd seen. I glanced from all the red slash marks on my sheet back to Jock, hoping I was right. Before I changed my mind, I took a reassuring breath and got to my feet. "We'll try it, then. Starting tomorrow."

I heard a tiny cheer and thunk. Right. Mata Hari spying on the other side of the door.

"And use the parking in back," I added. "We like to save the sidewalk for pedestrians."

He gave a curt nod.

I wasn't sure what I'd done or who Jock de Marco really was, but I had a feeling things were going to be different from here on out.

Mid-afternoon, I splashed through town on my way to Rueland Retirement. I turned onto Park Street, passed several century-old homes, and crawled to a stop in front of the sprawling two-story Victorian that housed thirty or so seniors.

I tapped the gearshift, waiting for the rain to stop pelting my VW Daisy Bug, my thoughts circling back to this morning. Had I made a colossal error hiring Jock de Marco?

I opened and clenched my hands, adding this to the growing list of things to worry about. Not only was I trying to run a decent salon, stay out of murder investigations, and put my mother out of her misery regarding Mr. Right. But now because of my impulsive nature, I had Mr. Loincloth starting work tomorrow. Well, I wasn't sex-crazed. I could work alongside a handsome man any day of the week. I worked beside Max, didn't I? Okay, so Max was…Max.

I could do this. Easy-peasy.

But what about Jock's other business? His past? He was evasive, and that bothered me. What's more, I'd hired him *knowing* he was secretive. This was worse than a blind date. I was inviting trouble. *Dumb, Val. Dumb.*

I pushed all the conflicting thoughts to the back of my mind, figuring I could torture myself later. The rain had eased up. It was now or never. I grabbed my supplies and dashed, head down, through the black iron gate and up the wide porch. I didn't stop running until my hand hit the huge oak door and I was inside the cavernous vestibule.

I tried to silence my heels from clicking on the hardwood floor in the hushed foyer, but it didn't seem to matter. Nobody was around. Unusual for this time of day. The twelve-foot-high doors were closed to the dining room, game room, and office, yet a habitual floral and medicinal smell filled the air. I even detected a whiff of pasta sauce. Marinara? Bolognese? Alpha-getti? I wouldn't place any bets on what had been served for lunch. With Ruby Taylor as cook, anything was possible.

The office door crashed open, and Evalene Delaney, the house manager, marched out, taking a quick look around. "Good day, Miss Beaumont." She clicked her army boots.

Guessing Evalene's age was nearly impossible, but she was a cross between George Patton and Mrs. Doubtfire, and she liked to run a tight ship.

"Good day," I said, trying my darnedest not to focus on her four stringy lip hairs or the wart nestled on her chin.

"The seniors are on a bus trip today," she said. "Gone to see that Polish singer Bobby Vubak in concert."

"Okay, I'll be leaving now." I turned, one toe already aimed for the door.

"Of course…"

Of course? No, of course! I was happy to move along, because to tell you the truth, Evalene scared the bejeebers out of me.

"Some residents stayed behind. Who was expecting you?"

"Uh, Nettie Wisz and Sister Madeline."

She narrowed her gaze on me. "Sister Madeline? She's been under the weather. Hillary Ayers took her lunch up to her earlier. Nettie, I'm not sure about. Check the halls. She's usually roaming them, looking for a good fight."

Evalene neither smiled nor laughed at that. She backed into her trench, the bun on top of her head the last thing visible as she shut the door.

Whew. I shuddered, then hauled my supplies up the small-scaled *Gone With the Wind* staircase to the second floor. I was about to knock on the first door on the left, but stopped myself and thought about Evalene's comment about Sister Madeline's health. It's true, she hadn't seemed well over my last few visits, and when I'd booked her appointment, she'd sounded worried. All she'd said was she needed to talk about the girl. What girl, I had no idea.

I heard a door chain slide in a lock to the right of the landing, and a moment later Hillary Ayers peeked out of her apartment.

"Hello, Valentine." She smiled.

Hillary was the Statue of Liberty and Princess Grace rolled into one. Her face was gently preserved for seventy or so, her golden blond hair was fixed into a perfect French twist, and her elegant pink sweater was buttoned once over a white blouse.

I set my load by my feet and asked why she hadn't gone to see Bobby Vubak.

"I'm afraid I'm not familiar with him," she said. "I was catching up on my reading. I've almost finished a moving biography on Joan of Arc. In fact, I should get back to it." She disappeared into her apartment as quickly as she had appeared.

I shrugged and rapped softly on Sister Madeline's door. I waited a few seconds, an affectionate warmth spreading through me like it always did when I was about to see her, or when I considered the unique bond we shared. A beautician and a nun. Go figure. But our friendship wasn't based on appearances, religion, or beliefs. It was more about trust and dreams. It was about how being a success was rooted in family and came from within. She was special, and I felt an ache inside from her recent decline.

I put my chin up and let myself in, calling out a greeting. I did this for the fragile residents so they wouldn't overexert themselves and rush to the door. Lately, I'd been doing this for Sister Madeline.

I placed my things on the sofa and gave my arms a brisk rub, eyeing the radiator on the wall to Sister Madeline's left. Silly heater. Never seemed to work. Yet the cool and lightly furnished apartment was oddly fitting for a nun. Apart from the ivory crucifix fastened above the mini sink, and the large gold-framed painting of *The Last Supper* hanging behind the sofa, the room was bare of decorations. Water steadily pinged into the kitchen sink, and the place smelled of pasta and sausage.

Like always, Sister Madeline faced the window in her frayed wingback chair. A small table sat in front of her, Bible and prayer book on the right. From behind, I could see the top of her delicate head as well as a white calla lily plant and a few other sparse plants that sat on the window ledge.

I pulled a brush and cape from my bag and sailed to the bathroom for a towel. I jabbered about the rain and how lucky she was to be nice and dry inside. She didn't respond, so I choked back my soliloquy. She was probably in the middle of a prayer. After a respectable minute, I crept closer, thinking if I gently brushed out a few tangles, I'd get her mind on her set.

I smoothed the brush across the top of her head with apprehension. Her half-eaten lunch sat in front of her, a fork rested slack in her hand. She hadn't spoken. Hadn't budged. Hadn't finished her meal. Had she done one of those things, I wouldn't have felt the uneasy tremor slide up my arm. I stopped brushing, and her head bobbed once.

Then *thunk*. Face first into a dish of lasagna. Red sauce splattered everywhere.

I screamed from here to Maine, hurling my brush almost as far. Then I hit the floor.

When I came to, Hillary was fanning me, and Evalene's large form knelt over me, her pebbly wart weaving in and out of focus.

"Are you injured, Miss Beaumont?" Evalene's voice was soft yet raspy. She hauled me onto a chair and handed me a tissue. "You're bleeding down your chin."

I tasted a mixture of blood and pasta sauce. "I-I must've hit my mouth on the chair." I dabbed my lip while Hillary continued fanning. "Sister Madeline. She's…" I couldn't get the rest out.

"Yes," Evalene hissed through her molars. "Dead. We heard you scream and we rushed in. When I couldn't get Sister's pulse, I called nine-one-one." Her lip twitched. "The police wish to know when there's a sudden death."

"Or a suspicious one." Hillary stared at Sister Madeline's lifeless body.

"Suspicious?" This was crazy. "It was probably a peaceful

passing." I swung my gaze from Hillary to Evalene. "Probably no need to get the police involved." I was sounding this out, more for me than for them.

"I agree," Evalene said. "But it's policy. It's fortunate most of the residents are out. I wouldn't want them alarmed." She took a final survey of the room, then marched, arms swinging, to the door. "I'll be back when help arrives." She closed the door behind her with a thud.

Hillary gently lowered the book she was using to fan me. *Huh.* Joan of Arc to my rescue.

"Poor soul." Hillary paled, tapping her fingers to her chest.

I helped her to a chair. Then I staggered to the kitchenette to get us both a glass of water.

"I'm not sure we should touch anything, Valentine. If the police are coming…"

"A glass of water won't hurt." Especially if it kept me from fainting again. Or throwing up. I downed the glass and grabbed another for Hillary.

While she was drinking, I took baby steps until I was beside Sister Madeline.

For dignity's sake, I wanted to pull her head back from the lasagna, but knew the police, or Hillary, wouldn't approve of this decision. Plus, I wasn't sure I could touch a dead person, even if I'd accepted the fact I was in the same room as one.

My pulse raced. I took a deep breath and angled close to Sister Madeline. Her left hand rested on her lap, palm up. An opened heart-shaped locket dangled from a gold chain in her hand. I bent to take a closer look, but the table was creating a shadow, making it difficult to see what was inside. It looked like a picture of a baby on the left and a photo of a young girl on the right.

Was this *the girl*? Clients were notorious for sharing secrets in the salon chair. Now I'd never know. In a trance, I reached to move the table.

"No!"

I clapped my hand to my chest. "Hillary! You almost

gave me a heart attack. Then we'd have two dead bodies."

She dabbed modest tears with a tissue pulled from inside her sleeve. "I'm sorry, Valentine. I was afraid you'd move something."

Very astute of her. I watched her fidget with the tissue, and her earlier comment came to mind. "Hillary, why did you suggest Sister Madeline's death as being suspicious?"

She shook her head. "I don't know. I blurted it without thinking. Being in Evalene's presence makes me nervous."

That made two of us. I grabbed my bag, thinking that for once I'd take a picture with my cell phone. "Sister has a locket in her hand," I said. "I only wanted to get a better look at the photos." I fiddled with the phone I rarely used and finally snapped a picture. And another. And another. *Drat.* Why did it always take more pictures than I wanted?

Hillary padded across the carpet as if it were safe to approach now that I'd paved the way. We studied the pictures I'd taken, squinting through the poor quality.

"The girl could be Sister Madeline," Hillary said.

"Perhaps." I enlarged the photo. "About nineteen or twenty."

It was no use. Between the blur and shots of my intruding fingers, we couldn't decipher anything. I dumped the phone back in my bag, and together we leaned our heads low.

"The only way to tell for sure is to pick up the locket," I said. "And examine it closely."

"I suppose." Hillary bit her bottom lip.

My skin crawled at the thought of touching the deceased, and Hillary didn't seem in any hurry to step up to the plate. Deftly, I pulled out my tail comb. I could use the pointy end to lift the locket without handling it.

Suddenly, the door flew open and two cops bounded in.

I shrieked and, on reflex, hurled the comb across the room. Hillary gasped. The cops ducked for cover.

"What the hell!" The uniform in charge rose, jerking

the pointy end of the comb out of the doorjamb. "Are you crazy?" He squinted at me good and hard. "Oh, it's *you.*" He didn't say this like he was glad to see me. More like he'd opened the door and saw his mean mother-in-law standing there.

I caught my breath and stared wide-eyed at Officer Martoli, who I recognized from the last homicide I'd gotten tangled in. Why did my sister have to work vice? Holly could've answered the call instead of this guy.

He sauntered over and gave the comb a good whack into my palm. "What other beautician would be lucky enough to find a dead nun? What's the matter? Not enough customers croaking at the beauty parlor? You gotta cross into other arenas?"

I cleared my throat. "Technically, I didn't *find* the last body."

"Uh-huh." He gave me a stern glare. "You gotta be Rueland's busiest broad." He jerked his head to the other cop, who was kneeling beside Sister Madeline. "Hey, Vince, I told you it'd be her. You owe me twenty bucks."

"Yeah, later." Vince waved a hand.

Martoli wasn't fazed by his uninterested partner. He gave me an eager nod. "So? How's the beauty business? Curl anyone's testicles, I mean, tendrils lately?"

I fisted my hands and tightened my lips. Several years before the murder in my shop, I'd apprehended another killer, using a perm rod and a lot of bravado. I wasn't proud of it. In fact, I hadn't realized perm-rod elastics could even stretch that far.

True, I wasn't an experienced cop like my sister or a well-respected detective like Romero. And maybe my methods of capturing criminals *were* unusual. And maybe I *had* come upon another dead body. Was that any reason to ridicule me? It *was* possible this one died of natural causes.

"What I want to know," Martoli mused, "is how you planned it?"

"Planned what? Sister Madeline booked the appointment and said she wanted to tell me about the girl."

"What girl?"

"I don't know. When I arrived, Sister was dead."

"Let me get this straight." He hoisted up his belt buckle. "You think someone came in here and killed an old nun so she wouldn't pour out her heart to her hairdresser? Maybe you want to borrow my badge and wear my gun since you're a regular Jane Rizzoli."

I saw red. The last thing I wanted to imply was there'd been a murder. I sure as hell didn't want to investigate one. Damn. Why hadn't I kept my big mouth shut?

I answered his questions and stormed out of the retirement home. Once I was in my car, I hit the gas and managed to travel a whole twenty feet before I jerked the wheel into a driveway, opened the door, and upchucked all over someone's mums. I swiped a hand across my mouth as a jogger ran by. He wasn't daunted by the huge rain puddles he was tapping through. Me, he gave a wary look and wide berth.

Perfect. Bad enough I had Jock stuck in my head like a throbbing toothache, now this. A dead nun. I repositioned myself behind the wheel and let out a heavy sigh. I tried to look ahead. Problem was, my next stop wasn't likely to brighten my day.

As the obedient daughter, I often checked in on my parents on Mondays. Today was no different. Five minutes in the door, I'd want to stab myself with my scissors. But after finding Sister Madeline dead, I needed to see my parents were okay.

They lived in a ranch-style house in Burlington, a fifteen-minute drive from Rueland, twenty if I stopped for Advil. Their home was like a bowling alley, and though they complained about descending the stairs to go to the basement, they never seemed to mind the two miles it took to walk from the bedroom to the kitchen. Still, it made them happy. Sort of.

I dragged myself out of the car and walked into the garage past their four-door blue sedan. *Uh-oh*. Cigar smoke. Likely, my father was wandering out back having a puff. Which meant one of two things. One of my mother's Ukrainian relatives was here, or a different kind of trouble was brewing inside.

I climbed the two steps into the house, the cigar stench masked by the usual smell of bleach. My mother met me at the door, apron fastened around her waist, no relatives in sight.

"What's that on your lip?" she asked. "It's not a cold sore, is it?"

I'd never had a cold sore in my life, but worrying was part of my mother's makeup. I figured she wouldn't like the truth, so I went with her theory. "Yeah, that's it, a cold sore."

"It doesn't look like a cold sore. It looks like you cut your lip."

There was no winning. Why she didn't team up with Holly, I'd never know.

"Mrs. Shales returned our plunger," she said, "and brought over the worst news."

Mrs. Shales lived next door to my parents, now, and in the old neighborhood where I grew up. Like she couldn't get enough of Bruce and Ava.

Despite my nausea, I kicked off my shoes and strolled into the kitchen. Mrs. Shales sat at the table behind a plate of gingersnaps. She had short brown frizzy hair like a Yorkshire terrier, and she resembled the Pillsbury Dough Boy. I gave her a warm hug, then sat across from her at the table. "What news?" I asked.

"I thought you would've heard by now." My mother pivoted toward Mrs. Shales and the plate of cookies. "The girl can't stay away from danger. Gets that from her father."

I debated taking a cookie since ginger was commonly used in aromatherapy to reduce nausea. Plus, my mother's baking was second to none. But I didn't think I should chance it.

"Retired after thirty years with the fire department," she continued, "he still loves taking chances."

I'm diligent, caring, and responsible. Patience, I lack. "Mom? The news?" It's like I was invisible.

"Do you know she caught Max Martell's friend's murderer? With a perm rod no less." She lowered her voice. "You remember Max. He's the one who wears women's panties."

"Mom!"

Mrs. Shales's rosebud mouth dropped open, and a chunk of cookie fell on the table.

My mother scraped up the crumbs and nodded at her. "Go ahead. Tell her."

Mrs. Shales swallowed thickly, probably wondering if she could leave now. "I got a phone call today from my friend Hillary."

"Hillary?" I disregarded the warning bells clanging in my ears.

"Yes. She's usually the epitome of calmness, but she was quite upset. A resident at the home died this afternoon."

"Resident?" An involuntary cough surfaced. "Home?"

My mother swung her head toward me, her brown hair bobbing softly. "Why are you repeating everything?"

"At Rueland Retirement," Mrs. Shales said. "Where Hillary lives."

There's no way on God's green earth I'd admit being anywhere near—

"You go there to do hair!" my mother proclaimed like Paul Revere crying, *The British are coming!* She planted her hands on hips. "Did you hear about this?"

I crossed my fingers behind my back. "I'm not the only beautician who visits retirement homes."

"Hillary's grateful *you* discovered Sister Madeline," Mrs. Shales said. "She would've fainted straightaway if *she'd* found the body."

"Uh, about the fainting—"

"What?" My mother went ballistic. "You found a dead nun?" She paced the floor. "Maybe you'd also like to help the FBI track down that Boston industrialist Levi Tazotto who slayed his mistress."

Mrs. Shales went white.

I rolled my eyes. "No, Mom, I like to stay local."

"You were always a smart girl. You could've been a nurse or a world-renowned pianist. But no, you pick hairdressing with a sideline of playing Charlie's Angels."

Traffic buzzed along the two-lane highway outside the kitchen window. The rain had stopped falling, but clouds were heavy. I stared out the window, waiting for the next enlightening thing to come out of my mother's mouth.

"You can't be happy finding ordinary dead people? A nun yet. Isn't that sacrilegious?"

And there it was. My mother left the Catholic faith when she married my father, who had a French and Armenian background and was raised Anglican. But she tapped her forehead and chest, mumbling, "Father, Son…"

Mrs. Shales bit her lip. Her gaze bounced from my mother to me like a ping-pong ball.

"Was she wearing a habit?" Gruesome as it might be, my mother wanted details.

"No," I said. "She was wearing a regular dress. No habit. No rosary. No cross dangling on a string. She didn't even have her Bible open. It was very uneventful."

She exhaled. "What am I supposed to tell your father?"

I was a grown woman; I had to worry about this? "Tell him I found a dead nun clasping a locket." Oops.

Mrs. Shales was trotting to the door but stopped suddenly, her flowered polyester dress swishing at her knees. "Locket? With pictures inside?"

Something in her voice told me things were about to get worse. "Yes. A young woman and a baby."

The second hand on the kitchen clock ticked by while she mulled this over.

I strode over to her, next to where my mother was already standing. "Do you know anything about the pictures, Mrs. Shales?"

She gave a slight shrug. "I know Sister Madeline used to visit the orphans at St. Gregory."

"In Metland?" A town ten minutes away. "Do you think the baby in the photo was from the orphanage?"

"I don't know. I just know Sister Madeline used to spend time there." She edged closer, a frown crossing her face. "There's something else." She paused, then whispered, "Virgil Sylas."

"Who's Virgil Sylas?" my mother and I whispered back in unison.

"Another resident at the home," she said. "And Sister Madeline's shadow. When I did my volunteer singing there, Sister Madeline would often join the group to listen. She was such a sweet thing. And then there was Virgil. Always by her side. If Sister moved to the refreshments, Virgil hovered. When she left the room, Virgil left. Strangest thing. Hillary noticed it, too. She was concerned Sister Madeline was involved with him."

I was going to hate myself for asking this. "Romantically?"

"Hillary described him as a loner."

It didn't make sense. If Virgil was such a loner, why crowd Sister Madeline? And why was I asking all these questions? I wasn't investigating anything.

"This Virgil," my mother said with a calculating eye. "Is he married?"

"I think he's a widower," Mrs. Shales said.

My mother nodded, giving me a hopeful look. I knew that look. Bad enough my dating life was beyond pathetic, now my mother was considering the old age home for sons-in-law.

"Hillary disliked how Virgil wandered in and out of Sister's apartment, but she never heard any commotion, so she kept quiet." Mrs. Shales wrung her hands. "Valentine, I don't get around much anymore, but I'm concerned about Hillary. Would you keep an eye on her?"

I wasn't sure how I got sucked into this conversation. Yet the whole thing *did* seem odd. I didn't know how Sister Madeline had died or what to make of the pictures in the locket. And I certainly didn't feel right about the situation with Virgil.

My mother arched a brow and tapped her toe. "Knowing Valentine, she's already planning a trip back."

Chapter 2

Tuesday morning, my cat, Yitts, repeatedly head-butted me, forcing me to sit up.

"Good morning." I made kissy sounds on top of her black head. "Visit to the vet today."

I'd inherited Yitts during my last murder investigation. I figured since I was giving her a new home, I'd give her a new name. I called her Little Lady, and because my speech devolved when speaking to animals, it soon became Yitto Yady. Yitts for short. After work today, we were updating her immunizations.

I was trying to enjoy the moment and put off the horrible memory of yesterday, but I was only prolonging the inevitable. I flopped back on my puffy pillow, reconciling myself to the fact I'd found Sister Madeline dead. What a relief it'd be to learn she'd died naturally. There'd be no investigation. And no reason for me to get involved.

I was thinking about this when the crystal beads from my table lamp caught my eye. I stared at them, glistening in the sunlight, and a lump formed in my throat. I loved anything that twinkled or glittered. Why was I lying here, almost in tears? I knew the answer to that before I even blinked.

It was Sister Madeline and the lack of sparkle in her

life. This was a woman I honored and respected. Her clothes were staid, her furniture worn, but that didn't take away from who she was as a person. I came back to the girl. Who was she? And if Sister Madeline was the young woman in the locket, then who was the baby? An orphan?

I had to lay to rest yesterday's nightmare. Today was a new day, and I had a business to run. I rolled out of bed and did some deep breathing and a few stretches. Yitts sat tall on my comforter, her lime-green eyes following my movements back and forth.

I turned my head from side to side and spotted my knit top from yesterday, sticking half out of the clothes hamper. I went over, lifted the lid, and stuffed the top inside. I wasn't sure why, but I took the top back out and put it to my nose. I inhaled a flowery hint of my Musk perfume, but I also detected leather. And citrus. Jock's citrus.

I recalled him staring at me like there was fire in his soul, and I flung the top inside the basket. "Stupid. Stupid. Stupid." I'd probably made the biggest mistake of my life hiring Jock.

Yitts crouched down, eyes raised at me.

"Don't look at me like that. I had to hire someone."

I ate, dressed, fed, and brushed Yitts, and on my way out the door, grabbed a sweater that was like the one Hillary wore yesterday. Before I knew it, I was going over Mrs. Shales's concern about her friend. Darn. Did I actually promise to check in on Hillary? I'd agonize about a visit later. I had other problems to attend.

I locked the door to my Cape Cod bungalow, ran down the porch steps to my car, and waved to Mr. Brooks across the street, starting up his lawnmower.

Five minutes into my drive, I opened the sunroof, rolled down the windows, and tossed my sweater aside. It was balmy for September, but signs of fall were everywhere. Trees lining Darling Street were already turning a beautiful orange, and a warm sweetness filled the air. I exhaled loudly and spread apart the slit on my skirt.

The warmth was steam piping from the chimney of Rueland's candy factory, the Peanut Gallery. Problem was I was hot. All because of some new employee.

I swallowed hard, picturing Jock's muscled body and large, strong hands. Suddenly, a truck screeched to a stop in front of me. I slammed my foot on the brakes nanoseconds before my little yellow car skidded into the truck's rear end.

I thumped my head back on the headrest and took a shaky breath. The truck driver poked his head out the window and hooted at women peeking inside Beaumont's front window. The guy behind me blared the horn, shouted a few choice words, then burned rubber to escape the scene. If this was any indication of what my day was going to be like, I was in trouble.

With my foot on the brakes, I did a double take of my salon. *Yikes!* Women resembling *Cosmopolitan* cover girls were lined up under the long striped awning. Max had obviously opened this morning as two women entered the front door. The next two in line leaned over the flower box, ogling inside.

Please, God, no casualties. I'd have to move to another state. At least the absence of sirens was a good sign.

I whipped into the parking lot I shared with Friar Tuck's, careened past the mini stone castle, and squealed to a stop behind the salon. The bakery's arrow-pierced donut revolved high on a pole above the lot, creaking and groaning as usual. The noise was subtle compared to the loud music and party sounds coming from my salon. I stalked past Jock's massive bike, on a mission, and entered through the back entrance.

Oblivious to the fragrant oils and nail polish smells that usually greeted me, I tripped down the hall past the bathroom and Ti Amo and Molto Bella—my two treatment rooms. I halted at the edge of the main salon and gaped at the three-ring circus in front of me.

Women jiggled their tushes and shook their shoulders. One had color mucked on top of her head. Another in rollers hip-hopped around the ivory-colored chairs. The hip-hopper twirled a flat iron in the air and narrowly missed bringing down the mini lights on the wall. Max and Jock didn't notice a thing. And why would they? They were too busy dancing with their own partners to Enrique Iglesias's blaring, rhythmic beat.

My eyes clouded over, and I could feel steam coming out my ears. Max and his *unleashing the wild side* advice. I could be a lot of fun, too, when the situation called for it. But I was trying to run a respectable establishment here, not a rave. This party was about to be crashed. I yanked off the volume. Ha! Silence.

Max jerked his partner free, which sent her hair-extension pompom through the air. She spun out of control and landed on Jock's other arm, dazed but delighted. Naturally.

Jock's half-buttoned shirt stretched across his massive chest, revealing a two-inch crescent-shaped scar on his ribs. The women slithered their hands up his abdomen, ignorant to the scar, but totally wrapped up in his presence. He smiled at them and spotted me with my hands on my hips. Dark thoughts wrestled through my head. He, on the other hand, looked quite cool and collected. He even had the nerve to grin.

I marched to the dangling hair extension, ripped it off the corner of a mirror, and pointed to my office, waiting for Jock and Max to take the lead.

"Traitor," I whispered to Max, slamming the door before his foot totally cleared it.

"Ow! You did that on purpose."

I gave him a merciless scowl, then shoved up against the desk and crossed my ankles. Enrique's voice wound up again in the other room. I paid no attention. I wanted answers here and now. Jock studied me. In the small room, it wasn't hard to see he was trying not to smile.

I tossed the hairpiece on the desk. "Somebody want to explain what's going on?"

"The ladies were only having fun," Jock said.

"I don't doubt that."

He nodded. "I admit I'm partly to blame."

"I'd say mostly to blame."

Max's eyes widened. "Do you two want to be alone?"

"You stay put," I ordered.

"Staying." Max's shoulders caved.

Jock waited until my eyes settled on him. "After you left yesterday," he said, "I asked Max if he could open up early. I like to get a head start on the day."

"Really."

"Yes. That a problem?"

"Not for me. Shows initiative. So, who are all the women?"

"Customers. I'm usually booked solid."

"I just hired you yesterday."

"Word travels fast."

I crossed my arms, forcing myself to hold his deep brown-eyed stare. I was in charge here, wasn't I? I had every right to be ticked. I wasn't going to be intimidated by blatant sexuality. I threw up my hands. "Could we at least keep the music below earth-shattering? I like Enrique as much as the next girl, but they may not be as thrilled about him in Rhode Island."

"I'll turn it down." Max dove out of the office before I could stop him.

Jock eased the door shut again, and the sensual lyrics to "I Just Wanna Be With You" hummed in the background. The power of the words, combined with Jock's closeness, had my blood pounding. Slowly, he turned to face me. "About the music…" His voice was low, eyes on me while he did up a button. "I'm used to working to music drenched in emotion. Italian. Latin. Will that be a problem?"

His shirt was damp, and an exotic, aromatic heat exuded from his body. I dragged my gaze from his glistening chest up his powerfully built neck. Oh boy. "I like all types of music."

"It's about the right atmosphere," he said. "Not just transforming an ugly duckling into a swan. Women like to feel cared for, like they count. If I can contribute to that in a small way, I'll do it."

How could I argue with the women-like-to-be-cared-for logic? It's a philosophy I tended to agree with. However, *my* compliments wouldn't be misconstrued as sexual.

With bent knees, he peered through my lashes, as if trying to read my thoughts.

I threw back my shoulders, staunchly in control. "Just don't forget who's boss." I slid past him into the mayhem of the salon, before he heard my beating heart.

The day progressed at a rapid pace. Between customers, I gave Max and Jock the short version of yesterday's visit to the retirement home.

Max's eyes got big. "Are you okay, lovey?"

"Good as new," I lied, touching my bruised lip. "And if you don't mind, I'd rather not talk about it." At that, I spun around and welcomed the next fashion model who was rolling in.

As it turned out, Jock was an exemplary employee. He worked steadily alongside Max and me, pleased every female who stepped in the salon, and rarely looked my way. Okay, he'd hardly noticed me all day. It's what I wanted, right? Women hiked up skirts as he shampooed their hair. Others slipped phone numbers in his pockets.

One blond paraded into the salon, reeking of lavender, wearing a tiny patch of material that might've been a miniskirt before the shrinkage. "Jock-Jock!" She planted a slutty kiss on his lips. It didn't help that she looked like a world-class supermodel.

Jock wiped her saliva off his mouth with the back of his scissor hand. "Be with you shortly, Bobbi." He gave her a sexy, hot smile that would've melted stone. It was so intense I had to look away.

And while I was looking elsewhere, I had to figure out why this bothered me. I didn't own him. What did I care if he kissed a client? He could kiss anyone he wanted as long as he did his job. He could kiss the croaky-voiced, tunic-wearing kid who worked at Friar Tuck's. He could kiss a dog, for all I cared. I was a fair boss.

Max leaned in, eyes on Bobbi. "Even on a good day, I could *never* look *that* gorgeous."

I shushed Max and his quick tongue. True, he had an eye for beauty and knew instinctively how to enhance a woman's appearance. Right now, I wished he'd keep his comments to himself.

I squared my shoulders, marched behind the folding screen between the nine-by-nine dispensary and the hallway, and faced my customer from the Ice Age. I thrust my chin forward and plunged into tweezing Mrs. Horowitz's whiskers. I wasn't going to be intimidated by the steady stream of goddesses wiggling through my door. Ha! They could throw their bras at Jock de Marco for all I cared. *I* had class. Maybe I wasn't a supermodel, but I, Valentine Beaumont, was known to turn a head or two.

A second later, the front door banged open. I held my breath and peeked over the partition, dreading another supermodel look-alike. What a relief when I saw Jimmy the Skink.

I'd known Jimmy O'Shea since ninth grade when he'd moved here from California. The Skink nickname evolved because, like a lizard, Jimmy had no neck to speak of. He did, however, have a long torso and short legs—ideal for creeping.

Jimmy had been one of those brave, nerdy kids who'd asked every girl out on a date. Every one had turned him down, me included. But unlike the throng, I'd regularly rescued him after the jocks locked him in the cafeteria cupboard. We'd developed a strange but amicable friendship, and Jimmy's attitude never changed. "Hey, man," he'd say. "If life hands you a lemon, like, make iced tea."

He scrutinized the salon and nodded. "Riiiiighteous." His curly bleached-blond hair sprung out on top of his reptilian body, adding a few inches to his shortness. "Like, what's transpiring here? Some sort of model search?" Then he spotted Jock. "Whoooooa. Who's the dude with the muscles? The Rock?" He squinted at the ceiling like he was searching for hidden cameras. "You can't fool the Skink. You got *Dwayne Johnson* working here?"

I guess if you shaved the blond hair down to the dark roots, you'd have a younger Dwayne Johnson, but I wasn't going to go there.

I folded back the screen, sat Mrs. Horowitz up, and whisked off her cape.

"Whoa!" Jimmy vaulted back, gawking wide-eyed at Mrs. Horowitz. "Major rude awakening."

Mrs. Horowitz hadn't been blessed with physical beauty. She had uneven skin tone, a crooked nose, and watery eyes, and beautifying her was a lot like piecing together a Picasso. But I liked the old girl. She was harmless, and her zany presence made her one of the family.

I bid Mrs. Horowitz farewell while Jimmy put on the charm with a few women. Then I introduced him to the man of the hour.

"*Jock?*" Jimmy gaped openly. "Like, far out! Jock the Rock."

Jock wiped hair off his wrists and shook Jimmy's spindly hand.

"Hey, dude," Jimmy winced, "you must bench press a *lot*."

"Not lately." Jock backed up to his client. "Too busy."

Jimmy dipped his head up and down, grinning at all the hot women. "Like, I can see with what."

"How 'bout you?" Jock asked. "You weightlift?"

Jimmy flexed his marble-sized biceps. "Yeah, man. I've been known to lift the odd barbell. Those five pounders are heavy. But it's groovy. Some chicks like us lean cuisines."

Jock nodded in agreement. I was looking for a place to gag.

Jimmy bobbed his head at me. "Hey, dudette, what's

the skinny on that old Mother Teresa from the retirement home? I hear she died."

"You mean Sister Madeline?"

"That's the one. I'm in and out of there all the time. I was dropping off tickets when I heard you found the reverent girl dead in her soup."

Jimmy had made a career of surfing waves off Cape Cod and watching sports since he was never good at playing them. Then one day he'd set up shop outside TD Garden, scalping hard-to-get Celtics, Bruins, and Red Sox tickets, and life took on a new meaning.

"It was lasagna, not soup, and yes, I found her."

"It's true? Far out! Was it like *The Exorcist?* Kinda spiritually spooky?"

Jimmy was a classic film and sitcom buff. If money could be made from ogling the screen, Jimmy would be a millionaire.

"No. It was more like finding one of *The Golden Girls.*" I had my own history with reruns.

"*The Golden Girls,* huh?" He thought about this good and hard. "Which one was she like? I hope it wasn't Bea Arthur. She rocked, but she had an attitude."

I rolled my eyes so far to the back of my head I could see my next thought. This was the sort of thing I had to put up with. If it wasn't flippancy coming out of Max's mouth, then I had Jimmy the Skink popping in, whiling my time away.

"Speaking of the spooky factor," he said, "there's some weird stuff going on at the seniors' pad."

"Rueland Retirement?" I gave him a skeptical look. "Define weird."

"I don't know. It's a vibe I got." He leaned in. "Like, when I popped in there on the weekend and saw old Virgil. The guy was acting strange."

"*Virgil?* What do you mean?"

"I *mean*, the dude was outside burying something in a pile of dirt. And it didn't look like a bone."

I didn't want to ask, and I could think of a dozen

reasons why I didn't want to know. But now I had two
people telling me Virgil was this side of strange. "What *did*
it look like?"

"I'll tell you this much, whatever it was, he was doing it
in secret. I passed through the front gate and saw him
shoveling away at the side of the house. I think I scared
the dude, because when I moseyed over and cried, 'How's
it hangin'?' he turned as red as my shirt, then grabbed a
brown paper bag from the ground, and slipped into the
side cellar door." Corkscrew curls shook over Jimmy's
eyes. "This town's falling apart. Like, weirdoes burying
stuff. Murders left and right."

"Who said anything about murder?" Honestly, there
was nothing suspicious about Sister Madeline's death.

"Come *on*, dudette. Get with the program. Everyone's
talking about it at the home. Sister Reverent didn't come
down for meals. Everyone knew it. Real good setup if
you're planning an execution."

"Because she ate in her apartment instead of the dining
room."

"Exactamundo," he said, missing the sarcasm in my
voice. "Like, anyone could sneak in and *whammo*." He
clapped his hands. "I'm glad I don't live there. I'd never
sleep, and the Skink needs his sleep."

"Nobody said it was murder. You can relax." Listen to
me.

He gave a throaty laugh. "Right. But if it *was* murder and
you were there. Like, far out. You keep stepping your L.L.
Beans in our fair town's slaughters. Dudette to the rescue."

Tilting his head back, he slunk over to Jock. "Like,
Jock, you know you're working for Wonder Woman?"

Jock hiked up an eyebrow. "You don't say."

"Yeah, I *do* say. Dudette snares crooks using these here
perm rods as ammo." Jimmy plucked a white perm rod
from the tray and twirled it in the air.

"Ammo." Jock folded his arms across his chest.

"Whoaaaaa. You said it. And you don't want to know
what this devil was wrapped around."

I yanked the rod out of Jimmy's grasp and threw it back in the tray.

"First," I said to him, wondering how I was already knee-deep in this mess, "I don't wear L.L. Beans. Second, what would *you* have done apart from letting a murderer get away?"

Jimmy gasped. "Come *on*, get creative. You could've used the rod like a slingshot. Let the guy keep his pride. Like, serious injury, man!"

"You had to be there."

"Hey, I'm only *too* glad I wasn't." He did a slithery arm wave in the air, then covered his crotch with both hands. "I'm not a sadist."

Oh, and I am. When was everyone going to stop bringing up the past perm-rod case?

Jimmy ambled over to Max, his Red Sox jersey hanging to his knees. He whipped out a couple tickets, flicking them under Max's nose. "Maximilian, dude. You and dudette? Major league game? Fenway? Friday night? Last of the season's games. Two primo tickets left."

Max snatched the tickets and waved them in the air. "Lovey?"

Jock bent toward me. "I love baseball."

"Too bad," I said, "there're only two tickets."

"Hey." Jimmy pulled out another ticket. "The Skink's always got extras for the VIPs."

"He's not a VIP." I narrowed my eyes at Jock and swiped the tickets out of Max's hand. "And a minute ago these were your last tickets."

"We'll take 'em." Jock slid the tickets from my palm. "My treat."

A fiery trail blazed from my stomach to my toes from the mere touch of his hand. I had a feeling my face was flaming, too.

"Hey, dude." Jimmy's gaze traveled from Jock's face to a brunette with a chest big enough to serve dinner on. "This has been *my* treat. Riiiiighteous."

If I'd had a pair of cymbals, I would've smashed Jimmy's

head between them for giving Jock the tickets. Slowly, he came back to reality, giving me the Skink grin.

"Can the dudette fit me in for a snipola? Going windsurfing at the Cape next weekend, and the locks are in the danger zone."

"Isn't it a bit past the season for windsurfing?" I shook a cape open for him.

"Not for this dude. The waves are righteous."

I gave him a righteous haircut, springing the last curl into place when a big, burly man with a police badge hanging down the front of his XXXL Hawaiian shirt sauntered into the salon. Jimmy took one look from the cop to the badge, threw some money on the counter, and hightailed it out the door.

Max ushered the man into my office, then dashed over to me sweeping the floor. "That man in there looks as if he eats little girls like you for lunch."

He was right. And I had no intention of becoming a convenience-store burrito.

Max grabbed the broom out of my hand and shoved me toward the front. I opened the office door, and the man rose from my chair, standing well over six feet. He was a wall of muscle and had a mound of frizzy hair sticking up from his head. He introduced himself as Detective Saunders. I'd seen him before, during the last case. Men of his stature were hard to forget. Seemed he remembered me, too.

"Valentine Beaumont," he said, "a.k.a. Wonder Woman. Cuts hair by day, fights crime by night." He sized me up. "I bet you could even wear one of those tiny belts with the big shield around your iddy-biddy waist."

I might've been flattered by the comparison, but the Wonder Woman jokes were beginning to get stale. "Detective, I don't mean to be disrespectful, but it's been a trying day. Could you save the cryptic humor and tell me why you're here?"

"Still sassy. Think that's what Romero liked about you?"

Hearing that name stabbed my heart.

I hated that rarely a day went by that I didn't envision Romero's hard, lean body, or the black stubble on his jaw, or imagine his deep voice, or picture that stupid Iron Man watch loosely strapped to his wrist. I'd craved his touch, his lips, his masculine scent.

My chest tightened from the ache, but I could be strong. I wasn't interested in where Romero was or what he was up to. He'd made his decision. He was moving on. *This* girl could move on, too. I didn't need updates. I had no desire for dating now anyway. He'd killed that notion. He was the last person I wanted to think about. "How is Detective Romero?" *Ooh.* Why did I torture myself?

"Aw, little lady." Saunders shook his head. "You know I can't divulge that information."

"I didn't want his social security number. I asked how he is."

"Why don't we leave it to Mikey to tell you how he's doing?"

There was a hint of sarcasm—or was it amusement—in his voice. I bristled. "Great idea."

He opened a notebook, the stone cop face replacing the best-buddy look. "I've been assigned the nun's case in Romero's absence." He peered at my desk. "And since there aren't any perm rods in sight, I'd say we're off to a good start."

I ignored that. "Have you determined the cause of death, Detective?"

"That's being investigated. That's to say, cause unknown at this point."

I gave him a silent glare. "What about the locket she was holding?"

"Probably going down memory lane before she slipped away." He flipped through his notebook. "Says here she planned to tell you about a girl. Any idea what girl?"

"No."

"Any idea why she'd confide in her hairdresser and not, say, the bartender down at Dino Hosta's?"

The muscles tensed around my mouth. "She was a *nun*. Not one likely to visit bars." All in all, I did good not climbing on top of his mountainous form and ripping out his hair at the way he was speaking to me.

"Now, look…" He chuckled. "This is one of them open-and-shut cases. A few routine procedures and I'll put this baby to bed. Is that clear?"

"Crystal." If he didn't stop talking to me like I was in pigtails, wearing knee-highs, and sucking a lollipop, I was going to shove one of my four-inch heels right up his keister. Sure, I was simply a beautician to the cops, and true, I didn't have their training, but I *had* solved two murders. Maybe they were feeling threatened and wanted me to go fix hair and stay out of their way. Well, he could be Mr. Secretive for all I cared. There had to be more to Sister Madeline's death; otherwise why was a homicide detective investigating?

He flipped his notebook shut and ducked out of my office as the sound of a mandolin and a Latin-tenor voice reverberated off the walls. I poked my head out the office door. Good. No orgies. Merely gorgeous females wearing longing smiles. Singing and smiling I could put up with. Max's one male customer even wore a delighted grin. Probably thought he'd died and gone to heaven. I shut the door, my mind racing at the possibilities from hiring Jock. If this grinning guy spread word about hot beauties in Beaumont's, potentially it'd increase the male-client population. I beamed. A positive side to hiring Jock.

I didn't dwell on this for long because my thoughts turned back to Sister Madeline. I remembered her on my last few visits, having cramped muscles and stomach pain. Even her hair seemed thinner. Out of concern, I'd told her she seemed weak lately, and maybe she should see a doctor. I'd felt bad for making that comment, and in light of her sudden death, that remark now haunted me.

I grabbed the phone and dialed Holly. I needed answers about yesterday's death—even if it was to satisfy my own morbid curiosity.

"How the hell do you keep uncovering dead bodies?" she asked. "That's just not normal."

Holly was three years my senior. She was born Christmas Day. I was born on Valentine's Day, hence the names.

"Have you been talking to Mom?" I asked.

"And half the police force."

Holly spent her days in Reeboks, tackling druggies and pimps while her husband played with lumps of clay in the name of art. Kurt wasn't a bad guy. He did father two adorable children, and he was a good dad.

"And you know Mom," she said. "She thinks one daughter playing with guns is enough. Plus, you were always her creative child."

Growing up, Holly had arm-wrestled boys and played with frogs. I'd colored Barbie's hair and designed her clothes.

"I heard Pete Saunders was coming in to see you," she said.

"Just left. The guy wouldn't make the grade as an informant. Could he be any more tight-lipped?"

"Sounds like Pete. What do you want to know?"

That was a loaded question since what I really wanted to know was what was going on with Romero. "How'd Sister Madeline die?"

"Look, it was likely a heart attack, stroke, or plain old age. It was sudden, right?"

Knowing that didn't make any difference when you had an overactive imagination and the Skink putting ideas in your head. Plus, Sister Madeline's need to confide plagued me, not to mention how sickly she'd quickly become. I had a creepy feeling there was more to this than a heart attack.

"What about poisoning?" I blurted.

"They'll look into it. Not every death spells murder, Val."

"This coming from a cop."

"You learn to be objective. You're lucky they're checking it out at all. They don't usually do autopsies on old people. But because of the state scandal last year about nursing and retirement home conditions, the coroner is being extra cautious. On top of which, he's backed up." She muffled the phone while she spoke to someone, then came back on the line. "Seems they're also looking into the residents' backgrounds. Do you know Hillary Ayers?"

"Yes, Princess Grace's double."

"She had a tax evasion issue fifteen years ago."

I thought about this. "Even if she was Sister Madeline's accountant, I don't see how that could make her a murderer."

"I didn't say this was murder."

"Then why are they doing background checks?"

"Covering all bases."

"You sound like Saunders." Open-and-shut case, my ass. "Couldn't they have given this case to another cop? That hair mound of his is distracting."

"You're absolutely right. I'll inform the captain right away that Saunders should be dismissed because of bad hair."

Dry humor ran in our family.

"Seems nobody can fill Romero's sexy boots." I could hear the smile in her voice, but the teasing made me heartsick.

"Forget *him*," I said. "I have."

"Don't be too hard on the guy. It's not his fault he was assigned that investigation."

I groaned. "*What* investigation?" It wasn't the first time I'd asked her that question.

"All I can tell you is he's on a high-profile case. I'm sure he'd be here if he could."

"I've got to go. My next client will be waiting." This was true, but more, I was tired of guessing Romero's latest exploits. We weren't married. He didn't owe me anything. Right?

I hung up and almost collided with Jock outside my door, accepting money and a kiss from one of his voluptuous clients. She left with a lick of her lip and a promise to return next week. Her hair didn't look bad either. I smiled as she toodle-ooed out the door. Then I rolled my eyes.

Jock caught this and backed me into the office, shutting the door behind him. "Okay. Out with it." He folded his arms across his chest.

"What are you talking about?"

"I want to know what your problem is."

"I don't have a problem." Honestly, the scantily clad females were starting to get to me, but I wasn't about to tell *him* that.

"Like hell. All day, you've been rolling your eyes, sighing, and when you strutted by Christina Rowan earlier, you swiped bleach on her *black* hair."

"That was an accident." I could be indignant when the moment called for it.

"Accident." His voice was tightly controlled. "I had to fix that *accident* before she ended up with a skunk stripe."

"I'm surprised you've noticed anything except breasts and buttocks. Do any of your clients actually own clothes and have names other than Ginger or Christy?"

"I didn't name my clients, and I happen to notice more than you think." He raked his eyes over my entire body like a pirate determined to pillage an innocent damsel.

My skin prickled, and I felt my nipples harden from his hot stare.

He glanced toward the door, then back at me. "Why do you have a problem with my clientele? They're quite happy to pay your prices."

It was a reasonable question, but I was on a roll. "I'm not used to patrons who resemble Playboy Bunnies thrusting their tongues down my staff's throats. What does your girlfriend think of all these women?"

"Actually, Molly Garr is too short to be a Playboy Bunny, and she only gave me a peck on the cheek. *And*, not that it's any of your business, but I don't have a girlfriend."

Duly noted. I couldn't see him with one woman anyway. A dozen women, yes.

"Have you ever heard of male clients?" I asked.

"I have male clients."

"I haven't seen any so far."

"That's because they can't get a booking." He stared up at the ceiling, then lowered his gaze to me with a sigh. "I get it. You want more male customers."

Yeah, that was it.

I crossed my arms, looking uppity. "I don't care who you work on, but could you keep the fondling to a minimum?" I didn't know what I was getting huffy about. Jock had a laid-back confidence that was alluring as all get-out, he was an amazing stylist, respectful in a sexy way, and okay, easy on the eyes. I was acting seventeen, but I couldn't help myself.

"For the record," he said, "I don't fondle my clients." He unfolded his arms, backed me into my desk, and worked his leg between mine, separating my skirt at the thigh. My car keys dug into my tailbone, but I ignored it. I was deaf to everything except my thumping heart.

He took his finger and circled my lips with amazing concentration. The silence intensified, the hum of a blow dryer in the main salon the only sound. "*This* is fondling."

I caught my breath, pretty sure it wasn't hairspray fumes trapped in my throat.

"By the way…" He opened the door a crack. "I need to leave early tonight and tomorrow." He slammed the door, leaving me with one thought. Who was this Jock de Marco?

At six o'clock, I hopped in the car, went home, stuffed Yitts in the backseat, and drove to the vet's. I tried not to let it bother me that Jock had left early. After all, he'd worked a hard day, exerting himself as much as Max and I had. Maybe even more. As long as he fulfilled his obligations, pleased customers, and didn't give me any grief, I wasn't going to worry about what time he was exiting the building.

I swung inside the Noah's Ark-shaped veterinarian's office with Yitts under my arm. Dorothy Taylor, the vet's assistant, was ready for us.

I knew Dorothy from band in school, and will always remember her thin form leaning forward during a performance, auburn pageboy swinging furiously while she gave the clarinet all she had. She was an excellent musician, though her chronically clogged sinuses often got in the way of her talent. What she'd needed was a combination of eucalyptus, clove, and tea tree essential oils.

I followed Dorothy into the examining room and waited while she adjusted her glasses and squirted nasal spray up her nose.

I put Yitts on the scale. "You okay, Dorothy?" I was asking for trouble with a question like this, but I couldn't ignore the sniffling or the heavy sigh that followed.

She frowned and nodded, and an unsettling feeling told me allergies weren't the only thing bothering her. A second later, a tear rolled down her cheek.

I didn't know what to say. I suggested aromatherapy for her allergies, but that didn't go far. Yitts stood with her front paws on Dorothy's chest and licked the tear off her face. I handed Dorothy a tissue. "Hey," I said encouragingly, "your hair's grown. Maybe you could come in for a trim sometime. Or a new style."

She dabbed her eyes. "How would a new style help someone like me?"

Dorothy was in a state. "Someone like who?" I said. "You're a nice person. You've got a great job at a vet's office, and you play the clarinet better than anyone I know."

She rolled her eyes. "Yeah. That's something that gets me lots of dates. Bad enough I have no life," she continued, "now I'm worried my mother's in trouble."

I took a step back. "What kind of trouble?"

"Cooking-at-the-retirement-home trouble."

Uh-oh. Occasionally, I ran into Ruby at Rueland Retirement. And I didn't like where this was going.

Dorothy slid up her glasses as if better vision would help her think more clearly. "Last night when I got home from work, she was acting strange."

"How?"

"She was cleaning windows."

"I don't get it."

"Valentine, my mother doesn't clean windows. She doesn't even clean counters. Kind of frightening considering she's a cook."

"Why was she cleaning windows?"

Dorothy leaned in. "Sister Madeline from the retirement home died. My mother's afraid they'll think it was her cooking that killed the poor nun."

"But your mother's been there for years. She must have a good reputation."

"She does have a reputation. It's just not that of the happy homemaker. Would you believe the other day we discussed vacuum cleaners, and she had to think for a minute where ours was?"

"I'm sure there's a logical explanation for Sister Madeline's death. Probably nothing to do with your mother's cooking." Listen to me. Hadn't I been considering poisoning as a cause?

"She's not a bad person. She simply has her own way of doing things." Dorothy petted Yitts. "Do you think you could talk to her, Valentine? She's always liked you, and you helped the police before."

I opened my mouth to respond, but she rushed on. "I work most evenings, so you could go to the house and talk to her in private." She sniffed. "I'd feel much better."

I didn't know how much better I'd feel, but I promised Dorothy I'd talk to her mother.

The veterinarian came in, gave Yitts her needles and a vet-to-pet kiss, and we left the office. I drove home, thinking about my promise to Dorothy and the other things I'd learned so far. I had a soft-hearted senior suggesting a liaison between two residents, and a surfer hinting at foul play. Now I had a chronic wheezer praying her mother wasn't a murderer.

What had Ruby served Sister Madeline that might've killed her? I'd climbed that grand staircase a hundred times in my mind, recalling the details. Calla lilies at the window, crucifix over the kitchenette, Sister Madeline face down in lasagna. Had the sauce gone bad? Was the sausage spoiled? Had anyone else gotten sick?

With the police suggesting Sister had died of natural causes, why was I hell-bent on making more of this? She had to be well over seventy. Maybe she did die naturally. But until I knew that for sure, I had to do something. Didn't I owe Sister Madeline that?

If I didn't do it for her, I owed it to myself. Though I'd tried, I'd never forgiven myself for working late the night my client and good friend Kitty Hibel suggested we meet for dinner. I'd missed the meal, and the next day, she was gone. Moved away. I knew she'd had personal problems, but I never found out why she moved so quickly or where she'd gone. And I never heard from her again. I'd screwed up with Kitty, and Sister Madeline had departed now, too, but I was going to honor her memory by seeing this thing through.

On top of Sister's case, I had another problem in the form of a sexy-smelling, motorcycle-riding, hunky stylist. I hadn't erased Romero totally from my mind or soul, but working a few more days beside Jock, and he'd be the person to do it. How was I going to resist temptation and guard my heart?

That, I was afraid, was the biggest question.

Chapter 3

Wednesday began like the day before with a fresh onslaught of supermodels traipsing through the front door. I hadn't had a chance to visit Rueland Retirement as I'd promised, but I planned to drop by the minute I finished work today.

It was the middle of the afternoon, and I was in my office, reading up on a new skin product. At least that's what I told the others. Actually, I was keeping a healthy distance from Jock, plus agonizing over Sister Madeline's death. I was tracing my steps back into Sister's apartment for the umpteenth time, when my best friend Twix Bonelli called, all breathless.

"You're not going to believe this!"

I hadn't talked to Twix in two weeks, and everything blurted out. "I just hired Fabio, unearthed a dead nun, have the Hooters girls in the next room, barely recovered from a visit with my mother, *and* I didn't get to Zumba last night to work out my frustrations. Try me."

There was a two-second pause. "You hired Fabio? The guy with all the muscles? And you didn't tell me?"

Twix had a thing for muscular men, a mouth-dropping-to-the-floor thing. I opened the door, peeked out, then collapsed on my chair and started at the beginning.

"A nun!" Twix said, once I'd filled her in on the basics. "Was it murder?"

"I don't know."

"Do you *think* it was murder?"

"I don't know."

"When am I going to meet this Jock?"

"I don't know."

"*Errr.* I want details the next time we clean."

Sanitizing the salon was our weekly to biweekly date with each other. Twix would fill me in on her life while we scrubbed sinks, and I'd tell her about my lack thereof while we washed floors. In payment for her help, I'd turn her into a fashion goddess instead of a mother of two, and we'd dine at Mr. Wu's Wok, owned by a tiny bossy Asian who made the best sweet and sour pork in the world.

"I have to tell you my news," she said, "while the pig finishes licking the spilled pablum."

The Bonellis' pot-bellied pig was their version of a dog. He was cute but hairless.

"I had to drive Tony into work this morning because traffic from the T was being rerouted. The whole city's in a tizzy over parking."

"Why? What's going on?"

"Hold on." She muffled the phone. "Junie, stop ripping off Joey's diaper." She sighed. "Lord, give me strength. Did I ever tell you how much I hate kids?"

"You run a daycare."

"And if you tell anyone I said that, I'll kill you. This is the latest. Junie discovered Joey has a penis, so she tied a gherkin on a string around her waist and said this was *her* penis. Now she's got the daycare kids asking for gherkins and strings. Last night, I ate half a jar of pickles to get rid of the damn things."

Despite her complaints, Twix was probably the best mother I knew. I only had to look in her eyes when she held her kids to know they lit up her world.

"What's happening in the city?" I asked.

"A movie's being filmed at Boston Harbor. Big tents,

trailers, and an actual pirate ship in the water with skull flags and everything. I heard it's going to be called *Caribbean Gold*."

Was I hearing right? "Why would they film in Boston if the movie's set in the Caribbean?"

She clicked her tongue. "Why'd they film *Gone With the Wind* in Los Angeles instead of Georgia? Why does Hollywood do anything? It's the movies!"

I grinned at Twix's usual overreaction.

"You should see the pirates," she gushed. "Tony has everything compartmentalized nicely. But *these* guys. *Whew!*"

"How do you know all this?"

"I dropped Tony off at six this morning, then got lost finding Storrow Drive. I ended up in this private lot. The kids were sleeping in the backseat. I had an hour before the daycare toddlers started rolling in, so I got out of the van and watched a swordfight. When the hero got stabbed, I gave one of my bloodcurdling screams. I couldn't help it. It was intense. A few stagehands stampeded over and grabbed me. I thought I was going to pee my pants I was so scared."

"What happened?"

"They offered me a part. They needed an extra with good vocal chords."

I couldn't believe it. Only Twix could fall in a pile of pirate doo-doo and come up smelling like a rose. "Are you going to do it?"

"Why not? A few early mornings and late nights. And the money's fantastic."

After work, I stepped outside and breathed fresh New England air. Thankfully, Friar Tuck's had turned off their fryers and were likely bagging day-old donuts. And with Phyllis gone, those must've been piling up.

I slid behind the wheel of my Daisy Bug and glanced

over to where Jock's bike had been a mere hour ago. Not even a drop of oil left on the pavement to verify today's presence. I sighed. What did it matter anyway? He'd told me he was leaving early. I wasn't going to get all worked up over where he was or what he was doing.

The French braid I'd put in my hair last night suddenly felt tight. I shook my fingers through the braid and undid it. *Ahh.* Wild and free. A welcome relief from the tension over the past few days. Maybe Max was onto something with his *unleashing the wild side*.

I set my buckled boot on the gas, cruised out of the parking lot, and headed for Rueland Retirement, thinking about the promises I'd made to Mrs. Shales and Dorothy. Since the residents were likely in the middle of their supper, I didn't think now would be a good time to talk to Ruby. And I didn't know what I was going to say to Hillary, but I figured she wouldn't be surprised by a visit, especially after our shared experience over Sister Madeline's death. That was my hope.

I turned from Darling onto Montgomery. Leaves drifting in clusters by the curb flew in the air as I rushed by. I slowed to a crawl on Park Street and watched a fire truck pull away from the retirement home and disappear around the corner.

I tucked a wave behind my ear and pushed down the panic sitting below the surface. First a death. Now what? I glanced at the home. No smoke. No harried observers. Things seemed normal.

I parked, entered the gate, and climbed the porch steps. Suddenly remembering Jimmy's speculation about Virgil, I trotted back down and hiked to a pile of dirt near the side cellar door. Thanks to Monday's rain, an earthy smell surrounded the area. An old spade leaned against the house.

Hmm. Jimmy was right. Looked like someone had buried something. Well, I couldn't start digging now. I'd have to come back later, when it was dark. I hurried back up the steps and opened the big oak door.

A slight shiver went through me from the cool temperature and a burnt odor. I was thinking again about the fire truck when Susan MacDonald's voice made me turn toward the recreation room. "B fifty-six!" she called.

As entertainment coordinator, Susan planned bus trips, shopping excursions, exercise classes, bingo, and movie nights. Odd they were playing games at suppertime.

I spun around and bumped into Evalene's G.I. Joe torso.

"Miss Beaumont." She clicked her boots, hands behind her back, hair in the usual tight bun on top of her head.

The hairstylist in me craved to yank out her bun and cover the crude grays with a warm color, give her soft curls, and wax the facial hairs. But I wasn't here to do a makeover. And what about the burnt smell? "Was there a fire, Evalene? I saw a fire truck leave. Everyone okay?"

"A Ruby Taylor catastrophe," she said. "We managed to put out the grease flames before the firemen arrived. Thank goodness. Carting thirty-five seniors onto the front lawn isn't high on my bucket list." She gave a heavy sigh out her nose. "Of course, this delayed tonight's meal. Susan put together an unscheduled bingo game to keep the residents busy until an alternate dish is prepared."

I nodded and took a casual look around. "Everything else okay since Sister Madeline died?"

"Yes." She gave me a distasteful look. Because I mentioned Sister Madeline's name? Or because I was asking too many questions? "The police said Sister probably died in her sleep, so we're moving forward."

Right. I scaled the stairs to the second floor and was halfway to the landing when I spotted Nettie Wisz below, hobbling toward the foyer with her cane.

"Dang things." She whacked an end table so hard, the cracking sound made me pull up short. Nettie was a regular customer who'd recently moved to Rueland Retirement. I liked Nettie a lot, though she was a master at disparaging remarks.

"What's that smell?" she asked. "Dead skunk?"

"Lordy, woman," Wit Falco said, bringing up the rear, "your voice could raise the dead."

"Good. Maybe it'll bring back Sister Madeline. And why don't you git." She swept him away with her cane. "I don't need you by my side. If I want a real man, I'll find Virgil Sylas."

"*Virgil!* Ha. That guy prefers plants to people. Even then, he wouldn't notice you if you had branches sticking out of your body." Wit took a step back and tugged his red suspenders. "But he'd probably like those tree trunk legs of yours."

Nettie tightened her fists. "At least he can talk about more than the price of Depends. Plus, he's a gentleman. He escorted Sister Madeline around, and I'm prettier than she was."

"Yeah, but she was saner. And nicer, too."

"Why you—" Nettie raised her cane.

Evalene swooped in and seized the weapon. "Let's calm down, shall we?"

Pitting Nettie against Evalene was akin to shoving David in front of Goliath. But what Nettie lacked in size, she made up for in attitude. She glared at Evalene's uniform and metal buttons. "Hand over my cane, Evalene, and stop pussyfooting around people. It's creepy."

I bounced back down the stairs, and everyone gaped open-mouthed at me like I was indeed Wonder Woman.

"Ha. You didn't forget about me, did you, Valentine?" Nettie swiped her cane from Evalene and stabbed it in Wit's direction. "After Sister's death, this old coot said that's the last we'd see of you. I told him you're used to people dying. Go ahead, tell him."

Her confidence in me was staggering, but I had to agree with the old coot. I had forgotten her appointment. If I didn't give her a fresh set, her white curls would keep parting like the Red Sea. "Why don't I set your hair after you've had your supper?"

"If there *is* supper." She cranked her head as Susan announced that bingo was over. "Fine. I'll see you after we eat." She jabbed Wit in the butt. "Come on, old goat. Stop ogling Valentine as if she's steak on a platter. Your teeth would fall out if you bit into a real piece of meat. And that ain't likely with Ruby's cooking."

They wandered off with Evalene following them, and I ascended the stairs, setting my mind on what I had to do. I took a deep breath and rapped on Hillary's door.

"I stopped by to see how you're doing," I said when she answered.

Hillary was dressed in a gray pencil skirt and blue pastel sweater. A simple strand of pearls graced her neck. Dark circles shadowed her eyes.

"I haven't slept much since Monday." She patted her cheek. "I must look dreadful."

"You look radiant as usual." Apart from the hollow eyes, I wasn't lying.

She asked me in and poured us apple cider. I took in the various potted plants, a flower-patterned sofa, and the smell of fresh-cut roses wafting from two filled vases. Quite a contrast from Sister Madeline's, though it was just as chilly, which explained Hillary's need for sweaters.

She tasted her cider, then frowned. "The police suggest that Sister Madeline took a nap and died in her sleep. But when she napped, she curled up on her couch. Plus, she appeared to be in the middle of having lunch. I know she could've died while eating, but...I don't know. It's been a huge shock. You think someone like Sister Madeline would live forever."

True. "Evalene said you delivered Sister Madeline's lunch on Monday."

"Yes. Evalene usually took care of it, but I was on my way up when she came out of the kitchen. She handed me the tray and asked if I'd mind." She looked at me sharply. "Is there something wrong, Valentine?"

I wasn't sure, and Holly's story about Hillary's run-in with the law plagued me. Her tax issue didn't make her a cold-blooded killer, but it did make me wary. I sipped my cider. *Stick to the matter at hand.* "What exactly was on the plate?"

"With Ruby, one can never be certain. But if I'm not mistaken, it was lasagna. And there was sausage, garlic bread, and a cucumber and tomato salad. Do you think Sister Madeline's death had something to do with what she ate?"

"I don't know, and even if there's an autopsy, it could take weeks to find out."

We sat quietly for a second, contemplating this. Then I recalled Mrs. Shales's concern. Careful not to divulge too much, I asked, "Did Sister Madeline have any regular visitors? Family? Friends?"

"From outside the home?" Hillary crossed her elegant legs at the ankle and angled them under her chair. "Not that I know of."

"What about inside?"

She grimaced. "I guess you could call him a friend."

"Him?"

"Virgil Sylas. I'd often hear him knock on her door and see him through the peephole."

"You sure it was him?"

"Yes. He'd say, 'It's me, Virgil.' Then he'd slip inside."

I leaned forward. "Did you ask Sister Madeline about their relationship?"

"I didn't think it was my place to pry."

Funny, it wasn't bothering me any. "Could Virgil have hurt Sister Madeline?"

"I'm not good at speculating, Valentine. Perhaps you should speak to him and judge for yourself. Now would be a good time. He often skips meals in the dining room." She stood. "Which is where I should be heading, if they've figured out what to serve us. Virgil's unit is around the corner and down the hall on the left. There's a philodendron outside his door."

I thanked Hillary and wandered the hall that had the rising smell of burnt wieners, cooked cabbage, and hard-boiled eggs. Tonight's gourmet replacement meal. Halfway down the hall, I spotted a lush green plant. Other doors had scarecrows on hooks or wreaths of silk flowers. I guess Virgil favored plants to fancy decor.

I stood for a moment beside the plant, concocting an excuse to be there. I couldn't very well ask if he had anything to do with Sister Madeline's death.

I knocked, and a thin man in an oversized shirt opened the door. Balding and stooped at six feet, he had a flushed face and broken capillaries—which needed laser, or vitamin K.

"Mr. Sylas?" I asked politely. "I'm Valentine Beaumont." I handed over my business card. "I'm making the rounds. In case you're looking for a new hairstylist, I usually visit here Mondays." I glanced at his balding head. What were the chances?

He thanked me for the card, slid it into his shirt pocket with a rubber-gloved hand, and started to close the door.

I put my hand on the door and gave a humble shrug. "I was supposed to do Sister Madeline's hair the other day, but when I got here…well, I'm sure you heard of her passing."

"Yes." His light blue eyes looked sorrowful. "We'd been friends almost from the day I'd moved here."

I smiled kindly. "You've lived here awhile?"

"Several years." He brightened. "It's such a beautiful community. The Boston area is so"—he gazed beyond my head, searching for the right word—"cultural."

I agreed. "You must've been shocked by Sister's death."

"I think we were all shocked."

I peered over his shoulder at the tropical forest behind him. Plants hung from the ceiling and covered most of the furniture. Condensation dotted the windows, and humid air sucked at my skin. I now understood why he was flushed. I clamped my mouth shut before he noticed I was gaping. Too late.

He nudged the door open wider, shrugging at my astonishment. "I'm a retired botanist. I guess one never totally gets away from one's work. Would you like to see more?"

He ushered me inside, and I did an itchy dance as sweat beads trickled between my shoulder blades.

"The heating system's irregular, but the plants love it." Clearly content in his world, he snapped off his gloves and cupped a scarlet bloom on a black-leafed plant. "Like this Canna Australia." He smiled. "Have you ever seen one before?"

I studied the flower. "No, but I do have a plant with similar black leaves."

He leaned forward. "Really? What species is it?"

"I don't know. It's too rotted to tell."

Virgil looked horrified, like he was staring at a certified plant killer. He shook his head as if to dismiss the thought. "This needs TLC. That's why I keep it here." He misted the plant with a nearby spray bottle.

I luxuriated in the cool vapor spilling my way, then shifted the conversation back to Sister Madeline. "Did you see Sister at all Monday?"

"Yes. In the morning. But she was fine when I left. I was told the police believe she died in her sleep."

"That seems to be the rumor."

"Do you think that's false?"

I didn't know what I thought, but I took in his gardening tools and a plastic bag of food scraps, and asked if Sister Madeline shared his love for plants.

"Somewhat," he said.

Likely true, since she only had a few struggling plants in her apartment. I let my gaze wander. "Does your wife like plants?"

He gave a bashful smile. "I never married." He set the spray bottle down, and I noticed his bare ring finger. He moved to the patio door and slid it open, bringing in a blast of fresh air and the earthy smell from outside. I could tell he wanted to get back to work, but I had one last question.

"Did you ever see Sister Madeline wear a locket? It had pictures of a baby and a young woman?"

He thought for a moment, then shook his head. "No."

For someone who stuck close to Sister, he wasn't a fount of knowledge.

He bent to look at the shallow crates on his patio that were filled with dirt, bark, moss, and other things that looked like they'd come from a forest floor. "I hate to rush you," he said, standing again, "but I must tend to my decomposers. They're so misunderstood."

I wrinkled my nose in confusion. Composers, I knew. Beethoven, Mozart, Chopin. "Decomposers?"

"Fungi. Mushrooms. They give structure to soil." He nodded at the bag of food scraps. "And that's food that nourishes them."

Virgil was likeable in an academic way, but Wit was right. This man preferred plants to people. I didn't want to say anything to tip him off about the dirt mound outside. I needed to see for myself what was buried there. I thanked him and followed the path out.

I dashed to my car and embraced the cool air. It took me a second to realize, but why did Virgil's heater work when the others didn't? Could the heating system have had any significance in terms of Sister's death? I tucked that thought away and hauled my portable hair dryer from my car. I ducked into the dining room and searched the sea of white heads for Nettie.

"She's gone to her room," Wit hollered. "Indigestion."

I nodded my thanks and plodded down the hall, dragging my hair dryer behind me past the ancient elevator. I often used the home's tiny salon when I had a number of sets and cuts, but for one or two clients, it was easier to simply visit their apartments.

I knocked and tried Nettie's door. Locked. *Darn.* I rapped louder and waited. I drummed my fingers on the wall. I counted to ten. I didn't like the ominous feeling prickling my skin. I reasoned just because one resident crossed the pearly gates didn't mean Nettie was meeting her there. In fact, I had a hunch Nettie's final destination called for much lighter clothes.

Okay, enough. I turned to get help when the door flew open.

"I was in the toilet." Nettie glowered. "Damned cooked cabbage gives me the runs, not to mention the chilly air." She yanked her sweater over her chest. "Is it any wonder with the heating off-kilter around here?"

Fifteen minutes later, I had Nettie nice and warm under the dryer. I cleaned up, then sat beside her and filed her nails. I figured I had nothing to lose, broaching the subject of Virgil and Sister Madeline. "Were they, um—"

"An item? I said that to rankle old ferret face." She stuck out her legs, crossing them at her saggy-nyloned ankles. "But Virgil stayed real close to Sister Madeline. I don't get all tingly for bingo or concerts, and Susan keeps volunteers going through a revolving door. All the same, most of us join the activities. Not Virgil." She clanked her rollers against the rim of the dryer. "He even flees the dining room with his food before one of us widows can make small talk."

"Maybe he likes his privacy."

"Could be. But one day last week I saw him go into Sister Madeline's apartment with one of his plants." She tipped her chin up, looking down her nose at me. "Does that sound like someone who wants privacy to you?"

I had no answer. Could there've been a past connection between Virgil and Sister Madeline? Or was this a case of pure friendship? Two people who didn't feel comfortable with the world, seeking solace with a kindred spirit. At least I could guess where Sister's plants came from.

I checked the dryer temperature with my hand, and Nettie squinted at me. "What's with all the questions? You suspect someone killed Sister Madeline? Because I can tell you who done it."

I lifted the dryer off her pink scalp with a thunk. "You can?"

She slanted on one butt cheek, closing the gap between us. "It's my opinion, for what it's worth, but I think Cook poisoned her."

"Ruby Taylor?"

"You got it, baby."

I stuffed the nail file in my bag and unwound rollers. "Why would Ruby poison Sister?"

"Because she doesn't know cyanide from rawhide. Someone's always rushing from the dining room, throwing up what's gone down. I'm surprised more of us aren't dropping like flies. Once, I complained. Know what she said? 'You don't like it? There's the cookbook.' What kind of an answer is that?"

I tapped a roller, thinking of Sister's recent appearance, then remembered Dorothy's concern. "Is Ruby still here?"

"Nah. She leaves the minute the food hits the table. Probably doesn't want to stick around to witness any casualties. Especially tonight, after today's fiasco."

I rooted around in my bag for my black oval brush. Great. Not here. Settling for another brush, I fussed and fixed curls around Nettie's hairline. She giggled like a schoolgirl. *Ha, Jock de Marco. You're not the only one who can put a smile on a customer's face.*

"Don't forget these." She opened my palm and placed two sparkly barrettes inside.

"Uh, wow."

"I knew you'd like them. All the hot chicks are wearing them. Even saw Kelly Ripa sporting a pair the other day. You ever seen *her* man? Hubba-hubba."

I fastened them to her hair, coated her with hairspray, and held up the mirror.

She grinned, angling her head this way and that. "Tell me Virgil won't notice me now!"

I went home, ate supper with Yitts, ironed tomorrow's outfit, and waited for the midnight hour so I could trek back to Park Street and unearth whatever secrets were hiding in Virgil's pile of dirt.

By ten o'clock I was done waiting. I threw on my

tailored black leather jacket, pulled on my black boots, stuffed my hair under a black beanie, and gloved my hands. Blackening my face would've completed the cat burglar look, but I didn't think I needed to go that far.

I grabbed a spicy pepperette to snack on, then locked up the house and drove to Rueland Retirement. The night manager would likely be on duty, but I didn't need to speak to her, and she didn't need to see me. I parked a few houses down from the home, gripped my bag, and stuffed my half-eaten pepperette in my jacket pocket. With a nervous sigh, I left the car and tiptoed down the sidewalk, limiting the clack of my boots in the still neighborhood.

The home was in darkness, except for a dimly lit lamp glowing from the music room, left of the front door. I breathed in relief. Likely, everyone was asleep. And the night manager—which is all I ever knew her as—would be camped in her office near the back entrance. I didn't think a glow would be noticed at the right side where I was heading. Darn. I still needed a flashlight to see what was buried. I reached in my bag for my cell phone, then remembered any time I'd tried to use the flashlight on it before; the icon had lit up but there was zero light. I took it out anyway and tried again. Nothing. I really had to get that fixed. I glanced at the distant streetlight. It would have to do. I just hoped the shovel was there.

I chucked the phone back in my bag, quietly unhinged the iron gate, and stepped onto the property. So far so good. Bag over my shoulder, I aimed right and crossed the lawn to the mound of loose earth.

My heart hammered in my chest, and my scalp was sweating under my hat. I didn't know if it was the heat from the pepperette or if it was nerves. But I couldn't stop now. I had to see what Virgil had buried in the mound. The spade, thankfully, was leaning against the side of the house. I went over to it, wrapped my fingers around the handle, and took one stride. The shovel dropped with a thud. *Shoot*. Heavier than I expected.

I bent over and clutched the handle again when a low

growl came out of the darkness. I turned my head and looked into the meanest, blackest eyes, glowing from the face of a big black dog. It bared its teeth, *grrr*-ing at me in an impolite tone, the streetlight illuminating the drool dripping from its mouth.

I felt my stomach drop and my voice shrink. Who knew Rueland Retirement had a watchdog? I fought back a scream and stared wide-eyed at the dog.

Killer growled, and I released the spade and slowly straightened. *Think, Valentine.* Throw him a bone. A branch. I patted my bag and felt my curling iron. Right. Wait. I groped inside my jacket and yanked out the pepperette. I whipped it toward the backyard and didn't waste time seeing if Killer would lunge after it. I ran as fast as my buckled boots would take me. I finally reached my car and collapsed with a sigh in the driver's seat.

I breathed in and out, waiting for my hands and legs to stop trembling. By now, Killer was at the fence, licking his lips, barking for more treats. All I needed was for the night manager to come to the door, or for Martoli or Saunders to cruise down the street and catch me pawing around the retirement home, looking like Catwoman. I took a final breath, and before anyone spotted me, I started the engine and roared away from the curb.

Chapter 4

Thursday was more of the same at work. Stunning supermodels. Different day. By Friday, I'd seen so much skin, I felt like I was working at the Playboy Mansion.

I wanted to go back to Rueland Retirement, but I was hoping to create some distance before I tackled Killer and revisited that scene. I was lucky I hadn't been caught. And I reasoned the mound would still be there. After all, how much digging could one man do? I'd go back tonight after the Red Sox game. This time I'd be armed. I'd stopped at Market Basket Thursday after work and picked up a hunk of meat. Maybe that would occupy the dog while I dug for gold.

Ruby Taylor was the next person I wanted to see. Granted, I didn't know what it would prove. Everyone knew Ruby's cooking was horrible, but did that make her a killer? I called the vet's, and Dorothy said she was working late. Now was my opportunity.

I finished cleaning my station for the day as two raven-haired knockouts strutted into the shop. Max, who knew my plans, shooed me away. "Do what you need. We'll lock up."

I scowled, my gaze traveling from Max to Jock. "Don't do anything you'll be sorry for."

Max gave a shrug, palms up. "How much trouble can we get into putting hair extensions on the Angeletti twins?"

My eyes narrowed warily.

"Go!" he insisted. "We'll all catch up at Fenway. And eat something. I can hear your stomach growling from here."

I *was* hungry. I grabbed my bag, rolled out of the parking lot, and took a deep breath as I hit the open road. I drove to a Selena Gomez tune, attempting to feel as free as her voice sounded, but I hadn't made the first set of lights when I began summarizing my week so far.

I was astonished I'd made it through four whole days with Jock in my employment. He'd received one marriage proposal, two propositions, and more ear licking than I cared to remember. Okay, maybe he tantalized the clientele. It was better than sending them off in a fury with fried hair or botched colors.

My thoughts ran to Phyllis and the flak my distant relatives had given me over letting her go. I reasoned Phyllis was no longer my problem, even if it meant ignoring rants that she was probably dead at the side of the road. Seemed no one cared about Phyllis when she was here. Now that she was gone, it was like Susie Sunshine was missing.

True, Max and I struggled to keep up with Jock's coiffing and curling talent. And with Phyllis gone, we were all too busy to take on the extras. Earlier today, I'd scratched down a reminder to advertise for another beautician, but that was a job I wasn't looking forward to.

I glanced at the car clock. Ten after six. Maybe Ruby did leave work after the food hit the table, but I didn't think she'd be home yet. I was in such a hurry to get this visit over with so I could get to the game, I hadn't even considered that.

I thought about buying a bag of chips to kill time and satisfy my hunger, but that thought was quickly replaced when I stopped at a red light. I noticed a cute miniskirt hanging in the front window of my favorite second-hand boutique across the street. I sat up. I needed a new skirt. After the week I'd had, I needed a new wardrobe. I looked back at the clock. I'd already accepted the fact I'd be late for the game. Ruby wouldn't be home from work for another half hour, and I was still hungry. But that skirt did look cute. Why not?

Thirty minutes later, I was back on the road with a new-to-me miniskirt, two matching tops, and a glittery bracelet. And it all came to less than forty dollars. What a deal!

Feeling I'd killed enough time, I continued driving south from town and passed homes with dirt lawns and scarred fences. I looked up at a battered sign, thinking I had to be close to Fife Street where Ruby and Dorothy lived. The worn sign was one indication. The dull feeling in my gut was another.

I batted around in my mind what I was going to say to Ruby. Should I ask what she'd cooked on Monday? How she cooked it? *Be yourself. And smile.* People reacted kindly when you smiled. It got me through Virgil's door.

I turned onto Fife Street and crawled up to the curb in front of Ruby's house. I felt nauseated with doubt, but I shut off the engine, took a major breath, and headed for the door.

Ruby's house was how I remembered it. Paint had been slapped on the bungalow a few times, but Ruby didn't care about matched colors or finished trim. I'd come here to do homework with Dorothy and could speak from experience—there wasn't much Ruby cared about.

It was almost seven when I climbed her front porch. Supper would be done at Rueland Retirement, and Ruby was probably already planning tomorrow's menu. Then again, maybe not. A floorboard creaked under my foot. I held my breath and took another step. Silence. I shuddered and rang the bell.

A tiny dried-up woman with short wiry black hair opened the door. Her eyelids were smudged in blue, her cheeks were flamingo pink, and her Spock-like eyebrows had been drawn with a sharp crayon. Ruby always did like makeup.

She squinted through a plume of smoke, sucking on a cigarette so hard, her cheeks folded in. "Valentine Beaumont." She hauled me in for a hug and exhaled into my hair.

I cringed, promising to spray myself with perfume before the ballgame.

"What are you doing here?" She held me at arm's length and gave a nod. "Never mind. Enter at your own risk."

I followed her and the ash trail into the kitchen, which had the same disorderliness as a mess tent vacated by a platoon of soldiers. She gave a bubbling pot on the stove a stir, then placed her cigarette in an ashtray that hadn't been emptied since the start of the millennium.

She crossed her arms over her chest and squinched one eye shut. "Dark-haired beauty Valentine Beaumont. What brings you to my humble abode?"

I prayed this would go well. "I saw Dorothy at the vet's, and I got to thinking it's been a while since you and I have said more than hi in passing at the retirement home." I gave an open-palmed shrug. "So here I am."

The corner of her mouth tipped up a hair. "You'll have to do better than that. You know what Dorothy's name means? Gift of God. I know my girl's worried about her ma."

She scooped a ladle into the pot, then slurped a mouthful of soup. It smelled like chicken, but one could never be sure with Ruby. She swiped paper plates off the table and flicked away a bread crumb, missing the ashtray. "Dang, I usually have better aim. Have a seat."

How anyone could operate in such filth was beyond me, but it was amusing in an oddball way. I brushed a dried noodle off a chair and sat down.

"So?" She lurched against the counter. "What did that child of mine say?"

I gave an earnest smile. "That you've been cleaning windows."

"Cleaning windows!" *Cough. Cough.* "And you believed her?"

She had a point. A blowtorch couldn't rid her windows of grime.

"Dorothy said you clean when you're upset."

"Yeah…I was a little upset. But I got over it."

I was going to have to spill the beans. "She's afraid you may lose your job over Sister Madeline's death." There. It was out on the table, such as it was.

Ruby spit into the sink. "Yeah, that'd be a real shame. I can't tell you how crushed I'd be." She siphoned her cigarette, then snuffed it out.

"You probably have nothing to worry about. And I'm sure Wednesday's fire wasn't your fault." Oops. Didn't mean to let that slip out.

"Ach." She flung a hand in the air. "I've had worse." She slid another cigarette to the corner of her mouth and lit up. "It's that darn dog that's troubling me now."

"Dog?" I looked around but didn't see any signs of animals.

"Rival, that black beast at the retirement home. Damn dog was moping around the backyard all day yesterday. Wouldn't eat or anything. He finally keeled over last night."

I blinked. "Dead?"

"Not dead. But he must've eaten something bad Wednesday night. When I arrived at work Thursday morning, he was farting up a spice storm. His intestinal tract was way off. Now everyone thinks I poisoned him."

I stared at her, suffocating inside. I'd poisoned Rival? With a pepperette?

"They rushed him to the vet, and Dorothy helped the doc flush him out or some damn thing. She called this afternoon. He's going to be fine. But they're keeping him one more night for observation."

I blew out air, relief flooding my core.

"Listen, girlie, stay and have supper with me. I got chicken pea soup here." She pointed to the counter ledge. "Tums are over there."

Except for a Friar Tuck's croissant, I hadn't eaten since Cap'n Crunch filled my bowl this morning. I was hungry. But I wasn't *that* hungry. "I don't want to impose. Really."

"No imposition. I'm used to quadrupling my recipes. And since Dorothy's working late, I'm eating alone. Now where are the bowls?"

"I'm going to a Red Sox game," I said, "which I'm already late for—"

"So, eat and run. I don't mind." She slapped a mixing bowl in front of me. "Sorry. Crate & Barrel hasn't delivered my new china."

Since I hadn't yet asked what happened the day of Sister's death, I agreed to stay for supper. We ate soup with serving spoons and ripped a French loaf apart with our fingers.

I wanted to steer the conversation back to Sister Madeline, when Ruby spoke up.

"I think it was the beans."

"Beans?" I pulled a chicken bone out of my mouth, then gave a startling burp.

"Yeah. I was making the lasagna when I realized I didn't have enough ground beef. Though I did have lots of beans. So, I loaded up the sauce with all the beans I could find. Kidney beans. Navy beans. Fava beans."

"Why the big dish? Hadn't most of the residents gone to a concert?"

She shrugged. "It wasn't a huge dish, and there were enough old farts to cook for. When the lasagna came out of the oven, Evalene had me make up a plate for Sister Madeline."

My stomach growled in dissent, and I backed away from the table. "Did you see where Evalene went with it?"

"No. She took the tray off the counter. Next thing I learned, Sister Madeline was dead." She squinched her eyes up at me again. "You don't think I killed her, do you?" She shook her head, the concern evident. "Sometimes I lose track of everyone's dietary needs, and Lord knows what pills they're all on. You don't suppose the beans did her in, do you?"

I didn't have a theory on the beans, but I couldn't see Ruby as a killer. My insides were churning, and I was trying to keep down another burp from the soup. I snatched the Tums off the counter and swallowed. "Let's hope it wasn't the beans."

Brookline Avenue was nearly deserted when I got to the city. Stragglers hurried past scalpers to the gates. Street vendors were closing, and gas stations that had stopped pumping for the night had cars sandwiched into every possible space. I needed gas, but it would have to wait.

I smothered myself in perfume to cover the stale smell of smoke, then paid an attendant forty dollars to sardine my car between a red jeep and a blue van. I dodged past people, looking for a bathroom when a hand gripped my arm and reeled me back.

"Hey, dudette!"

I wheeled around. "Holy cow, Jimmy. You nearly stopped my heart."

He gave a confident snort. "Yeah, I have that effect on women."

Lord, give me strength.

"Jock the Rock and Maximilian dude ducked inside," he said. "How come you're not with them?"

"Appointments." A slight exaggeration.

"Cool. Valentine the entrepreneur. Hey, you may even see that scary soldierlike dudette from the retirement home. She really digs baseball."

There was only one person he could be talking about. "Evalene?"

He gave a total body shake. "That's the one. With that bun on top of her head, I keep picturing her in one of those sumo wrestler outfits. It's like, wreaking havoc with my mind. But hey, I sell tickets to whoever wants them."

"Is that who you sold tickets to the other day at the retirement home?"

"Nah. Those were for my buddy's granny and her main squeeze. I had to go back since a few old folks were catching Z's. Boy, those seniors have the life of Riley! Shuffleboard, movies, naps, home-cooked meals. I could seriously get into that lifestyle." He looked at the ground. "Like, working's the pits."

Oh brother. "So, Evalene? Baseball?"

"Oh, yeah. When I went back in with this neat trim, talk got around to you. I told her how you scooped up the last good seats for tonight's game. And whammo, she bought a ticket in the nosebleeds." He smiled, obviously pleased with his salesmanship.

"So, she's here." A shiver racked my spine.

"You got it. You may see her in there." He pointed a thumb behind his head. "Like, if you're lucky."

The news of Evalene's presence and my unsettled stomach had me feeling anything but lucky. I popped two antacids, made a visit to the bathroom, and almost felt like new. Unfortunately, there was an irritating feeling I should be on alert. I kept my eyes wide as I bought popcorn and a soda and went to look for our seats.

Fenway was packed. Top of the fourth, Sox and Jays were tied. I hurried past crowded sections, breathing with relief that I didn't see Evalene.

I descended a ton of steps and stopped at my row on the left where four guys with beer bellies held up hotdogs. Their faces and bare stomachs were painted red, each with a white letter that collectively spelled *SOX*! The fourth guy was the exclamation point. Yeah. Great seats, Jimmy. Max and Jock were to the left of the guys.

I stared from the bellies to my butt-clinging turtleneck, black tights, and spiked boots. Perfect. I held my breath and excused myself as I carefully sidestepped to the left. I passed the last guy without getting smeared with paint and sighed. Then I tripped over Jock's leather boot. Half my popcorn flew in the air, the lid on my soda popped off, and soda sprayed everywhere. I landed backwards with a thump on Jock's lap and instantly struggled to get up. Jock held me down by the hips, apparently liking the feel of things.

I kicked his boot, which was sticking out into the row, and turned to meet him head-on. "You did that on purpose."

"I did so." He shoved my behind to one side and focused on the game.

Max held down my chair for me, then backed up and gave me a strange look. "Have you been smoking?"

Max not only took care of his appearance, but he had the corner market on men's cologne. Still cranky at Jock, I wiggled over to the middle seat, snapped the lid back on my drink, and set everything down. "I was at Ruby's, remember?"

He didn't respond, which was just as well. I was still processing Ruby's "bean" talk.

"Look!" He pointed to the field. "You're going to miss it. Pedroia has three balls." He giggled at that, but when he saw the unamused expression on my face, he swallowed the laughter, reached behind me, and tapped Jock's shoulder. "Think they'll walk him?"

Jock nodded. "Good chance, but I think they'll challenge him."

He was right. Pedroia whacked the ball and it disappeared in the stands. The crowd roared. The three of us jumped to our feet and hugged each other. Actually, I avoided hugging Jock and high-fived instead.

Max gave an ear-piercing whistle and waved down to the field. "Did you see that? Pedroia waved to me!"

During the seventh-inning stretch, Jock wandered the food stands. I updated Max. "I'm not getting any closer to figuring out Sister Madeline's death." Unless you counted Nettie's rantings.

"Maybe you're asking the wrong questions."

I gave him a blank look. "You're right. I should be more direct. How does 'Did you kill Sister Madeline?' sound?"

"Like you know one of those old fogies did it."

Why did I bother? "The most logical reason to murder someone old is to inherit their valuables. Yet as a nun, Sister Madeline lacked worldly possessions."

"True." He stuck a bag of chocolate-covered almonds in front of me. "She was a saint."

"They didn't come any nicer." I passed on the nuts. I didn't think I should tempt fate.

He crunched away, giving me a sideways glance. "You going to the funeral?"

"Are you kidding?" Funerals and I were a bad idea, unless you considered a major case of the giggles acceptable while everyone else sobbed. Visitation was the most I could handle.

"Yeah, you're right. The place will probably be a sea of priests and nuns. Last thing they'll need is an uncontrollable aesthetician in ribbed stockings and Gucci heels."

I cut him a deadpan glare. "I wouldn't necessarily wear Gucci. Anyway, a date hasn't been set for the funeral yet. Seems autopsies on seniors from retirement homes are keeping coroners hopping." We munched on our snacks and did some people-watching.

I turned to Max. "Have you ever seen Virgil Sylas at Rueland Retirement?"

Occasionally, Max joined me and took over the barber cuts if I was heavily booked with sets. It wasn't his favorite Monday activity, but lunch after usually put a smile on his face.

"Is he tall, dark, and handsome?"

"He's tall, thin, and balding. And he was close to Sister Madeline, but not romantically."

"Don't believe I've seen him before. And what's wrong with being close to someone? We're close, and we're not romantic."

I rolled my eyes. "It's creepy. He'd go in her apartment whenever he felt like it."

"How do you know that?"

"Witnesses."

"Hmm. What about Chef Ruby from 'Hell's Kitchen?'"

"Max, Ruby is sweet." I grinned. "In a demented way."

"Well? Did you learn anything?"

"She thinks she may have killed Sister Madeline with her lasagna." No need to share the dog debacle and the fact that I almost killed *it*.

"Wouldn't the whole retirement home be flat out like in Jonestown?"

"Most everyone else went to a concert that day. And maybe Sister Madeline's system reacted badly." I suppressed a burp. "Do you think eating beans could kill someone?"

He curled up his lip. "What kind of beans are we talking? Green beans or kidney?"

"Kidney. Fava. Navy."

"Major indigestion maybe, but I've never heard of anyone dropping dead over them. So, what are you thinking? Sister Madeline had an allergic reaction or was poisoned?"

"I don't know. But I need to go back and find my oval brush. It wasn't in my bag when I did Nettie's hair, and I think I left it in Sister Madeline's apartment."

"Just buy another brush."

"They stopped manufacturing this kind, and it's my favorite for brushing out roller sets. I'm not leaving it behind. And I might need you. Mind helping me out?"

"You want the truth?"

"No."

"Then I'd be happy to."

We heard the beer-belly guys suck in, then saw Jock and his bulging biceps cut by them. The guys nodded and made deep "yeah" affirmations, all the while holding in their stomachs. Something to aspire to was my guess.

"What'd I miss?" Jock sat in his seat.

"A couple of buxom blonds went up that way." I pointed behind us.

He took my finger and curled it into his hand, nestling it under his arm snugly.

I withdrew my hand and slouched back in my seat. I munched popcorn and gazed at him while he watched the game. His strong jaw dimpled when he smiled, his long windswept hair begged to be tamed, and he smelled like heaven. No wonder female clients couldn't control their lust. One look at Jock and they couldn't remember their names.

"You're going to go cross-eyed from staring," he said, without moving his head.

"I was looking at the scoreboard." Boy, was I quick.

"The scoreboard's that way."

Know-it-all. I jerked my head to the left and focused on a swarm of people on the stairs a dozen rows down, getting lots of attention from the crowd.

Several uniforms rushed down to the scene, keeping others back while two sloppily dressed men struggled to detain a man. The aggressor threw a punch at one of the men who was wearing a faded ball cap. The guy in the cap grabbed the assailant's arm and wrenched it behind his back, causing the guy to bend at the knees.

I strained to get a better look at the man in the ball cap, because even from a distance, there was something familiar about the way he moved and took control. He cuffed the guy's hands behind his back, and that's when I saw it. The Iron Man watch on his wrist and the glowing hands that kept time. For a split second, he raised his head above the crowd. His cap sat low over his forehead, and a dark beard covered his granite-like jaw. The watch could've belonged to anyone, but there was no mistaking the firm build and wide shoulders embedded in my heart. He glanced my way, and eyes blacker than the night zeroed in on me.

My heart stopped cold, and I couldn't swallow. I knew that look, and it burned right through me.

There was fumbling as the apprehended man thrashed around. The cops wasted no time ushering him up the stairs, out of sight.

I turned and craned my neck to see, then whipped back around in my seat, heaving for air. Jock was in conversation with the exclamation point guy beside him, and Max's eyes widened. "What is it, lovey? Looks like you had a nightmare. You're hyperventilating." He looked around for the cause and shoved Diet Coke under my nose. "Here."

I chugged soda between gulps of air.

"Wait!" Max rocketed to his feet, hand clamped to my shoulder. "Where is she?"

"Who?"

"The one person capable of giving *me* nightmares. Phyllis!" He snatched my drink, tore off the lid, and gulped it back. "Where'd you see her?" His gaze ripped through the crowd.

I yanked him down. "It wasn't Phyllis." I lowered my voice. "It was Romero."

He let out a heavy sigh. "As in sexy blue-eyed detective? Mr. Long Arm of the Law?"

"I'm sure of it." Which didn't make me feel any better. Two months had gone by. Why hadn't he phoned? Had he buried that spark we'd had? Was I that easy to forget?

"I see he's still got a hold on you. You're whiter than a cadaver." He slapped my cheek one way, then the other.

"Owwwww." I pressed my stinging skin. "What'd you do that for?"

"To put color back in your face."

"Sheesh. What color were you hoping for? Black or blue?"

"You guys going to catch the last inning?" Jock's voice was low. "Or would you rather take this out to the street?"

I jumped at my hunky new hire's voice. Then I scrubbed my cheeks, sliding an accusatory look at Max. What a day. Bad enough I wasn't getting anywhere in my search for clues, but I'd barely survived a Ruby meal, been slapped by a soon-to-be ex-employee, and now Romero was here, alive and well. I was thankful he was okay, but my heart sank at the thought that he hadn't wanted to see me.

The red-bellied guys cheered, signaling the end of the game. Max scooted out to pick up his car, and the guys filed out behind him, patting Max on the back. Winning made everyone buddies. After the cheering throng shoved to the exits, Jock and I climbed the stairs. "I'll walk you to your car," he said, taking my arm.

"I don't need a bodyguard."

"I gathered that. According to Jimmy, you're quite capable in the self-defense department. I'm walking you anyway."

"Look." I shrugged loose. I wanted to get the perm-rod story straight. "This murderer was fleeing. I jumped him. We wrestled in mud. I grabbed the first thing in my bag to stop him from beating me to a pulp. I'm not Lara Croft: Tomb Raider. I don't carry machine guns strapped to my back." My voice was close to hysterical, but I couldn't help it. "It's ridiculous. I get it."

He looked at me with amusement, folding his arms thoughtfully across his chest. "Did you try squirting him with gel? Maybe the mud would've hardened from all the extra hold."

I gave him a steely-eyed look. "Now you're a comedian."

"Thought I'd try it on for size."

"Go try it on somewhere else." I turned on my heels. "I don't need more jokes tonight."

"Okay. No jokes. This is downtown Boston. I'm taking you to your car."

No point arguing with a man when he was acting chivalrous. "Thank you," I said, begrudgingly.

We reached the top of the stairs, and I spotted Evalene standing still, holding up a wall as people jostled by. Why wasn't she heading toward the exit like everyone else? Why was she even here? Was it true she liked baseball?

"Valentine?"

I leaped at the voice and turned around. A dark-haired man in a sweatshirt and athletic pants approached us, waving his arm. Tony Bonelli. Twix's husband.

I let out a breath and slid my gaze back to the wall Evalene had been supporting. Lots of people. No Evalene. I didn't trust her absence. She was a lurker.

"You taking in a game?" Tony joined us and sized up Jock.

Tony was as Italian as they came. Hairy, handsome, swoon-worthy eyes. He was a good husband and had a decent job as a podiatrist for professional athletes. He was a head taller than me, but Jock was probably heads over everyone in Fenway.

"Yeah." I detected a mentholated ointment smell. "What about you?"

"Worked late tonight. Catcher has bunions. Figured might as well."

I looked up at Jock. "He works in sports medicine."

"Tony Bonelli." Tony smiled and extended a hand to Jock. "You're the new guy."

I hoped Tony had washed after touching the last pair of feet. Then again, maybe Smartass would contract athlete's foot while shaking hands.

"Twix wasn't joking. You have the arms of three men."

Jock cocked an eyebrow at me.

My face warmed. "His wife is my friend. I told Twix I'd hired a new stylist."

Jock nodded, and before he could speak he was pulled away by a client who was excited to see him at the game.

I turned back to Tony. "How's the movie going for her?"

"She's taking it seriously. Even gave herself a new name."

"New name? Why?"

He shrugged. "According to Twix, all movie stars use fake names. So, she and all the other extras are doing the same." He shook his head in disbelief. "She's been practicing her screams day and night. Said she may even give up daycare. Can you believe it? One line, suddenly she's Keira Knightley."

I did believe it. With Twix, it was all or nothing. "When does she start filming?"

"She's going in before dawn tomorrow." He looked at his watch. "Which means I better get home. It's daddy daycare tomorrow."

It was late by the time I left Boston. Jock offered to drive me home, but scrunching Jock inside my Bug was akin to cramming Hercules in a Matchbox car. That wasn't the only reason I didn't want him to ride with me. I'd sworn off men. Seeing Romero tonight had confirmed it. I needed to ignore the heat that continually flowed between Jock and me and block out the way he stroked me with his eyes. If only it was that easy. I swallowed a hard lump. I wasn't sure which was safer, but I leaned toward driving through Boston alone at night on an empty tank of gas.

Adding to my worries was Twix's new movie venture. She'd just gotten the job, but she knew *nothing* about acting. Plus, when it came to movie stars, Twix was impressionable. What's more, Twix didn't like driving into Boston during the day, let alone at odd hours at night. Heck, she was a big girl, right? She could handle herself. If Tony was okay with it, then that was good enough for me. After all, I had more pressing matters at hand.

The last thing I wanted to do was visit the retirement home. But with Rival recuperating at the vet's, it was now or never. I stopped at home, donned my jacket, gloves, and beanie, and this time remembered a flashlight.

By now, Rueland Retirement was in total darkness. I let myself in through the gate, trudged to the mound, and leaned my flashlight against a rock. I breathed easier knowing I wasn't going to be attacked by some overzealous dog. All the same, playing Nancy Drew at midnight wasn't high on my list of wild and crazy things to do.

Thankful that the spade was where I'd left it two nights ago, I dragged it over and started digging. It went in easily, and I concluded I wasn't going to unearth a treasure chest or another dead body. With a cool breeze sweeping in, the more I dug the stronger the mulch smell seemed.

After two solid minutes of shoveling, I hadn't hit anything hard—or soft, for that matter. I took a deep breath and wiped my brow. I was pooped. I fell to my knees and examined the turned earth. There was no weapon—which I'd been suspecting—or any other items. No money. No gold. Not even a measly bone. All I saw, mixed in with the soil, were eggshells, cabbage leaves, and other food remains.

How do you like that? I was digging in a compost pile. Virgil's compost pile. That's why no one saw him eating in the dining room. I suddenly remembered the plastic bag of food scraps in his apartment. He was taking his scraps outside and burying them when he thought no one was looking. Fertilizing. Big deal. I guess he must've been embarrassed when Jimmy cornered him. After all, what a shame throwing out Ruby's treats.

What did this prove? It didn't mean he killed Sister Madeline. Didn't mean he didn't either. And I wasn't going to sit around, shivering in the wee hours of the morning while I decided if Virgil had anything to do with a nun's death.

I heaped all the scraps back in the pit, put the shovel back, and dusted off my gloves. It was officially time to give up on the mound. But Valentine Beaumont was no quitter. I had my brush to retrieve. And once I got back into Sister Madeline's apartment, I'd do a different kind of digging. I shut off my flashlight and checked the neighborhood to make sure I hadn't been seen. Then I called it a night.

Chapter 5

I rolled out of bed Saturday morning, glad to be up instead of thinking of the men in my life. I'd done enough of that during my sleepless night. Of course, Romero couldn't be counted as a man in my life since he'd cut out of it months ago. But there you had it. Max was right. Romero still had a hold on me. In truth, my heart hadn't settled down since seeing his face again.

Then there was Jock. I thought about the way he insisted on walking me to my car last night after the game. Not only was he sexy and strong, he was also noble. He could probably leap tall buildings in a single bound. I still wasn't interested. I admit I took a right turn at sanity, hiring him. But we were both adults, right? Capable of working together, accepting one another's flaws, even if Jock didn't seem to have any flaws, which in itself was a flaw. *Erg.*

I showered, washed my hair, and styled it with hot rollers. I had work to think about. And Sister Madeline. I contemplated again about Virgil's compost pile and whether it had any bearing on her death. Seemed silly to consider, but at this point I was grasping at straws. Retirement home or not, Sister had been a client and someone I'd cared about. Plus, I couldn't stop thinking about the *girl*.

I ate some toast, stroked smoky eyeshadow across my lids, and because I needed to cheer myself up, I slipped on my new miniskirt, one of the matching tops, and my new glittery bracelet. Yitts stood paws on my thighs and tilted her head in curiosity at the sparkly bangle. Then she batted it hard, trying to get it off my wrist. In that instant, it occurred to me that someone else might have been curious about Sister's secret, but would they keep digging until they got to the truth? And would they kill over it?

After I brushed and fed Yitts, I filled my car with gas and cruised to the shop. The first surprise flew in at 10:05. Jock was cutting hair, Max was weaving waterfall braids, singing along with Tony Bennett, and I'd finished sweeping the floor. The air seemed to lighten, but then it always did when the Cutler twins came in.

"Don't be daft, Birdie," Betty said in her slight English accent. "If you want the sapphire necklace, get the earrings to go with it. Two for one's more economical."

"But I have Mummy's." Birdie patted her Smarties-sized sapphire earrings.

The twins were born in England fifty-odd years ago and lived in Rueland on a fancy estate. Mummy and Daddy had passed on years ago, and somebody had to spend their money.

"Fiddlesticks—" Betty bit back her next word and flicked her fingers on Birdie's arm quicker than a hummingbird's wings. "Bugger me! Who is *that* dishy thing?"

Everything silenced. Max stopped braiding. Tony Bennett left his heart in San Francisco, and Birdie and Betty's jaws dropped to their matching floral dresses.

I didn't need to follow their stare. I was getting used to the same question spilling off everyone's tongue. "That's Jock." I whacked the broom against the dispensary wall.

"He certainly is!" Birdie aimed her A-cupped breasts at him like she was at a firing range and Jock was the target. "Crrrrracking."

Jock caught his name and peered up from combing his client's silky red hair. He slid the comb in his shirt pocket and sauntered over real slow. His bare chest fought to break loose from the confines of his buttoned-up shirt. A plain shirt, really. Basic white, sleeves rolled to his elbows. On anyone else, one would hardly look twice. Yet here we were, gaping like he'd been rolled in diamonds.

"I feel a bit wonky," Betty gasped.

"I think I wet me knickers," Birdie sighed.

"Ladies." Jock shook their hands while I made the introductions.

Birdie demurely held onto his hand, taking his name for a test drive, revving the *k* in her throat. "Jockkkkk de Marco."

"J.D., if you like."

J.D.? They were here five minutes. I had five days' seniority; all I got was Jock.

"But Jock is more, *brrrrr*." Birdie slid up and down an imaginary pole, waiting on the perfect adjective. "Rrrrrugged."

He pulled her roughly toward him. "It's also more dangerous." He glanced at me, clearly amused by the twins.

Birdie trembled with excitement and pecked his chest like it was forbidden territory.

I, on the other hand, was looking for a place to barf.

"You're English." Jock removed her hand without offending.

Birdie smiled. "Blimey, you're a sharp one."

"Sounds like an accent from Chipping Campden way."

"Hear that, sister?" Birdie looked as if she'd discovered a genie. "He knows our home town."

He nodded. "I toured around there when I was in Europe."

She raised one eyebrow. "Aren't you a jammy chap, working with this posh ducky. We abso-bloody-lutely love Valentine. Look at her in that cute miniskirt. Isn't she a pet?"

He backed toward his client, giving me a penetrating stare that worked its way from my toes up. "Quite."

That word hung in the air like…London Bridge. Thank

you, Cutlers, for inspiring *that* thought. I wasn't sure what to make of Jock's story. I knew he'd globe-trotted, but gee, did he have to rub it in my face? And did every woman in the state of Massachusetts have to swoon when they met him?

Betty grinned at Birdie. "Wouldn't the kids at St. Gregory have a ball with him?"

Kids? I was walking Betty to my station but stopped short. "St. Gregory? You mean the orphanage in Metland?" I'd completely forgotten Mrs. Shales had said Sister Madeline used to visit there.

"It's more like foster care nowadays." Betty wiggled back on my chair. "But yes, we volunteer there. So rewarding."

I leaned in. "Did you ever see a nun there by the name of Sister Madeline?"

"Yes, Sister Madeline was often there. Heard the precious soul just up and died."

I quickly moved away from the details—me being one of them—surrounding Sister's death. "How long ago did you see her there?"

"Golly, it's been months, but she was always a blessed face."

I put a cape around Betty's shoulders, thinking about the girl Sister wanted to tell me about. Was she from the orphanage? I lowered Betty to the sink. "Did Sister Madeline ever spend time with a particular child? Maybe a girl?"

"No, pet. Not one child over the other. She was like an angel. She floated around and gave love to those who needed it most."

I shampooed Betty's hair, deliberating about the baby from the locket photo. It was such an old picture. On top of which, I didn't have the locket to show anyone. A visit to St. Gregory might answer questions.

Fifteen minutes later, Max and I slipped the sisters under dryers. I was making them tea when the front door crashed opened and a second surprise trooped in.

Phyllis.

I heard a smash and looked down. The teacup I'd been

holding had slid right through my fingers. Max screamed and snatched two tail combs, crossing them at arm's length to ward her off. I could almost hear gunslinger music echo as Phyllis slipped a cigarillo to her lips and folded her arms. Probably wondering what to make of the place since she'd been gone. She was towing a small man in a flowered shirt, plaid pants, and brown sandals over white socks. The smell of cheap cologne and Brylcreem wasn't far behind.

Max's eyebrows crawled up at the sight of Phyllis's stogie. For a moment, I thought he was going to fall over from shock. He lowered the combs to his sides and looked from the cigar in her pouty face to her large form. "I think Winston Churchill swallowed Phyllis."

Nobody said anything. We were all too speechless.

Phyllis's hair had been lightened to a brassy blond and had grown since summer. She was wearing a beige dress and beaded sandals, and cornrow braids weeded from her scalp. I didn't know if she was trying a new look or copying an old one, but with Phyllis, even seeing wasn't believing.

"Well?" She ripped the cigarillo from her mouth and click-clacked her head around. "Not much has changed around here."

Jock glanced up from his client, looking entertained. If I were in his place, I'd be asking what kind of funny farm this was, and how could I get fired. But I had a feeling he wasn't going anywhere. Yet. He straightened to his full height and gave Phyllis a solemn nod.

"Who's *that?*" Phyllis asked, hands on hips.

"Your replacement," Max said.

"My *what?*" she snapped.

"You know. Out with the old, in with the new."

"Well, I'm back. He can push on."

"News alert, Phyll. You were fired. Sacked. Given the boot. *Hasta la vista.* Remember?"

"Things have changed. I was in an emotionally distraught state."

"Like I am now." Max bit off a sigh.

"I needed to get away. I spent all my savings on a long holiday." She paced the floor. "But I'm a different woman now. I deserve another chance. So, you can get rid of Popeye."

Max hmphed two octaves higher. "Tell her, lovey. We're not ditching our gem for *this* imitation."

I picked up the broken teacup. "He's right, Phyllis. I'm not letting Jock go."

Jock raised an eyebrow at me, and my flesh tingled. I got a hold of myself, averted my eyes from his hot stare, and introduced him to Phyllis.

She circled Jock like a wrestling opponent, then gave him a curt nod. "He'll have to move over so I can get back to work."

A dozen responses ran through my head, all of them inappropriate. Truth was, we needed another stylist, and darn, I hadn't even placed an ad yet. Was I willing to stage twenty more interviews to find a gifted professional? After going through that ordeal and hiring *J.D.*, I doubted I'd ever find the perfect employee. Even if I persevered, it could take weeks to find a qualified stylist.

As bad as Phyllis was, there were some who didn't mind that she had no talent. Plus, I'd already taken enough family beatings over her absence.

Max slid the combs into his pocket and peeked over Phyllis's shoulder at the fine-boned man standing in her shadow. "And who is *this*?" His voice was playful as if he were peeking in the newborn window at Mass General.

Phyllis stepped back. *Crunch.* "Oops."

The man gaped down at his toe and tightened his lips.

Max rushed to his side. "Let it out, honey. You're in a room full of friends. We'll help you escape."

Phyllis jerked the guy away from Max and tucked him under her arm. "This is my friend. Tell them, Guido."

Guido shook his foot, then ran a finger through his black hair that was slicked into a duck tail. "I'm Guido Sanchez." He shrugged at Phyllis, like what else was there to say.

Jock, Max, and I stood in a row, gaping at the new man in Phyllis's life. Jock's mouth wasn't actually hanging. Max and I had simply mastered the art of looking dumbfounded.

"I met Guido at Zoto's Latino Dance Club in Boston," Phyllis said.

Max looked Phyllis up and down. "Were you a bouncer there?"

"No, you moron. I went there to learn how to dance. Guido's teaching me to salsa."

"Is that the same as teaching pigs to fly? 'Cause I'm having a hard time picturing this, Phyll."

She hiked up her chin. "I'm going to be a professional dancer. One day, I'll be on one of those TV dancing competitions. I'll make so much money I won't need to cut hair."

This was news to me. Up until now, Phyllis had no aspirations except perhaps where her next meal came from.

"What happened to sewing class?" Max said.

"I'm still sewing, but I finally found a store I like."

"You mean Barns & Stables carries your size?"

"*Plus*," she bulged her eyes at Max, "I needed something spectacular to sew." She smiled down at Guido. "Now I've found it."

"You're sewing Guido?"

"No, you dense idiot. I'm going to make a salsa outfit. You'll have to come to the club and see us sometime. That's if you can tear yourself away from the sangrias."

"I'll have you know I haven't had a glass of wine since you left. Of course, nothing lasts forever."

Where Phyllis had no lasting goals, Max had one—to get Phyllis. Not in an acquiring sense like accumulating books or coins. More like a vulture circling roadkill. And he was swooping low now. Meanwhile, Guido had stepped a foot back and was taking a good look around the shop like it was full of hidden treasures.

"What's with the cigarillo, Phyll?" Max wanted to know. "Candy cigarettes not doing it for you anymore?"

I shook my head as the familiar scene unfolded before my eyes. Max had gone two long months without seeing Phyllis, a lifetime of wasted one-liners. If I'd had better employer skills, I'd have stopped the quips several breaths ago. But in truth, I wasn't the world's best boss. I questioned my judgment, berated myself for making bad decisions, and in general struggled with how to handle employees. Typically, things picked up right where they'd left off.

"So, who did the braids, lovey? Lady Gaga?"

"A friend from the club did my hair, thank you very much."

"*Two* new friends. What are you paying these people?"

"Shove over," she said to Max. "I need to set up shop." She yanked her curling iron and scissors from her bag. Max mouthed *help* behind her back.

I pulled Phyllis aside. "Look, if I *let* you come back, you'll need to show some respect."

"To who?" she asked, like this was a new concept.

"*Everyone*. Maybe try a gentler approach."

She puckered her lips, frowning. "How's this? 'I'm pleased to serve you.'"

Max leaned closer. "Looks more like, 'My hemorrhoids are acting up.'"

A weary sigh left me. There was no way out. If Abe Lincoln could free the slaves, and NASA could put men on the moon, then surely I could allow Phyllis Murdoch to return to Beaumont's.

Jock strolled over, biceps draped around Guido's neck. He said something to him in Spanish, then nodded at me. "Guido's a repairman at Darling Heating & Appliances down the street."

"See?" Phyllis said. "We were destined to meet."

Jock grinned at her, then looked at me. "Guido was at the retirement home Tuesday."

Day after Sister Madeline's death. "Is that so?"

Guido gave a feeble smile under Jock's squeeze, which seemed more intimidating than friendly. "I'm in that old home a lot," he uttered quickly. "Their heating and cooling is loco." He ducked away from Jock's embrace. "Jis don't let the old ladies see me. They want to pet me like I'm a perro."

"Perro?" I asked.

"Joo know." He gave a shoulder jerk. "A doggy."

His size and jumpiness reminded me of a Chihuahua, but I put that thought aside and recalled Sister Madeline's cold apartment, Virgil's tropics, and Nettie's complaints. So, Guido was the man in charge.

"I can handle the old ladies. It's that Evalene that scares me." He muttered words in Spanish that sounded neither pleasant nor flattering, but they were heartfelt. "She was in her office when I came to do my job, papers flying everywhere. She was searching for somethin', man, but I didn't stop to ask for what. She reminds me of a fire-breathing dragon."

"Kind of like your date," Max said.

"Ah, no." Guido's voice softened. "Phyllis is a pussycat."

The work week finally came to an end—thanks to closing early on Saturdays—and the first thing I planned to do once I sank inside my car was head to St. Gregory. I didn't know if there was any significance to what Betty had said about Sister Madeline giving love to the orphans who needed it most, or if I'd discover anything about the girl or the pictures in the locket, but I figured I had nothing to lose by taking a drive there.

I was closing up shop when the phone rang. I trudged into the dispensary, opposite the front door, swiped a hair off the counter, and picked up the French provincial phone.

"It's Saturday," my mother said. "You don't have a date?"

I plunked myself on one of the wheeled stools and stared at the product-filled cupboards, contemplating how to answer that. Thing was, my mother wouldn't die in peace until I had a man to look after me, since I was incapable of looking after myself. I was amazed I could wash my underwear without being walked through the chore. My father was simpler. Eat. Sleep. Read. Nagging wasn't his department.

My gaze slipped to the lower cupboards that held products by the gallon, a pop-up tanning tent, accessories, and, up until the day I fired her, Phyllis's hidden junk food stash. "I told you, I'm not dating." I twined the curly phone cord around my thumb, thinking one of Phyllis's snacks would come in handy right about now.

"Then have supper with us."

Eating alone versus leafing through bridal magazines with my mother. *Hmm.* "I can't."

"Then Sunday. I'm making chicken, perogies, and green beans cooked Ukrainian style. Plus, I'm making pumpkin pie."

My mother was raised with the notion that cleanliness was next to godliness, food was a way to a man's heart, and everyone could be bought with dessert. Cultivating tender emotions was difficult for my parents, but pie said it all. I told her I'd be there Sunday. Then I locked up, hopped in the car, and made the short drive to Metland.

St. Gregory was a good-sized home that sat on roughly a dozen acres of land. A wide veranda and several upgrades suggested the more the merrier. There was a net-protected trampoline off to the side and a playground carpeted with a spongy brown surface. A group of kids ran around a huge slide, shrieking with joy.

I felt silly coming here asking questions about Sister Madeline, but if I wanted to learn about her time here, I had to suck it up. I shook my nervousness away, took a brave breath, and walked into the house.

A guy about forty was in the front room, behind a desk, downing a sub. He gave me an embarrassed nod and wiped his mouth clean.

"If I don't grab a bite now," he said, "there won't be time to eat once the kids rush in from playing."

I smiled over my shoulder to the window. It was mid-afternoon, and the activity in the yard was full steam ahead. I couldn't blame the guy.

I introduced myself and asked if he knew Sister Madeline.

"Yeah." He put down the sub and came around the desk to shake my hand. "Call me Scooter. Too bad she died. She was real sweet."

Everything I'd learned about her confirmed this. "Did she come here often?"

"Used to come in more. We'd all look forward to the day the bus brought her. But lately she was looking tired."

So, he'd noticed this, too.

"Age, I guess, creeping up on all of us." He shrugged, and his T-shirt molded to his tiny paunch in front.

I glanced at the "code and conduct" poster on the wall behind him and bit my lip. Would Scooter share any information? I didn't drive out here to turn back without asking. "Did Sister Madeline gravitate to a certain child when she visited? Maybe a little girl?"

He didn't need to think. "Nope."

Question number two. "Did she ever show you a locket with pictures in it? One photo was of a baby."

He shook his head. "Sorry, I'm not much help. All I can tell you is she prayed over these kids and held them in her arms like she was making amends."

"For what?"

"Beats me. Just a sense I got."

Visiting Evalene was next on my list. I'd left St. Gregory feeling stumped and a little choked up. It was the restitution comment that bothered me. What had Sister

Madeline done that required her to make amends? She was a nun, for Pete's sake. How terrible could it have been? I tried not to imagine all sorts of horrible scenarios. I was going to Evalene's. I didn't need bad visuals.

I talked to myself until I reached the outskirts of Rueland, stomach churning, palms sweating. I could do this. Evalene was an unconventional choice as a caregiver for the elderly, and true, she made me nervous. But I needed to see her in a different light. Maybe she was a carefree spirit, tiptoeing through the tulips with a bag of confetti, sprinkling the world with song and dance. Then again, maybe she was Hagar the Horrible and enjoyed stalking beauticians at ballgames.

I rolled to a stop at the end of Evalene's lane. She lived in a small white farmhouse that sat on a large chunk of land. The house looked well kept with a multitude of flowers and hardy shrubs. Neighbors were far and few. It wasn't the sort of place you'd want to live if you were into big-city nightlife, but Evalene didn't strike me as a salsa-dancing butterfly.

I grabbed my bag and slipped out of the car, asking myself again why I was here. A saner person would've skedaddled down the dirt road. *You're looking for information. Anything that might shed light on Sister Madeline's death.*

I stood at the screen door with knees shaking. *Okay, Valentine. Now what?* It was awfully quiet. Maybe she wasn't around. I spied an old jalopy in the driveway. Evalene's, no doubt.

I pressed my nose to the screen. *Hmm.* Tidy entry. I was about to knock when Evalene came around the front of the house in her khaki-on-khaki outfit.

She gave me a queer look. "Miss Beaumont? What are you doing here?"

Should I admit I saw her at the game? *No. Play dumb. Make something up.* "I, uh, was on my way to Green's Orchards to buy apples, and darn it if I didn't get lost." I gave an innocent smile. "Somehow, I ended up on your road."

"How nice." She straightened. "I don't get many visitors."

Was it any wonder?

We talked a bit about Green's Orchards, and then I asked how things were at work.

She released air through her nose. "Apart from Rival getting sick, work has been quiet. As I like it. Mind you, if I find out who hurt Rival, they'll have to answer to me."

I choked out a cough. Until a few nights ago, I didn't even know Rival existed.

"It's hot out," Evalene said at my discomfort. "Come in for a drink."

She dusted off her hands and boots and marched into the kitchen. I trotted in my heels behind her. She rooted around the fridge while I did a quick study of the room.

Sitting on the counter were dozens of glass jars with handwritten labels and cloth lids. Inside the jars were dried herbs. Rosemary, basil, thyme, warfarin, sage. Hold on a minute! *Warfarin?* As in rat poison? My father had once sprinkled warfarin in the back corner of his shed to get rid of a rat. Why would Evalene have a jar of it sitting beside her other herbs? Maybe I was reading wrong. Maybe the label said Wintergreen or Watercress. Maybe I needed my eyes examined. I blinked and stifled another cough. "You have quite a supply of herbs."

She handed me a water bottle, then sucked hers back. "I grow all my herbs." She wiped her mouth across her sleeve. "They're more," she paused, eyes on me, "flavorful."

Gulp.

I shot back some water and tried to sound nonchalant. "Is that rat poison?" I pointed to the jar next to the thyme.

"Yes." She didn't blink an eye. "I have pesky rodents that need euthanizing. Follow me. I'll show you my plants."

All righty then. We descended the steps into the backyard where a small herb garden sat next to row upon row of pastel-colored calla lilies. The white calla lilies were like the ones in Sister Madeline's room. I ignored the icky feeling in my stomach and watched as Evalene hiked into the flower patch and pinched a pink calla lily off at the stem.

"It's good I'm off for a few days." She stepped over a weed on her way back to me. "This garden needs attention." She handed me the pink calla lily. "Here. Take one."

"Uh, thanks."

"Hillary Ayers introduced me to calla lilies."

Hillary? I thought about her flower-themed apartment, and then Virgil's forest. Now I was knee-deep in Evalene's botanical garden. All three people had an avid love for plants. And all three were linked to Sister Madeline.

"You have a lot of green thumbs at the home." I waited a beat. "Like Virgil."

"Yes. He loves his plants."

"He seemed to care for Sister Madeline, too."

She gave me the same distasteful look she gave a few days ago. "They were together frequently. It wasn't a secret."

"Do you think one of the seniors was jealous of her? Someone like Hillary?"

"She was a nun, Miss Beaumont. Not someone many would turn green with envy over."

"Maybe because she was close to Virgil," I offered.

She wiped sweat off her brow. "That I can't answer."

I took another swig of water, and my nose twitched in anticipation at how she'd react to my next question. "Why did you ask Hillary to deliver Sister Madeline's food that day?"

Her eyes narrowed. "What do you mean?"

Steady, girl. "I understand you took Sister Madeline her food on a regular basis."

"That's right. She was too frail to come down to the dining room, and eating her meals on time often helped with the pain. That day, I was behind on my paperwork, so I asked Hillary to take it up." Her lips spread into a grin.

"Miss Beaumont, people die in retirement homes all the time. It's a fact of life, I'm afraid."

This was true, and God only knew if Evalene had anything to do with Sister Madeline's death. Either way, wouldn't she have acted more caring? More sympathetic? Trying to understand the woman was futile. I mean, who knew what went on inside the head of someone who kept a jar of warfarin pellets on her kitchen counter?

Not only was Evalene too emotionless. But she watched me as if *I* were guilty of something. The only thing I was shamefaced about was giving that damn dog indigestion.

Good thing she was off for a few days. My next course of action regarding Rueland Retirement was going back and retrieving my brush. Knowing I wouldn't run into Evalene would make my visit a whole lot easier.

Chapter 6

I did laundry the next morning, then hauled Yitts off her favorite black beanbag chair and harnessed her outside. Since I had at least until Monday to reclaim my brush from the retirement home, I made the most of my morning, cleaning and doing some thinking.

I trekked to the piano because tickling the ivories helped me reflect when I had a lot on my mind. If nothing else, it relieved stress.

I played for an hour, mulling over why I didn't buy that Sister Madeline died of natural causes. The rapid decline bothered me and, of course, her need to tell me about the girl. Deep down, call it a sixth sense, I knew there was more to this than a simple passing.

Maybe I needed to think about her theory on life. She'd had a strong faith and believed family was core to a good existence. Who was her family? Did she have a special love? Had she lived up to expectations? Darn. Why was I looking for trouble?

I gave my fingers a rest and checked on Yitts. She sat at the edge of the porch steps and wagged her tail at a couple of chipmunks chasing each other on the grass. Then she raised her head and sniffed smoke coming from Mrs. Calvino's cigarette next door. Five-star entertainment.

I finished playing one of my favorite Rachmaninoff

pieces, then cleaned the bathroom, washed out the litter box, and added fresh kitty litter.

I let Yitts in, padded to the kitchen to empty the bathroom garbage, and yelped when I saw the pink calla lily. I caught my breath. *Silly*. It'd been sitting on the counter in the vase I'd put it in when I'd returned home from Evalene's. I'd simply forgotten about it. I stared at the beautiful flower and felt like it was staring back, taunting me, like maybe there was something to this plant theory after all. I had to find out. But how? Who could I ask? I needed an expert. Wait a minute. What about my client Blair Dossan?

Blair was a microbiologist and worked at a pharmaceutical company in Arlington between here and Boston. Surely, she'd have come across toxins and poisonous plants at work. Even warfarin. I thought about Ruby and the beans. Blair would know about allergic reactions to foods. Instead of going on a rabbit trail on the computer, I'd get first-hand information from a professional. Blair wouldn't be at work today. And if she was like most people, she wouldn't want to be bothered on her day off. I'd call her on Monday.

My mother was in her apron when I arrived. She was adding whipped cream to pumpkin pie with one hand and stirring perogies with the other. My mother was the MacGyver of cooks. She could turn a flour crumb into a three-tiered Black Forest Cake—blindfolded. I noticed two extra plates on the table, and suddenly the aromas of cinnamon and sautéed onions didn't seem so appetizing.

"Why are there two extra plates on the table?" I dropped my bag, smelling fish bait.

My mother didn't flinch. "Mrs. Shales is coming for dinner with her grandson."

I backed toward the door. "Not Gibson. Tell me it's not Gibson."

She left her spot and dragged me into the heart of the kitchen. "One meal. It's been so long since you've seen him."

"Not long enough. It seems like yesterday I was staring at his chubby breasts in Mrs. Shales's inflatable pool while he farted bubbles in the water. And I still remember that snowy day he threw a chunk of ice at my back." I rubbed my spine. "That scar never went away."

My mother wasn't going to be put off by my objections. "So, he was a rambunctious boy. You haven't seen him since Holly's twelfth birthday. Remember how Mrs. Shales and I'd planned a party for them when he was visiting that Christmas? It was a good arrangement since he and Holly had birthdays a few days apart."

"So, invite Holly for supper."

"She's married, you're not."

Lucky Holly. "You planned this as a date?"

"Think of it as a friendly dinner. He's spending a few days at his grandma's to do odd jobs and cut the grass."

There was a light tap on the side door. "Hello, Ava?"

"Come in," my mother sang, giving me the *behave* look.

I tugged the hem of my top, giving a silent grunt. This meal couldn't happen fast enough.

Gibson shuffled in behind Mrs. Shales, his face expressionless. He was five-foot-three, like his grandmother, and still chubby. His wavy brown hair was parted down the center, and black-framed glasses sat on his nose.

I squeezed the stuffing out of Mrs. Shales and nodded at Gibson. I wasn't snubbing him. Gibson merely sent unhuggable vibes.

My mother put on her welcoming voice. "Gibson, you've grown into a nice young man."

The truth was, my mother didn't know if Gibson was a rapist or an axe murderer, but in her attempt to be hospitable, the verbal diarrhea spewed by the bucketful. Mrs. Shales and I stood there while my mother fired off one futile compliment after another.

Gibson hoisted up his pants and slunk into a kitchen

chair, signaling we could cut the small talk and start dishing out the grub.

My mother's keen food sense clicked in. "Get your father, dear. He's in the basement fixing the blender."

Since my father had retired from the fire department, he'd spent time watching TV while reading the newspaper, bowling with his buddies, and dodging my mother's chatter by fixing everything he didn't get around to when he was working.

I hiked a mile across the concrete floor and watched him fiddle with the blender. "Hi, Dad. Supper's ready."

"'kay." Conversation wasn't a great pursuit of my father's unless it related to him. He usually stuck to one syllable grunts and light banter that created little emotion.

We all gathered around the table. Gibson sat across from me, avoiding making eye contact from his magnified glasses.

"How's the Gippy?" my father asked, after grace had been said.

"Fine." Gibson scratched his head and a dandruff flake floated to his plate.

I choked back a gag and gaped at my mother. Even for her, this was an all-time low.

She overlooked my stare and zeroed in on my father. "How'd you like it if someone called you Brucey?"

He shrugged, like what was her problem. "I always got Brucey at the fire hall. Didn't bother me. Right, Gippy?"

"Fine." Gibson eyed the chicken.

"Valentine," Mrs. Shales said, "did you by chance speak to Hillary?"

My mother passed me the beans and a don't-spoil-the-evening glare.

I took the beans and passed them on. "She's doing okay."

"Do the police know how the poor nun died?"

All eyes were on me. "Uh, I don't believe so."

My mother was eager to change the subject. "Gibson, have some chicken."

Gibson piled on the chicken, added extra perogies, and slathered two spoonfuls of low-fat sour cream over everything. He was how I'd remembered him, only taller and quieter. I expected him to do something stupid like pour sour cream over my head or poke me with a fork under the table, but the rambunctious Gibson had disappeared along with the inflatable pool. In fact, helping his grandma with odd jobs sounded like a nice thing to do. I cut him some slack since he seemed no more interested in me than I was in him.

My mother beamed like a lighthouse at Gibson's healthy appetite. Feeding a man, in her books, was up there with cleaning sterling. "Your grandma tells me you're working two jobs."

"Yeah," Gibson said. "I drive a tow truck part-time and work at the computer shop."

"You're very enterprising. Maybe sometime you could update Valentine's computer."

I couldn't believe my ears.

"Do you have a card?" my mother asked.

"Sure." He pulled out a business card from his shirt pocket.

She took the card and raised her eyebrows at me. "You could use updating, right?"

My teeth were sore from grinding them. "No."

"I'm busy enough lately, anyway," Gibson said. "Setting up seniors with computers."

I shot him a look. "What seniors?"

"Folks at Rueland Retirement. Guess they want to stay current with technology." He grinned. "One lady even asked me how to search poisoning someone."

I dropped my fork, and my mother gave me a steely look. Before I could utter a word, she had me clear dishes and bring out dessert. She sliced Gibson a huge piece of pie, then placed a dish of chocolate squares in front of him. "Gibson, eat."

My father gaped from his plate to Gibson's. "How come Gippy gets a bigger piece of pie?"

My mother tightened her grip on the dessert knife. "You have to watch your weight."

My father was six feet and in good shape. Not once did he ever have to watch his weight. But cooking was serious business for my mother, and guests always received the biggest portion.

My father muttered something under his breath, then stabbed his pie with his fork.

After coffee had been drunk, my mother and Mrs. Shales cleaned dishes, and my father went down to the basement. I sat facing Gibson with my feet up on the chair beside me, getting back to the seniors and poisoning talk. "So, you've been spending time at Rueland Retirement."

Gibson nodded. "Yeah. For the most part, those old folks are sweet."

I nodded back, eager to hear more. "Who was the senior asking about poisoning?"

"I don't know her name, but she's a four-foot-eleven bully with that cane of hers."

My feet hit the floor. "Nettie Wisz?"

"Does she do a lot of complaining?"

"Yep."

"That's her. I showed her how to google information and got the hell out of there."

My mother did a final wipe across the kitchen taps, then handed Gibson a container holding the rest of the pie and squares. "In case you're hungry later," she said.

Never mind when my father was hungry later. You had to be a guest to get this special treatment.

My mother ushered Mrs. Shales and Gibson out the door, then veered to where I was leaning against the counter. "Well?"

I was still digesting the unusual conversation with Gibson. "Well, what?"

"What'd you think of Gibson? He has two jobs. That shows initiative. And he likes food. You'd never have waste." She didn't know when to quit. "I know what you're going to say. He's plump."

That's not what I was going to say, but I let her have the floor.

"Holly went through a plump stage when she was growing."

"Mom, Gibson's an adult. He's done growing. And not that it matters, but I've dated all kinds of guys, including plump guys. I'm not that shallow that the man I'm with has to have movie-star looks." Romero's movie-star looks came to mind, and I winced inside. So what? I wasn't *with* Romero. I was at my limit with her interference, but I put this as kindly as possible. "Gibson's not interested in me either. Can we say it was a lovely dinner and leave it at that?"

What I wouldn't leave behind was this information about Nettie and poisons. If I didn't learn anything else tomorrow, I'd get to the bottom of this disturbing news.

Chapter 7

I put out the garbage Monday morning and started my day with a visit to the sick kids at Rueland Memorial. The whole hiring-a-stylist process caused me to miss last week's visit, and then there was Sister Madeline's death...

I drove through the carwash, came home, and dragged the garbage can back to the garage. Then I flopped on the porch steps and waited for Max to pick me up so we could go to the retirement home together.

I considered how I was going to get into Sister Madeline's apartment without causing a commotion and what I hoped to learn while I was there. But my thoughts shifted to Mrs. Shales, then Gibson, then my mother and this continuous dating routine.

Gibson and I would never have matching His and Hers towels, but he wasn't a bad guy. He sat through dinner and only spoke when spoken to. He didn't toot once—that I'd noticed—though his eyes glazed over after his third chocolate square. Most importantly, he provided me with information about the case.

My thoughts turned to Nettie owning a computer and googling how to poison another human being. Had I missed something? It was clear the male residents adored Sister's sweet nature, and perhaps Nettie had been jealous of that. But did she have it in her to kill over it?

Max jumped the curb in his silver four-door and skidded to a stop in the driveway. I shelved my thoughts on Nettie and waited for the dust to settle. Then I opened the car door, threw in my bag, and buckled up.

"What happened to *you*?" he asked, hair gelled in front, diamond glittering in his ear. "Purple shadow on one eye, green on the other." He sniffed the air and used two fingers to wipe my bangs. "Plus, you have toothpaste in your hair." He licked his finger. "Mmm, spearmint. Wait." He reached over and tugged the hair on my crown.

"Yeeeeeow!"

He slapped three gel-hardened bobby pins in my palm. "They don't go with the toothpaste."

"Thanks." I threw the bobby pins in my bag, then rubbed my head and flipped down the sun visor. I almost shrieked again when I saw myself in the mirror. Boy, I had so much on my mind I hadn't even taken time to fix my hair and face after the hospital kids did their routine on me. Playing Mon Sac Est Ton Sac—My Bag Is Your Bag—was lots of silly fun, but it had its moments.

I slid Max a calculating look. Perfect as Barbie's Ken. Brown pants, trendy loafers, and a long-sleeved, white tight-knit top with brown piping around the armpits and square collar. At one hundred eighty pounds, Max's clothes alone could make him spokesman for Dolce & Gabbana.

"That hospital is going to kill you, lovey."

"No way." I fixed my eyes. "It's the one healthy thing I look forward to." I blinked over at him. "You should join me sometime. The kids would have a riot with you."

"I've told you a million times, a bunch of sticky-fingered kids in one room would give me hives." He screeched out of the driveway, taking the corner on two wheels. "So, whose legs are we breaking?"

Max usually jumped at the sight of a mouse. Today he wanted to play *The Sopranos*.

I did a mental sigh. "No legs. No breaking. I found out Evalene's off for a few days. Good time to search Sister

Madeline's apartment for my brush. And look for clues."

"I get it. No Nazi patrolling the grounds." He sped a few blocks, but I could see he was thinking about the big picture. "You have a key, right?"

"Wrong."

He squealed to a stop at a red light, and I smacked the dashboard with my hand before I went through the windshield. "*No?*" he demanded.

"That's the tricky part."

"Uh-oh. I don't like where this is going. Don't tell me you're going to sneak into Evalene's office and steal a key."

"I wouldn't lower myself to such tactics. *You're* going to steal the key."

"*What?*"

I grinned wickedly. "Relax. I'll ask Susan to let me in the apartment, if she's not in the middle of organizing an outing or playing bingo with the residents."

"What if she says no?"

"*Then* we'll sneak into Evalene's office and steal the key."

"Great. We're dead once Sergeant Bilko finds out. Why do I get the feeling we're walking into quicksand?"

"Because you're a drama queen. Now listen up. I also need to speak to Nettie Wisz. Seems she was searching the Internet on how to poison someone."

"She's what, eighty-five years old? Like she could kill more than an ant."

"Poisoning someone doesn't require strength." And I wasn't about to rule anything out.

He tapped the gearshift while a woman pushed a buggy across the street. "Ever wonder how we go from infancy to elderly so quickly?"

Oh brother. "Are you going to get all weepy on me? Because I only have one used tissue in my bag. Now pull yourself together. The light's green."

He floored it, and my head slammed against the headrest. "You know, lovey, that's the problem with you. You lack sensitivity."

"You can burn me at the stake later. There's something I want you to do when we get there."

He careened onto Park Street, swerved into the home's parking lot, and skidded to a stop. A man upwards of antiquity jumped on the lawn and shook his cane at Max.

I waited for my teeth to stop chattering, then took a deep breath. "See if Virgil would like a trim. I want your take on him."

We got out of the car, and I glanced over at the dirt mound. It looked the same as it had after I was through with it Friday. Rival was nowhere in sight. We entered the home, and Max skipped the stairs two at a time to the second floor where Virgil lived. I searched for Susan. Not seeing Evalene made me light-hearted. But I wasn't out of the woods yet.

Frank Sinatra crooned "Strangers in the Night" from the recreation room. I peeked inside and saw a dozen or so seniors ballroom dancing. Others less interested played cards on the sideline. Wit was one of those. Nettie cavorted by, held up under the armpits by Susan. Though I wanted a word with Nettie, Susan was my first priority.

I waved at them, and Susan gave an enthusiastic smile and escorted Nettie to Wit.

Susan was a small, middle-aged woman. Blond bangs framed her cherub cheeks, red-framed glasses sat on her nose, and a smile from ear to ear graced her face. I asked if I could retrieve my brush from Sister Madeline's apartment, and she smiled so wide her cheeks nearly lifted her glasses over her head.

"I'm not supposed to let anyone into Sister's room." She adjusted her glasses. "But since I'm in charge when Evalene's not here, I'm sure it wouldn't hurt if you went in." She handed me the key, then gave an exuberant handclap as though she wondered how else she could help.

I didn't know if it was Susan's cheeriness or the way she sang out her words, but she made me uneasy. She reminded me of tall, bright-eyed Candace Needlemeyer, my nemesis from beauty school, who owned Supremo Stylists, my biggest competitor.

Candace was blond and bubbly. Like Susan. But I learned long ago not to trust her lively manner. The first month of beauty school, Candace painted a moustache on my mannequin's lips. Second month, she poured chocolate pudding into my dye, ruining that color job. My third month there, she told the teachers I was stealing from the tip jar. When I graduated, I thought I was rid of her. Then a month after I opened Beaumont's, she opened Supremo Stylists three blocks away. She continually tried to outdo me in sales, number of clients, and qualified staff. During the last murder case, she even tried to steal Max.

I'm not saying Susan was rotten like Candace, but I questioned whether she was hiding something with all her brightness. Evalene was right. People died. Often in retirement homes. There wasn't anything cheery about that.

I thanked Susan for the key and asked if she'd seen anything strange last Monday.

She shook her head. "I was late for work that morning. My daughter and I were in Newton on Sunday, celebrating her eighteenth birthday with old neighbors." She gave a playful shrug. "We moms got a bit tipsy. But I made it here in time Monday to leave for the concert." She frowned. "I wish I'd stayed behind, though. I hate when one of our seniors passes away."

I thought of the dog's close call. "How's Rival? I heard he wasn't feeling great."

"He's all better, sleeping out back." The smile again from ear to ear.

I trotted upstairs to Sister Madeline's door. I took a deep, reassuring breath. I could do this. It was a vacant apartment. No need to get worked up. I opened the door and stepped into the cold, bleak room. Nothing looked like it had been touched. The tap dripped, calla lilies sat at the window, stillness surrounded me.

I wandered to the plants. They looked cared for, and

the soil was moist. Goose bumps covered my arms. It'd been a week since Sister Madeline's death. Had someone watered her plants? I remembered how Virgil reacted when I mentioned the rotted one I had. And I saw how Evalene cared for her garden. I didn't think either of them would want Sister's greenery to die, but wasn't entering a dead nun's apartment to water her plants taking things too far? And would Virgil even have access anymore? I swallowed down a lump and stoically moved on.

I found my brush tucked behind a cushion, Sister Madeline's fine hair embedded in the bristles. If the cops had searched the apartment, they'd obviously missed it or purposely left it. I went into the kitchen and searched cupboards for a baggy. Aha. I pulled one from a yellow box, slid the brush inside, and dropped it in my bag to clean later.

Since I was here, I stumbled into the bedroom to see what I could learn. The blue walls were bare, a twin bed with no headboard sat on the floor, and the dresser was plain. A pair of black shoes with laces stared at me, and suddenly I couldn't swallow.

I gaped down at them. Why was I choked up? They were a deceased person's shoes. Waiting to be filled. Only they wouldn't be filled. She wasn't coming back. A tear slipped down my cheek. Then another and another. They're shoes, damn it. Why was I crying? Because Sister Madeline had died alone? Because she'd lived a meager life? She was in a better place—she was a nun after all.

That didn't stop the tears from streaming down my face, ruining what was left of my botched makeup. I swept away the tears and forced myself to move on, away from the shoes. I sniffed and caught a glint of light from the crucifix in the other room. A simple object. And I cried some more.

I blew my nose with my last tissue. I needed to pull myself together. And I needed another tissue. I poked around in the dresser for one but felt disrespectful rifling through a nun's panty drawer. I closed the drawer with a bang, and something whooshed to the floor.

On all fours, I peered under the dresser. Stuck inside the baseboard was something that looked like a playing card. I pulled it out and stared at a Catholic prayer card with a depiction of the Virgin Mary holding baby Jesus. I wiped my nose with the back of my hand and flipped the card over. The Lord's Prayer was on the back, and written in small print at the bottom was an address and *Sisters of the Divine.*

Sister Madeline had belonged to a convent in the Berkshires, but until now, I didn't know it was to Sisters of the Divine. I smoothed the card with my thumb. It'd been something like ten years since she'd left the convent to come here, but as far as I knew, the nuns had been her only family.

I dug in my bag for my cell phone and, after a few minutes of routine struggling, found the convent's website. It was basic in design and limited in data. There were no pictures and no contact number. A map showed directions to Stockbridge where the convent was located.

Since I'd learned little about Sister Madeline from anyone here, including Scooter from the orphanage, the convent seemed the logical place to get information. Especially about the photos in the locket. And the best way to learn anything would be by going there. I tucked the card and phone in my bag and met Max on the landing.

"Get what you needed?" he asked.

"Yes. You?"

"Yep."

We flew down the stairs and were six steps from the bottom when Max tripped, did a nosedive, and somersaulted to the ground. He whacked his hands on the floor and gave his head a dazed shake.

"Aha!" Nettie pulled her cane from the stair rung. "Escaping, Mr. Max, without saying hello?" She dropped her cane and tackled him.

"*Aaah!*" Max screamed like a child being held down by a doctor with a long needle.

Nettie always did have a soft spot for Max. She smooched his cheeks, and Max slapped his hands on the ground for freedom.

"Valentine! Help!"

Holding in from peeing my pants, I reached down and lugged Nettie to her feet. Then I turned to Max, flattened to the floor, eyes glazed at the ceiling. "It's over." I tapped his toe. "You can get up."

Nettie tugged down her skirt. "Next time, don't stay away so long. We need real men around here."

I wasn't sure what kind of real men Nettie was talking about, but she missed the boat with Max. He had all the right parts. He was just selective how he used them.

I told Max to meet me in the car so I could have a word with Nettie. I needed to get to the bottom of this googling poisons business. He gladly agreed and dove for the door.

I turned around in time to see Nettie rip a paper off the hall bulletin board and stuff it in her skirt pocket. Without even a glance over her shoulder, she leaned on her cane and hobbled down the hall.

I fast-tracked to the board and spotted Gibson's card nailed to the cork beside dozens of other business cards. There was a blank space where the paper had been that Nettie had pilfered. *Think fast, Valentine. She's getting away.* "Yes! Woo-hoo!" I did a fist pump in the air.

Nettie turned around and creased her eyebrows. "What's all the hollering about?"

I unpinned Gibson's card and hurried over to her. "I've needed someone to do upgrades to my computer." I waved the card in the air. "At last, I've found him. How lucky is that?"

Nettie rolled her eyes. "Are you this happy when your mail comes?"

I faked studying the card. "I've had so many problems. I need someone reliable."

"Yeah, Gibson knows what he's doing."

"You know Gibson?"

"Not intimately." She winked. "But he got me going with the basic computer stuff."

"Good to know. So how do you like owning a computer?"

"Not much. I'm too old to learn new tricks. Still, it's better than watching TV. I can sit at my desk or lie in bed and have all the info I want at my fingertips."

"What info is that?"

"Just stuff." She rummaged around in her pocket and turned away. "I gotta go."

"Uh, Nettie?" I said to her back. "What did you take off the board?"

She spun around and shot me a sharp eye. "What board?"

I pointed behind me.

She hesitated, then pulled the crumpled paper out of her pocket and handed it to me. I unfolded it and stared from the supper menu in my hand back to Nettie. This is what she lifted off the board? Was she scrapbooking menus?

She rolled her tongue around her dentures like she was deciding what to say. "So, arrest me. I walked off with the menu."

"Because?"

"What do you expect? With all that's happened around here—first Sister, then Rival—I did a little research on my own."

I shook my head, confused. "You're looking up menu items?"

"I'm saying I don't trust Ruby's cooking. If there's something fishy going into our meals, I want to know about it. And the Internet tells you how to detect bad food. I may not live to be a hundred, but I sure as hell don't want to drop dead tomorrow from food poisoning."

Her reasoning had merit. I was just glad she wasn't using the Internet for the wrong reasons. I said goodbye to Nettie, strolled toward the front exit, and bumped into

Susan who was coming out of the recreation room. I pulled Sister Madeline's key from my bag and accidentally dropped the prayer card at Susan's feet. My eyes widened in horror at my carelessness, and before I could swipe it up, she knelt and picked it off the floor.

"Did Sister give you one of these, too?" She handed me the card in exchange for the key.

"Uh, yeah." I slipped the card back in my bag.

"I think Sisters of the Divine used to send her those cards so she could hand them out." She smiled. "Such a wonderful ministry."

Since she brought up the convent, I asked if Sister Madeline had ever returned there.

"Not that I know," she said. "I think the Boston area became home."

I said thanks, then left and piled in the car beside Max. I perched a leg on the seat and turned toward him. "I've been thinking."

Max fanned his face. "Lucky you. I'm still having gag reflexes."

I grinned. "So, Nettie's hot for you. She'll get over it. What'd you find out?"

He swallowed. "Virgil's gay."

"What? How do you know?"

"Honey, I know gay."

"Did he tell you that?"

"People don't usually begin talking about their sexual preferences with a stranger, but there were innuendos. And when I asked to use the bathroom, the garden path accidentally led me into his bedroom. That's when I saw the calendar on his night stand."

"I take it the calendar wasn't of Playboy Bunnies."

"Not even real bunnies. But there were a few firemen's chests that would've gotten your ticker pumping. It did mine."

"A calendar's not much to go on."

"Open your eyes, lovey, and smell the cologne. The man's gay. And he never married."

I visualized his bare ring finger. "That's not proof." Then I remembered Virgil's "cultural" reference when talking about the Boston area. Was this what he'd meant?

"What proof do you need? Not every gay man drinks fruity cocktails, keeps an impeccably clean house, or speaks with a lisp. There are those who look and act like regular people."

"Is that so?"

"Indubitably."

"It blows my theory of Virgil being romantically involved with Sister Madeline."

"Then work on a new theory. What'd you find out? Did you get your brush?"

I patted my bag. "Also cleared Nettie of any wrongdoing. She's only taking precautions before eating Ruby's cooking. I also found this." I handed over the card. "Like I said, I've been thinking."

He scanned the prayer and squinted at the small print. "Let me guess. You're planning a visit to Sisters of the Divine." He brightened. "In the Berkshires!" He bounced on his seat. "I smell a road trip. Can I go? Huh? Can I? Can I?"

I plucked the card back. "I'm going for one day. You've got to hold down the fort. With Phyllis back, you two can fill in for me." I dropped the card in my bag. "And be good. That means no quarrels or jokes about her weight."

He slumped in his seat. "Did you have to spoil the moment?" He started the engine and grinned. "At least Jock will be there. I'll be good."

"Can I have that in blood?"

I treated Max to pizza bagels and fries. After he dropped me off at home, I drove to the shop. The first thing I did when I got there was scan the appointments to see which day I could go to the convent. I couldn't leave tomorrow because there were some I couldn't switch or cancel. Thursday and Friday were busier days and too late in the week. It had to be Wednesday. I'd leave things in Max's capable hands.

An anxious tremor shot through me at that thought, but I straightened my shoulders and tried to think positively. It was one day. What could happen in one day?

I did some cleaning before Twix banged on the back door at 4:15. The daycare kids had been picked up, Tony was home fixing the swing set, and Twix was on fire.

"So? How's Fabio?" She dropped her bag on one of the ivory-colored hydraulic chairs. "Is this his station? It is, isn't it? I can feel his sensual oils on the armrest." She stroked the Italian leather, rubbing against it like a lovesick teen.

Oh brother. "Are you for real?"

"I knew it." She snatched a brush off the counter. "Is this his favorite tool?"

I dumped rollers in the sink. "May I remind you, you were changing diapers until fifteen minutes ago?"

"Killjoy."

I added soapy water to the sink and soaked the rollers. "I'm more interested in hearing about your movie. How's it going?"

"Phenomenal. I even chose a new name for myself, strictly for acting, of course."

I grinned, remembering Tony sharing this news at the Red Sox game. I sloshed the rollers around in the soapy water, waiting for Twix to come out with it. She grinned and danced around, brush in hand, enjoying making me wait. I finally flicked my soapy hands up in the air. "Well?"

She tossed the brush back on the counter and held her arms out wide. "You're now looking at the talented, the irreplaceable, Desirée."

I held back a chuckle at her dramatics and grabbed a towel. "Desirée, huh?"

"Yeah. Isn't it dreamy?"

"That's one word for it."

She threw her hands on her hips. "Hey, if it's good enough for Neil Diamond, it's good enough for me."

Naturally.

"Nobody on the set knows me as Twix Fitzpatrick Bonelli, the cheeky Irish girl from Rueland, now married and a mother of two. I'm simply Desirée." She grabbed the broom and swept in all the crevices that were normally ignored. "And between us, it's kind of fun being someone else. All that testosterone is making me horny as a toad. Must be the long hair and pirate clothes. To be honest, my screaming isn't all that fake. One of the stuntmen even gave me a ride home. Said he had to come to Rueland anyway."

"What does Tony think about all this?"

"Are you kidding? He's Italian. He's happier than hell when I come home and jump his bones." She stopped sweeping. "What's wrong? You look like you lost your best friend. Which is impossible because I'm standing right here."

It was the Italian comment. I didn't keep things from Twix, and it bothered me I hadn't told her about Romero. What's more, I couldn't get him out of my head. I was trying real hard, too, but seeing him at the Red Sox game brought on longing, tormenting me to no end. I reached for the dustpan and angled it on the floor. Then I gave her the long story. How we'd met during the last homicide, how arrogant he was, how klutzy I was. His sexy voice. My betraying heart.

"Are you crazy?" She swept bits of hair and dirt onto the dustpan. "He's Italian. They're notorious for being unfaithful, womanizers, gamblers, *and* bad fathers. Run the other way *fast*."

"*You're* married to an Italian."

"Which is why I can say these things. I've seen evidence of this in Tony's family."

I wasn't going to be swayed by ethnic labels. Before I could tell her that, she shook the broom in midair. "And if Tony even looked at another woman, I'd cut off his balls."

"And *my* name makes headlines."

She swiped the dustpan from me. "Take my advice; Fabio sounds like a better catch. He's not Italian, is he?"

"No. Jock's from Argentina."

"Ooh. Forget the cop."

If only it were that easy.

Chapter 8

Tuesday morning rolled around, and Phyllis, Max, and I were in the dispensary, our hangout between customers, eating Boston creams while I went over my plan to visit the convent the next day.

"What's this all about anyway?" Phyllis sat on one of the wheeled stools, twirling her unlit cigarillo like she was in a boardroom making global decisions.

I stood in my thin-weave navy sweater dress with my back to the microwave. Max sat on the other wheeled stool and gobbled a hunk of pastry, likely to keep from criticizing Phyllis's latest getup. "While you were picking out Guido from the pet store," he said between chomps, "Sister Madeline died."

"Who's that?"

Max rolled his eyes. "Nobody. Go out and light your cigar."

Phyllis knew I did hair at the retirement home, and she'd often heard me mention Sister's name. A four-year-old could sustain interest better.

She slammed her fist on the counter and looked at me point blank like something had just registered. "You're not involved in another murder case, are you?"

"Technically, no." Obviously, she wasn't eager to relive the salon homicide from several months ago. I couldn't blame her.

Max filled her in between bites, and I tried not to gape at her Pocahontas outfit. I was far from perfect, and there were things I knew nothing about, like stock market trends or how to change the oil in my car. But I knew fashion. Phyllis went with a theme and did it to death. Today's dress had fringes and printed totem poles, and a feather stuck up from her braids.

I licked custard off my finger, thinking about her choice of wardrobe, when Jock sauntered in with a big container of fruit salad. "You're late," I said.

He dropped the bowl on the counter. "Traffic was bad."

"Traffic bad every morning?"

"Lately, yeah."

Jock rode in from Cambridge—minutes from Boston—and he'd said all he was going to on the subject. I poked away anyway because of an idea niggling my brain. "Do you think traffic has something to do with that movie production?"

"Could be. I'll try not to be late tomorrow."

"Good, because you three will need to run things while I'm in the Berkshires."

He gave me a slight nod. "You taking a holiday?"

"No. Visiting a convent."

The corner of his lip crept up. "Was it something I said?"

"Don't flatter yourself. I'm simply looking into Sister Madeline's past."

He nodded.

Max sprang to the cupboard for bowls. Phyllis eyed the fruit, twirling her cigarillo. Me, I was aggravated, looking to bring Mr. Come-and-Go-as-I-Please down a notch. Saturday, he'd brought in a veggie tray. Today it was fruit.

"Why do you always cart in rabbit food?" I ripped my donut apart. "Can't you cook?"

"Last time I checked," he said, "you couldn't barbeque steak in a microwave."

Max giggled.

I fired him a look, then turned my attention back to Jock—acting all indignant.

"By the way," he said, "I do cook. And if you're nice to me, you can come over and handle my range."

A grape dropped out of Max's mouth and went unnoticed by everyone but me. "I probably wouldn't know what to do with it when I got there." I bent over and tossed the grape in the garbage.

"I'd take your hand and guide you."

"Save it for your bimbos. I'm sure they'd like a lesson in cuisine."

We were back to the same old theme, but I couldn't help myself. His ego and the daily procession of curvaceous women were having a negative impact on me. Not that I needed to be top dog, but I was starting to have one too many erotic dreams at night with Jock in the lead role.

My forehead felt hot, and I sensed the rose by my chignon wilting. Sexual tension was escalating between us, and I wasn't sure what to do about it. I was swearing off men. Right? I wasn't interested. Even if I was a bit fascinated, Jock was not my type.

"Those bimbos are paying your rent," he said.

"This building is paid for, buster, not that it's any of your business." That was a lie. His bimbos *were* paying the mortgage, but sheesh, give the guy an Argentinean pope, suddenly he's Mr. Righteous.

I forked a cherry into my mouth, and Jock's eyebrow went up. That did it. I would not give into the sexual innuendoes. Period. I put my back to him and watched Phyllis, slouched over her bowl, gobbling fruit salad.

"Phyllis, you're drooling." Max wiped juice from her chin. "And could you put the cigar down? You look like Sitting Bull."

She slapped his hand away. "That's an offensive racial stereotype, mister."

"You're right. And I apologize to every Native Indian

for the travesty sitting in front of me. Now put the cigar down."

"It's a cigarillo, for your information." She glared out at the stations, and her eyes got as big as two compact mirrors. "What's *that* doing here?"

All eyes zoomed to Evalene's calla lily sitting in the vase on my station. Figuring it'd die a lonely death at home, I brought it into work. "It's from Evalene." I smiled grimly. "She grows calla lilies in her garden."

"I hate calla lilies," Phyllis said. "The whole species should be wiped out."

"We're not too crazy about *you*." Max collected the bowls. "But you don't see us hiring a hit man to erase *you* from this world."

"Ha. Ha. Why don't you take a bite of that flower, funnyman. We can all have a laugh."

I frowned. "Phyllis, what are you getting at?"

"Calla lilies are poisonous," she said, matter-of-factly.

Max yelped like a poodle and leaped to Jock's side.

"What do you mean, they're poisonous?" I asked.

"One bite of any part of that flower and you'd drop dead. Stem, root, leaf, doesn't matter. It's too dangerous to have in here."

My neck gave an irritating spasm. "Where'd you hear this?"

"Anyone who knows plants can tell you."

What scared me most was she almost sounded as if she knew what she was talking about. I thought about Yitts and her natural tendency to seek out new things. If she'd jumped on the counter, taken a bite of the calla lily while it was at home and then died, I'd never forgive myself. My heart thumped with relief that I'd brought it here, even if I wasn't sure about Phyllis's theory.

"If you don't believe me, ask your client, that Dossan lady. Isn't she an expert on that?"

Blair. Darn! I never did get back to her. I left the trio and disappeared into my office before it got busy. I called MicroPharmLabs where she worked and spoke to her assistant. She told me Blair had a slot Friday after lunch. I'd have to skip out of work to see her, but I wasn't about to get choosy.

The first batch of customers trickled in, followed by the seductive sound of tango music. Of course. We couldn't have quiet with Mr. Argentinean Lover here.

"Oh, Joooooock," panted a female voice. "Don't stop!"

Okay. By the sound of water running and pump bottles squirting, Jock was shampooing his client's hair. Still, I tensed.

"Max, darling," said another voice, "no one cuts hair like you."

I smiled. Max never disappointed.

"Ouch!" An angry voice louder than the others. "You pinched me with those things."

Phyllis. I grimaced. It'd been months since we'd lost any customers. Goodbye to being in the black. I stormed out of the office and held my nose high as I passed Jock and his concubine. I mean, really. The whole breathy thing was plain annoying. I stopped short at the edge of the folding screen where Phyllis attempted to tweeze a squirming woman's eyebrows.

"Do you want this done or not?" Phyllis pressed her hands on the woman's face.

I felt my blood pressure rise. How'd I end up in this industry? It's not like I didn't have any other aspirations in life. I had a musical background. I could've been a concert pianist. I could've played Carnegie Hall. I could've been in the Boston Pops. Memorizing thirty pages of music had to be easier than waiting for the inevitable.

Phyllis threw up her hands. "How am I supposed to pluck your eyebrows with you wriggling like a snake?"

So much for a gentler approach with clients.

The woman bolted off the chair and ran to the mirror. "Where are my eyebrows?" She felt her forehead. "You tweezed off my eyebrows! I look like the Mona Lisa!" She snapped up her purse and narrowed in on Phyllis. "I'd like to know where you got your license."

"I can show you," Max said. "But I'd have to buy a box of Cracker Jacks."

The client stomped to the door, scowling back at Phyllis. "You not only look crazy, you *are* crazy!"

"That's what I keep telling her." Max always had to have the last word.

Everything quieted down after the lady left. Then Guido ambled in with a smile on his face and a CD in his hand. He wrapped his arm around Phyllis, stood on his toes, and gave her a smooch on the cheek. Max gave me a look that said, *the fun was about to begin*. I texted him a mental message that said, *not a word*.

He blinked innocently, pretending not to see my glare. "And how's Guido this morning?"

"Hokay." He nodded and took another look around the salon. Nobody seemed to notice his interest in his surroundings, and I shrugged it off. He was a curious being, not unlike Yitts.

He focused back on the group and waved the CD in the air. "Thought joo people would like to listen to Gloria Estefan and Ricky Martin shake it up."

"We'd love to!" Max cried.

All I wanted to hear from Guido was news that he'd been back to Rueland Retirement and of any other strange sightings he may have had. But I didn't get a chance to ask a thing.

Max popped the CD into the player and pumped up the volume on the trumpets and drums. The windows shook, the ground pulsated, and I thought I saw a crack in the mirror.

All eyes were on Guido as he salsaed around the room, whipping Phyllis into a circle like she was Twinkle Toes. Her braids clacked, her head spun right to left. I had to hand it to her. She was more graceful than I would've guessed, and with more practice she might've realized her dream of being on TV.

Max sailed by with Phyllis's client and her walker, and before I knew it, Jock's hands slid on my hips from behind. Suddenly, I was conscious of the open back on my sweater dress.

My breath caught at the feel of his warm, hard body pressing into me. I tried to untangle myself from his embrace, but it was useless. He bent slightly, and the hollow of his cheek cradled mine while he led with his own erotic version of the salsa.

When the song ended, Jock unspooned me, his lips brushing my flushed cheeks. "Thanks for the dance," he whispered in my ear.

I breathed hard, shivering at his words. Then I tugged my dress into place, attempting to gain control of the aroused state I was in. "Is there anything you *can't* do?"

"Like?" He didn't even have the decency to gasp for air.

"Oh, I don't know. Swimming with sharks comes to mind."

"Sorry. Done that."

Grr. "You cut hair, you've toured Europe, you speak Spanish, and you salsa. Were you also born with castanets, snapping the cha-cha?"

"You mean the flamenco."

Ooh. I marched to my office to gain some distance, ignoring the sweat trickling down my neck. Jock strode in behind me with a *God save me* look on his face, and shut the door. I grabbed a water bottle from my desk and took a gulp. He took the bottle out of my hand and studied me as he chugged the rest. Then he wiped his mouth with the back of his hand. "It bothers you I have other talents?"

"No. It bothers me you *think* you're so talented. And that's my water." I looked away from his large hands that were moments ago pumping me against him. "What would happen if a Frenchman walked through the doors? Would you *parlez-vous français* with him?"

"*Probablement.*"

I whacked my palm against my forehead.

"So, I lived in Europe and speak three languages. What's wrong with that?"

"Nothing!"

He shook his head in frustration. "You know, if I'd guessed you were going to be this kind of boss, I'd have taken a job at Supremo Stylists. Candace Needlemeyer practically bent over backward to hire me."

Say what? "I'm sure she'd bend over any way you wanted." I could feel steam hissing out my ears. First, she'd tried to lure Max away. Now Jock? "And if you want to work for that Medusa, then don't let me stop you." I threw open the door, whooshed by a trio of gorgeous women, swooped up dirty towels, and raced downstairs.

While I was down there, I tried to understand my attitude. I was normally a happy, polite person. Yet my guard was always up around Jock. Why did he bring out the worst in me? What was it I didn't trust? And what was Candace up to? That snake in the grass.

I stuffed laundry in the washer, poured in soap, and flicked on the machine. A moment later, footsteps pounded down the stairs.

Jock stalked into the room and banged the door shut. He crossed his arms, his face like thunder. "You want to tell me what I did wrong?"

If I knew, I would. I stared back, muscles tense, angry at myself for caring more than I should.

The room grew smaller by the minute. He tilted his head and put his hands on his hips, studying me hard.

I exhaled. "What!"

"I'm trying to figure you out." His icy look sent prickles down my spine. "You hire me, then act as though you can't stand being around me. Frankly, I'm beginning to wonder why I wanted to work with you at all. You're sexy as hell, but you're damned hard to get along with."

My face got hot at the sexy comment. "That's… that's…because…"

He frowned and his dark eyes smoldered.

I could feel myself getting lost in those eyes, but I remained tough. "Because you're arrogant. You think every woman you meet is going to lie down, begging for sex."

"That'd be nice."

I fumed, tight-lipped.

"Believe it or not," he said, "I don't like clingy women. A guy likes a challenge."

"Ha. Even *that's* arrogant. I dated enough guys like you. I'm not interested in repeating my mistakes."

He closed the distance between us, cupped my face with his hands, and forced my head up to meet his gaze. He held me that way for the longest moment. "Does this look arrogant to you?"

I fought to gain control. *Not interested. Not interested.* "Look," I finally said, avoiding his probing stare. "Sister Madeline's death is preoccupying my mind. I'd just like to get through a normal workday without incident."

He stepped back a foot. "And you think I'm causing an incident."

Shrugging a maybe with one shoulder, I passed him and yanked on the doorknob. "No. Tell me this isn't happening." I spun around. "You locked us in."

He stepped toward me in the confined space, lifted me up, and set me aside. Then he jiggled the doorknob.

"Gee, why didn't I think of that?"

Ignoring my sarcasm, he examined the hinges and hydraulic closure. "Any tools in here?"

I scanned the room. Furnace. Water heater. Softener. Stray tools from when my father oiled or repaired things. I picked up my pink-handled hammer. "How's this?"

He looked from the feminine hammer to me like he wasn't surprised. "I don't think so."

"Wrench?" I asked.

He grimaced.

"What about this file?"

"Let me see that."

Minutes dragged by while he fiddled with the hydraulic closure. I stood back and watched his biceps flex and his butt tighten.

"How's the view back there?"

"Wiseass," I mumbled.

"Pass me the hammer." He stretched back his arm.

I thunked the handle of the hammer in his hand, hard.

He looked sideways at me, which sent a spark right down to my groin. Then he tapped the hydraulic arm, wormed the file around, and sighed.

"Great," I said. "Everything else you can do. Getting us out of a locked room, you fail."

He tossed the tools on the ledge. "I see this as more of a blessing than a failure."

"Care to explain?"

His eyes darkened, and he got this incredibly sexy look on his face. He pinned me to the humming washer and wove his fingers through mine. The vibrating machine was stimulating and stirring and...*oh boy*. Where in God's name was Max? He never missed a thing. Now when I needed him, he was Mr. Invisible.

Jock grinned. "I could take the door off, but I could also use this time to teach you a few friendly gestures."

I leaned back, gaining some space. "I know an Italian gesture, but you may not like it."

He rubbed my lower lip with his thumb. "I was thinking of a French gesture that involves a kiss."

Hot. Hot. I tried to sidestep away from Jock and this damn pulsating machine, but he dragged his thumb down my collarbone, between my breasts, and drove his hands on my hips. When I wouldn't look at him, he gave an incredulous laugh.

"You want me, Miss Valentine. That's what this is all about. Only you're too stubborn to admit it."

I opened my mouth to object but didn't know what to say. Was I that transparent? Was I on guard because of fear my true feelings might surface? His alluring cologne swam through the air. I swallowed dryly, my knees almost caving from the heady exhilaration seeping daily into my pores.

Another set of footsteps pounded down the steps. Thank goodness—help. A second later, the door burst open and a man stood there, chest heaving, lips tight.

Black stubble shadowed his jaw, his hair as wild as the look on his face. His intense sapphire eyes darkened when his gaze landed on me.

Romero.

Brutally handsome didn't come close to describing him. I stared, my breath almost taken away.

Max must've told him I was down here.

Unblinking, he turned his cold, stony gaze from me to Jock. I broke free from Jock's grasp as if I'd been caught with my hand in the cookie jar. Romero glared at me, and blood rose to my face. I wished he yelled or did the Italian arm-waving thing, but he remained silent.

"I better check on Tawny." Jock gave Romero a curt nod and left the room.

Romero looked as if he wanted to explode, but he folded his arms, impressively keeping things under control. "Did I interrupt something?"

His deep voice hit me harder than I thought possible. I wanted to run into his arms, to feel his warmth, to recapture what we'd had months ago when we were dancing on that yacht. But I didn't dare move. Instead, all the hurt rushed to the surface. His absence. Why he hadn't called. I wanted to know where he'd been, whom he'd been with. More importantly, why was he here? Regrettably, his hard stare told me nothing.

I was boiling inside, deciding what to say, when he blew out a sigh like he had it all figured out. "Guess that's a yes." With no explanation, he turned on his heel and climbed the stairs.

I felt cheated. Stunned. "Good riddance," I shouted, my pulse knocking in my throat.

Ooh. How dare he look at me like that! *He* was the one who left with no goodbye. I heaved a sigh, trying not to think of the past budding emotions, the heat, or the magic we'd shared. I was ticked. I refused to be filled with self-doubt.

The rest of the day I was in a fog. I wanted to block out Romero's drop-in. I walked on automatic pilot past

Max doing a guy's cut and Jock bleaching a swimsuit model's hair. I sensed conversations, but mostly everything was a blur. I wandered into the dispensary, lugged out a gallon of hairspray, and filled four spray bottles. Phyllis was beside me, cigarillo dangling from her lips, braids clicking as she scrubbed perm rods in the sink. I wanted to rinse out the jug, but she was elbow-deep in lather. I strode to the bathroom, dumped the last tablespoon of spray into the toilet, rinsed the bottle in the sink, and returned to the dispensary.

"I'm going out for a smoke," Phyllis informed me.

"Fine." Since taking up cigarillos, Phyllis would pop out back for a puff, then stamp back into the salon, reeking like Smoky the Bear.

I pored over the appointment book, deciding which customers I'd reschedule with Max while I was in the Berkshires and which unlucky ones I'd leave with Phyllis. Suddenly, a loud *whoosh! boom!* came down the hall. I dropped the book, bolted from the room, and slammed into Max, darting in the same direction.

Phyllis staggered toward us, arms out front like Frankenstein, smoke rising from her barbequed braids. Her face was sooty, and a burnt cigarillo drooped from her lips, ends curled up like a cartoon stick of dynamite. "Ohhhhh," she moaned, smelling up the air with charred hair.

I slapped my hand to my mouth while Max pried the cigarillo from her lips. Jock squeezed by us both, checked to make sure there was nothing burning in the bathroom, then took Phyllis's outstretched arms and helped her to a chair.

"I threw a match in the toilet on my way out." Phyllis shook her head in slow motion. "Then a blue flame swirled up and...*booooom*."

I didn't explain about the hairspray or that I was in a Romero-induced fog when I poured it in the empty toilet bowl. But I was full of guilt. I could've killed Phyllis or scarred her badly. I led her into Ti Amo, laid her out on the facial bed, then cleansed and soothed her skin.

"I'm fine," she said, pushing my hands away thirty minutes later. "Stop fussing."

I helped her up. "All right. But will you be okay if I'm gone tomorrow?"

"Just don't leave me any challenging customers." She clutched my wrist. "I don't want any unappreciative types."

I promised. It was the least I could do.

I locked the front door, threw the day's deposit in my bag, and scanned the rest of the shop, double-checking things were unplugged and put away. Since Sister Madeline's death, I'd hardly had an opportunity to be alone in the salon after everyone had gone.

I breathed and exhaled slowly. The quiet relaxed me and helped me unwind. Let's face it, with Jock here, Beaumont's had turned into a zoo—Jock being king of the beasts.

I set my mind on tomorrow. Guaranteed long day in the mountains. Shoot. Tonight was Zumba class. Should I go or shampoo my hair and grab a bite to eat? My feet were killing me, and my stomach was empty. Okay, Zumba wasn't top priority. I promised myself to sweat blood and tears next week.

I kicked off my heels and finished the remaining fruit salad. Since Romero had stormed into the salon, my heart was at war with my stomach. Fruit might not have been the best choice, but it stayed down. I wiped my mouth and slipped in Adele's CD. I needed to lose myself in some soul music, and hey, I could do my own Zumba. I padded barefoot around the shop, pretending I was JLo. I undid my bun, shook my hair loose, and swept it forward into the sink by my station. Swaying my hips to the music, I shampooed my hair.

"Practicing for a dance job at For Your Eyes Only?"

I screamed like a banshee and peered at Jock through sudsy strands with my head upside down in the bowl. He leaned against the edge of the hall wall, a stack of folded towels in his arms.

I stood there helpless, pawing for a towel. "Is that what you do in your spare time? Visit strip joints?"

"Too busy for that."

He had a point. Though, apart from work, I wasn't sure what he was busy with.

"I thought you left," I said.

He held up the stack. "Towels were forgotten." We both knew why, too, but neither one of us chose to go there.

He stuffed towels in each of the other stations' cupboards, then sauntered over to my station, where I was still head-upside-down in the sink. Hair dripping. No towel. Backside of my sweater bare. Adele's sultry voice crooned in the background. No mistaking, Jock heard her, too. He squeezed in slowly to my right and almost spooned me again while he bent to put towels away. "I could help you with that," he said softly, his warm breath grazing my bare back.

Tingles swept across my spine, and my knees suddenly felt weak. "Thanks. I can shampoo my own hair."

He put one hand on my hip as he shut the cupboard door, then effortlessly lifted me, turned me around, and deposited me into the chair, sopping hair and all. As soon as my derrière made contact with the seat, I planted my feet on the ground, ready to bolt.

"Move off that chair, and I'll straddle you."

Okay, I'd let him think he had the upper hand. Water dripped down my face as I inched my head back toward the sink.

"Look up," he said.

"Pardon?"

He handed me a mirror. Liner had run down my cheeks, and blush blotched my skin like chickenpox. I was a cross between a goth and one of Phyllis's makeover clients. I plunked the mirror on my lap, blinking a you're-not-so-perfect-yourself look. Damn it.

He lowered his head and carefully wiped my cheeks. I fought to concentrate on Adele's voice, but his lips were extremely close, and his exotic scent was clouding my senses.

Finally, he moved on to shampooing my hair, massaging my scalp with his fingers. I closed my eyes and breathed easier, enjoying how the smell of the strawberry-scented shampoo blended with his enticing aroma. As much as I wanted to flee, there was also a part of me taking pleasure from his strong, caring touch. No doubt, he knew what he was doing when it came to a woman's hair. And I'm sure it didn't stop there.

I choked at that and slit one eye open at his muscles flexing beneath his shirt. His tanned skin glistened with a sheen of exertion. I held my breath and let my gaze travel down his chest to where I'd once seen his scar.

Had he been clawed by a bear? Knifed by a crazy lover? Spent time in jail? He had the shaggy-haired, dangerous look depicted in those action movies. I let out a breath and felt my legs grow warm. No wonder he had women panting. He was a sexy mystery.

He threaded vanilla-mint conditioner through my ends, then leaned against the counter while the conditioner did its thing.

"You have beautiful hair," he said.

"Thank you."

He nodded without smiling. "Who was that, this afternoon?"

"Romero?" I tore away my gaze and stared at the ceiling. "He's a detective."

"I figured. He had *cop* written all over him." He took the hand mirror off my lap and rehung it. "Is that all he is to you? A cop?"

"He's also a friend." I was taking liberties, but what the hell.

"Friend? If looks could kill, sweetheart, you'd be pushing up daisies."

"You're wrong. He was merely surprised to find us like that."

"Like what?" I caught him grinning out of the corner of my eye. "Oh, I see. He's *that* kind of friend."

I wasn't certain what Romero was. In fact, I wasn't sure about anything where Romero was concerned. The one thing I knew positively was I'd be leaving for the Berkshires tomorrow morning in hopes of getting solid answers about Sister Madeline. Worrying about anything else would only add to my frustrations.

I leaned my head on the side of the sink and turned to face him. "Why are you here anyway? The towels could've waited until tomorrow."

"I wanted to give you something earlier."

I scanned the room from a lying position since he wasn't helping me regain my seating. "Where is it?"

He angled toward me, rested both hands on the sides of the sink around my head, and bent down until our lips nearly touched. "Here."

He closed his eyes and kissed me with the sweetest, softest kiss I could ever have imagined coming from his lips. Then, as if an underlying volcano ruptured inside him, he leaned into me, cupped my face with his hands, and deepened the kiss until a hot sensation mounted inside me.

He paused to look in my eyes, then raised my jaw, and kissed me deeper. I justified the kiss by admitting I was human. I wouldn't think of Romero. Walking away in July. Pretending not to see me at the ballgame. Storming out of the salon today. My wet hair dripped on the floor, and my heart pounded as I curled my fingers through Jock's hair.

He took his fingertip and tucked a curl behind my ear the same way Romero once had, and everything crashed to a halt. I pressed his chest away and sat up, wiping my mouth. "You should leave."

"Why? Because I kissed you, or because you liked it?" He didn't wait for a response. He reached under my neck, arched me back like a wishbone, and kissed me long and hard. I didn't want to think about Romero, but I couldn't help it. Seeing him again was too fresh, and his rugged face wouldn't erase easily.

Panting, I broke off and pushed Jock away with more force. "*Please*, go now."

He licked his lips and nodded. Without another word, he left.

Chapter 9

I got up early the next morning, packed a light lunch, and gave Yitts extra food in case I was late getting back from the Berkshires. I spent twenty minutes and ninety dollars' worth of makeup giving my face that natural look, and before I could tell myself this was a crazy idea, I locked up and headed for the mountains.

Within half an hour, I was out of the city, taking the scenic route west. I passed by people canoeing in the bluest lakes and flew by farmlands and trees turning reddish gold. I had the windows down and music cranked up. The sun beamed warmly on my sleeve and reflected my sparkly earrings on the dashboard. I refused to dwell on Jock or yesterday's kiss. It was a one-time occurrence, done in the heat of the moment. He'd probably already forgotten about it. And so could I.

The morning wore on. I stopped once to stretch my legs, and by the time I arrived at the convent, it was almost noon. Crazy or not, I had arrived.

Sisters of the Divine was an ancient two-story red-brick building. It looked more like an enormous house than a convent. The high-pitched roof gave way to dormers, and three chimneys stemmed evenly across the rooftop. A church with a tower crowned with turrets sat to the right of the convent.

I got out of the car in awe. I suddenly felt out of place with my hair in braids, dressed in a fuchsia-striped hoodie and pink-hemmed jeans. I looked down at my feet. And pink heels. Right. Well, I wasn't here for a job application.

I hitched my bag over my shoulder and climbed the stairs to the main entrance. My palms felt clammy at the thought of Sister Madeline walking these steps, existing inside these walls. What had her life been like? I visualized the locket she'd been holding when I found her dead. Again, whose pictures were inside? I took a huge breath, shook off any negative doubt about being here, and entered the convent.

A hush in the air shrouded me, along with a musty smell that never left old buildings. My strappy heels tapped the scarred wooden floor while an organ played in the distance. So *Phantom of the Opera*-like. Two nuns swished toward me in full habit, asking if they could help.

"I'm looking for the office," I said, clasping my hands to keep them from shaking.

They pointed down the hall, smiled benevolently, and continued on their way.

I walked down the hall and stopped outside a room I figured was the office. I heard a loud *bumpity-thump*, then a female's voice.

"Dang. I mean, shoot. I mean, oh shit." The last word came out in despair.

Forgetting my nervousness, I peered around the corner and saw a young nun in a dark jumper and white veil, sitting on the floor. She was surrounded by several cloth food bags that had obviously toppled from a huge stack. The frazzled novice wiped her brow, frowning at the mess.

I grinned at an acorn squash at my foot, picked it up, and handed it to her. Then I asked if I could speak to the reverend mother. The novice looked at me with a mixture of awe and fear, like this type of request wasn't usually heard, and by someone in dangly earrings and high heels.

"Do you have an appointment with Reverend Mother?" she asked, eyebrows raised.

I smiled. "No, I'd like to speak to her about one of the nuns who used to live here. Sister Madeline. She was a client of mine."

Her eyes grew big and round, probably wondering who I was that I would have a nun as a client. Or maybe it was because she'd heard Sister Madeline's name mentioned before. "I'll, um, see if Reverend Mother is avail—"

"It's all right, Sister Agnes." A tall, handsome woman walked into the office from an adjoining room. She was seventy-five or so and was draped in a black habit with stiff white cardboard poking out around her face. I wasn't sure if I should bow or curtsy, but I was pretty certain I was in the presence of greatness.

"I'm Reverend Mother Margaret," she said to me in a firm but pleasant tone. "Please come."

I tightened the grip on my bag and walked over to join her in the next room. She tilted her head past me as I approached the doorway and, without missing a beat, gave a compassionate smile to the novice. "Next time, Sister Agnes, try to find substitutes for those colorful words."

Sister Agnes lowered her chin, her cheeks a deep shade of red. "Yes, Margaret Mother."

The reverend mother arched a brow at her.

"I mean, Reverend Mother Margaret," Sister Agnes corrected.

The older nun sighed as if she hoped for better days, then led me into a dark wood-paneled sanctuary. She passed a wall lined with books and took a seat behind a massive desk. A painting of the Virgin Mary hung to her right, and a black-and-white photo of the convent grounds sat on her left.

She motioned me to a straight, hard-backed chair. After I sat, she smiled and folded her hands on her desk. "Now, what can I do for you?"

Act calmly. She's not a saint. She's a person. And you're here on business. I put on a brave smile and gave her my card. "I used to do Sister Madeline's hair at Rueland Retirement."

"I see." She slid on a pair of black-framed glasses and scanned the card.

I bit my lip. "And I'm the one who found her body."

She put my card down and formed an *O* with her mouth. "That must have been difficult for you."

She had no idea.

I fingered the prayer card in my bag, then took it out and passed it to her. "And I found this."

She nodded, understanding. "Which led you here."

"Yes."

She thought about this for a moment. "And why are you here, Valentine? Was there something about Sister Madeline or her death that you wished to share?"

"Well, yes." I collected my thoughts. "Sister wasn't herself lately. She'd grown unusually weak and unwell. And this had concerned me."

I waited for the reverend mother to say something, but she didn't need to; the look on her face told me this news came as a surprise.

"Then a few days before her death," I continued, "she phoned and booked an appointment, saying she needed to tell me about the girl. I didn't know what she was talking about, and making this declaration was unlike her. She was a nun. Others confessed to *her*. But it seemed urgent, and she sounded worried, maybe even scared."

Her eyes widened. "For her life?"

"I don't know. When I found her dead, she was holding a locket in her hand with old photos of a young woman and a baby. It was the first time I'd ever seen the locket, but it looked as if it was dear to her. As I studied the photos, I couldn't shake the urgency in her voice about the girl."

I also couldn't erase the other things I'd learned since her death. Like the residents' odd behavior at the retirement home. The meals. The calla lilies. The orphanage. None of these shouted foul play, yet something didn't feel right. How did I reveal I was going on a hunch? Hard as it was, I met her stare. "I'm not certain Sister Madeline died of natural causes."

Reverend Mother Margaret stood and gazed at me from head to heels as if she were trying to distinguish good from evil. I lifted my eyebrows, striving to look angelic instead of like a whore at a garden party. I zipped up my hoodie a notch, having the distinct feeling this conversation was over.

"Did Sister Madeline ever tell you her story?" She came around the front of her desk. "How she came to be at Sisters of the Divine? Why she ended up at Rueland Retirement?" She leaned on the edge of her desk, looking at me from above the rim of her glasses.

"No, and if I'd known she'd had a family, I wouldn't have bothered you."

"If you have suspicions about her death, why not turn it over to the police?"

Boy, she was good.

I thought about Saunders and Martoli's flippant attitude toward the case, and I restrained myself from balling my hands into fists. "The police are doing their own basic investigation, but I felt I owed Sister Madeline the dignity of uncovering the absolute truth."

"Fair enough." She smiled kindly. "I can help you with the locket and will share something that touched me many years ago. I wouldn't reveal this if our dear departed were still with us, but since she's been called Home, I will assist where I can."

I was humbled. "Thank you."

She pushed off from the desk and strode over to a beam of sunlight shining through the window. Her back faced me, but her voice was clear. "Sister Madeline, born Irene Guillaume, came knocking one night on that door you entered today. It was May 1965."

She turned around and shivered, as if remembering. "It had been one of those raging nights, thundering and lightning as if God Himself were rocking the world. The storm had knocked down powerlines and trees. And here was this fragile, starved bird at our door, eight months pregnant, begging for help." Her gaze shifted from somewhere in the distance back to me. "Part of our mission at that time, other than feeding the poor, was to take in unwed mothers."

Her words were interrupted by another *bumpity-thump* that came from the next room, along with more muttering. Sister Agnes and her food bags.

The reverend mother did a slight eye roll in the direction of the outer office, then gave a patient sigh, and continued. "Naturally, we welcomed the dear girl in her time of need."

I was on the edge of my seat. "What about the baby's father?"

"She didn't reveal who that was, and we had to respect that. When she had the baby, she decided to give it up for adoption. We prayed over her and for the well-being of the child." She shook her head sadly. "Such a difficult decision for anyone to make. But she seemed at peace."

"And after that?"

"She left for a short time, maybe for two months, but came back, giving her life to the Lord."

I pictured the locket. "The photos." I cocked an eyebrow. "Sister Madeline and her baby?"

"It would seem so." She settled behind her desk again, and I waited a moment before asking the next question.

"Was the baby adopted?"

"Yes. But several years after the adoption, the parents died in a terrible car crash. I don't know what happened to the child after that." She grimaced. "Sister Madeline never talked about it further. I believe the poor girl was tormented. She spent many years in the chapel, asking for forgiveness. She knew in her heart God forgives sincere repentance, but no one can explain the depths of human guilt."

I recalled Scooter's claim that she was atoning for something at St. Gregory. Likely, he was right. Atoning for giving up her child. Or was she atoning for the sin of getting pregnant out of wedlock? Perhaps she asked for forgiveness because of how she got pregnant. My breath caught in my throat at this. Was she involved with a married man? Did she feel she was too young to care for a baby? What about her economic background? The questions kept coming. "And her visits to St. Gregory?"

She nodded. "Even when a nun retires, she'll do a small amount of work. This could be visiting foster homes or even spending time with other seniors. St. Gregory was the place of her choosing. It's been ten years since she left Sisters of the Divine, and though a nun would normally retire at the mother house, we made this allowance for her to live closer to the orphanage. I believe giving there was how she wanted to live out her remaining years."

I thought about this and the children at St. Gregory. "Did Sister Madeline ever try to locate her child?"

"As far as I know, she didn't." She took off her glasses and stood. "There are many adoption agencies throughout the Catholic Church. Abiding Hearts was the one that arranged the adoption for Sister Madeline. My prayers were that the toddler was adopted again."

I thanked her for her time, wrote my home number on the back of the card in case she thought of anything else, and walked to the door. My hand was on the doorknob when one last thought occurred to me. I turned around and smiled. "You never said, was the baby a boy or a girl?"

"Girl."

The girl. Had to be. My pulse picked up with this realization.

I sprinted outside into the warm sun, jotted down Abiding Hearts Adoption Agency on one of my business cards, then crossed the parking lot. Was there any point in pursuing this? The adoption wasn't related to the case. Sister Madeline had given up her daughter over fifty years ago. Surely the grown woman had moved on and likely wouldn't care to learn if her birth mother had died.

This may have been true, but I couldn't ignore the

burning question that kept haunting me. What had Sister Madeline wanted to tell me, especially if it was regarding her daughter? Did she know where her daughter was? Did she have something to give her? I was considering other ideas when movement in the bush to my right caught my peripheral vision. Simultaneously, a dark, unmarked car pulled in and swerved over beside mine.

Romero angled out of the car in a sports jacket and jeans that were molded to his body. His dark hair was windblown, his face unshaven, his expression dour. Still, at the sight of him, my heart twisted and my throat went dry. Plainly, I lost all thought in the other direction.

He placed his hands on his hips. "Now I find you at a convent?" His voice was hard, cynical. "Do you have any other surprises in store?"

I slung my bag in the car. "None that I care to share with you."

I knew he was more ticked at seeing me with Jock than finding me here, but I widened my high-heeled stance like Clint Eastwood in a spaghetti western. "What do you care anyway? You can't even pick up the phone to ask." And again, no talk of where he'd been.

My heart was tripping all over itself, but I refused to give in. "Not that I'm interested, but why are *you* here? I don't imagine you're looking for me."

"I'm here on Sister Madeline's case."

"Ha. That's rich. Your buddy Saunders said this was an open-and-shut case." I crossed my arms in front of me. "And I thought *he* was in charge."

"Things have changed. Now *I'm* in charge." He sliced me a look full of distrust and no adoration. The sentiment stabbed me in the chest. Well, he could eat my dust. I wasn't going to stand around, being rejected again. I ducked into my car and yippee-ki-yayed out of the parking lot like a tumbleweed whipping down a ghost town road. Once the dirt settled, I glanced in my rearview mirror. Romero gave one of his famous head shakes, then stormed into the convent.

Watch out, Reverend Mother. He was one to reckon with.

I wound down the mountain on one of the quieter highways, trying unsuccessfully to wipe Romero's face from my mind. I'd gone two long months without seeing him. Now I'd seen him three times in five days. What was up with that? And why was *he* investigating Sister Madeline's death? He was supposedly on some high-profile case.

I munched on the grapes and cheese I'd packed, attempting to rid my thoughts of Romero. Only it wasn't helping. The food dropped to an empty pit in the bottom of my tense stomach.

I stopped for a Diet Coke and continued down the mountain, sipping my soda while putting things into perspective regarding Romero. He had no reason to react like I'd cheated on him. So, Jock and I were sort of in an embrace. Big deal. Romero had left me standing on a yacht. No hint of where he'd gone or what he was doing. Not even a phone call.

I thought about the few times I'd passed his house, totally by coincidence, of course. His grass had been cut, and there were no signs of piled-up mail. What did that say? "If Romero wants to act like an ass"—I plunked my drink in the cup holder—"then he can kiss mine goodbye."

I spun the radio dial around, in the mood for hard rock. I got Carrie Underwood singing "Jesus, Take the Wheel." I listened for a minute and found myself cooling down, my mind wandering back to Sister Madeline and the adoption.

Eyes on the road, I rooted around in my bag, past bottles of nail polish and hairspray, and pulled out the business card I'd written on earlier. *Abiding Hearts Adoption Agency*. Fifty-plus years was a long time ago. I wasn't sure what, if anything, I'd learn, but I'd look into it when I got back to Rueland. That was my last thought before a colossal force slammed into me from behind.

My head bobbed forward, and I lurched off the road. Stones crunched under my tires with me keeping a death grip on the wheel. What the *hell*? Trying not to panic, I looked ahead for a soft shoulder wider than two feet where I could pull over, but there was no sign of the unpaved ground broadening.

Muscling back on the road, I stuck my arm out the window and turned my head, catching sight of a huge black grille. I signaled that I was okay. Then I motioned for the driver to follow me. Thoughts of car insurance and repairs started clouding my mind, but I told myself I was fine. That was the main thing. Then I was banged again.

I missed the guardrail by inches, fear escalating inside me. Who was this lunatic? The highway had practically been deserted. I hadn't passed any vehicles or tailed anyone. What did they want with me? *Think, Valentine, think.* If I couldn't stop, what did that leave? I glanced in the rearview mirror. The black grille's monstrous mouth looked ready to swallow Daisy Bug whole. Right. I flattened my foot to the floor like a NASCAR driver and shot ahead, but the mountain was a twisting, turning terror trap. I let up on the gas in time and swerved hard to the left around a bend, tires squealing.

I darted my gaze to the side mirror. What kind of vehicle was back there anyway? As if I'd know. I squinted, going around another curve, and got a better view. It had tinted windows. And it was black. An SUV. Or truck. Or Jimmy, whatever that was. It was big. I knew that much.

While I congratulated myself on being observant, the vehicle thumped me again. My heart leaped in my chest, and I blinked in shock. *Okay.* I tightened my lips. *This was do-or-die.*

I grabbed my soda, which was the closest thing I could find, and pitched it out the window. Then I pawed through my bag, desperately tossing anything I could get my hands on. Combs. Dye. Glitter.

Vaseline?

Good for scrapes and dabbing on hairlines before coloring. All right, now wasn't the time to split hairs over proper protocol. I stuck the tube out the window and squeezed it dry. Ointment coiled through the air and splattered on the tank's windshield, adding to the mess of gold glitter, smeared dye, and a tail comb that was sticking up at the base of the windshield.

"Yes!" I screamed, surprised at my own accuracy.

The vehicle rocked behind me, wipers squishing grease across the glass. Meanwhile, my heart hammered above the din of the speeding motors. I flung the tube on the floor and was immediately *thunked* again. Metals clanked and my head rammed the steering wheel.

"Ooh!" Now I was getting mad. I shoveled the rest of my grapes into my palm and gave them a mean toss out the window. I wasn't stupid enough to think they'd have much impact, but at this point I was willing to try anything.

Punching around inside my bag, I yanked out my fuchsia nail polish. *This* may have an impact. I unscrewed the lid and opened the sunroof. I was about to fling it back when I hit a sharp corner. I curled around it on two wheels, knocked the bottle out of my hand, and sent polish all over me. *Crap.* I scooped up the bottle, sailed it through the air, and hit my target squarely on the hood. The vehicle zoomed right and left, wipers beating faster, pink polish spreading across the windshield.

Finally, an exit! I took the cutoff, hoping I'd lose this lunatic. No luck. The vehicle sped down the ramp after me and banged into the side of my car. Squealing my brakes, I did a 360 past signs and guardrails, finally crashing into a rocky ditch off the side of the road. Everything went still except for dust that kicked up around me, creating a thick fog.

I listened for the return of the black beast, but the

vehicle was long gone. Wonderful. I dropped my head back in a daze and waited for the world to stop spinning. I took a shaky breath and prayed I wouldn't throw up. I hated throwing up. It was gross, it made me cry, and bits of food stuck in my throat.

I calmed myself and peered out the windshield. Why hadn't the dust settled? I swallowed nausea and bolted forward. That wasn't dust. Smoke was fanning from under the hood. Not only did some creep try to kill me, he'd wrecked the one thing I didn't owe any more payments on.

"*Shit!*" I didn't often swear. It made me feel undignified, like a ruffian with tattoos and missing teeth. I checked the mirror to make sure I still had my teeth, then gawked down at my fuchsia-lacquered clothes and back up at the smoking hood. "*Shit!*"

Okay. I wasn't hurt. I felt my forehead and winced. Well, I was a little hurt, but I was alive and in one piece. Even if I was stuck on a mountain in a banged-up car, with black clouds rolling in.

I frowned at the steering wheel. Odd, my airbag didn't pop out. What else could go wrong? I opened the door and *whoosh*. Airbag. Shards of plastic flew everywhere, and the force pinned me back. Naturally. The finishing touch. The airbag deflated, and I put a leg outside the car and fell ass-backward onto the rocky ground.

My head hit the edge of the road, stones pressed into my palms, and I could almost taste burnt rubber. I lay there, holding back sobs, staring up at my pink-spotted Bug, almost wishing a speeding bus would finish me off. At least it'd be a quick death. I rolled my gaze down the deserted road. Figured, not even a possum ambling along.

I attempted to pick myself up, but my heel wrenched between two rocks, and pain shot up my calf. I gave myself a second to catch my breath, then worked my foot loose, keeled over, and threw up.

I lifted the hem of my hoodie and wiped my mouth and nose. Then I reached in the car for my Diet Coke. Right. No soda. That was ammunition miles back.

Smelling nothing but vomit, I dug to the bottom of my bag, sighing with relief when I felt the smooth plastic water bottle I'd packed this morning. I lugged it out, unscrewed the lid, and rinsed my mouth with water.

If things weren't bad enough, now I needed to find help.

Logic told me I should call the local police. Yeah. No way was I going to introduce myself to another town of cops.

Romero couldn't have been far, but I'd choke down my hairspray before I asked him for a ride.

If I called my parents, my mother would go on about my predicament until I threw myself off the cliff.

Twix was out. She'd either be dealing with kids or practicing her screams.

What about Jock? Right. After that hot kiss yesterday? I gave a laugh, but it was a laugh masked in fear. No way. He'd be up to his elbows anyway with fawning clients.

Max and Phyllis would be busy at work, too. I might as well call a tow and swallow the bill I couldn't afford. Unless I tried the last reliable person I knew. My sister.

I grabbed my cell phone and punched Holly's number.

"Unbelievable!" she said, after I told her my slightly tamed story. No use getting her all worried. "And you're okay?"

I swiped my cheek and noticed a bit of blood on my fingertip. Of course. The airbag explosion. I'm lucky I didn't lose an eye. "Yeah, for the most part."

"Then let me get this straight. First, you've been asking me—and probably half the town—questions about Sister Madeline's passing. Then you did what any good detective would do; you went to the convent to probe some more. Stop me if I've got any of this wrong."

Smartass. I could've called Romero if I'd wanted to be raked over the coals.

"And on the way back down the mountain, someone plowed into you. Any idea why?"

I flattened my lips. "Maybe I'm on the right track about Sister Madeline's death, and someone's not happy about it."

"Mmm-hmm." She clicked her tongue. "When are you going to learn to leave things to the police?"

Considering how the cops had handled the case so far? "Probably never."

"That's what I thought." She sighed. "Hold tight. Someone will be there soon. I'd come myself, but I'm due back in court in fifteen minutes." She paused. "You sure you're all right?"

Sudden tears stung my eyes. Holly was a cop, and she was bossy, but she'd always be my big sister. I said I was fine, disconnected, and lowered myself onto a boulder.

I eased my aching foot up and rolled up my pant leg. Fabulous. My ankle looked as if I'd been dancing all night in spikes, which I'd been known to do. I smiled grimly, hearing my mother's irksome advice about dressing for comfort, not fashion.

The wind had picked up, and I felt cold air slice through me. I wrapped my arms around myself and started to panic. What if it was true? What if someone was angry because I was digging into Sister Madeline's death? But who would be enraged other than a killer? Which would prove my theory that there *was* a killer. And who knew I was in the Berkshires other than my staff?

I looked around. Darn. Why hadn't I paid closer attention when I'd exited the convent? A prickly itch up my arm told me someone had been lurking in the bush by the parking lot. What if that someone was the driver of the black monster, and that person returned to finish me off?

I heard a plop. Then another. And another. I looked down at big, wet raindrops splattering the boulder. "Okay, already," I shouted at the sky. I flipped up my hood, climbed back in the car, closed the sunroof and windows, and waited for help.

I was on alert when a truck slowed, and the driver hollered out his window. "You okay?"

I put my window down a crack and told him help was on its way. I wasn't totally convinced of this myself, but I gave a firm smile, and he did a thumbs-up and continued on down the ramp.

Twenty minutes later, there was a knock on my window. I must've dozed off because I flinched at the sight of Romero leaning on the door, wind and rain lashing his face.

"You okay?" he shouted through the downpour, his hair soaked, water dripping off his unshaven jaw.

Telling my heart to calm down was useless. I rolled down the window and gave a sheepish nod.

He did a quick sweep of my body. "Grab your bag."

I wanted to run my fingers through his hair and kiss him madly, even if it was during a downpour, I was covered in stale vomit, and he was the last person I wanted to see. How could anyone look so sexy and be ticked off at the same time? "I'm waiting for help."

"I'm it."

"What?"

"You wanted Iron Man?"

I had him once, I thought regretfully. Now we were distant strangers.

The look on his face said he wasn't in the mood for an argument. *Fine.* I hoisted my bag over my shoulder, stepped out of the car—forgetting my twisted ankle—and fell into his arms.

He scooped me up and held me close. The familiar scent of his Arctic Spruce deodorant mixed with rain sweetened the air, overpowering my stench. Shame overcame me, and I avoided his eyes. I knew when I looked pathetic. He placed me on the passenger seat of his unmarked car and yanked the seatbelt.

"I can do it," I said with as much pride as I could muster.

He gave me a short stare that might've said *don't bother talking* and continued to buckle me in. When he snapped the seatbelt in place, he paused. Probably considering his next move. My insides were roiling. My chest felt tight. I sat on my hands so I wouldn't do anything stupid or impulsive, like caress his rugged jaw or slap his face; I wasn't sure which, but I wanted some kind of reaction. Thankfully, before I could do either, he slammed the door and walked around to his side.

He slid onto his seat and tugged a pad and pen from inside his jacket. "First, do you want to tell me what that smell is?"

I looked down at the dirt and dried bits of vomit clinging to my hoodie. Could I die now, Lord? Save me from this embarrassment?

"And what is that pink stuff all over you?"

I bit my bottom lip, attempting to hold my composure.

"Oh no." He gave an exasperated sigh. "Is this going to be another one of those perm-rod stories?"

I shook my head, biting back tears.

"But it's going to be just as good."

His sarcasm couldn't top the humiliation I already felt. *Fine*. He wanted to know what happened? I swallowed my dignity and filled him in on the chase and how I'd hurt my foot, subtly slipping in the sick part.

I had to give him credit for not laughing at me for the idiotic ways I'd saved myself. There were a couple of times *I* would've gaped jaw-down at my story, but he kept the grin off his face and remained professional. "All right," he said. "Give me a description of the vehicle that veered you off the road."

"It was black."

He scratched this down and waited.

"And big."

He lowered his pen.

"And it was loud."

"Did it go vroom-vroom or putt-putt?"

"Okay!" I swiped a tear off my cheek before it went noticed. "So, I don't know what type of truck or van…or jeep it was. I know it was powerful."

"You didn't by any chance get the license plate."

License plate? "No."

He rubbed his jaw. "Let's see. We've got a big, black,

loud, powerful vehicle. We're still sitting on the fence about the vroom-vroom or putt-putt part."

I folded my arms, anger replacing tears. "Just look it up in one of your books."

"Sure," he said, "and I'll get back to you anytime between now and eternity."

I thought about how he'd disappeared from my life. "In other words, don't expect to hear from you."

He gave me a dagger look for that. Then he called a tow truck and the local police and shot out of the car, probably gaining distance so he wouldn't throttle someone. That was dandy with me. I wasn't too crazy about his attitude either. *And* I wasn't thrilled that he'd called the local police. That was only inviting trouble. Whoever did this was from Rueland. Had to be. Why waste time with distractions here? He popped open his trunk, grabbed a raincoat, and threw it on while he waited.

What seemed like hours later, a police car and a tow truck pulled up. The two men got out of their vehicles, shrugged on their raincoats, and formed a huddle with Romero in the pouring rain. After a few more minutes went by, Romero jogged back to the car and ducked his head inside. "Police want to talk to you about what happened." I frowned, and he gave me a nod. "Don't worry. By the time he's heard the whole story, he'll be glad to let us handle it from here."

I blew out a sigh. As much as I hated to admit it, I was relieved Romero was in charge.

He stuck out his palm. "Meanwhile, give me your license and Triple A card."

I dug out my license and handed it to him. "I don't have Triple A."

"What?" He waved his arms. "You drove over two hundred miles alone up a mountain and you don't have Triple A?" He pressed the heel of his hand to his neck and kneaded.

I stole a glance at him, sensing a touch of concern. Angry concern, but beggars couldn't be choosers.

He mumbled something that sounded like *unbelievable*, then slammed the door.

He gestured to the cop that he was welcome to talk to me, and it struck me that even when Romero was aggravated, he was still decent. Darn him for making me feel something for him.

He must've told the cop about my sore foot, because instead of me hobbling to the police car, the officer joined me in Romero's. I gave him the bare bones of what happened, and *he* didn't seem put out because I hadn't caught the license plate or know the make of vehicle. He thanked me for my cooperation, gave me a reassuring smile, then put up his hood to his raincoat and joined the other men.

Through the whipping wet wind, Romero pointed to my car, then toward the highway. The tow truck driver nodded as if he was taking directions. The cop left in his cruiser, and ten more minutes went by while Daisy Bug was hooked behind the tow truck. The driver disappeared back on the highway, and Romero took a last look around, then slanted into his car. Wordlessly, he handed me my license and shrugged off his raincoat. "He's taking your car back home to Bruno's Garage." He tossed the coat in the backseat and gave me a sidelong glance. "That okay? It's on me."

I nodded like an admonished child. "I'll pay you back."

"No need," he said, reading a message on his cell phone.

I scowled at my situation, then sat there silently while lightning stabbed the sky.

He tapped away on his cell phone, looking out the window once. "Storm's getting worse. It's not going to be a nice drive."

I remembered Reverend Mother Margaret mentioning the severity of the storm the night Sister Madeline had arrived. "I'll take my chances," I said, wanting to get home.

He shoved his phone in his jacket pocket and cut me a frosty look. Then he buckled up, put the car in gear, and headed in the same direction the tow truck had gone moments ago.

It took us almost an hour to go twenty miles down the highway. The wipers went full speed but couldn't keep up with the torrential downpour. We pulled over several times, waiting it out, heater warming our legs. Finally, we came to a police car angled at a road block. Two cars had turned around in front of us, but Romero wasn't going anywhere until he spoke to the cop. He edged closer to the cruiser and rolled down his window.

"Falling rocks and mudslide around the bend," the uniform shouted through the wind and rain. "Couple of trees down, too. Sorry, folks. Road's closed. Mess won't be cleaned up until morning."

What about Daisy Bug? Did the tow truck pull her through all this?

"How's I-90 look?" Romero asked.

"Also closed. Powerlines down. If I were you," the cop said, "I'd stay put for the night."

Romero gave the cop a nod, rolled up his window, and made a U-turn.

"What are you doing?" I asked.

"Turning around. There's a place ten minutes back down the highway where we can rest."

"But I have to get home." That wasn't totally true. And Yitts had enough food to last another day. Truth was, my emotions were all over the place, and I didn't trust myself around Romero. Last thing I needed was to be stuck here alone with him.

He shook his head. "Did you hear the man? Road's closed." His cell phone hummed, and he pulled over to look at the readout. "Tow truck barely made it through the mudslide. Warned us not to chance it."

Grand. I was glad to hear the tow truck driver was safe and that Daisy Bug would make it down the mountain, but now a different kind of fear flowed through my veins. I glanced miserably from the black clouds to the brooding expression on Romero's face. Right. Guess he wasn't ecstatic about being alone with me either.

I thought back to yesterday and how he'd thundered down the basement stairs to the laundry room. I wanted to ask why he'd come? Did he want to apologize? Check up on me? Reunite? One of my greatest fears was falling hard for a man, then being betrayed. Wasn't that why I stopped dating? Afraid I'd be rejected again, I kept quiet.

After an eternity of driving in torturous silence, thousands of lights flickered through the blurry windshield, framing the peaks and valleys of a beautiful Victorian-style inn. We rolled by luxurious iron gates and my heart fluttered—which I tamed quickly.

"How did you know this was here?"

He circled a graceful fountain statue of a naked woman. "Been here before."

Oh? With whom?

I almost missed the smile tugging at Romero's lips as he pulled up under a large canopy. Ignoring my protests, he carried me into the lobby and lowered me on an Elizabethan chair beside a roaring fire in a stone fireplace. I got back on my feet because I'd left my bag in the car.

"Stay put," he ordered. "I'll park and get our bags."

Our bags? What was *he* packed for? Hiking the Appalachian Trail?

As if reading my thoughts, he said, "I always come prepared."

Bully for him. I had no overnight bag. No clothes. Not even a measly toothbrush. Only my beauty bag that was now depleted of items.

I fumed but sat down, eyeing the spa and gift shop signs pointing down a hallway. My heart lifted. Maybe I should explore the inn. I glowered at my foot. Or not. I watched a businessman, then a couple of lovebirds check in. I bet they'd be going to the spa and gift shop.

With nothing else to do, I clicked my nails on the antique end table. Wait. Why weren't my nails clicking? I peeked at my hand. Chipped nail polish. Jagged tips. Dirty cuticles. I squealed so hard inside I could feel pressure come out my ears. My foot gave a throb, not happy about the state of affairs either. "Wait your turn," I muttered, reaching for my emery board. Right. No bag. Romero was *fetching* our bags.

Needing something to do, I peered down at *The Boston Globe* on a large coffee table. Business tycoon Levi Tazotto's face was plastered on the front page. The heading read *Tazotto Finally Captured!* What had my mother said about the industrialist? He'd murdered his mistress? I quickly read the short blurb and learned the details of the arrest had not yet been made public.

I limped to the far side of the coffee table to read another account when I spotted a local paper. In light of my highway mishap and my growing suspicions about Sister Madeline's death, I hoped this paper would have something on her demise. I flipped through it but didn't see a word on Sister Madeline. Or the convent, for that matter. And why should I? Everyone seemed to think she died a simple death. No need for a news story. I doubled back anyway to make sure I hadn't missed anything.

My head was buried in the pages when I heard a man clear his throat. I glanced up and caught Romero glaring at me, bags slung over his shoulder, key in one hand. Whoa. One key?

He dropped the bags and nodded at the paper. "Looking for something?"

"No." I wasn't about to share any speculation about Sister Madeline's death. Now that he was on the case, he was probably brimming with information. Never mind that. What was with the one key?

"And didn't I tell you to stay put?" He pressed his lips together and sighed as if he wasn't sure what to do with me. Romero. New York City tough cop. Uh-huh. I'm sure he knew exactly what he wanted to do with me, and this thought made me nervous in more ways than one.

"I'll carry you to the elevator," he said with cold detachment.

I studied his face. I wanted emotion, right? Emotion wasn't always filled with heated words and flared tempers. "I'm fine. Really."

I sized up the elevator, then stared down at my foot, silently negotiating with it to get me there. Taking a deep breath, I inched along with the grace of a toddler in high heels.

Romero pressed 3, the top floor, bags in hand, looking as if he were on his way to a torture chamber. I stood beside him, fiddling with my hoodie strings. If things had been different, this night could've been the beginning of something great. A bead of water dripped from his hair onto his shoulder, and my heart gave a thump.

I attempted to look aloof despite my foolish desires. "So, you've been here before."

"Case I was on." He shot me a sideways glance. "I didn't spend the night."

Relief washed over me at the same time the elevator doors opened. I limped into the elevator, focusing on the present, not what-might-have-been. We rode to the third floor in tense silence, the pain in my foot nothing compared to the knot in my chest.

We arrived at a room and he opened the door, then handed me my bag. "I'll be next door, making some calls. Then I'll be over with some ice."

Ice. If he thought I was in the mood for cocktails, he was sorely mistaken.

He placed my room key in my palm. "Better elevate your foot. It's swollen."

Thanks for noticing. I gave him a tight-lipped smile and slammed the door behind me.

Chapter 10

I lugged my stuff to the bed built for a giant and tried not to swoon at the soft, romantic décor. Terry bathrobes were neatly folded on a chair, and the smell of rosemary mint coming from tiny burlap bags soothed my temper. I would've loved nothing more than to pour myself a hot bath, but with half an hour left before closing at work, I needed to see how things had gone today. With the way my day had panned out, I wasn't expecting a positive report. I flopped on the bed, grabbed my cell phone, and dialed the salon.

Max picked up. "Beaumont's Massage Parlor and Strip Joint. We're hiring."

"Max!"

"I'm joking. I knew it was you."

I hoisted my foot up on the bed and rolled my eyes.

"I saw that," he shot back.

Max and I had worked together for so long we almost knew what the other was thinking. I grinned despite myself. "What's been happening there?"

"The usual. Women dropping like flies around Jock, begging for his number and anything else they can get their hands on."

I remembered how Jock liquefied me with one kiss. All right, it was two. No. It was three! And I welcomed them.

I shook off the tingles that flooded me. "And Phyllis?"

"She's the manure that attracts flies."

"Max!"

"What? You asked. Okay, she's fine. With her eyebrows singed off, she crayoned a pair and unsuccessfully glued on false eyelashes. She looks like Bozo the Clown, and she's flaunting what's left of her cornrows. I wish you could've been here when she swung her beads around, lost her balance, and fell on top of Mrs. Benedetti." Max laughed. "You know Mrs. Benedetti. She takes crap from no one. Ahhhhh, it was beautiful."

"Mrs. Benedetti's coming tomorrow for a wax. Why was she there today?"

"One of her Mafia sons was treating her to a hairdo. Phyllis was the only one free."

"Her sons aren't in the Mafia. I don't think."

"They carry guns and they never smile. And they're always in black."

"Lots of people wear black. And maybe they have a permit to carry a concealed weapon. Maybe they're private eyes. Gunsmiths. Maybe they belong to the National Rifle Association."

He chewed on that, and I plunged ahead. "What about you? Anything I should know?"

"Few cancellations because of the storm. Guido brought us tacos for lunch." He stalled. "Uh, also…" His tone changed.

"What, also?"

His voice lowered. "About fifteen minutes ago, a woman came in and pulled Jock aside. When they were done talking, Jock said he had to leave."

"What?" Gone one day, yet something would happen.

"Don't panic, lovey. Phyllis and I will finish up tonight."

"Who was she?"

"I don't know. She didn't look like the multitude who've been swooning over him. She was short, blond, and jowly. Fairly standard, no special markings."

"Sounds like you're describing a cocker spaniel."

"Plus, she was wearing a black T-shirt and had one of those lanyard-keychain-y things around her neck. And she wasn't real smiley."

"Maybe she's in the Mafia."

"Funny."

It actually wasn't. I had a bad feeling about this. "Did Jock say why he had to leave?"

"No. And I didn't think you'd mind. I asked myself, 'What would Val do?'"

"Did you conclude I'd say he had a job and couldn't go?"

"No."

He was right. I would've watched Jock waltz out the door because that's the take-action type of boss I was. "Is he coming back?"

"Said he'd see me tomorrow. What's happening at your end, Kemosabe? Hey, are you at the convent?"

"I was there at noon. On my way home, someone forced me off the road. My car's being towed to Bruno's."

"Wow. You okay?"

"Except for a twisted ankle and a closed highway, which means I won't be back until tomorrow morning. I'm at a place called Eden Winds Resort."

"Are you kidding? I've read about that place. Number one spot in New England for lovers. Too bad you don't have one of those."

"It's one night. I think I might survive without the male species."

"How are you getting home?"

There was a knock at the door.

"Hold on," I said to Max, then hopped to the door.

Romero held up an ice bucket. "For your foot." He backed me into the room, went directly into the bathroom, and grabbed a towel.

I stood there like a dummy. Romero was the toughest cop I knew, mentally and physically. And here he was bringing me ice for my foot. When he came out of the bathroom, I was perched on the bed, smiling my gratitude, phone in hand. "Checking in at the salon."

He gave me an unreadable look and set the ice wrapped in a towel across my foot. "Didn't mean to interrupt," he said. "Here. Put this on your ankle." Before I could even say thanks, he was gone.

I blinked at the door. Did he think I was talking to Jock?

"Who was *that*?" Max asked.

"Romero." I sounded flushed, but I couldn't help it. The man took my breath away.

"He's making resort calls now?"

"He picked me up when my car got sideswiped."

"Uh-huh. He happened to take a day trip to the Berkshires in hopes of saving your fanny on a mountain." He sighed. "Our man in blue is *such* a Prince Charming."

"More like he's on the case and paid the convent a visit."

"Hmm. Did he tell you where he's been the last two months?"

"No. We haven't really talked." Understatement of the year.

"Now you've got all night to talk." There was mischief in his voice. "I gotta go. Phyllis is picking beads out of her cleavage." He paused. "Be careful with that male species…that you don't need."

I rang off and caught a whiff of myself. *Oof.* I needed a shower. I glanced longingly at the sprawling bed, my eyelids fighting to stay open. I rolled over. A two-minute nap wouldn't hurt anything. I'd test the mattress. I yawned and smoothed my fingertips along a silky pillowcase. Probably a three-million thread count. Like the expensive shirts Jock wore. Same quality. Same rich feel. I buried my nose in the pillow and caught a clean spicy scent. Enticing, again like Jock.

Whoa. I jerked the pillow away from my face. What was I *doing*? I wasn't on a romantic quest, pining over Jock—I eyed the door—or Romero. I was here on a mission. Maybe not *here* here. But I had other things on my mind. Mystery things. Sister Madeline things. Adoption things. I wasn't too thrilled about Jock right now or his wanderlust attitude.

I yawned again, punched the pillow, and stuffed it under my head. And who was this lanyard-toting woman anyway? Jock wasn't the type to drop everything for anyone unless…unless maybe she wasn't just anyone? Maybe she was his sister, or his aunt. Or his wife. I sat up with a start, eyes wide. He'd told me he didn't have a girlfriend. He hadn't said anything about a wife. Was he leading a double life? Pretending he was Mr. Carefree, Mr. Living It Up when there was a little missus at home? Ha! I knew it all along.

Mistrust burned inside me. Since I couldn't relax now, I snatched my phone and did a search on Jock de Marco. Why hadn't I done this sooner? I tightened my lips. Right. My world didn't revolve around computers and Wikipedia. And maybe I took people at their word.

I scrolled through names and found Jock linked to the salons where he'd worked. Everything he'd told me was there in black and white, from training in Rome to working in Los Angeles and Chicago. Apparently, both salons had maintained consulting relationships with Jock. Fabulous.

Wait a minute. What was this? I went back to an older search result. *Navy firefighter Jock de Marco, recuperating from an abdominal wound while onboard the USS…ship provides fifty percent of the air support for Afghanistan troops…expects to make full recovery.* Holy crap! Jock was in the navy?

Maybe this was another Jock de Marco? I clicked the article and pulled up the thumbnail picture. Definitely Jock, dressed in full navy uniform. He looked a tad leaner, his jawline was more pronounced, and his hair was buzzed to nothing. Reluctantly, I had to admit Jimmy was right. Jock could pass for a younger Dwayne Johnson. His scar was from a wound that happened—I looked at the date— almost ten years ago.

My heart jumped into my throat at the memory of Jock checking the bathroom yesterday after Phyllis's unfortunate explosion. Seemed we had a real-life hero amongst us, and it added a whole other sexy dimension to Jock de Marco. Yet that didn't explain the lanyard woman or where he was sneaking off to—not that I was sure I wanted to know. I dropped my phone on the nightstand and sighed. And what in creation was a navy firefighter doing working in a salon? Was this some sort of joke?

A while later, I felt a vague awareness of a presence beside me. I forced my eyes open, expecting to be licked by Yitts. I blinked. No Yitts.

Romero sat on the edge of the bed. *Damn.* With all that had happened today, I must've fallen into a deep sleep. The side of Romero's hard-muscled back faced me while he stroked my foot. Something purple and fuzzy trailed from his lap onto the bed.

I pushed down the excitement I felt from his touch and elbowed to a sitting position. "How'd you get in here?"

He pointed to the connecting door. "It was unlocked."

"I'm supposed to believe that?"

He examined my foot. "How is it?"

I flexed it, masking a cringe. "Better. That sleep helped."

"Good. The hotel gave me a wheelchair. We'll use it for dinner."

I warmed at the thought of a romantic dinner, then frowned at the wheelchair nonsense.

He read my expression. "You'll find the pain worsens as the night wears on."

"I didn't realize you also had a degree in medicine."

"Impressive, isn't it?"

I slumped back. "I'm not getting in a wheelchair."

"You will, if I have to handcuff you in." His voice was deep and hard-edged.

"You'd use brute force to restrain me?"

"In a heartbeat."

Blood surged in spots I didn't want to think about, all

because I was envisioning Romero and me and handcuffs. Darn Romero. He possessed an irresistible confidence that overpowered everything. In my most adult-like manner, I huffed indignantly.

He swiped my strappy heels off the floor, his Iron Man watch sexily draping his wrist. "Tell me this isn't all you've got for footwear."

I gaped at my dainty heels dangling from his strong hands. "Reverend Mother had to cancel our tennis match, so I left my Nikes at home."

He lowered my shoes and raised an eyebrow at me. Suddenly, I had a dreaded feeling he'd bought me practical granny loafers in the gift shop.

My heart almost seized out of panic. "Tell me those aren't orthopedic shoes you're hiding there."

"No orthopedics," he said, "but when you're not being wheeled, you'll be carried."

Better than sinking my feet into granny loafers. "Okay. I know when I'm beat."

His eyes challenged mine. "Sweetheart, you wouldn't know you were beat if I straddled you on all fours with your hands locked above your head."

Holy smokes. *Was it hot in here?*

He came around the side of the bed. "Thought you might need to change your top." His gaze roamed to my cleavage. "Not that I mind the one you have on."

Instinctively, I looked down. My zipper had dropped several inches while I was sleeping and revealed my pink, lacy bra. My hands flew to the pull and closed the gap.

"This is the closest thing I could find." He tossed me a purple chenille hoodie.

My voice got lost, and I felt all velvety. It wasn't diamonds, and it wasn't a room full of roses, but this was the third nice thing he'd done for me. I'd been a pain in the ass earlier and said some stupid things, and he'd reciprocated, first by paying for a tow, then the ice, and now with a simple hoodie. "Thanks." I nestled the soft feel under my chin. "I guess I'll take a shower now."

He nodded and left to check out the weight room. I hopped on one foot into the gold-toned bathroom, dragging my bag behind me.

"Wow." I stared from the huge martini-glass sink framed in smooth stones to the cotton plush towels, to the shower that resembled a glass tulip. I limped to the mirror and almost screamed when I saw myself. My hair and clothes were slashed in pink polish. My eyes were red. There was a small cut on my cheek. And regurgitated food decorated my hoodie. Was it any wonder I couldn't find a man?

I fished through my bag for nail polish remover, nabbed a few cotton pads from a jar by the sink, and went to work scrubbing myself clean. I ripped out my braids, showered, and brushed my teeth using a complimentary toothbrush and tube of toothpaste. I put on my new hoodie, then my jeans, and worked a miracle with my hair and face. I wasn't supermodel caliber, but I wouldn't send anyone shrieking from the mountain resort either.

Heavy rain continued to batter the ground outside. Swaying branches flicked the lobby window. The dining area was set back from the main entrance and was much cozier, almost shutting out the storm. It was made up of four separate rooms that a sign in the lobby explained were a living room, a parlor, and bedrooms at the turn of the century. Our dining room was elegant and intimate. A dimly lit chandelier hung from a high ceiling, and miniature hurricane lamps glowed on each of the eight tables.

Romero wheeled me up to our table and took the seat across from me. I was hunched in my wheelchair, like Whistler's Mother, and he sat back, looking breathtaking. He'd removed his sports coat, which left a black fitted crew neck and a clear view of his well-sculpted shoulders and muscled chest. And he smelled all male.

He leaned in, clasped his hands on the table, and nodded at my purple hoodie. "Nice."

I looked from his eyes that pierced me with that brilliant blue, to his hair that was dry but unruly with waves curled at his neck. I exhaled at the sheer beauty of this man. "Thanks. It was an extravagant gift."

"Not at all," he said, eyes not leaving my face. "Why were you at the convent today?"

So much for small talk. "You mean this isn't a social gathering?"

He cracked a grin.

How much did he know about my involvement? He obviously knew I'd found Sister Madeline's body. But did he know I'd gone back to her apartment? Taken a prayer card from her room? "Why were *you* there?"

"That's police business."

Typical cop response. "Okay. Mine was beauty business." I was proud how indifferent my voice sounded.

"Funny, the reverend mother wasn't sporting any makeup or wild hairdo after you left."

"I can imagine how she looked after *you* left."

"Care to elaborate?"

I shrugged. "You have a certain effect on people."

He lowered his voice to almost nothing, eyes dilated. "Do I have an effect on you?"

I blushed at that, thankful for the dim lighting.

The waitress appeared at the table before I could find my tongue. She was dressed in a long flowing black skirt, a high white-collared blouse, and her hair was swept into a loose Edwardian bun. She looked straight-laced and self-denying, yet the way she eyed Romero—a look I'd seen on women before—was anything but turn-of-the-century timidity. Probably wondering if he was as hot out of his clothes as he was in them.

She pushed down a swallow, set bread and water on the table, and took our order. A minute later, she was back with a seductive smile and a bottle of red wine. Her smile wasn't lost on Romero. He thanked her for pouring the wine, then caught my eye and winked.

I trembled at the wink because it was sexy and oozed confidence. It said *I like you…a lot.* Yikes. Was the old Romero back? I was so nervous, I felt heat rise from my toes. The room felt like a sauna. And boy, was I thirsty! I reached for my water and knocked it over. *Clumsy.*

Romero caught the glass before it hit the floor, and I went for my wine. I was a poor drinker, but I was desperate. I swallowed a healthy gulp and sat up straight. Mmm. Bubbly. And sweet, like punch. No harm in a few more sips. To courage, I silently cheered, tasting more.

Romero sat back with a predatory look in his eye.

"Bread?" I held up the basket, feeling a sudden tingle spread through me.

He buttered a slice, eyes on me.

I blinked through the wine rush. "So, you're working this case."

"I am now. I just came off a major indictment."

Was this what had kept him away for so long? I wanted to ask but didn't want to ruin the night when it had only begun. "Does that mean Detective Saunders is out?"

"Let's say Shredder's helping in another capacity."

"Shredder?"

"You don't want to know."

"Try me."

"His nickname goes back to a repeat offender's slippery fingers, a meat slicer, and Shredder's innate sense of justice."

"Is that legal? Shredder cutting off someone's fingers?"

"I didn't say that."

I sighed. "What about this case? Are you going to say anything?"

He chewed on his bread, thinking about this. "What do you want to know?"

"What you found out about Sister Madeline today."

"Probably the same thing you learned, except you didn't have the locket to show anyone. But I imagine you gave an accurate description."

I grimaced, then swallowed more wine.

"The woman in the picture was Sister Madeline," he said. "The baby was her child."

I nodded that I'd already learned this, and because I knew what was coming next, I put my head down, pretending I was interested in my wheelchair's brakes.

He waited until he caught my eye. "So, you're taking up detective work again."

I wasn't going to share my personal reasons for wanting to see this through. My past regrets were my own. And some things were none of his business. I raised my chin in defiance. "Sister Madeline got very weak very quickly. And—"

"And did you ever consider maybe she was sick?"

"Yes, I did, but she would've told me." I stared him down through another shot of wine.

He shook his head, like what was the use in arguing.

"And last time I talked to her, she sounded different, scared. She said she had to tell me about the girl. Two days later, I found her dead. Sue me for feeling responsible."

Romero sat back while the waitress placed our meals in front of us. Once she cleared the room, he leaned in. "Why is it every time there's a dead body, you feel responsible?"

"It's who I am." I tossed back more wine.

He glanced at the ceiling as if the ornate moldings would help him figure me out. Getting no answer there, he blew out a sigh and stabbed his ribeye.

I felt hot inside. Was it the wine on an empty stomach or the anxiety of being near him again? I wanted him to explain the last missing few months. I wanted to know if we'd had anything before then, or if it had all been my imagination. My prime rib stuck in my throat, so I threw back more wine.

"There's talk Sister Madeline died in her sleep," I said.

Romero nodded, assessing this. "Sounds like something Shredder would say."

"Why would he say it if it wasn't true?" I gave a tiny burp and felt the room revolving.

"There's a teddy bear inside that man. He probably

didn't want to alarm the old folks. But I *will* say she wasn't shot, stabbed, strangled, or drowned."

"Gee, I wasn't sure about drowning since her apartment looked like Boston, *hic*, Harbor." I fumed inside. "I can see I'm not going to get anywhere with you." I knew who'd give me answers. Holly, that's who.

His eyes bore into mine. "How'd you know about the convent?"

I made a loud, floaty sigh from who knows where, vaguely aware he'd asked a question. I took another swig and eyed an empty glass.

He gave me a stern nod. "You're going to get drunk if you have any more wine."

I saluted my glass high in the air, deaf to his advice. He stared at me like he was weighing the consequences, then shook his head and poured me more wine.

The more I drank, the more I could see through Romero's game. In fact, things became crystal clear. They don't tell you that when you're sober. All he wanted from me was information on Sister...uh...Mackaline's death. The sneak. He didn't care one iota about me. No siree. Well, I wasn't going to tip my...my finger. If he thought he'd learn anything from this girl, he was waaaaay off.

"I'll tell *you* somefink," I slurred. "I'll bet you didn't know Girvil's a composter."

"What? Who's Girvil?"

"Aha! What kind of police work are you? Virgila lives near Sister Magdalene."

"Madeline."

"That's what I said."

"I think you've had enough for tonight." He set the bottle on the floor out of sight.

"Hey!" I shouted. "Bring that back. I want to finish the bottle."

"Fine." He poured most of the wine in his glass, dribbling the rest into mine.

I shoved my glass in the air for a toast. "You cheated. You only gave me a tea-poon."

He came close and lowered his voice. "I'm glad you're in a wheelchair because it'd look embarrassing hauling a drunk woman out on my back."

"I'm not drunk. You're jealous 'cause I know more about Sister Macnamine's death than you." I swayed in my chair, squinting at the wine sloshing on the tablecloth. *Oops.* I lifted the table skirt and swiveled to look under the table. Did this thing have wobbly legs?

Romero's eyes burned into me, and another sizzling jolt ripped through my body. Didn't matter much anyway since I was already on fire. "Ooh, it feels warm in here." I flung my head around. "Who's being so loud?"

Two couples gawked at me. Probably heard the loudmouth, too.

The waitress appeared with the check, giving Romero a tight smile. He told her to charge it to his room, then calmly wheeled me out to the elevators. What a cutie. I pitched my head back at him with a carefree smile, then gazed at the sparkly ceiling tiles.

"Look at all the diamonds," I called out. "I love diamonds, but only the clear-cut ones." I hiccupped. "Don't ever buy me the cloudy ones. They're cheap."

"I'll remember that."

He opened the door to my room and dropped me on the bed like a sack of potatoes. Grumpy puss. I had my arms wrapped around his neck, but he untangled himself from my grip and held me by the shoulders before completely breaking free.

I sat on the bed in a stupor, not ready to give up. I wasn't entirely sure where my mind was at, but it felt important to put my all into this moment. I squirmed to the edge of the bed and slid my tongue across my top lip. Then I smoothed my hands up his toned chest, giving him my best sultry look.

At my touch, Romero's breathing slowed and his body froze. The hunger in his eyes was unquestionable. He lifted me off the bed and pulled me in until we were hip to hip. My heart was beating wildly, and I thought I would faint from desire. He cupped my head with his powerful hands and stared deep into my eyes.

A second later, he threw his hands down. "I've got to be crazy falling for you."

I wasn't sure if I'd been insulted, but I fingered his mouth, wanting more than anything to feel his lips on mine. My arms and legs snaked around him, my breasts crushed his abs.

He felt hard in all the right places, yet he swore under his breath like he was holding back. Maybe he was crazy, but I knew he wanted me.

I backed up to the bed, sliding my knees on top of the mattress, pulling him with me. I slithered my hands down his abdomen and around his hips, giving his rock-hard butt a squeeze. "You want to play?"

His feet didn't leave the floor, and I was running out of ways to get him to loosen up. "You have no idea," he said, groping my hair, "how hard I'm restraining myself."

My gaze lowered to his pants. I had some idea.

Suddenly, my cell phone rang, sending me reeling back on the bed. Romero put the phone to my ear. I groaned.

"Valentine? Is that you?" My mother mumbled something to my father.

I groaned louder, hearing her voice.

"Sounds like a dying dog," she said to my father. Then the line went dead.

"My lother." I flung out my arm, phone in hand.

Romero put my phone back on the nightstand, grasped my hands, and pulled me to a sitting position. "I better go. It's not my style to take advantage of an inebriated woman."

"I'm not kneebriated," I argued.

"Sugar, believe me. You're inebriated. I'll be next door if you need me."

"I need you now." I flopped back on the bed. I wasn't into casual one-nighters. Still, frustration cuffed me in the stomach.

"What you need is rest. And your mother will be calling back any minute."

A beat later, my cell phone pealed again. I grabbed it to keep my head from spinning off while Romero disappeared through the connecting door.

"'lo," I said, pressing my temple.

"Valentine?"

"Yesh, Mom." Damn Romero and his cleverness.

"What are you doing in the Berkshires?"

Holly, the rat-fink, must've snitched on me.

"Did you have an accident?"

"It's complishated. What'd Holly tell you?"

"I haven't talked to Holly, and why are you slurring? What happened? Did you go to the hospital?"

"I'm fine." My head was starting to pound. My stomach wasn't feeling good either. "If Holly didn't tell you I was here, who did?" Then it struck me. Max.

"Gibson told me."

"Who?" My state of awareness wasn't all there.

"Gibson. You know. Mrs. Shales's grandson."

"Gippy," shouted my dad in the background.

I was more confused. "How does Gibshon know I'm here?"

"His company towed your car this afternoon. Gibson was at the garage when the driver pulled in. Are you hurt?"

"Just my pride," I mumbled. I'd save the ankle story for when I was up for warnings of amputation.

"What are you doing in the Berkshires? Your father said there's a convent in the mountains. Is that where you went? To find out more about that nun?" There was muffling, then she said, "You talk to her. She's your daughter."

My father came on the phone. "Is the car totaled?"

"I hope not. They took it to Bruno's."

"Good choice. I'll go see him tomorrow morning. Here's your mom."

I heard my mother mutter her unappreciative thanks, then she cleared her throat. "Will you be home tomorrow, dear? Mrs. Shales wants to talk to you. Her friend Hillary's disappeared."

I sat up so quickly, hot nausea rose in my throat along with a sense of impending doom. I tried to think rationally about what could've happened to Hillary, but all I could do now was promise to come by the next day.

I disconnected and calmed my stomach. I was a sweaty mess. I clawed at my hoodie and jeans and left a trail of garments on the floor until I was down to my bra and lace undies. Relieved to be rid of my clothes, I hobbled to the bed, blew a kiss toward Romero's room, then passed out, face down on top of the covers.

Chapter 11

I woke early the next morning in the same position. My neck was stiff. My head throbbed. I rolled off the bed, limped to the bathroom, and stood stone-faced in the mirror. Everything was a blur, but I could tell I looked pathetic. My hair stuck up, my eyes were puffy, and black liner had bled down my face. For a nondrinker, I had the mother of all hangovers.

I washed my face, brushed my teeth twice, then dragged myself around the room, looking for my shoes. I dropped to my knees and lifted the bed skirt. No shoes. I plunked myself on the bed, ignoring the coconuts clapping between my ears. Straight ahead, I saw my heels dangling on the doorknob of the connecting door. I didn't put them there. *Did I?*

My tongue felt like sandpaper, and my stomach threatened war if I didn't stop moving. I swallowed a few times, stretched back onto the pillow, and tried to bring last night into focus. Wheelchair, yep. Dinner, yep. Wine, yep. Hotel room, yep. Romero, ye—*uh-oh.*

I choked at the vague memory. I didn't throw myself at him, did I? After convincing heaven and earth I wasn't interested in men? I did. I jumped Romero. *Valentine, how could you?* That was my mother speaking. No, my mother wanted me married. It was the inner tortured me, crossing her arms, aghast at my aggressiveness.

Thinking of my mother, I recalled her news about Hillary. My stomach did another tumble that had nothing to do with alcohol. It was the strange things going on at the retirement home, from Ruby's cooking and Virgil's plant fetish to Nettie's poison search. And now, Hillary's disappearance.

I closed my eyes and said a quick prayer. "Please let Hillary be alive and well."

There was a knock at the hallway door. "Amen." I opened my eyes, pushed off from the bed, stepped down too hard on my ankle, and collapsed to the floor. Shoot. I had to pull myself together. I rubbed my ankle, yanked on my jeans and hoodie, and answered the knock.

Romero stood there, clean-shaven and totally edible, smelling like he'd walked through an herbal shower. His black T-shirt that would've hung to my knees held snug to his trim body.

He looked me up and down, a twinkle in his eye. "I hope you don't usually greet room service like this." He carted in coffee and orange juice and set them on the table.

I finished zipping up my hoodie and patted down my hair. In a charming gesture that bordered on seductive, he smoothed his finger across the scab on my cheek. Then he glanced down. "How's the foot?"

I caught my breath and found my voice. "Not bad." I did a jog on the spot. Oh boy, that wasn't wise. Not trusting myself to speak, I held up a finger while the nausea passed.

"Coffee?" He reached for the paper cup.

I shook my head. "Don't…drink coffee."

"Why doesn't that surprise me? How 'bout breakfast?"

I stared at him miserably.

"Juice?"

I took the bottle, chugged it back, and swiped my mouth with the back of my hand.

He grinned, seemingly enjoying himself.

I wasn't going to let it get to me. We all had our embarrassing moments. Mine happened to occur when Romero was around. I inhaled deeply and exhaled. "How much wine did I drink?"

"Two small glasses."

"What?" I slapped the bottle on the table. "You sure?"

"I *can* count that high."

"I thought I emptied the bottle."

"You had help."

"Then why aren't *you* hungover?"

"I don't get drunk."

"Oh, I forgot. Do you also walk on water?" Ignoring the grin, I gawked at his abs, partly out of an itch to touch him and partly because I was piecing together the fresh shirt. "Clean clothes?"

"Never know when you'll need a fresh shirt." He smoothed his chin. "Or a clean shave."

Right. The overnight bag. He didn't have to be chipper about it. Mr. Take On the World.

Half an hour later, we checked out of the resort, toting a breakfast of oatmeal muffins to the car. The early morning sun beamed over the horizon, drying the hood from last night's rain. If I'd been feeling better, I would've taken in the glorious morning, drawing hearts with my finger on the window.

Instead, I got in the car and chastised myself for driving up the side of a mountain like Miss Marple. Ha. More like Wile E. Coyote, almost getting killed coming down. No matter where I turned, there was the Road Runner—or another *R* person—honking and laughing at me like the fool I was. To top it off, I got liquored up. Life of the party. What was I thinking? I gave my head a shake and stole a glance at Romero studying the road.

He was right. Shredder was right. My mother was right. Better I concentrate on hair. Leave the investigation to the police. I had a steady establishment, a good location, and a decent staff. My thoughts drifted to Max, Jock, and Phyllis. Brother. With all the shenanigans lately, it's a wonder I had any business at all. Despite that, it was a new day, and I had unfinished matters. "I'm sorry I was a pain last night. I don't usually throw myself at men."

He slid me a sideways grin, then slipped on his shades. Tingly jolts went from my brain to my pelvis. Lord, this man was sexy. As much as I'd wanted to feel his lips on mine, I begrudgingly respected the fact he hadn't taken advantage of me. The guy had morals. That was huge.

Smiling to myself, I flipped down the sun visor and almost shrieked in the mirror at the red pimple on the tip of my nose. Where'd that come from? Perfect. Went with the rest of the look. I slammed the visor back into place and glared out the window.

The drive had made me sleepy, and I couldn't keep my eyes open. A while later, I woke to the sound of Romero's cell phone ringing. I stretched my neck and focused on the Boston sign flying past us.

"Change of plans," he said, disconnecting and whipping off the next exit. "I need to stop by the FBI field office."

"Where's that?"

"Boston."

"Do I ask what for?"

"I don't think the lieutenant would appreciate me confiding the particulars of an FBI investigation to a nosy beautician…no matter how sexy she is."

My heart did a leap considering how bad things got yesterday. "You think compliments will shut me up?"

He didn't answer, but I knew what he was thinking.

I folded my arms and tightened my lips. "Will I at least be home before work?"

"Promise."

We fought traffic, pileups, and detours in Boston. Romero swung off the main artery, turned onto a side street, and slammed the brakes behind a caravan of cars.

"Damn!" He tossed his shades on the dash. "Half of Hollywood's here." He threw the gear into park. "Stay put." He hoofed it down the street to a couple of cops directing traffic.

I took an easy breath, admiring how Romero conferred with the uniforms. Then my gaze meandered to the action, noise, and gunfire at the dock. This had to be the movie Twix was in. She was right. It was exciting. More. It was infectious. I scanned the costumed crowd, searching for Twix. Mesmerized, I got out of the car and moseyed toward the cordoned-off area.

I didn't see or hear Twix, but a pirate fight scene captivated me. One by one, buccaneers plunged into the cold water, leaving a long-haired, puffy-shirted pirate to save a woman tied to a post. After he unwound her, he gave her a deep, unyielding kiss. I swallowed hard as I experienced that kiss as if it were on my own lips. Like I knew how it felt, how it tasted. Like those savage hands had taken control of my body...

"Cut!" someone shouted close to the scene, and the kiss ended.

Whew. I expelled a breath I didn't know I'd been holding.

Romero advanced on me, his expression grim. "Why is it every time I tell you to stay put, you disappear?"

"My friend's in this movie," I said. "I was looking for her."

"Should I buy popcorn while I wait?"

I huffed. "You don't have to get snippy about it."

He rolled his eyes, hands on hips while I got in the car. He slammed my door and trekked around to the driver's side.

"How are you going to get out of this traffic jam?" I asked.

He slung his cop light on the roof. "Buddy up there gave me another route." He wove through stopped cars and crawled past the private area for movie personnel.

"Must feel good to be king," I said.

He swerved around a pedestrian. "Has its moments."

I kept my eyes peeled for Twix, then almost swallowed my tongue. "*Stop!*"

Romero squealed the brakes.

A petite blond woman in a black T-shirt, wearing a lanyard around her neck, threw a towel over the shoulders of the pirate in the puffy shirt. He pulled off the long wig and eye patch, turned my way, and handed them to her.

I banged against the headrest and slid down in my seat, my heart racing. A second later, I peered wide-eyed out the window and watched Jock step into a mammoth trailer.

"What was that all about?" Romero asked.

"Nothing," I said. "You can go."

"You sure?"

"Yes. *Go!*"

By the time Romero had popped in at the FBI field office and then dropped me off at my house, it was a quarter past eight. I asked another round of questions about why we'd stopped, and all I got was a "You know you're cute when you're persistent?" and a flick on the nose.

In other words, he wasn't going to tell me a thing. That was fine with me. I pursed my lips, opened the car door, and primly thanked him for the ride.

Yitts was in the middle of the living room floor when I stepped into the house. She was chasing one of my bobby pins that had a pink silk rose glued to the end. She took one look at me and bit down possessively onto the bobby pin, ready to dart away. I let her have her fun and went straight to her food dish. "Sorry I didn't make it home last night." I filled her bowl. "There was this accident. I hurt my foot."

She abandoned the bobby pin and wound herself through my legs, not bothered I was limping slightly, but plenty grateful she was getting fresh niblets.

I filled her water cup that sat by the bathroom sink, recalling how it used to be my rinsing cup when I brushed my teeth. That was up until the day she licked the water in the cup while I was brushing. I was pretty giving when it came to my cat. I shared my house, my bed, even the odd morsel. The water cup was going too far. It was officially now her water bowl. My new cup stayed hidden in the cupboard.

I went into the kitchen to get a drink for myself. I downed a glass of water and pressed the answering machine blinking beside my pink, heart-shaped princess phone. One message, and it was from the reverend mother. "I realized after you'd left," she'd said, "that I should've suggested you contact Sister Francis. She was close to Sister Madeline in their younger days, and she may remember something surrounding the adoption. She's currently working in the Boston area." She recited a phone number and wished me good luck.

I jotted the number on a scrap piece of paper and looked at the time. Wasn't even eight-thirty. Too early to call someone I didn't know. I'd try later. I threw the paper in my bag, excited that this may be a lead. Then I called Max for a ride to work. If anyone could get me there before opening, it was Max. By the time I heard his brakes screech to a stop outside, I'd whipped my hair into a bun, fixed my face, and changed my clothes.

I slid in the car, and his jaw dropped to his knees. "What. Did. You. Do?" Max should've been a journalist. He was always looking for a story.

I slammed the car door and buckled up. "What do you mean?"

"You've got afterglow all over your face, and what's that on your nose?"

"The afterglow is called a hangover, and *this* is a pimple!"

"Why do you have a pimple?"

"Oh, I don't know. It erupted to finish off a perfectly miserable day."

"What about the glow?"

"There's no glow! Nothing happened."

"Uh-huh. If you say so." He roared the engine and squealed out of the driveway.

"You're worse than my mother. The truth is I got so drunk I was speaking in tongues. And if you don't stop at the 7-Eleven for Clamato juice, you can forget a Christmas bonus."

"You had a religious experience with Romero?"

"I'm saying I got loud, drunk, and obnoxious. And earlier in the day, I puked."

He wrinkled his nose. "And he's still speaking to you?"

"Thanks. Like I don't feel bad enough."

At work, I nursed and elevated my foot every chance I had. Thankfully, it didn't balk, crammed into my Yves St. Laurents all day.

Jock carried on his high-speed pace as if he wasn't swashbuckling at Boston Harbor earlier this morning. Just as well. I wasn't sure what to say regarding his movie secret. Or his navy secret. And though avoidance did have its appeal, the right moment to talk hadn't presented itself.

Currently, Mrs. Benedetti and I were holed up in Molto Bella. Mrs. Benedetti had enough leg hair to braid cornrows up her thighs. The sudden interest in waxing was commendable, if late in life. I gently slathered a strip of wax on her calf, patted and molded it to her leg, then *rrrrrip.*

"*Aaaaah!*" Mrs. Benedetti struggled to a sitting position to clamp her leg.

"*Aaaaah!*" I screamed back, my head about to pop off. "I'm sorry, Mrs. Benedetti," I breathed. "I know it's painful."

"Mamma mia." She rubbed her satiny leg. Smiling at the feel, she clutched the sides of the bed and lowered herself. "Go again. I didn't deliver eight bambinos by being afraid of pain."

I waxed. She screamed. I screamed. That's how our session went. After she lumbered off the bed, she squeezed my arm. "I'll be back in three weeks, and I no want that Phyllis working on me. She's *pazzo!*" She pinched my cheeks so hard I tasted blood.

"*Pazzo.* Right. I'll make sure I'm available."

After Mrs. Benedetti left and Max and Phyllis cleared out, I plunked down at the computer in my office and sucked back an Advil with Clamato juice. Then I searched Abiding Hearts Adoption Agency online. Nothing came up. And the other agencies listed had been established within the last thirty years. Figured.

I picked up the phone and punched the large number pad, hoping I'd reach Sister Francis. The number Reverend Mother had given me was for Prayer Up Press.

The man on the phone said Sister Francis would be in tomorrow and to come by at five o'clock for an interview. He gave me directions and hung up. I stared at the phone. What just happened? Interview for what? I put down the phone and chugged back the rest of my Clamato juice. I'd see Sister Francis tomorrow. Wasn't that the main thing?

I wouldn't get anywhere until I had wheels. So I called the garage to see when I could pick up my car. Bruno garbled about transmissions, rear panels, and wheel axles. I clicked what was left of my nails on my desk, waiting for the time. A day. Maybe the hour. I got, "Check Monday."

Great. End of the day and no car. I'd have to call my parents after all. On second thought, I could always get a rental. Okay, that was a waste of money I could use on a cute new pair of shoes. Setting priorities was important. And I still had to pay back Romero for the tow. I bit my lip. Calling my parents was the best option. I needed to talk to Mrs. Shales about Hillary's disappearance anyway.

Rotting banana peel, perm-soaked end papers, and other stale smells wafted into my office. Of course. Nobody had taken out the garbage. I shut down the computer, thinking I'd call my parents outside after I took out the trash. I went into the dispensary, emptied the last bits of hair from the dustpan into the garbage bag, then dragged the bag down the hall along with my things.

Jock bumped into me as he came up the stairs with one of his salad containers. He took the garbage bag from my hand and followed me out the back door, offering a lift.

We hadn't been alone since the kiss, and I realized now was my opportunity to talk to him. I'd been wrestling with what to say all day. Moreover, I was suppressing the warmth spreading through me because I'd been working beside a sexy navy firefighter. I didn't know where to begin. His years in the military? His life in the movies? Did I tell him to quit the film, or else? Beaumont's was thriving because of Jock. Was I going to risk losing him because of a movie? Maybe he was working undercover. Maybe he wasn't a hairstylist at all. No, that couldn't be true. His hands were magical. Nobody satisfied women like that without knowing a thing or two about hair.

He tossed the garbage in the Dumpster, and I locked up and hiked over to his monstrous black motorcycle. Now that I was standing beside it, my heart stuck behind my tongue. "You want me to get on *that*?"

"It's only a bike." He tucked the container inside one of the saddlebags by the back wheel, then zipped up his leather jacket.

"I don't ride Harvey-Davidsons."

"It's Harley-Davidson, and considering everyone else is gone, I'm your last option."

"Still nope."

He straddled the bike, snapped on his helmet, and rumbled the engine to life. Then without looking back, he scraped his heel on the asphalt and angled out of the parking lot.

I stood there for a solid minute, surprised he left. "*Pazzo!*" I repeated Mrs. Benedetti's term. Whatever it meant, it sounded appropriate. I dropped my keys in my bag and pulled out my cell when the thundering bike returned. It ripped around Friar Tuck's and screeched a perfect donut six inches from my heel.

Jock flipped up his visor, opened a saddlebag, and pulled out a helmet. "It's all warmed up. Get on."

My mother was on her hands and knees, tugging out annuals when the roar of the motorcycle caught her attention. She tossed a clump of discarded flowers into the wheelbarrow and gave a quizzical look our way. Probably wondering if the Hell's Angels were on a rampage.

Jock helped me off the bike, then whipped off his helmet and nodded at my mother. I took off my helmet and almost kissed the ground that I was in one piece.

The woman who gave birth to me, who always offered advice and butt into my life, stood comatose. I wasn't going to encourage conversation, so I made the introductions brief, thanked Jock for the ride, and said goodbye.

My mother wasn't having any of that. She edged closer to the god in black leather. "You're a friend of Valentine's?" Clearly, Jock was the jackpot, and my mother was about to collect her winnings. My father, meanwhile, was in back, mowing the lawn, missing the show.

Jock looked down at me. "I like to think we're friends. I work for Valentine."

I thought my mother was going to have a stroke. "You work for her?" She glared at me.

"I guess I forgot to tell you. Things have been busy at the shop, so I hired Jock. Um, also can I borrow the car?"

She blew a stray hair from her face, ignoring my request. "I see I miss a lot when I don't make it into the salon."

"Phyllis is back, too," I said, figuring I might as well lay it all out.

My mother didn't care about news of Phyllis or the car. She invited Jock to stay for supper as my father came from around back, straw hat on his head, rake in hand. Oh Lord. This was heading in the wrong direction.

Thankfully, Jock said he had to go. Good thing. All I needed was to sit at a dinner table with Ms. Matchmaker and Mr. Navy Firefighter Movie Star. By the time he roared away, my father had wandered up to us. He removed his straw hat and pressed it to his chest. "Did you see those biceps, Ava? I've only seen arms like that on Arnie." That was Arnold Schwarzenegger, for anyone who wasn't on first name basis with famous people like my father.

I talked to my dad about the car and let my mother examine my ankle and question the scrape on my cheek.

"I'd be getting your foot checked," she said. "Nora Koney's mother-in-law, Sharon, lost her foot to gangrene. It all started with a sprain." She went back to pulling out flowers. "Oh, I almost forgot. Wear something nice for your date tomorrow night."

Date? "What are you talking about?"

"Your date with Reverend Cullen's nephew Harold. It's at eight o'clock, so be ready."

What? "You've got Reverend Cullen fixing me up now?"

"It's not like that. He came for a visit, and we got talking about your business."

"I'm waiting for the connection from my business to my private life."

"Well, we must've mentioned you being single."

"We?" I picked up a clump of flowers she'd thrown on the ground.

"I don't remember how it came out, but Reverend Cullen thinks you're a super girl."

"And he's terribly concerned I'm not hitched."

"I may have initiated that part of the conversation."

"Uh-huh." I pitched the flowers in the wheelbarrow so hard dirt flew everywhere.

"Now, dear." She got to her feet. "He simply brought up his nephew. I thought you might be interested."

I changed tactics before I screamed. "You *bet* I'm interested. If he's related to Reverend Cullen, then this guy must be a real sex fiend."

"Don't be disrespectful."

"Then *you* date Harold."

"Fine." She dusted off her hands. "You tell Reverend Cullen you don't want to see his nephew."

"What's his number?"

"Don't worry the poor boy's new in town and doesn't have any friends."

Errr. "*Okay.* You win. I'll go out with him."

I threw one more heap of flowers into the wheelbarrow, then ventured next door to Mrs. Shales's house. I hoped the next conversation wouldn't be as depressing, but I wasn't going to hold my breath.

Mrs. Shales lived in a gingerbread house with lots of color, swirly wooden trim, and a stone-edged walkway. It was smaller than my parents' house with more warmth and less disinfectant.

Mrs. Shales was reading on her porch swing when I crossed the lawn. She looked up at me and put her book down. "I'm glad you're here." Strain soaked the politeness in her voice.

"I hear you had upsetting news," I said.

"Your mother seemed upset herself. Are you okay? I hope Gibson didn't cause any trouble when he told her about your car." She searched my eyes. "Did he?"

"No. No trouble." That was a lie. My mother probably baked all night because I'd had an accident. Once, Holly blew curfew by three hours, and by two a.m., my mother had baked enough spice muffins to stock a Dunkin' Donuts. I woke up the next morning to the most glorious sight and the smell of cloves and cinnamon. There was no place to sit, but who cared? It was the best breakfast in history.

Mrs. Shales patted the swing, gathering her dress under her leg to make room for me. I jumped on board, and we rocked gently.

"I went to see Hillary yesterday," she said in a soft voice. "Got up my nerve to drive and everything. When I got to the retirement home, she was gone. All her stuff had been moved out." She shook her head. "I didn't see this coming. Hillary never said anything about moving." She wrung her plump hands, concern flooding her eyes.

It was time I asked a few questions of my own. "Could

Hillary have been hurting financially? Maybe she couldn't afford the retirement home?"

She made *tsk-tsk* sounds with her tongue. "You're referring to the tax scuttlebutt, right? That's what Hillary called it."

"Yes."

"It's followed her around all these years. Trampled her dear departed husband's reputation. And of course, Hillary's, by association. All nonsense. The poor man took bad advice when he was on town council. He was a good man, Valentine, and the issue was cleared up." She pushed off with her stubby feet to get the momentum going. "Hillary was not hurting for money. Quite the opposite, I'd say."

I smiled at her obvious love for her friend. "Do you have any idea where she could've gone?"

"No. Her kids live far away, and I know she has a brother, but I don't recall where he lives. Hillary's always been a private person. But maybe that's who she's with."

"Hmm. I'll drive by Rueland Retirement. See what I can learn."

"Would you?" She brightened.

I hopped off the swing. "You've got my word."

My father had a real sense of humor. When he offered me the old black-and-white cruiser he'd bought at a police auction fifteen years ago, I thought it was the funniest thing I'd heard. The car rarely left the house and was only ever used as a backup. If I'd thought for a minute he'd offer it in my hour of need, I would've contemplated other reliable options. Like hitchhiking.

"It runs like a charm," he'd said. "And you've got your phone for emergencies."

The only emergency I could foresee was driving it into a wall to put me out of my misery. My father had never repainted the car, and this lent itself to massive teasing in high school, then beauty school when I occasionally had to drive the black-and-white. Now I was about to relive that nightmare. "I hate to sound ungrateful. But what about the blue car?"

My father shrugged. "We're taking Tantig to New Jersey for a few days to visit the cousins. The cruiser isn't the greatest on gas mileage."

"What if I get pulled over for impersonating a police officer?"

"Nobody's going to pull you over." Easy for him to say. He wouldn't be the one behind the wheel.

I sighed at his lack of concern. I guess I couldn't expect my father's aunt to sink in the backseat of a gutted-out police car, could I?

At the moment, I sat outside Rueland Retirement, gathering my nerve to go back into the home with more questions. I looked around the darkening neighborhood, thinking that wasn't my only problem. I hoped I wouldn't be seen getting out of the barebones cruiser. Of course, this was like expecting a five-ton elephant to go unnoticed on a tricycle.

Just my luck, my archenemy from beauty school, Candace Needlemeyer, drove by in her red Corvette. I didn't know makes or models of cars. But I knew Corvettes. I loved my yellow Daisy Bug, and it suited me fine. But I'd dreamed of owning a red 'Vette ever since I could remember. Candace-the-surgically-carved-nose-in-the-air-Needlemeyer, who had already tried to steal Max out from under me—and who was now working on Jock—had already gone through two Corvettes. Two marriages, too. But that was another story.

I squinted at the cutesy license plate, HOT BAE, embedded in my soul, as she sailed by. Then to my horror, the brake lights went on, and she peeled an inch of rubber backing up to where I was parked. I squinched down in my seat, but Candace had x-ray vision in those baby blues of hers.

The passenger side window slithered down, and the

shine from Candace's lip-glossed, collagen-plumped lips almost blinded me. "Valentine Beaumont," she purred. "Driving around in your dad's police car again? I thought they scrapped that thing years ago."

"Nope. Runs like a charm." My knuckles strained white on the steering wheel from pounding it good naturedly.

"Shouldn't you be at work? Oh, wait. You only work on men's genitals."

"Ha-ha-ha." *Don't be goaded*, I told myself, pressing my foot to the floorboard beside the gas pedal.

"I'd love to work on that new employee of yours, but it seems he's too busy making it in the movies."

I straightened in my seat. "How do you know about that?"

"What do you think? I live under a rock?" She fluffed her hair with her long fingernails. "He's using you, Valentine, until he makes it big. Then it'll be so long Beaumont's." She revved the engine. "I'd love to stay and chat, but I've got a hot date with a surgeon."

"Plastic surgeon?"

"How'd you know?" She waved. "Ta-ta!"

She zoomed away, and I blew out air. Who cared what Candace thought? Driving around in her fancy sports car. Dating a surgeon. *Pff.* At least she didn't get Max. I thought about Jock and groaned. Was he using me?

I stared at the retirement home, getting over myself and my worries. The home was quiet, and Rival was nowhere in sight. I was armed, too. I had a whole container of my mother's chocolate chip cookies, along with a full cooler of her home cooking, since I bailed on supper. I should've flung a cookie between Candace's flapping lips, for the satisfaction. I was ready to toss Rival any number of items if he showed his ugly face.

I ate a cookie, then trekked to the porch, the last of the setting sun on my back. For the heck of it, I glanced over at the compost pile. Should I decipher what the residents had for dinner? Surprisingly, the mound looked untouched. In fact, the soil had settled to ground level.

Hmm. Maybe Virgil was eating more of his meals instead of composting them.

I mounted the steps, thinking everyone was probably tucked into bed. That's where I wanted to be, but the day wasn't done yet. I tiptoed into the foyer and passed Evalene's office, my nose giving an involuntary twitch. I didn't know if she was gone for the day, but I wasn't taking any chances. The door was closed, no light shining beneath. Good enough for me. Of course, that left the night manager.

I was on my way down the hall to her office at the back entrance when I heard voices and laughter in the recreation room. Maybe I'd catch the night manager here. The double doors were closed and again there was darkness under the crack. I turned the handle anyway.

"Who let the light in?" yelled a voice that sounded like Nettie. "Can't you see we're watching a movie?"

Momentarily forgetting about the night manager, I slid inside the room and watched two grumpy-looking men on the screen fight over a beautiful woman.

"Look at Matthau's nose!" Wit stood. "My nose has more character than that actor's."

"Your nose looks like your knees," Nettie hollered. "Bumpy and hairy. Now sit down. You're blocking the view."

Wit wiggled his tush at Nettie. "Why don't you pick my hairy nose, old woman."

Nettie jabbed him on the seat of his pants, and he flew forward.

I stood against the wall, stifling a laugh, when Susan scurried to my side. She gave me a tiny shove out the room. "Those two." She smiled. "They really like each other."

Sure. And that was foreplay.

She looked at her watch. "Are you here to do hair, Valentine?"

"No. I came to see Hillary. She has a special hair ornament for me," I lied.

"Oh, Hillary's gone. Left a few days ago while the rest

of us were on a bus trip to Salem. I think Paula helped her with her last few belongings as it was late when Hillary left."

"Paula?"

"The night manager. She's home with a sick child tonight. I'm filling in for her." She moved to the foyer table and jotted something down on a piece of paper. "Here's her number if you want to talk to her. Maybe she knows about the hair ornament."

Drat. "Thanks." I slipped the paper in my bag. "Mind if I look in Hillary's room anyway? Maybe she left it behind."

Susan shrugged. "No problem." She pulled a key ring out of her pocket, detached a key, and handed it to me.

I held onto the key, forcing back the uneasiness rising in my throat. When Susan had given me the key to Sister Madeline's room, it had been a single key. No chain. No ring. No other keys in sight. Had she detached Sister's key from the ring so she could quietly enter her room without anyone noticing? And if she had, what was she doing in there?

A sudden memory came to mind from one of my prior visits: Susan leaving Sister's apartment. She'd taken a cursory glance over her shoulder as she'd shut Sister's door. Had she simply been checking on the nun? Reading to her? Playing cards? It was my understanding that Evalene acted as main overseer of the residents. Still, Susan did have a set of keys.

The cause of Sister's death was undetermined, but I kept coming back to poisoning. What if Susan had been slowly killing the nun? She had opportunity. She had access. The only thing she didn't have, as far as I could see, was motive. She was a happily married woman with a teenage daughter. What reason could she have for wanting Sister Madeline dead? Suddenly, Reverend Mother's words came back to me. Sister Madeline had arrived at the convent in 1965. Susan looked the right age to be born around that time. But so were lots of women. Millions probably.

I thanked Susan for the key and climbed the stairs. I reached the landing and heard a soft thump from Sister Madeline's apartment. I frowned. Was it my imagination? I put my ear to the door. Then I bent to see if there was light coming from inside. No light. No more noise, except for my heart pounding like a drum, overpowering movie sounds from downstairs. I tried the door. Locked. Chalking it up to nerves, I shrugged and glanced down the steps.

Susan was at the bottom, pointing to the apartment to the right. I shivered at her smile and gave a thumbs-up. Then I moseyed over to Hillary's and unlocked the door.

The smell of roses had disappeared from Hillary's apartment. In fact, everything had vanished, except for some potted plants on the window sill. Two of the plants were calla lilies.

Prickles ran up the back of my head. Calla lilies were poisonous, said Phyllis, our local expert in every field. Now the idea had me creeped out.

Shaking that off, I pulled the paper Susan had given me out of my bag, dug out my cell phone, and punched in Paula's number.

Sandrift Boulevard was in West Heights—fondly known as Snob West. It wasn't Beacon Hill in Boston, but it also wasn't the sort of neighborhood where auctioned-off police cars drove. A few of my wealthier clients lived here, and Birdie and Betty Cutler lived beyond Snob West—where the real money was.

I parked in front of a large two-story house. It had an octagon-shaped glass atrium on the east side, and a flagstone path to the front door. I sat in the cruiser, working up the courage to ring the bell. Mrs. Shales was right, and Paula had confirmed it. Hillary had moved to her brother's. I'd also asked Paula if she'd seen or heard anything suspicious at the retirement home around the time of Sister Madeline's death, but seeing as how she worked nights, she was no help.

I thought about Mrs. Shales's story about her friend and tried to put things in perspective. Even recalling conversations I'd had with Hillary didn't help. I had this squirming doubt I didn't know the real woman. Maybe she was a fraud. Maybe she killed Sister Madeline.

Okay, the tax evasion thing. Nonsense, according to Mrs. Shales. That was her husband's issue, not hers. And how would that make her a murderer in any case? The calla lilies? Obviously, a favorite. She even had Evalene growing them. And having potted flowers didn't make her a murderer. Or did it? I remembered Hillary's disclosure about Virgil Sylas. All of a sudden, I found it odd she knew his every visit to Sister Madeline's apartment. What did the woman do? Keep her ear glued to the door? Or was she trying to point the finger in a different direction?

She did deliver Sister Madeline's plate the day she died. What if she'd mixed chopped calla lilies with the cucumber salad? She appeared at my side quickly after I'd found Sister Madeline. Maybe she was waiting for the outcome. I rolled these thoughts around in my head, along with the latest question. Why did Hillary suddenly move out of the retirement home? That in itself was suspicious. Not to give any warning? Or leave a forwarding address to a good friend?

I reread my handwriting and the house number I'd jotted down, thanks to Paula. Then I looked back up at the house. If I was an idiot for knocking on a stranger's door this late at night, I wanted the right door.

I grabbed my bag, slung it over my shoulder, and walked the flagstone path to the porch. I rang the bell, and a dignified-looking man opened the door, a sweater tied over his polo shirt.

I introduced myself, and before I could explain why I was there, he asked, "Am I in trouble with the law?" He nodded at my—for lack of a better word—car.

"No." I glimpsed over both shoulders, pretending I didn't know what he was talking about. Damn it.

"Good. I just got back from a day of sailing. Afraid I might have exceeded the speed limit in my haste to get home."

I explained how I came to see Hillary, and minutes later I was sitting on a rocker in the atrium, facing her.

"The truth is, I was spooked," Hillary said from her wicker chair. "I keep going over Sister Madeline's death in my head. You and I in the room with her. That locket. The baby's face. It's given me nightmares."

I swallowed at the memory. "The baby was hers. And that was Sister's picture in the locket."

"I figured as much. I took a good hard look at my life and decided it was time to move on. I have children to visit, and my dear brother built a spacious guesthouse for me, hoping one day I'd come to stay." She reached over and patted my lap. "It's not Rueland Retirement, but I'm happy here."

I liked Hillary, and I wanted to believe everything she'd said. Trouble was, there were too many unanswered questions plaguing my mind. For now, I'd let this rest. I still had a few other leads to follow up before I passed judgment on Hillary Ayers.

I bulldozed through my front door and dropped my parents' ancient cooler on the floor. I sat on the cooler and rubbed my foot. My ankle was much better, but it felt tender under my fingertips. I'd elevate it the rest of the evening. "Promise," I said to my tootsies.

I filled Yitts's bowl with niblets, then unpacked eggplant parmesan, chicken, half a peach pie, and the cookies. I bit into a drumstick and ripped off a piece for Yitts. She sniffed it, backed up, and meowed. Yitts wasn't much of a carnivore. She reached her paws up my legs, sniffing the air.

"No pie for you," I said, finishing my drumstick. "Go eat your nums."

I hobbled to the bathroom with my bag and the container of chocolate chip cookies. I ate two cookies while I ran water in the tub. I poured in a healthy dose of vanilla foam bath, then replenished my bag with some items I'd lost during the car chase.

Settling into a cozy hot bath, I sank lower and lower until the fragrant bubbles caressed my neck. *Aaaaah.* I'd been dreaming of this all day. Yitts jumped on the tub ledge and pawed at the bubbles. I closed my eyes, grinning at her antics, when Romero's face and predatory smile came to mind. *Huh?* How'd he get in my dreams? It certainly wasn't because he made me laugh. I stirred restlessly in the water, my body temperature suddenly rising from other passionate thoughts Romero provoked. I reached for the cold-water tap when my cell phone rang. Yitts flew off the ledge. I lunged for the call.

"I was worried about you on that mountain," Holly said.

I sank back in the tub, grabbing another cookie. "If you were worried, why'd you send Romero to my rescue?"

"He was heading to the convent yesterday morning. I'm sick of arresting pimps and druggies. I begged him to take me along."

"What'd he say?"

"One Beaumont in his life was more than he could handle."

"Ha-ha." I gave a sarcastic look into the phone, but it was wasted. So, I chewed my cookie instead.

"You behaved for him, right?"

"Define behave."

"*Valentine.*"

"Well? After he abandoned me, do I let him walk back into my life?"

She gave a throaty chortle. "I would."

"Moving on. How do you find out if a child was adopted fifty years ago?"

"What exactly do you want to know?"

"The identity of the child. She'd been adopted once, but the parents had died. I want to know if she was adopted again. Where she grew up."

"First, there are strict privacy laws attached to the records of birth parents and adoptees. You can't walk into an agency and ask them to hand over files."

"Duh. I know that."

"Good. Having said that, usually you start at the agency in the town where the adoption took place."

"I tried. No longer exists."

She sighed. "Sorry."

"That's okay." I thought about my appointment tomorrow with Sister Francis. "I know someone who may be able to help."

I no sooner let my hair down and slipped into my baby-dolls when there was a knock on the door. Brother. Couldn't a girl have a quiet night? Yitts darted under the couch. I pulled my pink Pooh nightshirt over my baby-dolls and opened the door a crack, leaving the chain on.

Jock stood on the front porch, holding a bottle of wine and a white envelope.

"What's that?"

He gave a slight nod. "Peace offering."

What for? The kiss? Disappearing from work? Coming in late? Not telling the truth? I gave him a skeptical look.

"Thought we'd have a drink."

After last night's fiasco? No way. "It's ten o'clock. And how did you know where I lived?"

"Max." He looked over my head. "You going to let me in?"

"No."

He lowered the bottle and glanced over his shoulder at the cruiser. "You have company?"

"Just the ghost of police cars past."

He looked at me strangely.

"That metal in the driveway, according to my father, is going to take me from point A to point B for the next several days. Unless I shoot it first."

He grinned in a boyish fashion with his head down. Part of his charm. "You were cool toward me today. Figured you were still mad from the other night."

Was I? Jock had been a thorn in my side since I'd hired him a mere ten days ago. He did what he pleased at work, when he pleased. He lied by omission about his past as a navy firefighter, not to mention his part in the movies. He toured the world like a bandit on his bike and experienced things most of us dreamed. He was a hero to men and a god to women. And here he was on my doorstep, looking as luscious as peach pie, asking for forgiveness for a kiss a wiser woman would've seen coming. His dark eyes searched mine, weakening my legs and my resolve. *Ooh.* I slammed the door.

Then I undid the chain.

"Nice shirt." He stepped over the threshold.

I looked down at myself, suddenly embarrassed. The only thing standing between us was a flimsy nightshirt and even more flimsy baby-dolls. I placed my palm on his chest, stopping him from taking another step, denying I liked the warmth of his body under my touch. Then I thought about the scar on his abdomen and threw back my hand quicker than if I'd touched fire. If he wanted to keep his past a secret from me, I'd play his game. For a while.

He kicked the door shut, nodded approvingly at the living room, then looked from the Pooh phone on the end table to me with the same mystified expression Romero had given when he'd first seen it. They had *that* in common. I flattened my lips. So, I liked cute phones!

He kept in a grin, circled one arm under my legs, and swept me off my feet.

"I—"

"Shhh." He planted me on the sofa, dropping the envelope on the floor.

It made a chinking sound, and I picked it up. "What's this?"

"I don't know." He set the wine bottle on the coffee table. "It was sticking out of your mailbox. Thought you might want it."

I narrowed my eyes at him. I guess it *was* possible I hadn't seen the envelope for myself when I got home tonight. I ripped it open and found a crucifix dangling from a blue rosary. I flipped the envelope over. No return address. Only a postmark. "Stockbridge, Massachusetts." I looked at Jock and froze, instinct telling me this was a warning.

"It's about the nun," he said.

I nodded. "That's where I was yesterday."

"Know anyone who would've sent it to you?"

"Maybe Reverend Mother, thinking it'd be helpful." As soon as the words were out, I knew they were false. After all, wouldn't she have mentioned it in the message she'd left?

We stared at the rosary that had strangely made its way into my hand. I looked away, misty-eyed, hiding the terrifying emotions climbing to the surface. Feelings I'd been down this road before. Was someone stalking me? Trying to scare me? I put the rosary back in the envelope and went to the kitchen for a wine glass for Jock.

I thought about calling Romero, but he'd insist on coming over, and with Jock here… Yeah, forget that idea. *Put it out of your mind*. Right. About as easy as forgetting you had a blinding pimple on the tip of your nose. I slid the envelope on the counter and reached in the cupboard for a wine glass when the lights went off. Alarmed, I rounded the corner.

Jock finished lighting the candle on the coffee table. He leaned back with one arm draped over the sofa. "Too much light."

Whew. No one cut the power. It was only Jock dimming the lights. *Yikes! Jock dimming the lights!*

His gaze was on me. "Come here."

I couldn't read his eyes at the best of times, but in the darkness, I was a ship without its sails. "I'm fine here, thank you." Forgetting about the wine, I sank on the opposite end of the couch, knees knocking, thinking I was better off agonizing over the rosary.

"You need to relax." Jock pulled me closer and massaged my neck. "There's nothing you can do right now anyway about the rosary."

"I beg to differ. You ever hear of worrying?"

He gave me a reprimanding look. "Maybe I should stay the night."

"I don't think so." I yawned and moved away from his expert touch. "And as nice as all this is, I do need sleep."

"Then we're good? You're not going to sic your cop friend on me?"

I smiled. I didn't doubt for a minute Romero could take on Jock. True, Jock had muscles on top of muscles, plus he had a distinguished navy background. But Romero's toned, tight-assed physique was second to none. And his status as a detective was impressive. Okay, it was a turn-on.

I nodded. "No sicking."

Jock did one of his deep laughs. "What's going on between you two?"

I shrugged. "Something started a few months ago. Then he was gone."

"He walked out on you?"

"I think it was work related. He hasn't actually explained it."

The candlelight danced in his eyes as his fingertips moved down my shoulder. "Then you're not involved."

I wasn't sure how to answer that. And I was all too aware he was staring at me.

"You're beautiful when you're caught off guard."

I felt my skin flush. "Need I remind you that you work for me?"

His fingers stopped roaming. "And I'd do anything you say."

My breath snagged in my throat. Jock had the ability to melt a woman by entering a room. He was mysterious, sexy, and commanded respect. What's worse, we were alone. Before I did something I regretted, I stood up. "You better go."

He gave me a short stare like maybe he was considering a repeat performance of the other day. Heat rushed through me at the thought. But I was wrong. He got to his feet, gave me a half-hearted smile, and without saying another word, he left.

I exhaled loudly and locked the door. Damn, he could be sweet. And persuasive. And if I wanted to stay in control of my feelings, I had to toughen up where he was concerned.

I put the wine in the kitchen cupboard, blew out the candle, and went to bed. Burying myself under the covers, I rewound the night, once again thinking about the rosary. Did it belong to Sister Madeline? I was sure I'd never seen it before, but something told me I was getting close. Close to what? A killer? The truth? What was the truth?

These thoughts were keeping me awake. Then I realized I'd forgotten to brush my teeth. I yanked off the covers, stomped into the bathroom, and saw the chocolate chip cookies. What the hell. I scarfed back two, carried the container into the kitchen, then tramped back into the bathroom and brushed and flossed like nobody's business. Finally, I collapsed into bed, snuggled deep under the covers, and took a long breath. The last thing I did before I fell asleep was thank God Thursday had come to an end.

Chapter 12

I got up the next morning feeling achy all over. I made a lame attempt to stretch, then padded into the bathroom, scolding myself for working yesterday. I slung my foot on the toilet seat, expecting the worst. *Huh.* Swelling was totally gone. How'd you like that? Perfect timing. I was finally going to see Blair Dossan today, and later I'd see Sister Francis. I wanted to look my best, and at this point, my best meant not hobbling around.

Yitts jumped on the sink, rubbed her nose against mine, and meowed. Translation: *My water cup is empty*.

I fed and pampered Yitts, then peeked out the window. Grass was dewy, sky, brilliant blue. High expected over seventy. Massachusetts in the fall.

I washed up, lined and sparkled my eyes, then secured my hair low to one side with a flowered elastic. I dressed in a cap-sleeved yellow dress that dipped across the collarbone in front and shoulder blades in back. Modest but fetching. I slid on earrings and walked into the living room.

Yitts was on the floor, tangled up in the rosary. What? Little thief must've stolen it from the counter.

I unwound the blue beads from her head, put the rosary in the envelope, then walked it, like a grenade, to my bag. I pushed it to the bottom, thinking how glad I'd be to pass it on to Romero. And no time like the present to make that happen. It was 7:45. Likely, he was already fighting crime. I tried his cell phone anyway. No answer. I left a message that I needed to speak to him and hung up.

I ate fruit and yogurt for breakfast and placed a small dish of pineapple on the floor for Yitts. Once I was ready to go, I stepped outside in my yellow platforms and saw Mrs. Calvino already hard at work, feet up on the railing, phone cradling her neck, cigarette tarnishing her fingers. I waved, futile as it was.

Cruising to work, my thoughts shifted from Mrs. Calvino poisoning her lungs to Sister Madeline's possible poisoning. I had nothing to go on, but the calla lilies nagged me. And I kept seeing that jar of rat poison on Evalene's counter. That got me thinking how easy it'd be to sprinkle a meal with a tasteless, odorless poison. Even if calla lilies were chopped and mixed in with the cucumber salad, white flakes would've easily been detected. Back to Evalene who kept poison next to spices. She was strange, but murder?

What reason could she have had to do away with a sweet, harmless nun? Had Sister Madeline complained about something at the home? Was she too much of a burden? There was no sense analyzing Evalene's thought process. It gave me shivers thinking about it.

I stopped for donuts at Friar Tuck's, then made coffee, slid in a Bruno Mars CD, and unlocked the front door. I perched myself in the dispensary and checked my appointments. If I stayed on schedule and switched one client to another time, I'd get to MicroPharmLabs in Arlington after lunch. Only problem was, before seeing Sister Francis, I'd have to come back for a couple mid-afternoon appointments for customers who I already knew wouldn't switch to another time, or let anyone else work on them.

I'd have to head out a second time, but it wasn't like I'd have far to go. Prayer Up Press was east of Lynnfield. Fifteen minutes, tops. The appointment was made, and the sooner I got answers to my questions, the better I'd feel.

I made a quick call to the Stockbridge post office about the envelope, and barely got off the phone when I heard Max and Phyllis bickering their way down the hall. Their squabbling spoiled the Bruno Mars song, not to mention the peacefulness in the salon. I didn't want to get involved in their spat, so I stuck my nose in the appointment book.

"You slob," Phyllis said to Max. "You didn't shave today."

"Neither did you. What's your point?"

I flipped pages, ignoring them.

Max tugged Phyllis by her charred braids to the dispensary doorway, gawking at me like he was surprised to see me. "What's with the police car?"

I sighed. "I'm borrowing my father's prized vehicle until mine's fixed."

This satisfied him, likely because he was in the middle of antagonizing Phyllis. "Let's hear Val's opinion," he said to her.

"Let's not." I didn't have a clue what they were arguing about, but I busied myself by dialing my client who needed switching.

Max and Phyllis quarreled in hushed tones. Max stretched back Phyllis's eyelids and rushed her to the mirror. I rescheduled my lady, hung up, and strode over to the two of them.

"Okay, Max." I was a beggar for punishment. "What's this about?"

"I told Phyllis, now that she has a man, she should drop a few pounds and alter her face."

Phyllis arched her arm and gave him a clout in the stomach.

Max doubled over. "I'm only trying to help. You want to keep Guido happy, don't you?"

She jerked away to her station. "Guido doesn't care what I look like."

Max dropped open his mouth, then snapped it shut, clearly at a loss for words. He grabbed a tube of red lipstick from the makeup stand and held it up to Phyllis. "Here. Try this."

I watched Max color Phyllis's lips, and this had me thinking. Phyllis liked red lipstick. Millions of women wore red lipstick. Nothing wrong with that. Except red lipsticks had a higher lead content than other colored lipsticks. If women unknowingly wore something potentially harmful, how easy would it be eating food laced with tasteless poison? I was pondering this theory when Jock appeared around the corner.

His hair was gelled back into a short ponytail, he was freshly shaved, and he smelled like leather and exotic cologne. He wore black jeans that were anything but plain on his body, and he had on a pink Armani dress shirt. I smiled inside. Not many men wore pink for fear they'd be teased, but I had a feeling no one laughed at Jock. He stood there, confident, alluring, seeing the appreciation in my eyes. And he winked. Flustered by the wink, I banged my knee on the cupboard door. *Ouch!*

Jock, all serious, mouthed, "*Hi.*"

There was a lump in the back of my throat, making it impossible to swallow. I mouthed "*Hi*" back, remembering my latest resolve to toughen up. Okay. How could I keep fighting this attraction for Jock when he was here daily tantalizing me? Yet thirty-six hours ago, I was trying to seduce Romero. And tonight, I was facing another blind date. Gosh. I sounded like a trollop. Next, I'd agree to date Gibson.

Max waved a brush in front of my eyes. "Earth to Val." He grimaced at Jock. "Will you stop already with the good looks? You're putting our female staff into a coma. Right, Phyll?"

We all turned to Phyllis. A cigarillo hung from one side of her red made-up lips, a licorice dangled from the other.

"It's no good, dear." Max yanked the licorice from her mouth. "God made you a woman, not a walrus. Now put away the tusks like a good blubbery mammal, and let's get down to work."

The good-naturedness ended when another of Jock's bosomy clients led Birdie and Betty Cutler through the front door, followed by Phyllis's pedicure client. Minutes later, the right side of the salon fogged up with steam.

"This water's boiling!" Mrs. Krulicki hoisted her knobby knees above the steaming basin, her usual pallor like raw beef juice.

Phyllis yanked her legs down. "What you're saying is I'm burning you." She rolled her eyes in my direction. "I mean, let me add cold water. You'll be more comfortable."

She was making an effort, I told myself. All the same, I spied the first-aid kit on the top shelf in the dispensary. Then I peeked at Jock. Like I didn't have enough to worry about with Phyllis, now I had to fight not concentrating on *him*. I thought I was doing an amazing job, too. The Cutlers were under the dryers, their hair well on the way to being dry. I was shampooing my client's color off next when a spritz of cold water hit my bare back. I arched my body and screeched, slamming down the tap.

I gaped over my shoulder at Jock. He aimed a squirt bottle at me, ready to fire again. What was this all about? Trying to get my attention when I was deliberately ignoring him? Well, I held a lot more power than a measly squirt bottle. Scooting to the other side of the sink for protection, I clutched the hose high, pointing it straight at him. My client, the poor soul, was held hostage in between.

"You wouldn't dare." Jock took a bold step closer.

"Wanna bet?" Me, suddenly Miss Confidence.

He strutted over until he was six feet from me and my customer—a nurse from Rueland Memorial. Good thing, too. Jock would need medical attention when I was through with him.

"Uh, I don't think he's kidding, Valentine." She peered up at me.

"I'm not either." My eyes locked with Jock's, my insides exploding in every direction.

He leaned sexy-like, stealing everyone's gaze from

magazines, mirrors, and pedicures. Then he loosened the nozzle tip. Slow. Deliberate. Eyes on me. There was a hush in the salon. Everyone waited with bated breath. He was serious. *Ha.* Two could play at that game.

In one quick movement, he planted both feet wide and grabbed Max's water bottle off the counter. With double barrels, he shot water at me in a long steady stream, splashing my neck and the entire front of my dress.

Screaming, I fired back. Water sprayed everywhere, but I hit my target. Jock's shirt turned deep rose. It clung to him like plastic wrap, the wet material intensifying his washboard stomach. There was squealing and laughter, but I was deaf to it all.

Tossing the bottles aside, Jock seized me *and* the hose. Everyone sucked in air, wanting to know what would happen next. Incapable of doing anything, I swallowed, wishing I could rewind the scene.

Betty rapped on Birdie's dryer hood. "Wake up, pet, you're missing the hanky-panky."

Birdie opened her eyes wide and clapped her hands. "Ooh, this is going to be jolly good!"

The nurse sat up, sudsy color trickling down her cheeks. "Kiss her, ya damn fool."

Jock let go of the hose and dipped me back so far, my ponytail swept the ground. He stared into my eyes, and I knew he was thinking about the kiss from the other day. Thankfully, he only gave me a wink, then whirled me back up, amidst the cheering and clapping.

I caught my breath while he undid his soaked shirt one button at a time.

Mrs. Krulicki squinted through the steam. "Is he going to take it off?"

Everyone swiveled their heads from Mrs. Krulicki to Jock's abdomen.

Waiting.

Jock tugged his shirt out of his drenched pants.

The twins' dryers clicked off, and everything went silent. Jock hooked his thumb inside his belt loop, and my gaze traveled a few inches lower. I tried to keep from gasping. Everyone inhaled like they'd noticed it, too.

Mrs. Krulicki lunged for her purse. "Where are my heart pills?"

"*Blimey!*" Betty gaped at his crotch. "What a stiffy!"

Birdie gasped. "I need water!"

"Bugger the water!" Betty gulped. "Who's got sherry?"

I was a few minutes late by the time I got to MicroPharmLabs. Blair met me at the entrance and led me past rooms with beakers, test tubes, and microscopes. When we arrived at her office, she offered me a seat and settled her tall, classy frame in an executive chair behind her desk. The sun streamed in, falling on her short auburn hair that she had tucked behind her ears.

"You're wearing a dress with water stains?" She gave a puzzled smile. "You're usually flawless. What gives?"

I squirmed in my seat. I hadn't stopped to reflect on the water fight I'd had with Jock this morning. But now that I thought of it, the whole thing had been sexy, flirtatious, and fun. I'm sure my face was still tingling from the incident. "I had a battle with a hose."

Her eyebrows shot up. "I'd say the hose won."

I gave a shy grin, aware it was likely bigger than I'd meant.

She grinned back. "So, what's up? Normally, it's me booking with you."

This was true. Usually on her day off, without her lab coat on, or glasses laced around her neck.

I filled her in on Sister Madeline's death and what I'd seen when I'd found her. "What I'm not sure of is cause of death, but I have a feeling she was poisoned."

She looked amused. "I know about your past involvement with homicides, but don't you think you're jumping to conclusions?"

"I can't let it go."

She nodded. "Like a disease. Gets in your blood." She smiled. "For the record, I'm a microbiologist, not a toxicologist, but I'll help where I can. What do the police say about her death?"

"Seriously? You'd think they were guarding the Hope Diamond. The most I can get out of Romero is that poisoning's a possibility."

"Hey, how is that cousin of mine? I never hear from him."

I tried to forget Blair was a second cousin to Romero and that she'd attended his sister's wedding a few months ago. The same wedding where I was left holding the bouquet. I blushed.

"That good, huh?"

I leaned in, wanting to talk about the case, not Romero. "Blair, what happens when someone is poisoned?"

Her expression turned serious. "Basically, everything shuts down, ending with respiratory failure. Do you have any idea what could've poisoned Sister Madeline?"

"This sounds eerie, but she was surrounded by people who adored calla lilies. Are they really poisonous?"

"Let me put it this way. I wouldn't keep them in the house if I had children."

"What about rat poison?"

"Warfarin?"

"Yes. What would happen if a person swallowed it?"

"There's a warfarin-based drug for humans—a blood thinner. Brand name is Coumadin. The rat poison's been around much longer, and when you give it to rats in huge doses, their blood thins rapidly and kills them."

"So, if Sister Madeline ate warfarin pellets intended for rats, could it have thinned her blood enough to kill her?"

"Depends on how much. Testing her blood could've determined if her INR or platelets were too low."

"Then you don't think warfarin could've killed her?"

"I didn't say that. I'm only answering your questions. Something else to be aware of: warfarin is both odorless and tasteless." She thought for a moment. "If there's an autopsy, and warfarin was the cause of death, this will all come out sooner or later."

With the backup on autopsies for seniors? Later, more likely. "What about an allergic reaction to something she ate?"

"It's possible. People have anaphylactic reactions all the time. Could it have killed her?" She shrugged. "Again, anything's possible."

I was running out of options, and for all I knew, Sister Madeline could've choked on a piece of food. Or had a stroke or heart attack, or about a million other things besides being poisoned. But while I was here, I kept firing questions. "What about arsenic?"

"Like warfarin, it depends on the amount administered. A large dose will kill within days, if not hours. It was a convenient killer years ago because it was also odorless and tasteless. One thing you should know, if arsenic is in the bloodstream, it'll be present in the hair."

I recalled Sister's unusual hair loss. "I'd learned about arsenic in hairdressing school, and how it enters the bloodstream through hair. Up until now, I'd never given it much thought." This reminded me that I'd stuffed my brush in a baggy when I was in Sister Madeline's apartment. The police may have already taken hairs from the brush in for testing, but now that I was here, it wouldn't hurt to ask. I pulled out the baggy. "The hairs on this brush belong to Sister Madeline."

She slid her glasses on her nose, then twisted in her chair toward the window, holding the brush up to the light. "This is quite a find."

She put the brush down and plucked off a single strand, pointing to the hair end. "The closer arsenic is found to the tip, the older the exposure." She slid her finger to the opposite end. "Closer to the root, where the hair is newer, the more recent the exposure." She laid the hair on her desk like a jewel, then slanted back in her chair. "I imagine you see the same pattern when doing colors.

People, like me, come in for their monthly fix-ups, and you fill in the roots, right?"

I nodded. "Retouches."

"How fast would you say hair grows?"

"On the average, half an inch a month."

She grasped the strand. "This piece is about three inches. If the exposure was recent, it'll show up here by the root. Can you leave the brush? I'll cross-section the hairs and test them. Give me a few days. It's been busy, but I'll make this a priority."

When I got back to Beaumont's, Phyllis was sprawled out on the floor, wailing.

"What happened?" I rushed to her side.

Max gaped down at Phyllis. "Jock answered the phone and handed it to Phyllis. I got the feeling it was bad news. After she hung up, she collapsed on the floor."

I looked over at Jock. He had two female clients on the go and two more waiting at the front, but like everyone else, he was focused on Phyllis sobbing.

"He's dead," she moaned. "Deaaaaad."

"Who's dead?" I asked.

"Guido."

Max rolled his eyes. "The Lord giveth, and the Lord taketh away."

"Max!" Blood pounded behind my eyes.

Jock helped Phyllis to her feet and set her in her chair. Phyllis had chucked the false eyelashes and was batting hopelessly at Jock, soaking in his attention.

"What happened, Phyllis?" I asked, bringing her back to why she was crying.

She tore her gaze away from Jock and flung her head back, wailing. "My Guido's dead."

"We heard that part," Max said.

I gave him one upside the head, then dampened a cloth and soothed it over Phyllis's forehead. "Who called?"

"Guido's sister, Tia. She said Guido's boss phoned. Guido didn't show up for work today. Nobody had seen him since he worked at the retirement home yesterday. Then kids found him floating in the Charles River."

"I'm so sorry, Phyllis."

"*Waaaaah.*"

I didn't know how to comfort her, but I thought talking things through might help. "When did you last see Guido?"

"I don't know. A few nights ago. We danced at the Latino Club, then went for a drink. After that, he dropped me off. He phoned here yesterday morning," she sniffed, "while you were chin-wagging with handsome over there. That's the last I heard from him."

I resisted the temptation to peek at Jock. "What did he say?"

"Something about finding a treasure."

"What kind of treasure?"

She frowned. "I don't know! He was going to tell me more later, then…*waaaaah!* We were going dancing tonight, too. *Waaaaah!*"

I cuddled her despite her runny nose, howling cries, and my hammering head.

"Here," Max said. "Let me get one of your cigars."

Phyllis shuddered. "I'm never smoking those again. They'll only remind me of Guido."

Max lowered the corners of his mouth. "You can always find another Guido, Phyll."

"Another Guido!" Phyllis gawked at him, and I flung the cold cloth onto my forehead. "Guidos don't grow on trees! He was my soul mate. We were like Napoleon and Josephine. Rhett and Scarlet. Romeo and Juliet."

"You forgot Laurel and Hardy."

The cloth dropped in my palm with a wet thwack. I gave Max a sharp glare.

"What!" He gaped at me. "There's a resemblance."

"Take off the rest of today," I said to Phyllis. "Tomorrow, too."

"Yes, go home," Max said. "It's not like you can do any more damage here."

He pushed Phyllis out the door, and my stomach did a double flip. First Sister Madeline had died. Now Guido. Were their deaths connected? I hadn't known Guido well, but I couldn't forget how he'd scrutinized the salon whenever he'd been here. Like he'd been looking for something. Had someone killed him? Or were the police going to say he'd gone for a swim and accidentally drowned? The fact that he'd dated an employee—and relative—hit too close to home. Tinges of fear traveled down my neck. Was I in danger? My staff? My family?

Guido had made repairs at Rueland Retirement. Suppose he saw something he shouldn't have? Something incriminating like an item the killer wanted to hide, or some weird behavior. Maybe he'd seen Susan doing something shady, and she'd smiled her way out of an explanation. Or maybe Guido overheard a secret conversation and was found out. Could he have been killed to keep him from talking?

But what did any of this have to do with a treasure? Was he part of a murder plot? Did Sister Madeline have money I didn't know about? After all, Hillary was rich, and I hadn't known about that.

The day carried on. I looked after my choosy customers, and we all filled in for Phyllis, which as it turned out wasn't difficult. Clients weren't lining the street for her like they did for Jock. Max whistled his way through blue-haired ladies, and I thought about Phyllis's loss. "You could try to show a little sympathy," I said to Max between choruses.

"Believe me, I'm crying on the inside."

A while later, the front door opened, bringing in sounds of cars cruising by at an easy pace. Then Romero stepped around the corner. His hair was neater than usual, and he was wearing dark dress pants, a tie, and a white shirt that accentuated his broad shoulders and lean waist. The women in the waiting area sucked in at the sight of him, then exhaled dreamily as if they'd been shot with morphine. I understood their reactions. Romero was like a drug. Easy to get hooked on. Hard to let go.

A smile washed over my face, and warmth spread through my body. I was a sucker for a man in a shirt and tie. I slid my client under the dryer and stepped one unsteady foot in front of the other until I was standing under Romero's strong jaw, inhaling his fresh scent. I looked up into his face, tempted to embrace him. I knew we were being watched, so I fought the urge.

Romero took his finger and flicked my chin. He didn't care who was watching. "I got your message. How are you?"

Anyone else could ask that question, and I'd give a perfectly lame *fine*. When Romero asked it, *woo*. My legs felt wobbly, and my heart raced. "Better today, thanks."

"Do I ask about the old cruiser out back?"

I sighed. "It's my father's idea of a joke. I'm driving it till my car is fixed."

He gave me a grim look. "You really need to get Triple A."

"So I heard." I tugged at his purple and teal psychedelic tie. "Going somewhere?"

"Returning from court." He wrapped his hand around mine. "I thought of you when I put this on this morning 'cause you like bright colors."

"It *is* bright."

His gaze slid down my dress, his fingers following a stain down low. "What happened here?"

My breath hitched in my throat, and every nerve came alive from his touch. On top of that, I suddenly became conscious of Jock in the background. "I…uh…we had a bit of a water problem earlier."

He glanced over my shoulder. "Is that why Mr. Universe has his shirt hanging loose?"

Darn. He didn't miss a thing. "Unfortunately, he got most of the…uh, problem."

He gave Jock a solemn nod, then focused on me. "Can we talk in your office?"

"Yes, she can!" Max chirped from his station, fluttering a finger wave at Romero.

We entered the office, and Romero clicked the door shut. "Are you really okay? You've been through a lot lately. Any more urges to placate yourself with wine?"

I didn't trust myself to speak about the drinking incident. Besides, what was there to say? I was tipsy? Okay, I was flat-out drunk, but he needed to know I didn't usually drink. "About that…"

He grinned. "What?"

He was going to make this hard for me. "My, uh, wee indiscretion."

"Indiscretion! You were shouting at table lamps."

"They were gaudy. Someone had to say something. And I can't be held responsible when I drink."

The grin widened. "I'll have to remember that."

"Not that I don't enjoy discussing my flaws, but may I ask why you're here? Was it to totally humiliate me, or is it about Guido Sanchez?"

He sighed. "Tell me you didn't help discover that body, too."

I sniffed, all indignant. "No, I did not."

"Good. We've still got questioning to do. *No* interfering."

I wriggled under his bossy tone, thinking about this new development. "His death is linked to Sister Madeline's, isn't it?"

He folded his arms. "How do you jump to these conclusions?"

"I know he did repairs at Rueland Retirement. And he told Phyllis he'd found a treasure. What I'm not sure about is where he'd found this treasure. But I know he was last seen at the retirement home. Say what you want, I have a feeling the treasure comment is related to all the other strange things going on."

He stared at the ceiling like he was trying to make things go away. Unfortunately for him, I was still standing there when he looked down. "You're not going to listen, are you? You're going to go out there and get yourself hurt."

I studied his face. "You think Sister Madeline was murdered. Of course. That's why all the warnings. You know someone snuffed out that poor nun. I bet you also think the same person killed Guido. I bet he didn't drown at all. I think he was murdered and then dumped in the Charles River." There, I said it.

"First, Miss Detective, there are a lot of unanswered questions regarding Guido Sanchez's death. Unlike *you*, a trained detective doesn't make rash assumptions or jump to conclusions. That's how we avoid getting ourselves in hot water."

"Oh, I forgot. You, big cop. Me, dumb-dumb."

He pinned me against the wall and cupped my face. He shook his head, his mouth so close I could've licked his lips. Blood thrummed in my veins, and my core began to shake. If he didn't kiss me, in one more breath he'd have to scrape me off the floor.

"All right," he said, releasing me. "You want to know? Preliminary testing is in. It looks like Sister Madeline was poisoned. But there's conflicting evidence on the poison."

I sat in my chair, exhaling the hot spark sizzling through me. "Meaning?"

"Further testing."

I swallowed. "I have a lead on the poison."

"Come again?"

"I took Blair hair samples from the brush I used on Sister Madeline."

"Blair?" He blinked. "Brush?"

"Blair, my client, your cousin—whom you never call."

"Now you sound like my mother. And what are you doing taking potential evidence to a microbiologist working at a pharmaceutical company?"

"It couldn't hurt." I huffed. "And the brush is mine. She's going to test the hair for arsenic."

"Arsenic. You want to tell me how you came up with that?"

"No. But I will tell you arsenic enters the bloodstream through hair."

"You're incredible. We'll need to look at this brush." He stared at me. "This doesn't mean I approve of your snooping. The other day on the mountain was no accident. That big, loud black vehicle that veered you off the road? That was intentional, sweetheart."

"Then I guess now's not a good time to tell you about the rosary."

"What rosary?"

"The one that was delivered to my house yesterday from Stockbridge. The one I tried calling you about."

"And?"

"I looked into it. Nobody at that post office remembered anyone coming in the past few days with an envelope that jingled. The man on the phone said the envelope could've been weighed at any station but had to have been mailed from that location. Delivery takes one to two days, which means whoever tried to end my life could also be the person who sent that envelope."

Romero scratched his head out of frustration, and a lock of hair swept over his forehead.

"You need a haircut," I said.

"Stop changing the subject." He threw his hands on his hips. "I want the rosary, and I want it now."

Boy, snitty or what. I reached behind my chair and plucked my bag off the floor. I rummaged to the bottom until I found it. "Here. It's all yours."

He took the envelope. "Did you touch the rosary?"

"Maybe?"

He rolled his eyes. "Good thing we've got your fingerprints on file." He opened the envelope and examined the rosary with the tip of his pen. "There's fur on this."

I shrugged innocently. "My cat sort of got into it."

"Your cat." He shook his head. "Do you know who the rosary belongs to?"

"No."

He closed the envelope, then sat on the edge of my desk.

"There's something else. Sister Madeline had terminal cancer."

"Cancer!"

"Yes. Which is likely why she was so weak. The disease aged her. And she refused treatment. She had two years at the most."

I thought about the last few times I'd been in Sister Madeline's apartment. She'd had bouts of abdominal pain, but was this from the cancer or from being poisoned? This news was confusing. Why kill her if she was already dying? The obvious answer was the killer didn't know she had little time left. Still, something didn't feel right.

Romero wrapped his fingers around my ponytail, tugging lightly. "What are the chances of us getting together after my shift tonight?"

I shrieked inwardly. "Slim to none?"

He tightened his lips and jerked his head at the door. "Is this something I should know about?"

"What do you mean?"

He threw me his tough-cop look. "The new guy."

"Jock?"

"That's the one. I saw the way he looks at you. He wants to see more."

"I've seen *you* look at me the same way."

He pressed his leg against mine in an intimate manner. "That's different."

Good thing I was sitting. My legs were untrustworthy, and my heart was pumping erratically. "Well, you're wrong. Did you see the beautiful women out there? They're waiting for him."

"The only beautiful woman I know has amber eyes and a huge water stain down her dress."

Beautiful? Inside, I was doing the happy dance all over my desk.

"We need to talk." He stood. "About us."

The dancing stopped. "I know."

"What's so important tonight?"

"A date."

"Break it."

"I can't."

"Care to explain?"

"Not really."

"I'm not letting go."

"Don't."

He had his hand on the doorknob. "I need a few words with Phyllis."

"She's gone."

"I'll find her."

It was four-thirty when I left work for the second time today. I jumped in the cruiser, merged onto I-95, and slipped in and out of lanes with ease and zero tailgaters. People either thought I was on my way to an emergency, or they wanted to distance themselves from the lunatic in the outdated police car. That was fine with me. Friday afternoon traffic was gearing up for the weekend, and I had a big date tonight, thanks to my mother and Reverend Cullen. I had no intention of being late. On the other hand, if I *were* to get stuck in traffic and missed my date…

No, Valentine. Don't even think it.

Prayer Up Press was a square, white two-story. A large colorful banner of a cross hung on the parking lot side of the building. I pulled into the small lot, took a self-assured breath, and went inside. I told the striking raven-haired woman in a red blouse, sitting behind a metal desk, that I had an appointment with Sister Francis.

The woman blinked wide. "Valentine?" She jumped to her feet, reached over the desk, and threw her arms around me. "It's me, Cleo." She pulled back her long, bouncy hair. "Cleo Papadopoulos."

"Cleo?" I swallowed. Twice. "I haven't seen you since high school. How are you?"

She smoothed her hands down her black pencil skirt and collapsed on her chair. "Never better, now that I can bend over to tie my shoes. I lost a bit of weight."

And she looked great. My main memory of Cleo was of her eating baklava on her way to bio class every morning. It was a good pre-lunch snack, she'd said, plus the smell of cinnamon and honey offset the odor of formaldehyde. She'd had a point, and who was I to argue? She'd always shared her baklava with Twix and me.

"I lost one hundred pounds, ditched my old wardrobe, and traded my glasses for contacts." She flashed me her diamond ring. "Married, too, with two kids. Want to hear the crazy part? I married Danny Maldonado. You remember Danny. Wild kid. Curly black hair. Mischievous smile."

Cleo and Danny. *Huh*. "You had the hots for Danny."

"Hots! I was in love. After high school, I went to Greece with my family. Came back a year later a size ten. I went to college and bumped into Danny. He remembered me. Get this. He didn't think I was fat at all. Isn't that sweet?"

She eyed my left hand. "What about you? Married? Kids?"

"No. And *no*."

"Interested? I know this guy. He's all man. Greek, too. I could match you up."

"No thanks. I'd hate to deprive my mother of that job."

"Gosh, I'm sorry."

"Don't be. I have a salon. Couldn't be happier." Like I had the world by the tail. Changing the subject, I repeated that I was here to see Sister Francis.

"Oh." She smiled. "You're the five o'clock interview."

"Interview?"

"Sister Francis writes a spiritual column here at the press. It's educational and theological in its approach, but it interests women who have a desire to enter monastic life. Part of her job is to answer questions and give guidance." She shook her head like maybe she had me all wrong. "Do you?"

"Do I what?"

"Have the desire?"

"For what?"

"To be a nun."

"*Me?*"

"Yes." What she wasn't saying was that I was floundering in my personal life. Closing in on thirty. No husband. No kids. Maybe a life change was in order.

I tried to see myself in full habit, walking the quiet halls of Sisters of the Divine, but the trouble was I *couldn't* see it. "Um, no. I'm good."

"Then what are you doing here?"

I explained about Sister Madeline's death and told her about the baby and the adoption. "I need to know what happened to that child, Cleo. And Sister Francis may be able to help."

She looked at me sharply, like she was weighing the odds. "I'm supposed to screen anyone who walks through that door, and you're not here to ask about Sister's column or about monastic life."

I folded my hands, angelic-like. "No, but I'd appreciate it if I could speak to her."

"I'll let you, on one condition."

"Name it."

"Come out to dinner with Danny and me tomorrow. It's been so long since we've talked."

"What's the catch?"

"No catch. Simply a nice foursome."

"Cleo—"

"It's one dinner. If you don't like him, you never have to see him again."

"Yeah, I'm familiar with the blind date concept."

"Good. I'll call him and set it up. You heard of the Belly Flop on Boylston? Great Egyptian food, excellent belly dancers."

"Okay." Feeling like I'd been hoodwinked, I followed Cleo into Sister Francis's office.

The nun was barely five feet tall, and her face was

covered in wrinkles. Dressed in a plain blue dress and modest veil, she scurried around the office like someone in her twenties instead of her seventies, taking papers from a photocopier and stacking them on a pile on her desk. Her eyes were sharp, her manner pleasant. Cleo gave a brief explanation why I was there, then left us alone.

Sister Francis smiled at my yellow dress. "The color of sunshine." And just like that, I adored this pint-sized woman. She pulled out a chair for me to sit on, then hurried around to the other side of her desk and hopped on a chair.

"Sister Madeline and I roomed together at the convent, once upon a time," she said. "I'll miss her. She had a beautiful heart."

I agreed.

She looked me over, and by the kind expression on her face, I knew she wasn't passing judgment on my hair or makeup. "And you want to know what happened to Faith after the parents' car crash."

"Faith?"

"Sister Madeline's child."

"Yes. Do you know if she was adopted again?"

She tapped her fingers on the desk. "She stayed at St. Gregory in Metland for a year after the accident."

"St. Gregory?"

"Yes. Lovely foster home."

Now I understood why Sister Madeline had wished to serve there. In some way, it must've brought her closer to Faith. "Did Sister Madeline see Faith during that time?"

"No. But she worked with adoption services for a period." She gave a tiny shrug. "That's when the laws weren't so strict. Since Faith had been adopted once through the Catholic Church, Sister Madeline hoped to find out if she'd been adopted again." She smiled, and her wrinkles seemed to disappear. "Ended up, a couple who lived in Newton adopted Faith."

Newton. Where had I heard that town mentioned before?

"But they left there and raised Faith on Martha's Vineyard." She pursed her lips. "My memory's not what it used to be, but I believe the couple's last name was Hewitt. Orville and Blanche Hewitt."

She hopped off her chair and came to my side. "I think Sister Madeline realized she had to let go. That's the last thing she'd ever said about Faith."

By the time I'd pulled into my driveway, I'd gone over the recent events from today. Guido was dead, Sister's hairs were being tested for arsenic, I had a lead on her child, and I had another blind date to contend with.

Guido had worked down the street from Beaumont's at Darling Heating & Appliances. Tomorrow was Saturday, and since we closed early, I planned on popping into the store and asking his boss a few questions. Maybe he'd shed light on who Guido really was. I chewed on my lip, thinking about Phyllis. If she needed more time off to grieve, she could have it. I wasn't worried about losing business because of her absence. What I was most worried about at the moment was my upcoming blind date.

How did I get in these messes? No action in months, and here I was going on a date tonight, and one tomorrow. Set up by a friend I hadn't seen in eons, and Reverend Cullen yet. How absurd was that? I was a big girl. I could find my own dates, couldn't I? And there *was* Romero. Okay, maybe there was nothing in writing, but there *was* something there. I only had to feel his hungry look on me, and I'd be all goose-bumpy and hot. And what about Jock? *No, don't go there.*

I checked for messages when I got inside, then ate most of my mother's eggplant parmesan. Yitts was sleeping on the black beanbag, whiskers twitching, back paw trembling. She slept through my meal but came running when I poured niblets into her bowl.

I showered to Kylie Minogue's "la-la-la" song, pushing

away all the stress of the day. I'd have fun tonight, if it killed me. The air had cooled, so I slipped into a brown turtleneck and brownish black jeans. I yanked out my ponytail, brushed my hair straight down, and added a dab of pomade. Then I swept the bang low over my left eye and tucked it behind my ear.

Next, I searched the closet for black heels. Yitts grazed past me and stepped on my Jimmy Choos, hiding in the corner. I swallowed dryly. Last time I wore these, I was covered in mud, having yet another confrontation with Romero. Gingerly lifting Yitts out of the way, I tugged out the shoes and carried them to the kitchen garbage. I scraped dried dirt from the heels, shedding old, unkind thoughts about Iron Man while I was at it.

I slid into my heels when the doorbell rang. Eight o'clock on the dot. I shut off the music and braced myself. Then I flung open the door and stared down at a short young man. He was wearing large-rimmed glasses, a windbreaker, and pleated pants. His light brown hair was combed neatly, and he had large front teeth and curved eyebrows that seemed to ask the question *why*. So, this was Harold.

I looked down at my heels. Admittedly, I liked my men taller than me, or at least looking like they'd graduated middle school. I was tempted to change into flats but cringed at the thought. I smiled at Harold, and he handed me a box from the Peanut Gallery. "My uncle said you liked nuts."

I grimaced. "Thank you, I think. Would you like to come in?"

"No," he squeaked. "I would like to go now."

I locked up and we walked down the porch. "Where's your car?" I asked, turning to him.

"I haven't got one. My uncle dropped me off."

Perfect. "Why don't you tell me where we're going. I'll pick the mode of transportation."

He scratched behind his big, floppy ear. "The Rueland Fall Festival."

"Great. That's walking distance."

"I can't walk. I have bad arches." He looked down at his orthopedics. "Plus, I have asthma." He whipped out a puffer from his windbreaker in case I didn't believe him.

"Okay. I'll drive." I wheeled around and Harold bumped into me. I steered him to the car, opened his door, and helped him buckle up.

"I've never been in a police car before." He looked around the interior, fidgeting with his puffer. I tried a few icebreakers, but his quick responses told me he was nervous enough without thinking of things to say. I tightened my grip on the wheel, and we drove on in silence.

I pulled into the fairgrounds and eased into a parking spot, recalling the good times I'd had here as a kid. The music, lights, and rides. Smells of cotton candy and caramel popcorn. Heaven. I unleashed Harold from his seat and waited in line while he unzipped his wallet and paid the admission fee. He counted his change and safely tucked his wallet away.

"You're new to Rueland," I said, once we walked through the gates.

"Yes." He tripped, then crunched an empty drink cup.

I stopped walking while he pried the sticky lid off his shoe. "Harold?"

"Yes?" He looked around as if the class bully was hunting him down for a wedgie.

"How old are you?"

He squealed like I'd asked for ID. "How old do you think I am?"

"Harold?"

"Okay, okay. I'm thirty."

"If you're thirty, then I'm forty."

"Really? You look pretty good for forty."

I rolled my eyes, then placed my hands on his trembling shoulders. "Harold, you are not thirty. Now come clean."

He slumped his shoulders. "How's twenty-eight?"

I shook my head.

"Twenty-five?"

I crossed my arms.

"Okay! Twenty-one. I swear."

I was robbing the cradle! "Does my mother know I'm dating a twenty-one-year-old?"

"I don't know your mother. My aunt just said this lady would show me around."

Lovely.

Screams sounded above us as the mini rollercoaster dipped, curved, and circled above the crowd. Oh well, the night was young—no pun intended. Might as well make the most of it. I gave an enthusiastic smile, and Harold peered up at me.

"Harold, why are you staring at me?"

"Your teeth are amazingly white. What's your secret?"

"Toothpaste."

"I took tetracycline when I was a kid. My teeth turned gray."

"There're lots of remedies for that. You should talk to your dentist."

"Yeah?" The stare again.

"Now what!"

"I was thinking how lucky I am to be with you, Valentine. You're not exactly the girl next door. You're classy." He frowned. "I'm a catastrophe."

"You're not a catastrophe, Harold. You need to think positive."

He gave a dopey grin, his discolored teeth pressed against his bottom lip. Oh boy.

"How 'bout a rollercoaster ride?" I said.

He shuddered. "I get motion sickness if I even step on a ladder."

I scanned the park. "What about the Haunted House?"

He squinted past my shoulder. "Night blindness. I wouldn't find my way out alive."

We ambled toward the arcade. Kids pulled their parents' sleeves, begging to fish for rubber duckies or toss hoops. One child slumped on the ground, holding his finger, howling.

"It's only a scratch from the fishing pole," his mother said, shaking her head, but gladly accepting a Band-Aid from the fishing booth man.

Harold gripped my sleeve.

"What's wrong?"

"That kid," he gasped for air. "He's bleeding."

"It's a scrape."

The mother applied the Band-Aid, and the man stuffed a plush blue dog in the boy's arms. The kid was all smiles.

Harold, who had looked away, tightened his grip. "Is the blood gone?"

"Yep." I grinned. "Blood's gone."

"*Whew!* I'm glad that's over."

We trotted on, stopping in front of a shooting gallery. A guy, not much younger than Harold, was behind the counter, hollering for takers, swinging a huge panda in the air.

I looked down at Harold. "Wanna shoot up the Western scene?"

"Loud gunshots nauseate me."

I was out of ideas. "Harold, what *would* you like to do?"

"I'm kind of hungry. I could go for pizza."

It was going on nine o'clock. Why not?

We moseyed up to the pizza stand and each ordered a slice of pizza. I chose a supreme with everything on it. Harold decided on cheese.

"Why don't you have pepperoni with it?" I asked.

"Too greasy."

"What about sausage?"

"Too spicy."

"Onions?"

"Gives you bad breath."

I gave up.

We got our humongous slices, and my mouth watered with anticipation. We found a bench to sit on, and Harold leaned over to inspect my pizza.

"You're not going to eat that, are you?" he asked.

"What, my pizza?"

"Those mushrooms."

I stared at the mushrooms. "They came with the pizza. Of course I'm going to eat them."

"I'd think twice about that if I were you."

"Harold, what are you trying not to say?"

"Only that mushrooms are poisonous."

"Some, but they wouldn't put poisonous mushrooms on pizza."

He shrugged as if to say, "It's your life," then went to get extra napkins. While I chewed my first mushroom, Harold blotted grease off his pizza, squeezed it dry, and ripped off a tiny piece. He examined it, lifted the cheese, and carefully placed it on his tongue.

"Are you going to live? Or is the cheese poisonous, too?"

We ate our pizzas when curiosity got the better of me. "Harold, what are you doing in Rueland?"

He peered up at me through his lenses. "I got accepted into Harvard Medical School. I'm going to be a doctor."

I choked on a green pepper. "Doctor! You can't stand the sight of blood."

"I'm hoping I'll get over that part."

"Do you have a second career in mind?"

"Promise you won't laugh."

"I promise."

"I've always wanted to be a male model."

"What's your third choice?"

"See? You think it's dumb."

"It's not dumb. One of my clients is a model, but they lead a different life. They have dreadful schedules and hardly any social life because they're usually on shoots, sleeping, or traveling."

"That's okay. I don't have a social life either."

"Presuming you had a third choice. What would it be?"

"Probably an artist. I love to draw."

"Really?"

His eyes lit up. He whipped out a folded piece of paper from his pocket. "I drew this at church this afternoon while I was waiting for my uncle." On it was a famous depiction of Jesus, sketched with unparalleled, intense emotion.

I gasped from the realness. "Harold, you're talented!"

"You think so? I like hanging around the church, sketching copies of the pictures. I don't know if there's a calling for that type of art, but there's so much expression in biblical characters' faces."

"You should show your uncle. He'd be proud."

He was beaming, and his voice sounded positive, strong.

For some reason, I was back to thinking about Sister Madeline, her life as a nun, and the child she gave up. Why did it feel like there was a connection in all this to her death? Like the biblical faces were a clue Harold was handing me on a gold platter. Was there something in Sister Madeline's face I should've seen when she died? Some fragment of information? Kind of hard to notice anything when she was covered in pasta sauce.

What about a resemblance to someone I'd seen around the retirement home? But who did I know that had her soft features and delicate eyes? This stumped me. I knew of no family. Yet Susan's friendly face came to mind.

Harold smiled like I'd thrown him a bone, and before he asked any more juvenile questions, I thought now would be a good time to take him home. The night wasn't all bad. I got to go to the fair, I met a nice boy, *ahem*, and possibly I had a clue in disguise.

Chapter 13

The pounding on the door got me out of bed at six-thirty the next morning. I slogged into the living room, wiping the cobwebs away. This better be important. I swung open the door to Phyllis, standing on the porch, hair frizzed out like an orangutan.

Yitts hissed and dove under the couch.

"You up?" Phyllis pushed past me.

"Uh, actually—"

"I'm up, too. I'm so up I'm pulling out my hair. I'm coming back to work. I can't sit at home anymore, moping."

"You were home half a day."

She waved her arms. "Grieving's hard work."

My gaze traveled down her body. I could've sworn she'd donned the same dress yesterday, only something was different. "You sure you're ready?"

She paced the floor. "I drank a gallon of coffee and decided I'm better off without Guido."

"Huh?"

"The greasy turd was just using me. Digging through my purse when he thought I wasn't looking. Always borrowing money—and you know I don't have a lot of that. I was getting real sick of it, too. A few days ago, I caught him red-handed, stealing the gold bracelet

Grandma Maruska had given me. He's lucky I didn't give him a black eye. The slimy creep. Probably stole one time too many from someone else, and they tied a rock to his bony ankle and tossed him in the Charles River."

I blinked wide-eyed, my mouth gaping.

"Can I use the bathroom?" She stomped past me.

Yitts crawled out from under the couch while Phyllis did her business. Then Yitts's water cup clattered, and the door burst open.

"That's better." Phyllis hustled back into the living room. "Good water, too. I'm going to keep a cupful by my sink from now on."

Yitts and I looked at each other. I knew what she was thinking. *That woman drank my water.*

I refilled Yitts's water cup, and a few hours later, met up with everyone at work.

Max stood alongside me in the dispensary, gawking at Phyllis. I'd gotten over the initial hair shock, but Max was in a stupor. "What in heaven's name happened to you?" he asked her.

"I took out my braids."

"I can see that. The question is why?"

"They were a reminder of Guido."

"Now you remind *us* of an ape. Look at you. Dress on backwards, hair looking like it went through an eggbeater."

"If you don't leave me alone"—Phyllis made a fist—"I'm going to sock you from here to next week."

Jock opened his mouth to speak, then closed it. A wiser man was never born. He grinned at me like this was better than sex, and I felt my breasts tingle.

This was how the morning went. Max antagonized Phyllis. Phyllis threatened Max. Jock sent me sexy smiles and unspoken thoughts. And I took stock of my products, making sure all items were accounted for since Guido had been in the shop. I broke away from the madness and went downstairs to the laundry room. If I was going to question Guido's boss today, I had to be prepared. Maybe if I returned a tool Guido had left behind when he, at no charge, fixed something, I wouldn't come across like I was snooping.

I picked up my pink-handled hammer and felt a warm jolt spread through me, recalling the scene with Jock and the locked door. I fingered the hammer delicately, then tossed it back on the ledge. I needed something less…pink. Aha. A tape measure. I had two or three of these floating around. I could part with one easily.

I climbed the stairs, went straight to my office, and tossed the tape measure in my bag for later. I sat down to pay some bills when the phone rang. It was Cleo.

"A friendly reminder about our date tonight," she said.

"About that—"

"Unh-uh. See you at seven. And dress Egyptian. It's a fun place." *Click.*

Egyptian. Right.

I hung up, mad at myself for not getting out of the date. Wait. Cleo worked at a respectable press. Surely the guy she was setting me up with wouldn't be all bad. At least I'd gotten the information I needed from Sister Francis. I'd even learned Sister Madeline's baby was named Faith—if she was still called Faith, and not something else…like Susan. Hold on. Susan? Newton? She was in Newton the day before Sister Madeline's death. Celebrating her daughter's birthday with old neighbors. Was this a coincidence or a clue?

If the Hewitts lived on Martha's Vineyard, then that's where I was going. They'd clear this all up.

I got on the computer and learned there were two Hewitts listed on Martha's Vineyard. An R. Hewitt and an O. Hewitt. Betting the O was for Orville, I searched and found the address, then ransacked my desk drawer for a brochure I'd stashed away of the ferry schedule to Martha's Vineyard. I studied the departure times. Tomorrow at eleven.

Max poked his nose inside the office. "You ready for this?"

"It better be good."

"Oh, it's good. We transformed Phyllis from an ape to a kitten."

"*Max.*"

He gave a shrug. "All right. She'll always be a primate in here." He patted his chest. "But her hair now resembles a human's." He glanced at the pamphlet. "What are you doing?"

I tossed the brochure on my desk. "Taking a day trip tomorrow to Martha's Vineyard."

He studied me for half a second. "Tell me later. Come on."

I rounded the corner and Jock whisked Phyllis around in his chair. Gone was the damaged, scorched bush. In its place, soft mahogany curls framed her face—which had been professionally made up.

"Phyllis! Wow!" I said. "The beads were okay, but this is…wow."

Phyllis blinked coyly. "Yes. Jock's amazing."

"Ahem." Max tapped his toe. "I *did do* the makeup."

After three blinks, one of her eyes glued shut. She reached up and twisted her eyelashes, making it worse.

Max slapped her hand away. "I told you to wait before you fiddled with them." In one quick motion, he ripped off the false eyelash.

"*Aaaaah!*" Phyllis arched back in her chair.

"Don't be a baby." Max squirted glue on the eyelash, then put Phyllis in a headlock. Moments later, in a grand sweeping motion, he removed his hand from her face.

Phyllis admired herself in the mirror. Max fussed with her curls. Jock stared at me like he was searching the depths of my soul.

My heart skipped around inside my chest from his intense gaze. *Get a grip. You made your position clear. This is a work relationship. Nothing more.* Then why didn't this calm my thudding heart?

After work, I drove down the tree-lined street past the

drugstore, Dilly's Florist, and Kuruc's European Deli. I pulled into the angled parking on the left between the bank and Darling Heating & Appliances. I did some banking, then strolled back to the appliance place.

I entered the store and spotted Ralph the owner, a friendly guy I made small talk with when I saw him at the bank or the deli. He finished hooking up a refrigerator and wandered over to me. I gave him the tape measure and said Guido had left it behind a few weeks ago.

"Shifty little guy," Ralph said, bouncing the tape measure in his hand, "but he could fix almost anything."

"How long did he work here?" I asked. "I never saw him around."

"Only here a few months. Left with the truck Thursday morning. Never made it back to the shop."

"Did he ever mention a treasure to you?"

"Ha. As in a pirate's treasure? No." He placed the tape measure in my palm. "We have dozens of these. Keep it."

I nodded. "You have any idea what happened to him? Know of any enemies?"

He shrugged. "Like I said, he was shifty, but I never gave him access to the safe or till, so he never caused me any trouble. Can't speak for anyone else."

I didn't learn much more. I said thanks, dropped off the tape measure at work, and drove to the mall where I made a few special purchases. Then I headed home to freshen up for my date at the Belly Flop. Dress Egyptian, huh? I scrounged around my closet and found a veil and low-waisted harem pants I'd once worn to a Halloween party. They were made of gorgeous teal organza.

A surge of excitement piffled through my veins. Oh, what the heck. They'd be fun. I pulled out the matching top with sparkly gems planted along the neckline, and tugged it over my head. I wrapped my hair into a high bun, freed a few curls around my face, and attached the veil with a gemmed barrette. Then I slid into sandals with tiny gold coins that dangled from the straps.

Yitts hopped around me, pulling the drawstrings on my harem pants. I fed her and was almost out the door when the phone rang. I stared at the Pooh phone, then peeked around the kitchen corner at my pink princess phone, flashing hysterically. Okay already.

"You wouldn't do your best friend in the whole world a favor, would you?" Twix asked, when I picked up.

"Depends." I cradled the phone while I retied my drawstrings.

"On what? If you asked *me* a favor, I'd drop the kids and run."

"All right! What do you want?"

"I'm shooting my last scene tonight, then there's a wrap party. Tony's driving me in, but he needs to be available for Junie who's going to a birthday party. So, I need a ride home."

"Anything, except that. I have this blind date, and—"

"Your mother on the warpath again?"

"Not my mother. Cleo. From high school."

"Cleo Papadopoulos?"

"Yes, now Cleo Maldonado. Married wild Danny."

Twix laughed. "Wait. She works at some religious press. Is this date related to the nun's case?"

"Indirectly."

"Who's she setting you up with?"

"No clue, but it could be a late night."

"Gotta go. Tony's backing out the van. Listen, it's not an emergency. I'll get my honey J.D. to drive me home. Toodles."

"Wait!" J.D.? What were the chances? Hold on. Twix hadn't met Jock yet. She wouldn't have the foggiest notion he was one and the same man. And Jock would only know Twix as Desirée. But I could be wrong. Anyway, it's not like I was worried. Twix wasn't a cheater. And Jock wasn't a secret I was trying to keep. Plus, he had a motorcycle. Twix had almost been killed on a bike when she was a teen. She'd never be caught anywhere near one.

I looked at the phone in my hand. "Have a good time."
I smiled, imagining Twix whooping it up at the party. Then
I hung up and headed out the door.

I toured through Boston's flashy theater district, parked
in the first spot I saw at Boston Common, and hiked back
down Boylston in my lightweight sandals. I rubbed my
sore feet once I got to the Belly Flop. This date better be
wrapped in gold. I looked up at the neon blinking sign and
watched the *B* turn into a genie. Forget the gold. This guy
better be dripping in diamonds.

Snake-charmer music welcomed me as I stepped past
delicate sheers into the hazy cedar-incensed restaurant.
Feeling like I'd stumbled into Cairo's marketplace, I
looked for Cleo amidst people dressed in costume like me.
I found her in a Cleopatra-type white dress, sitting on a
floor pillow behind a low table. I collapsed on a green
cushion across from her and told her she looked stunning.
"So?" I looked around. "Where is he?"

"The guys are in the bathroom," she said. "But he's tall,
dark, and handsome. And he likes to joke around."

I relaxed a bit. "I like a sense of humor."

She glanced over my shoulder. "Oh! Here they come.
Ready to meet the man of your dreams?"

I tightened every muscle in my body with excitement.
If Cleo ended up with Danny, surely, I'll end up with—

"Baaaaabe!"

That voice! *No.* It couldn't be...

I spun around and stared at a tight leather crotch,
ruffled shirt opened to the waist, and large gold
cross dangling on a chain. I peered up. "Not *Craig*!"
Nearly everyone in the room was clad in Egyptian
costume. My former blind date—Apeman—was
dressed like an outdated lounge singer. He swiveled his
hips, and I ducked before his cross clunked me on the
forehead.

"You two know each other? This is great!" Cleo beamed from us to Danny, who sat next to her, cute as ever, dressed like a pharaoh.

Craig dropped on the yellow pillow beside me, struggling to fold his legs under him. Finally, he settled for one knee bent, the other folded in, his gut spilling onto his lap.

"This little beauty and I go way back," Craig said.

"Heh-heh." I couldn't get more excited than that. "How are you, Craig?"

"Never better. You know what they say. It's hard to keep a good man down."

"Yeah, I think you told me that on our last date."

"Ha. Could be. How's the pussy?"

"Craig!" Cleo gave him a disapproving look, then smiled at me apologetically. "I told you he was a joker."

"I'm not joking. Vallie told me she had a kitten. Peed all over the place."

Darn. I had to give him credit for paying attention to something I'd said that night. At the time, I didn't have a cat. I fabricated one in an effort to dump him. I sighed and gave a brief explanation. "My cousin Faren works with Craig at the dealership."

"You bet she does," Craig said. "Can't get her to go out with me, though. She's too stuck on that boyfriend of hers. Moron, if you ask me, but some chicks like the dull type."

He yanked out his Porsche medallion keychain, cleaned his ear with a key, then scratched his gold tooth like it was a lottery ticket. I was going to kill Cleo, right after I wiped the sweat drenching my neck.

"Hey, babe." Craig elbowed me in the ribs, almost knocking me off my pillow. "Don't get hot and bothered yet. We got the rest of the night to get down and dirty."

"Steady, big guy." Danny leaned close to me. "Between us," he whispered, "I can't believe my wife set you up with this Casanova."

I gave him a bleak smile, baffled by the same thought.

The emcee jumped on the platform and asked for volunteer belly dancers.

Craig took his hairy hand and cranked up my arm. "Here's one who's got a body that can gyrate."

I ripped away from his grasp. "Unh-uh."

Unperturbed, he got to his feet. "Okay, I'll do it!" he shouted to the emcee. "Just keep those girls off me. My pretty lady might get jealous."

He strutted to the stage and swirled his hips, and Cleo apologized for her error in judgment. "Craig's been to church a few times. I thought he'd be different." She gave me a coaxing smile. "You've got to admit, he's not as bad as those horrible dates we had in high school."

I couldn't remember any date being as horrible as this.

The audience roared with applause at Craig's belly routine. A moment later, he flopped on the pillow beside me, sweat pouring down his face.

"Whoa, babe," he said to a passing waitress, "I need a cold one. Hey, Vallie, how 'bout Sex on the Beach? My favorite drink, remember?" He used my hand to mop the sweat running down his temple. "Might put you in the mood."

I swallowed dryly, wiping my palm down his sleeve. "My mood's calling for Kaopectate."

"Kao-what? Sounds like mouthwash to me." He flicked the waitress's bikini tassel. "Make that two Sex on—"

"No!" I said. "I'll stick to Kao—Diet Coke, thanks."

We ordered our meals, and the minutes ticked by. I tried to move away from Craig blowing in my ear, and instead listen to Danny's story about a strange coincidence at work. But at this point, I was doing well not throwing up.

"That's nothing." Craig dismissed Danny's story as trivial. "Want to hear a good one?"

We were all prisoners. It didn't matter what he said.

"We leased out one of our top-of-the-line Toyotas."

He tipped toward Danny as the waitress brought our meals. "This baby packs a powerful V-6."

Car talk held no appeal to me, so I put my head down and concentrated on eating.

"The truck went out Tuesday night," he continued, "and one of the guys from the garage spotted it on his way to work Thursday morning. It'd been ditched a few blocks away, smashed up with this glittery pink goop caked all over it."

Truck? Pink goop? My fork slid from my hand and clattered onto my plate.

Craig nodded at me, sensing my shock. "Yeah, right? What kind of gearhead would abuse a ride like that?"

This was too much of a fluke. A familiar fear haunted me that this was the truck that tried to bump me off the mountain. "What color was the truck?"

"Color!" He chuckled, pulling me in by my veil and cuddling me. "It was black, honeydew. *Yeeow!* That's what you remind me of. A luscious, ripe melon."

I flattened my hand against his face, forcing it in the opposite direction.

"Anyway," he said, "the boys are looking at it. Depending what the internal damage is, we may write it off."

"Who leased it?" I asked. "Did you get his ID?"

"Looks like the ID was fake. Guy just disappeared, so we called the cops." He shook his head. "Gas tank was empty, too. That baby must've been on the road all day." He licked my bare shoulder. "I wouldn't mind riding you all day, babe."

I learned all I needed to know about the truck, and I was at my limit with Craig. I semi accidentally knocked my drink onto his lap and got up. "Oops, sorry, but I've got to go."

Craig scurried off his pillow, grabbing a napkin for his pants. "Come on, honeydew. Don't get your panties in a knot." He swung his head toward the stage. "Let's dance."

"Stay," Cleo begged me.

"I can't. I have kitty litter to clean. But thanks. It was good seeing you and Danny again."

"Let me walk you out," Craig offered. "Give you my number."

"I've got your number," I said, and took off.

I showered off Craig's finger marks when I got home, then pulled on my baby-dolls and slid under the covers. I curled up into my favorite sleeping position and was almost dead to the world when I heard *clunk-clunk swish-swish*. Probably some cat scrounging for food in a neighbor's garbage can. I'd had enough excitement for one night. I blocked out the noise and cuddled deeper under the covers.

Seconds later, there was a soft knock on the front door, then the sound of a vehicle screeching down the street. I bolted upright in bed. The scrounging cat I could overlook. But nothing good could come from a knock and a car speeding off at this hour. I took a steady breath and crept to the living room window.

Everything appeared calm outside. Inside, my heart was racing. I squinted at the streetlight, then at shiny red puddles that looked like paint leading to the house. I flicked on the light and opened the door. It wasn't paint. It was *blood*. And it was smeared on my door in the shape of a cross. The blood dripped, already forming a small pool on the doorstep.

Bile rose in my throat, suffocating the scream trying to get out. I started hyperventilating. Then I started choking. I couldn't calm myself. I ran to the railing, slouched over the ledge, and hurled pilaf and kebab onto the ground. Once I was sure I was done, I staggered into the house and wiped annoying tears that always accompanied retching. I washed my face, brushed my teeth, and was still shaking. Only now, dampness had crept into my bones, and my teeth were chattering.

I crawled into a white sweater that hung to my knees and covered my fingertips. Then I called Romero and waited with Yitts by the window until he arrived.

Ten minutes later, a squad car pulled up, followed by Romero in his truck and an ID unit. Before everyone fanned out, Romero spoke to his team, the Pied Piper of cops in a leather jacket, T-shirt, and jeans, giving strict orders and stern looks.

Once everyone was busy, Romero met my gaze through the window and motioned for me to let him in through the back door. His shoulders were squared, his mouth grim. The look said he wanted this over in a big way. That went double for me. Yitts jumped off my lap and ran into the bedroom. I bit my bottom lip, went to the back door, and let Romero in. I wanted to snuggle in his arms like a scared kitten, but he looked anything but cuddly.

He reached out and pulled something from my hair. "Rice?"

He'd already seen me at my worst. Would anything else surprise him? "I, uh, got sick."

Sighing, he wrapped his arms around me and rested his chin on top of my head like someone who didn't care if I was a mess. Contrary to how I looked and smelled, his worn leather jacket was the best scent I'd inhaled all night. His gun jabbed my waist, but even that was welcome. I buried myself deeper into his arms, wanting to stay this way forever.

He drew me back into the living room. "Let's go over this again."

The ID unit removed samples off the door, and I repeated what I'd told him on the phone.

He took it all in, then steadied his gaze on me. "Come home with me." There was concern in his voice that brought a swell to my throat.

"I can't."

He pulled away. "Val, this isn't a game of hide-and-seek. First the accident, then the rosary, now this."

I didn't answer. I didn't trust myself to speak without crying.

"Well?"

I swallowed. "I'll be fine."

One of the cops popped his head through the doorway. "Mikey, we got all we need."

"Thanks, Nick." Romero frowned at me, then went outside to debrief. A minute later, he was back, slamming the door behind him. "What is it with you? Trying to prove you're tough? Okay, I concede. You're tough. Now come home with me."

"I'll be fine."

"Yeah, you said that already." He exhaled. "You're acting"—he waved his arms— "*pazzo!*"

"*Hey!*" There was Mrs. Benedetti's word again, and it didn't sound nice. "What does that mean?"

"*Crazy.*" He shook his head as if to say he'd never understand me. "Where's your hose? We've got all the evidence we need. I'll wash down the door."

I overlooked the *crazy* remark because part of me knew he was right. "I'll do it before the sun comes up. Leave it."

He studied my eyes, and his unyielding look softened. "At least let me stay awhile." He came forward and held me until I stopped shaking. After one more attempt at getting me to change my mind, he dragged me to the door. "Lock this behind me, hear? Anything else strange happens, call. I'll be here in a minute."

I nodded, wanting more than anything to go with him, but I couldn't. What's more, I couldn't explain why. That made hot tears swell again.

He gripped my shoulders and looked deep into my eyes. Blinking back tears, I stared at this man I was falling for, this first-rate cop who'd seen the ugly side of death. Iron Man. Afraid of nothing. Yet concern filled his eyes. He embraced me tightly, then walked out the door.

Chapter 14

I woke up at six the next morning in a tangled mess on the floor. I kicked off my comforter that was twisted around me and yanked my barrette out from under my head. I glared at the gemmed accessory and scowled, remembering last night's date. Ugh. I refused to start the day envisioning Craig, especially when I had more cheerful things to think about. Like the bloody door.

I dragged on yoga pants and a black shirt, then stumbled into the living room and peered outside. The grass looked dewy, and the dark sky was giving way to bright blue. I took a grateful breath that Mr. Brooks across the street wasn't out yet, gearing up his power tools. Then I saw movement to my left. Yikes. Mrs. Lombardi, who lived kitty-corner across the street, was walking her poodle, Chester. Mrs. Lombardi's son was a priest, and I could imagine what her reaction would be once she spotted the bloody cross on the door. I ducked from the window before she noticed me.

"*Aaaaah!*"

Yep. There it was. I caught her scooping up Chester. With knees bent high, she sprinted down the street. Lovely. Now she'd go home and anoint herself with a bottle of Cabernet.

I tried to forget about what Mrs. Lombardi or the rest

of the neighborhood would think. I armed myself with vinegar and a scrub brush, and was looking in the kitchen cupboard under the sink for rubber gloves when there was a *rat-tap-tap* on my door. Brother. Who else was up at this hour?

I got off my knees, went to the front door, and gaped at my landlord. "Mr. Jaworski?"

Why was I surprised? Mr. Jaworski arrived on the first of every month with suspicious eyes and greedy palm up for the almighty rent check. He was a shorter version of the grim reaper, and it was hard to get warm and fuzzy over him. But he *was* punctual. Which was about all you could say for him. I slammed the door in his face and dashed for his check.

"Valentine," he hollered, knocking. "What's this all over the door? You having wild Halloween orgies?"

I opened the door again. Pools of blood had dried on the doorstep in front of Mr. Jaworski's Velcro running shoes. "Halloween's not for thirty more days."

He stretched his head past my shoulder, getting a good look inside. Then he turned back to the artwork on the door. "I told you I want no wild parties. I said, 'No wild parties in my house.' Remember?"

"Just kids playing pranks, Mr. Jaworski. I was about to clean it up." With that, I stuffed the check in his palm and banged the door in his face.

A second later, I heard him grumbling down the walkway. "Water your plants, why don't you! They're half-dead. Crazy kids."

I shook my head at Yitts. "Orgies. What does he think I run here? A cat house?"

As soon as the coast was clear, I darted outside and pitched vinegar at the door to erase the lingering smell. Forgetting the rubber gloves, I scrubbed and hosed everything clean with my bare hands. I wanted to make this quick. I had a ferry to catch to Martha's Vineyard.

I was about to put the hose away but sprayed my flowers first. Mr. Jaworski was right. They did look half-dead. Of course, it was the first of October. Everyone's flowers looked half-dead.

I showered and was tugging on my underwear when Max called.

"You still going to Martha's Vineyard?" he asked.

"Yes." I wrestled into my bra while trying to keep my hot pink high-heeled phone to my ear.

"What's wrong? You sound off."

"Nothing." I readjusted the spike. "I had a bad night. And this morning's not going so peachy either."

"You're going to save me from my imagination and explain that, right?"

"Later."

"Does this mean I can come?"

"Don't you have plans for the weekend?"

"Not really."

Max didn't talk a lot about his personal life. He thrived on listening to Phyllis's endless sagas and my lack of a life. What a pathetic trio we were. Of course, Jock's night was probably jam-packed with creative entertainment. What's worse, Twix would've been hanging onto his every word. I'd catch up with her later. "Can you be here by eight-thirty?"

"Can do."

I hung up and hustled into jeans and a white top that sat off the shoulders. I swept on mascara and tied my hair into pigtails. Yeah, I was going on thirty, but who cared? I fed Yitts, let her out for air, and because I needed comfort food, I ate a bowl of oatmeal. By the time Max knocked on the door, I'd brushed my teeth and was relatively together.

He handed Yitts to me and wrinkled his nose. "Have you been pickling?"

"No." I slipped off Yitts's harness, then slid on the new open-toed stilettos I'd treated myself to after the last case.

"I smell pickles."

"Not pickles. Just vinegar. Come on."

We drove to the Cape, left the car, and hopped on the ferry by eleven. The waves were wicked, but the sun danced over the water, not a cloud in the sky. I sat inside below next to Max and regaled him with the sordid details of my night.

"That's an awful story," he said, a shade under vomit green.

"You're the color I was when I saw the bloody door. Do you want to go above, get some air?"

Max was in designer jeans and a gray polo shirt with the collar up. His stubble was perfectly groomed. Dark shades covered his hazel eyes. He turned from the window and took a long swallow. "I'm good here. So, who are we nabbing today?"

"What makes you think we're nabbing anyone?"

"Deductive reasoning. I know you don't like saltwater taffy, and it's too cold to lie on the beach, so I figured door number three. Valentine the sleuth rides again."

"Well, relax. We're not nabbing anyone. I simply want to talk to the people who adopted Sister Madeline's baby. See if they can shed light on her whereabouts."

He glanced out at the waves. "Have they always lived on the island?"

"They lived in Newton around the time they adopted the baby." Again, I pictured Susan saying she'd once lived in the same town. Again, was this a coincidence?

A strong wave splashed against the ferry, pitching us to one side. Max's face went white, and he hung his head between his knees. I rubbed his back till the nausea passed.

"I don't get it." He sat up. "What does Sister Madeline's baby have to do with anything?"

"Maybe nothing." I didn't know if there was any merit to my theory that Susan MacDonald could be Sister Madeline's daughter, but I had to find out. Susan worked in a retirement home. If she were a killer, who was to say she'd stop at killing one resident?

"If it was nothing," Max said, "I wouldn't be sitting here with green gills."

"Give me the day. We'll see what turns up."

"We could be dead by the end of the day. I hate to tell

you this, lovey, but you haven't had luck lately in the detecting department. Need I remind you of the accident on the mountain?"

I thought about this and Craig's revelation that a guy had leased the truck that bumped me off the road. Oh. Crap. I'd forgotten to share this new development last night with Romero—if he didn't already know. Say this news was true, that would eliminate Susan from causing the car crash.

"Stop being a drama queen. You wanted to come today." I grinned and wiggled my toes, liking how comfortable my new, somewhat expensive, shoes felt. "And nobody's dying. You may lose a finger or two, but nobody's dying."

Max spread his fingers, then whimpered and clutched them to his chest.

I shook my head. "What happened to wanting to be my bodyguard a few months ago?"

He ripped off his shades and gave me his deadpan stare. "If you remember, I wasn't exactly volunteering for the job. I thought Mr. Long Arm of the Law might be interested in protecting your fragile boo-tay."

"He's not here. You'll have to do." I patted my bag. "Anyway, no need to worry. I've got my arsenal right here."

"That's a relief." He slid back on his shades.

We were approaching the island when my cell phone chimed. I yanked it out of my bag and plugged my other ear.

Blair's voice came on. "Arsenic was definitely present in Sister Madeline's hair."

My blood pounded. "You're certain."

"Judging by the tests, arsenic was used consistently and in small doses. The autopsy report should confirm this."

"What's going on?" Max asked when I clicked off.

I shushed him, then wandered to the window and called Romero. "I heard from Blair," I said when he picked up. "Sister Madeline's hair contained arsenic."

"Forensic's already on it. According to the medical examiner, fat from the sausage in the digestive system would've sped up the toxic effect. Alcohol's known to do the same thing, but there was no trace of alcohol here. The ME estimates time of death around two-thirty."

"Then she *was* murdered."

"Looks like it. We've had the cook detained for questioning all morning."

"The *cook*. Ruby?"

"That'd be the one."

"Sure, her cooking's horrendous, and maybe the odd resident has stomach ulcers because of it, but that doesn't make her a killer."

"Further questioning will determine that."

"You're barking up the wrong tree."

"We'll see."

"Fine. I also have news about the vehicle on the mountain."

I pictured him behind a messy old desk, mulling this over. "You mean it wasn't big, black, and loud?"

"You may pay for that comment later."

"I look forward to it. Tell me your news."

"It was a Toyota truck." I gave him the dates and dealership where it was leased.

"Impressive. We've got the report from the dealership. By the way, the only prints on the rosary were yours and Sister Madeline's. By all accounts, the beads belonged to her."

"That means someone stole them and went to the trouble of mailing them to me from Stockbridge."

"That's what it means. Listen, there's a deranged person out there who has it in for you." He paused. "Where are you anyway? It sounds windy."

"On my way to Martha's Vineyard."

"Let me guess. You're not shopping for hand-blown glass or saltwater taffy."

"You guessed right."

"Would it matter if I said turn around?"

"Probably not. I wouldn't know the first thing about hijacking a ferry."

"You could always convince them with a perm rod or two."

"Oh, ha. That was a joke, right?"

"Just be careful."

I rang off, and we docked at Vineyard Haven.

"What was that all about?" Max wanted to know as we shuffled toward the exit.

"They're detaining Ruby for questioning about Sister Madeline's murder."

"Why?"

"Because they found arsenic in Sister Madeline's system, and she died roughly three hours after eating lunch."

"So? Is Ruby the only one capable of poisoning someone?"

"My point exactly. And what about motive? I can't see the appeal for a cook to knock off an old nun. Plus, Sister Madeline didn't make it down to many meals. Especially near the end."

"Which means someone had to take up her food. Someone who could've regularly salted her meal with arsenic."

"Correct."

"Who delivered her meals?"

"Hillary did the day of her death."

"She's regal and lovely. Strike her off."

"Max, this isn't a beauty contest. Attractive people are still capable of murder."

"That's what it means in *my* books."

We stepped onto shore, and Max's color returned to a healthy shade. "Do you have any other ideas?" he asked.

Before I could answer, a little girl plowed into Max, squealed at her mistake, and ran off, turning around to stick out her tongue.

"Did you see that?" He stuck out his tongue back at her.

I grinned. "She's a kid."

"That's no excuse."

"Right. Why don't you chase her down while I do what I came here to do?"

He gave the kid a final squinty eye, then threw his hands on his hips. "Sarcasm doesn't become you."

I looked heavenward and counted to three. "Come on."

Chapter 15

We ambled the cobblestone streets, the smell of fries and warm fudge overpowering the odd whiff of raw fish. My phone wouldn't pick up a signal once we docked, so I asked around for directions to the Hewitts' street while Max gazed through store windows. He stopped at one shop that had huge colorful glass globes hanging inside. His eyes got big and round. "Friendship balls!"

"Beautiful." I glanced from him to the map I'd purchased.

"I've got to have one."

I whacked the map against my thigh. "What are you going to do with a friendship ball?"

"Hang it. What else?"

"Could we do this later? I don't want to catch the last ferry out."

He waved me off and drifted into the boutique.

I groaned and tucked the map in my jeans. Then I meandered around the store. Not seeing much to tickle my fancy, I stood by the window and watched weekenders jam the narrow street, filling their bags with fishermen doodads and lobster trinkets. Standing still in front of a jewelry shop across the road was a person in dark glasses and a baggy black hoodie. The hood was up, covering the face that was staring straight ahead. I couldn't spot anything else because of the mob, but a familiarity nagged at me.

I backed away from the window, then sidestepped to the door to get a closer look. By the time I reached the storefront, the hooded person had vanished in the crowd.

I swallowed air. Probably a tourist waiting for a diehard shopper to hurry up. I sighed. I knew the feeling. Suddenly, there was a tap on my shoulder. I jumped and spun around. *Max.* I scowled at him for scaring the bejeebers out of me.

His smile was wide, and he held a box big enough to house a fifteen-pound bowling ball.

I huffed. "Did you have to buy the biggest one in the place?"

"Yes."

"Now we have to lug *that* around." Oh Lord. Why had I allowed him to come?

"I'm not asking you to carry it, am I?"

"And don't get any ideas."

"I won't, but see these cut-out handles on *both* sides?"

I slid him a not-on-your-life glare.

"So, that's the way it is." He trampled along. "Sourpuss. You're all accommodating when it comes to your customers, but away from work, you're not so agreeable. I know! You could get a friendship ball, too. Guaranteed to cheer up that disposition. Might even help in the romance department."

"I don't need help. I've got dates coming out the ying-yang. One more date, I'll faint from so much romance."

"You could still use a nicer outlook. I'm sure Jock would agree."

I stopped abruptly. "What does Jock have to do with this?"

Max stopped beside me. "Don't pretend you haven't noticed he's into you. And, girlie, one look at him tells you he's h-o-t, *hot*!"

My face burned. "Jock has enough excitement everyday with his half-naked clients."

"*Ooh*. Your eyes are turning green."

"Are not."

"Are too."

I heaved a sigh. "I'm merely saying I'm not his type. What would Jock want with me when he's got a harem to choose from?"

He looked me up and down. "Maybe he likes the wholesome type."

A moment lapsed while he reconsidered his words. "So, you're not Goody Two-Shoes. You're still the most genuine, caring person I know."

"A second ago, you were calling me a sourpuss."

He tapped the box. "You're multifaceted."

I smiled and started walking again. "Maybe Jock's not *my* type."

"You mean dead?" He trotted along beside me. "Come on, lovey. Wake up and smell the perm solution. Here's a man coming onto you like a stallion onto a mare, and you're whipping on the chastity belt. What's your problem?" He peered over at my poker face, then took a gigantic breath. "*Ohhh*. It's the good detective."

I kept walking.

"I understand fully. With a bod like his, and those blue eyes and black lashes." He sighed dreamily. "I could get lost in those eyes."

I veered off the main street. "Listen, it's been a busy week. I simply want to speak to the Hewitts and get home. Could we put off the fantasizing?"

"Ten-four, Miss Two-Shoes." He trailed behind me, banging his box against his leg. "But you're no fun. Does Mr. Long Arm of the Law know you're a real killjoy?"

"I don't know. Why don't you ask him?"

"Darlin', if I call that sexy cop, it won't be to talk about you."

This is what I got for being an equal opportunity employer.

We wandered a few more side roads and came to the Hewitts' street.

"We've bumbled into Dullville," Max said, facing the Hewitts' clapboard house.

"Shhh. They might hear you."

"So, what if they do? What are you going to say?"

"I haven't worked that out yet."

"Wonderful." He rapped his box nervously against his leg.

I shut him out and walked past two beat-up bicycles leaning on kickstands in the gravel driveway. Suppressing butterflies in my stomach, I stepped onto the single-plank porch and rang the bell. A thin, elderly woman opened the door. She was wearing a tattered dress and scuffed shoes. "Mrs. Hewitt?"

"Yes?" She took a cautious look over her shoulder, cupping her hand to a scar on her neck.

Since I had nothing else planned, I decided honesty was the best policy. I introduced myself and Max and told her we were friends of a nun who had just died, and we were trying to locate the child she'd given up over fifty years ago. I left out the part that Sister Madeline was murdered.

Blanche's mouth dropped open with the news. She recovered quickly when an older man in a soiled undershirt stormed to the door, shoving her aside. Orville, no doubt.

He was bald and had a nose that looked as if it'd been flattened by a steamroller. He was also unshaven, though his stubble didn't hold a candle to Max's. He gripped a coffee mug in his calloused hand, his breath smelling nothing of coffee. His eyes were assessing, angry, and he scrutinized me through glassy corneas. "What do you want?"

I repeated my blurb, then gazed past his shoulders. The house had a rank smell but seemed tidy enough, except for the empty whiskey bottles littering the kitchen counter. I gave a smile I didn't feel. "Could you tell us about Faith?"

"Who?" He belched, then hiccupped.

"The baby you adopted fifty years ago."

"Don't know what you're talking about." Orville wasn't what you'd call a happy drunk. He waved me off and staggered into the living room.

The three of us followed, the tension palpable. I stationed myself beside a worn chair, telling myself to be brave. Max continued banging his box against his leg.

"It's been so long," Blanche said. "We'd forgotten that name."

"Forgotten?" I asked.

The banging sped up, and I turned to Max, tight-lipped. "Could you put that down for one minute?"

He set the box down, huffing loudly.

"She came to us as Faith, but we renamed her after Orville's aunt. Let me find a picture." She lifted a photo album from a wall shelf, dusted off the cover, and opened it.

Orville waved his arm lackadaisically. "Who wants to look at old pictures, you stupid hag?"

The guy didn't strike me as the honeydew-calling type, but this went beyond insulting.

"We couldn't have kids of our own," Blanche said, "so we adopted." She scurried to her husband and opened the album like it was a treasure. He took the book and whipped it across the room, flinging her hand away for good measure.

"I think it's time we leave," Max said in a shaky voice.

"We're not going anywhere." I was surprised at my pluck, but I needed to see this picture.

Orville emptied the last of a bottle into his mug, gulping booze like there was no tomorrow. And at the rate he was going, there was a good possibility there wouldn't be.

Blanche crawled after the album with bruises on her forearm and burn marks on her wrists. She picked up the album, tiptoed over, and handed it to me. I lowered my eyes and gaped at the frighteningly big child with a wart on her chin, staring out at me.

"Evalene?" Max said, wide-eyed over my shoulder.

Blanche gave a hopeful nod. "You know Evalene?"

I frowned at Max in a plea for silence.

"Uh, it says so under her picture," he said.

It's like the wind had been taken out of her sails. She

held her wrists tenderly as we gawked at the photo. Evalene as a kid was not an easy image to fathom. But there she was, sullen-faced, standing almost as big as her adoptive parents.

I thought back to the hooded stranger in the street. The eyes were shrouded, but the chin was distinct, wart and all. My heartbeat quickened. Was Evalene on Martha's Vineyard?

All the similarities to Sister Madeline began to fall into place. Like Evalene's frown that had an unusual curve and dimple between her brows. The frown she gave when I came to, after finding Sister Madeline dead. The same frown Sister Madeline used to give when she was embarrassed about her inability to keep her hair tidy. There were other nagging habits, like Evalene's blatant indifference toward Sister Madeline, her close watch on Sister's apartment, plus, the meal deliveries. Efficient caretaker? Or calculating killer.

Orville brought me out of my stupor. He ripped the album from my hands, then flopped on a chair and leafed through the pages. "What's all this got to do with Evalene?"

I swallowed and it hit me. Evalene was the *girl* Sister Madeline wanted to tell me about. Question was, did Sister Madeline know it? Was this what she wanted to confide in me?

I took a breath before I went on. "Sister Madeline held dear a locket with pictures of her and Evalene as a newborn. Though Sister gave her up, I think she would've wanted Evalene to know she'd passed away." This seemed like a moot point now, since, if nothing else, Evalene certainly knew of Sister Madeline's death. "I didn't come here to upset you."

"Ach." He swilled his drink.

I turned to Blanche. "Did Evalene know about her birth mother? That she was a nun?"

"Yes. She left for good after we told her. Said life was going to get interesting now."

I recalled the repulsive look Evalene always gave regarding Sister Madeline, and my voice caught in my throat. "Meaning?"

"I don't know, but it chilled me to the bone. Evalene could do that to you sometimes."

"More than sometimes," Max muttered.

"After she finished high school, she took the ferry off the island. Never returned."

Orville swayed to his feet. "Didn't like living under our roof. Said we were horrible parents. Ingrate." He belched. "Heard she married some drunken bum, then got dumped." He chugged his drink and stumbled back, narrowly missing the corner of a cupboard. He missed the end table completely, shattering his mug as he landed hard on the floor.

Max shrieked and picked up his box. "Now I *really* think it's time to go."

Orville took a stab at getting up, but gravity had a pull on him. After several attempts, he gave up and dozed off.

"Orville's never had it easy," Blanche said. "He works hard at the fish market. It's a demanding job for someone his age."

That explained the rank smell. I didn't ask why he worked. It was obvious they were barely getting by. We thanked Blanche, and I suggested she use peppermint-flavored toothpaste to soothe her burned wrists.

She didn't bother fabricating a lie. "I'll try that."

I was so depressed when we left I didn't hear a word Max said. He jibber-jabbered all the way back to town, but all I could think about was the life Blanche had endured with Orville. She was either a victim of abuse or else one clumsy woman. Then I thought about Evalene. Was she a victim as well? I couldn't blame her for escaping that life, but how'd she end up at the retirement home?

"Let's eat," Max said. "All that gloominess made me hungry."

We traipsed along the main street, me keeping my eyes peeled for Evalene cloaked in a black hoodie, Max scouting for restaurants. He stopped and pointed over my shoulder. "This'll do."

I turned and looked up at the sign. "Choco-Fudge House? What do you suppose we'll get here? A fudgeburger?"

"Don't knock it. Haven't you seen that new study on dark chocolate? Lowers high blood pressure and stimulates endorphin production. You should load up on that for your next date."

"My endorphins are fine, thank you. And I hate dark chocolate. Blech!"

He set down the box and planted his hands on his hips. "Well? Where do you want to eat?"

I spotted a fish and chips place across the street. "There. It doesn't look busy."

We found a table and ordered fish, fries, clam chowder, and a couple of Diet Cokes.

Max slid his mammoth box on the chair beside us and rested his arm on the lid. "So, Evalene's involvement was what this jaunt today was about."

"A while ago, I would've said yes to that. But somewhere along the case, someone else started to look suspicious."

"Someone like Susan MacDonald?"

I blinked at him in surprise. "How did you know?"

"Remember Monday when we went to get your brush, and Nettie tackled me on the stairs?"

I grinned. "How could I forget?"

"When I was sprawled out on the ground, I looked up at the second-floor landing and saw Susan enter Sister Madeline's apartment."

"Why didn't you tell me this before?"

He shrugged. "I didn't think much of it. Sister Madeline had already been dead a week. But you were intent on this case being a poisoning. Then the next day at work, Phyllis saw your calla lily, and she went on about how deadly they were. I remembered you telling us about the calla lilies in Sister Madeline's apartment, and seeing

Susan go into her room was fresh in my mind. I played with a few scenarios, wondering if Susan could've minced the flower and somehow gotten Sister Madeline to eat it."

I blinked again and exhaled. "That's some deducing."

He shrugged. "But then I figured, naw, Susan is too friendly to be a murderer. So, I eliminated her."

I rolled my eyes. "Naturally." Based on what Craig said about the driver of the truck that had bumped me off the road, I'd already decided Susan wasn't behind the wheel, and therefore likely not the sender of the rosary.

Max tilted his head. "You think Evalene could've killed Sister Madeline? Her own flesh and blood?"

"I think it's a good possibility." I filled him in on my talk with Blair. "Evalene had a jar of warfarin sitting on her kitchen counter. Considering she was no stranger to poisons, and seeing as how arsenic was found in Sister Madeline's system, maybe Evalene hid a jar of that somewhere else."

"Like at work. And sprinkled it on Sister Madeline's food."

"I'd bet on it. Evalene took up Sister Madeline's meals daily. Even if she didn't, she could've intercepted, sprinkled the food with arsenic, then passed off the tray to an unsuspecting person, like Hillary."

Our fish and chips came, piled high on a basket lined with red-and-white checked paper.

"Go ahead," I said, as another waitress brought the clam chowder. "I'll eat the soup first."

"You don't have to tell me twice," Max said, emptying half a bottle of ketchup.

I crushed crackers into the bowl when I caught a glimpse of the hooded person, peeking in the diner at us, hairy wart in full view. "Evalene!"

I grabbed my bag and leaped for the door.

"Hey!" Max shouted. "Where are you going?"

I didn't have time to explain.

"Wait!" I charged in my stilettos down the cobblestone road after her.

Lots of tourists turned around. Not Evalene. She kept running, her G.I. Joe torso not stopping for anything. I hadn't gone ten feet when my heel snapped off between two stones, and *whump*. I fell flat on my face. My bag tipped open, and my perfume and favorite FACES lipstick scattered onto the street, along with my brush and battery-operated clippers. I snatched everything up and threw what I could into my bag, then almost strangled myself swinging it over my shoulder.

Evalene disappeared behind a building. I followed, clippers still in hand, bopping up on one shoe and down on the other.

I rounded the corner of the building, and Evalene barreled into me. I reeled back from the impact, and the clippers sprang to life, hit her chin, and made mincemeat of her wart.

Blood spurted in my face, and I lost my balance and fell. I wiped blood from my eyes and grabbed her by the army boot.

"Let go!" she yelped, dragging my body several feet through a cloud of dust. She kicked away my hand and smashed a store's flowerpot on my back.

I shrieked and arched my spine in agony.

Evalene regained her footing and took off. A second later Max showed up, looking satisfied from his meal, sucker twirling in his mouth, box under his arm. He jerked his sucker loose and gaped down at me panting for air. "What happened to you?"

My eyes stung from blood and dirt, my feet were starting to blister, and my back had taken a beating. If my life were about to end, I was going to make the most of it. I spit out some dirt and scrambled to my feet. "Give me that."

He tightened his grip on the box. "What do you want with my friendship ball?"

"I've got to stop her!"

"Who?"

"Evalene!"

"That was her?" He clung tighter. "I paid two hundred dollars for this."

I poked him in the ribs. "She's getting away!"

"No fair," he squirmed. "You know I'm ticklish."

We saw Evalene trip and struggle to her feet, one hand glued to her chin.

"Oh, all right," he moaned.

I lifted the thick glass globe out of the box and hurled it down the road like a bowling ball. It bumped along the cobblestones, missing a few bystanders, and took Evalene out at the knees. She dropped on top of the globe, and it smashed into a million pieces.

"Strike!" Max shouted.

I hobbled down the road and stooped over Evalene. She was on her back, writhing in pain, blood dripping down her chin. I heaved for air. I really had to get back to Zumba. I plopped on a boulder to catch my breath, arms on my knees.

Max was right behind me. He swiped a piece of glass off the ground and pointed it at Evalene. "You're lying on my friendship ball."

She clenched her teeth real slow. "If you like, I'll roll over. You can *pluck* it from my *ass*!"

"That's okay." He cringed. "It's yours now."

Tourists gathered around, staring at us like we were a Barnum and Bailey act. Evalene scowled at the crowd, then narrowed her eyes on me. "I knew you'd show up here first chance you had."

I was still panting. "Why'd you do it, Evalene?"

"Do what? Kill my mother? End that worthless repairman's life?"

"Killing Sister Madeline's a good place to start."

She reddened, and a look of grief crossed her face. "She had to pay for giving me up. For what I lived through." She wrenched a piece of glass from her backside and stabbed it in the ground. "How could you understand? Did you grow up in a house of horror? Have alcoholic parents?" She shook in anger. "Were you beaten as a child,

Miss Beaumont? Beaten until you wished death would come?"

"No," I said, softly.

She curled her fingers around the collar of her hoodie and ripped it away from her neck, revealing long, jagged scars on her chest. "This is only half of what that lecherous animal did to me. One night, I took his fishing knife and threatened to kill him if he ever touched me again. Then I left."

Raw misery reflected in her eyes, and I pitied her for living in that madhouse. I waited a moment, then asked, "How did you find Sister Madeline?"

"That poor excuse for a mother told me where she was." She leaned over and spit out blood. "I wasted half my life, living in that nun's shadow while she stayed sheltered on that mountain. Kept tabs on her, so to speak." She gave a laborious sniff, her chin smeared with blood. "Then I learned she'd moved to Rueland Retirement. It took a while to get a job there, but I did. This was my opportunity."

"To slowly poison her," Max added.

"I like to think of it as tormenting. Like how I was tormented all those years as a child!" Her voice was hoarse from emotion. "She *abandoned* me! What kind of mother does that to her child?" She wiped her eyes. "Not only did she reject me, but she went to work at St. Gregory, giving other kids the love I was denied. She didn't deserve to live."

Words stuck in my throat, everything suddenly clear. "You followed me down the mountain."

She took a measured breath like she was trying to calm herself. "I was certain you'd go there. Especially after Susan had mentioned your conversation about the convent."

I remembered dropping the prayer card in front of Susan on Monday, and how our conversation had rolled around to Sisters of the Divine. *Thanks, Susan.*

"Calling your salon confirmed it. I learned you were at

work Tuesday. But when I called first thing Wednesday to book an appointment, chatterbox behind you said you were gone for the day."

I glared over my shoulder at Max.

"Well? How did I know it was her?" He gnawed on his fingernail.

Evalene smirked. "I'd already rented a vehicle in case my crapola car was recognized."

"But a man leased the truck," I said.

She didn't seem fazed by this news. "Must've been the ball cap that threw them."

"Not to mention the whiskers and linebacker's body," Max mumbled.

"What about ID?" I asked. "Driver's license."

She shook her head in disdain. "I was on the street when I was a teenager, Miss Beaumont. Getting fake ID isn't hard." She dabbed her chin. "I wanted to believe you were paying your respects to the nuns, but when I saw you exit the convent, I couldn't predict what you might have said inside." She tightened her lips. "I'd just mailed that rosary, too, hoping you'd back off. But you were becoming a real pain. An accident seemed the only way to be rid of you for good."

I imagined Evalene sealing the rosary in an envelope, and a shiver sliced through me. "I take it you also painted my door last night."

She grinned. "You like fat rats, Miss Beaumont? I have several butchered at home."

Max wiggled his eyebrows up and down as if to say Evalene was certifiable. He wouldn't get any argument from me. "What about Guido?" I asked.

"Ha. Day after Mommy Dearest died, I was tearing my office apart. I'd gone through her mail but couldn't find where I'd stashed it."

"Opening someone else's mail is a federal offense." Max pointed his sucker at her. "You could go to jail for that."

Evalene stared right through him, likely unconcerned.

"I enjoyed keeping tabs on her, seeing who she contacted, where her interests lay." She puckered her lips, and her eyes got that slitty look. "Then that oily turd Guido showed up to install new thermostats. I let him and his dirty toolbox in one of the apartments, then came back to my office and found the mail I'd been searching for. I resealed the envelopes and slipped them back on Sister Madeline's bedroom dresser. That's when I saw the rosary. I pocketed it as an afterthought."

She yanked out another shard of glass and tossed it by her feet. "I might've taken the rosary, but I wasn't a born thief. Not like Guido, eyeing the seniors' valuables like he did. And when he thought I wasn't looking, he stole loose change in one of their apartments." She coughed. "This past Thursday morning, he was back to finish the wiring in Sister Madeline's apartment. I went to check on him, and he said he'd found something I'd want, and I could have it for a price. If I didn't cooperate, he'd tell everyone the secret." She shuddered. "I didn't know what he'd found. But I'd had too many secrets in my life. There was no way Guido Sanchez was going to blackmail me."

"So, you killed him." The something Guido had referred to was obviously the treasure he wanted to tell Phyllis about. The oily turd.

A *waft-waft* of a helicopter drew near, but Evalene didn't seem to notice.

"I asked Guido to reconsider," she said, "but he wasn't feeling too magnanimous. Nobody saw him come in that morning since everyone was at fitness class. The fool even parked his truck a block away, complaining he couldn't find anything closer. It was perfect. I choked the life out of him and locked him in Sister's apartment. I went home after my shift, then snuck back that night while the movie was playing. I was going to dump him in the elevator and throw his skinny body in the river. But you showed up again, so I hid in Sister Madeline's apartment with the body until everyone had gone to bed."

I winced inside, remembering the muffled sound that night inside the apartment.

She looked over my shoulder in alarm and hastily crawled to her feet. She staggered a few yards but didn't get far when Romero and the cavalry closed in.

Romero knelt by my side, and the uniforms seized Evalene and hauled her away in handcuffs.

A sigh escaped from the crowd. I was just glad the whole ordeal was over.

I watched the mob disperse, then took in Romero's brown sports jacket, Reeboks, and tight-assed jeans, hugging his thighs. Macho and entirely mouth-watering.

"You look pretty rough." He tugged one of my pigtails. "You all right?"

I nodded, blinking from his face that was two days beyond a five-o'clock shadow, to my scrapes, my dirty white top, and my irreparable shoe.

"I'm fine," Max said. "But your girlfriend here stiffed me with the bill."

Romero smiled at Max, then shifted his gaze back to me. "The cook told us everything. From Evalene delivering the meals, to Ruby witnessing her sprinkling food with what Ruby thought was salt. But it wasn't salt, and because Evalene did it in secret and never put the shaker back, Ruby got suspicious. That's when we moved in. We found arsenic locked in Evalene's office. Tests will confirm the poison." He shook his head. "This had been going on for months, if not years. With arsenic building in the nun's system and cancer killing her at the same time, she didn't have a chance."

I got to my feet with Romero's help. "So how did you know to come here?"

"While Ruby was giving her statement, we impounded the truck and dusted for fingerprints. Evalene's were all over it. Guess she finally slipped up. Plus, we resurrected her old file. Found mostly petty stuff. But when we connected the adoption, her past life on the streets, her job at the home, and Ruby's account, I figured you were onto something." He grinned, and tiny lines creased the corners of his eyes. "And because I have an innate sense where you and trouble are concerned, I didn't want to wait for the ferry to get here. So, we brought in a helicopter."

Max *ahh*-ed with a loopy smile, and I was trying to decide if I'd been insulted.

Romero wiped a smudge off my nose. "How'd you suspect her?"

I didn't go into my previous suspicions about Susan. What was the point? "It was a few things. The calla lilies. The warfarin. Plus, the contemptuous look she always gave whenever Sister Madeline's name was uttered."

"A look?" I could tell he was trying his damnedest not to roll his eyes.

"Okay. Maybe it's not a smoking gun, but it's what I noticed."

He rubbed his neck in frustration, something I was getting used to seeing him do. He lowered his arm and sighed, his stare long and hard. I didn't know what he was thinking, but every part of me was overheating under his scrutiny.

He reached into his jacket and pulled out my broken heel. "What are we doing with this?"

I gazed down at my ruined shoe. For once, I had no answer.

"And that's your bad ankle."

I ignored his reference to the mountain accident and bopped up on my heeled shoe. "It's fine."

"Yeah?" He slid his arm under my legs and swooped me up.

There was a delightful sigh behind us, and we both turned to stare at Max. "Maybe you should carry him," I said. "He's had a rough day."

It was after ten when I got home, tired, dirty, and sore. The most energy I had was to shower, fill Yitts's bowl, and hit the hay. I was shutting off all the lights when I saw the answering machine blinking. I pressed play, dropped on a chair, and heard Twix's voice.

"Where are you when I need to talk? I wanted to tell you what I discovered last night." She giggled. "It has to do with J.D. And guess what? I'm no longer afraid of bikes!"

I sat up. Twix liked to have fun, but she wouldn't have done anything she'd regret. Would she? She was happily married and a mother of two. Unfortunately, Jock could be persuasive, and now more than ever, I questioned his moral standards.

A hard knot punched me in the stomach. Twix had daycare in the morning, which meant it was too late to call now. Anyway, what would I say? Stay away? You're married? He's taken? Right. Jock didn't belong to anyone. So why was I aggravated? I mulled this over. Tomorrow I'd get to the bottom of this. Desirée would have to come clean.

Chapter 16

First thing Monday morning, I called Bruno's Garage and learned my car was good to go. Now to phone my father to see when I could swing by so we could pick up my car. The cruiser had been an experience, but I missed my yellow Bug.

I also knew my mother would be waiting to hear about my date with Harold. Since there was no way around it, I'd tell her the truth. I gave it a shot. It didn't work out. *C'est la vie.*

I called their number, and my mother said my father took Mrs. Shales to Hillary's for a visit and was buying kielbasa at Kuruc's. Kielbasa was a staple in my parents' home, so that didn't surprise me. But I smiled at the news that Mrs. Shales was again in contact with Hillary—a woman who, after having one brush with the law, was again innocent, despite earlier doubts. Seemed their friendship would last forever.

My smile faded when I thought of my own friend Twix and this thing with Jock—if it was a thing. I glanced at the clock. Already eight-thirty. Twix would be up to her eyeballs in her morning routine with the daycare kids. On top of which, Mondays were her busiest day of the week. I'd have to wait until later to find out what happened with J.D.

I took a deep breath and told myself to chill. Everything and everyone would be fine. Twix. Mrs. Shales. Hillary. Ruby. Even Phyllis would live to tell the tale from this ordeal. Now that Evalene was in custody, the world as I knew it would return to normal.

This meant I had all day to concentrate on other things. Like buying groceries for one. There was zilch in the fridge, and I'd polished off my mother's leftovers days ago. I'd get groceries right after I visited the hospital kids and picked up my car. Thank goodness I had nothing booked at Rueland Retirement. I didn't think I could handle a morning there, rehashing the case.

I ate a banana for breakfast and looked outside, noting gray skies. Perfect. Damp weather equalled unruly waves. I squashed mousse through my hair, shook my head, and scrunched the ends. It looked wild, but after what I'd been through yesterday, kinky waves were nothing.

I went heavy on the makeup to match the wild hair, then dressed in a partly leather black top and fitted black pants. I slipped on my biker-chick ankle boots, took the garbage out to the road, and backed out of the driveway.

I did my usual routine at Rueland Memorial and left relatively unscathed. Only half a dozen hair extensions tangled my hair, and black nail polish covered my nails. By the time I arrived at my parents', I had most of the hair extensions pried off my scalp. The black nail polish I kept. It went with the outfit.

"Where's the funeral?" my mother asked, when I arrived at her door.

"There's no funeral." Thank the Lord.

"You should be in bright colors with the murderer being caught."

Evalene's arrest had made the news, and my mother had a point.

She marshaled me into the kitchen that smelled of bacon, toast, and coffee. "Want me to scramble you some eggs? Or there're pancakes. And juice."

I was starving. "Juice and pancakes are good. Thanks."

She served me and a second later disappeared down the hall for her sewing kit.

I turned and watched her go, then ate my pancakes, thinking about her comment on the case.

Now that Evalene was off the streets, I should've felt at peace that Sister Madeline's killer had been caught. But since I'd gotten up this morning, I'd suppressed a peculiar sensation. Sort of the feeling you get when you leave the house and you think you left the door unlocked, and it nags at you until you march right back to check and see it was locked all along. That's how I felt. Like the door was open. But Evalene was the key, so logically, the door was closed tight. She'd admitted to killing Sister Madeline and Guido. Then why was I bothered?

My mother banged her sewing kit on the table, bringing me out of my reverie. She pulled a clean pair of my father's underwear out from her apron pocket and threaded a needle.

"What are you doing?" I asked.

"Your father has holes."

"So, buy new underwear."

"He likes these." My mother was happy in her life of servitude. Why rock the boat?

She repaired holes, and I ate pancakes, deciding how to bring up the topic of Harold. I'd worked up my nerve to shatter her dreams when she said, "I hear you went out again with that fellow you call Big Man from the car dealership."

"Big Man?" *Darn.* Craig must've blabbed at work to my cousin about our date, and Faren likely told her mother, Lorna, who couldn't wait to spread the news to her cousin, my mother.

"Seems Big Man has a thing for you." She looked up from her sewing. "He told Faren he'd like to swizzle your sticks. What does that mean, dear?"

I rolled my eyes until I could see out the back of my head. "I don't know, Mom. I don't speak baboon. And it's not Big Man. It's Apeman." I gulped my drink.

"Why do you call him that?" she asked. "I'd like to meet him. Why don't you bring him for dinner?"

I snorted juice out my nose. "I'm going to respond to all three comments. Then I don't want you to mention his name ever again."

"You haven't told me his name."

"All the better. First, I call him Apeman because he drags his knuckles on the ground, has hair covering every conceivable spot on his body, and he acts like an ape. Second, you will *never* meet him. And third, the only place I'd like to bring him to is Boston Harbor, with a cement block chained to his ankle."

"Valentine! That's awful."

"Yes! *He is!*"

My mother looked confused. "Then why'd you go out with him again?"

"It's a long story, but the short version is I didn't know he'd be my date."

"Don't you think you're being too hard on him? After two dates, maybe he's softened."

"You aren't listening. The only thing soft on that Neanderthal is his belly. Wait. His brain is soft, too."

She tied a knot in her thread and cut it loose. "Your dad was all macho when I met him. But he softened in time."

Please. Picturing my father in leather pants and a gold chain around his neck was like visualizing Robert De Niro in a tutu.

"What are you going to do about it?" she asked.

"About what?"

"Your situation. You've got men clambering all around you. Like Gibson." She pursed her lips. "Now there's a thought."

"Gibson's a bad thought."

"What about Harold? You haven't told me about your date."

"Mom, Harold's still weaning from the bottle."

"He couldn't have been that bad. I was talking to

Reverend Cullen yesterday at church. He said Harold's had
a rash since Saturday."

"A diaper rash?"

"Sounded like hives."

I thought about Harold's food issues. In my
subconscious, a bell tinkled. Of course, because it was
Harold, it was a bicycle bell, and I had no idea what I
should've been recalling. When we ordered our pizzas
Friday night, he wouldn't have pepperoni, sausage, or even
onions. And God forbid he try a mushroom. "All he ate
on our date was a cheese pizza."

"Whatever it was, I suggested calamine lotion to
Reverend Cullen. It must've worked. He called this
morning. Harold's rash has disappeared. They think it was
the mini California strawberries."

I bit my tongue from making any more baby jokes. The
truth was Harold was sweet. Just not my kind of sweet.

A grin played on my mother's face. "What about Jock?
Why aren't you dating him?"

I squirmed in my chair. "It's complicated, but if he
proposes, I'll inform you."

"I know why you aren't thrilled about any of these
men."

I dropped my fork on my plate and leaned back.
"Okay. I'm game. Let's have your theory."

"It's that detective."

My pulse thumped, and a stupid grin came out of
nowhere. Fighting the grin, I stared at the table, afraid my
heart was going to leap out and land there. "What
detective?"

"The one Holly works with," she said. "The one who
keeps saving your tushy. The one you won't bring home to
dinner."

She had me on all three counts. I avoided her eyes and
picked up my fork. "He's…he's—"

"Special?" She put her needle and thread away, smiling
like she knew something I didn't.

My father poked his head in from the garage. "Ava.

Kielbasa." He tossed her the wrapped meat and looked at me. "Ready?"

Boy, was I.

After I paid Bruno for fixing my car, I settled behind the wheel, sprayed a mist of perfume to rid the interior of oily mechanic smells, then headed for the grocery store. I might've needed healthy food in my cupboards, but I also had a craving for chocolate. *Milk* chocolate.

I liked grocery shopping as much as having a pap test. I hurried along with my cart, throwing in apples and oranges, when there it was again. That odd feeling that something was forgotten, missed. I looked over my shoulder in case someone, like Evalene, was trying to spook me. Ludicrous. She was in custody. Rueland's finest had led her away. I glanced around the produce department and saw a few seniors, a mom and a toddler, and a guy stocking squash. There were no monsters. No Evalene. Still, I was edgy.

I shifted my stare to the left of the produce stocker and stopped dead in my tracks, gaping wide-eyed at a bin of plain white mushrooms. Like the kind on my pizza. The decomposers or fungi Virgil nurtured at Rueland Retirement. The food Harold said killed people.

Wait a minute. Virgil? Mushrooms? Food that killed people? I gulped back the lump climbing my throat and steered my cart closer to the mushrooms. In a trance, I picked up a handful and sniffed their earthy smell. Fear rose inside me. Virgil's compost pile had the same scent. So did the crates on his balcony.

I recalled his statement about table scraps being food for his decomposers, decomposers that were misunderstood. "They give structure to soil," he'd said. Virgil was odd, but had he been using compost to nurture poisonous mushrooms? Were they at the heart of what he'd meant about being misunderstood? More importantly, were they the real cause of Sister Madeline's death? Couldn't be. That would make Virgil a murderer. And he adored Sister Madeline.

I felt sick inside like when I'd discovered Sister Madeline dead. I was focused on the memory and didn't realize I was crumbling the spores in my fingers.

"Excuse me!"

I let out a deafening scream, throwing mushroom pieces in the air. Hand to heart, I turned and glowered at the squash stocker.

He scowled back. "Did you need help?"

I exhaled. "No, thank you. Just deciding which mushrooms to buy."

He scooped up several large portobellos and shoved them under my nose. "Would you like to crush these, too, or do you have a thing for button mushrooms?"

He stomped away, cutting a look over his shoulder that said he could do without people like me.

I glanced around, then stuck out my tongue. So, it wasn't mature. It was his fault for startling me in the first place. I paid for my groceries, made for the parking lot, and unloaded bags in the trunk, head down, thinking about Virgil's breeding ground. I hoisted a 24-pack of Diet Coke into the trunk when I heard, "Hey, dudette!"

I hit the trunk lid at the sound of Jimmy's voice and almost dropped the carton. "Frick and frack." I rubbed my head and shoved the soda in the car. Then I spun around and glared at Jimmy.

"Oops, sorry." He looked contrite, dressed for the beach in board shorts, a T-shirt, and sunglasses hanging on a string around his neck. Like it was July instead of October. Which reminded me, Jimmy had planned to go to the Cape this past weekend.

I gave my head a final rub. "How'd the windsurfing go?"

"Couldn't make the whole weekend work," he said, "but Sunday was a blast. Best waves ever." He smiled eagerly. "You know the coolest thing? I was skipping curls when the waves got all choppy, and this helicopter flew at rocket speed toward Martha's Vineyard. Something was going down, and I don't mean like helicopter rides. What a *rush*." He patted his belly. "But I came home to no grub. Hence, the grocery store."

Jimmy obviously hadn't heard the news on Evalene's arrest, or that the helicopter was the one Romero had commandeered. For a second, I thought about enlightening him on the capture, but I didn't feel like his *dudette to the rescue* remarks. Moreover, I had this unsettling feeling about the case. I slammed down the trunk lid and motioned toward the grocery store. "There's a guy in produce who'd love to hear that story."

Jimmy nodded in the same direction. "Yeah? Rock on. Hey, speaking of the Rock, how is that dude?"

"I take it you're referring to Jock."

"Like Jock the Rock, man." Jimmy got that faraway look. "I was selling tickets the other day down at Boston Harbor when I saw him stunt-doubling in that pirate movie *Caribbean Gold*. There's more to that dude than meets the eye. Cutting hair by day, stunt work by night. The guy's cryptic, like Superman. But I can dig it."

Sheesh. Did everyone know about Jock's movie role?

"I lost track of time, but later he blew past me on his Harley with this screaming chick on the back."

My heartbeat almost stopped. "Screaming chick?"

"Yeah, like ear-splitting. I thought the sky was falling. Weird thing is, it took me back to high school. Like I shoulda known that voice."

I heaved Diet Coke on the counter and hauled groceries into the cupboards, my mind on what Jimmy had said. So, Jock took Twix home. *Of course*. He was obviously the stuntman who'd given her a ride a week ago, since he was "going to Rueland anyway."

J.D. *Ooh!* He'd get J.D. from me, flirting with a married

woman. I dialed his cell number. Nothing. Darn. We'd talk, if I had to strap him down to do it. My palms got sweaty imagining that. I swiped them on my pants and rammed olives in the fridge. Then I grabbed the phone again. I had more important things to think about than Jock de Marco.

I had to tell Romero I was heading to Rueland Retirement to speak to Virgil. I was hoping to avoid going there today, but my anxiety level was rising, and I had to deal with this sooner than later.

I called Romero's cell and got voicemail. Shoot. I needed to talk to him *now*. I dialed the station, and Shredder started by saying it was Romero's last day in court. "So, how's the hair biz?" he asked. "You ever want to change careers, I hear they're hiring at the bowling alley."

Sarcasm from Shredder was the last thing I needed at the moment. Anyway, I had nothing to feel ashamed of. So what if I used a friendship ball to take out a murderer. It worked, didn't it?

"Let Romero know I called," I said, choosing the high road. "Tell him I'm heading to Rueland Retirement to speak to Virgil."

"Will do."

Shredder wasn't a bad guy, but he had a thing or two to learn about how to treat a lady. Between my anxiousness and the confrontation, I felt a chocolate attack coming on. I banged cupboard doors and poked my head in the fridge like a mouse after cheddar. Nothing. No German Chocolate Cake. No brownies. No chocolate muffins. And my mother's chocolate chip cookies were *finito*. I just put away a bunch of groceries, and I had nothing with cocoa in it. I smacked my hand against my forehead. How stupid could I be? Must've been the infuriating encounter with the produce guy that threw me off the chocolate trail.

I stuffed the carton of soda in the fridge, and two cans rolled out, plunked on the floor, and fizzed by my feet. Great. What else could go wrong? Yitts cautiously stepped into the kitchen and licked the floor. I gently pushed her aside, wiped up the mess, and placed the cans in the sink to deal with later.

I arrived at Rueland Retirement and pulled up behind two police cars parked by the curb. Had Romero already gotten my message?

I stood outside the huge oak door, my nose twitching, my stomach wound tight. I clenched my hands into fists. *Everything's going to be fine. Just get it over with.* I walked inside and met Susan MacDonald doing traffic control in the foyer. Police had taken over Evalene's office, and seniors loitered about. Romero was nowhere to be seen.

Susan shook her head at me. "Everything's topsy-turvy with Evalene gone."

I set aside my unease and watched two cops haul boxes out of Evalene's office and another carry out a spare pair of her army boots. I didn't know if Evalene would need her boots where she was going. But I did know justice was being served for her part in all this.

"Is there anyone who can step in?" I asked.

"That would be me. We're having a meeting with the owners tomorrow." She flipped through half a dozen envelopes in her hand. "On a cheery note, I'm supposed to give you this." She handed me a white envelope with my name written on the front.

I stared at the envelope, the rosary delivered in another white envelope still fresh in my mind. I swallowed. Ridiculous to think like this. It was probably a lunch invitation. I stashed the envelope in my bag to open later, and Susan apologized, saying she was needed elsewhere. "Between answering questions for the police, and this event"—she waved the envelopes in the air—"I don't know if I'm coming or going."

"That's fine," I said. "I came to see Virgil Sylas."

"Virgil? He went out a while ago." She bit her lip. "Or

did he? Like I said, it's been crazy. With the crime scene tape now up on Sister Madeline's door, I can't even water her plants." She gave a small smile. "I got in the habit when she was sick, and now with everything that's happened, I should clear them out." She shrugged. "It's just they gave me a reason to feel her presence."

I nodded, eyes down. Max was right. How could I have suspected Susan of murder when she was genuine and caring? Hadn't she even filled in for Paula, the night manager, when she was home with a sick child? I straightened and told myself I was merely following leads. Nobody said detective work was easy.

Since Susan couldn't recollect Virgil's steps, I hiked up the staircase, turned the corner, and went down the hall to his apartment. I stood outside his door and glanced down at my trembling hands. *Stop it. If he's home, you'll have a friendly chat. THEN you'll tell him you suspect him of murder.* I cracked my knuckles and knocked on the door.

There was muttering and movement inside. Finally, the door opened, bringing a blast of warm air into the hallway.

My eyes widened. "Nettie?"

"You were expecting Martha Stewart?"

"No, I was expecting Virgil. Is he here?"

"Left a while ago. I thought you were cutting his hair. Anyway, he let me in since my apartment's colder than one of them ice hotels. Virgil's pad is the only place they got the temperature right. With Guido dying, it'll be eons till they get that straightened out."

I was already at the corner when she shouted, "Did you get the invite?"

I cried yes and flew downstairs. Virgil was up to something, and I wasn't going to stop running until I found out what it was.

Chapter 17

I didn't know why Nettie thought I was cutting Virgil's hair, but I went down a floor to the petite salon in case he was waiting for me. He wasn't there, so I searched the rest of the home. I even checked around the compost pile since Rival was sleeping out back. The shovel was propped up against the side of the house, and the pile had been freshly stirred. I didn't know what to deduce from this, but Virgil's whereabouts were gnawing on me. Had the search of Evalene's office scared him off? Did he finally crack under the strain of Sister Madeline's death? Did he flee Rueland? The USA?

Maybe Evalene was guilty of Guido's murder, but I was sure Virgil was responsible for Sister Madeline's. What I didn't understand was why he did it when he seemed devoted to her.

I looked around, pondering what to do next. The police cars were gone, Virgil had disappeared, and I was sitting on a time bomb. I remembered the envelope Susan had given me and pulled it out of my bag. It was a wedding invitation from Nettie Wisz and Wit Falco. I sighed with satisfaction. Maybe their wedding was the silver lining in all this. I'd go, if I survived the case.

I shoved the invite back in my bag and got in my car. Waiting for Romero to get back to me was torture, but I couldn't sit and do nothing. Best thing to do now was to clean the shop. Better than driving myself crazy with worry, or waiting for the phone to ring.

First, I stopped at the 7-Eleven and bought two big Hershey bars. My stomach was in knots, and I didn't have a huge appetite, but there was a lot to be said for sugar and cocoa at a moment like this. I put the car in gear, took Broadway to Montgomery, and sucked on a chocolate slab.

I looked at the car clock, my mind coming back to Twix. I pulled over to call her, but it was almost two. She'd be playing dress-up or finger-painting by now. *Face it, Valentine. You're not ready to hear the J.D. discovery.* Right. I *wanted* to hear it. I wanted every sordid detail, but I wanted to hear it from Jock first. I needed him to look me in the eye and tell me he was having an affair with my best friend. Yeah, that's what I wanted. I pulled back into the lane. Who was I kidding? I wanted to hear no such thing. Plus, if Jock gave me his smoldering look, I'd pee my pants.

I inhaled more chocolate, stomped into the shop, and armed myself with disinfectant. I scoured Jock's station, muttering miserably to myself. I tried to concentrate on cleaning, but my eyes kept seeing him in his puffy pirate shirt and eye patch.

I whipped the wet cloth in the sink, my heartbeat thumping in my chest. Even with Jock's secretive side and all the movie business, I'd gotten used to having him around. I looked forward to seeing his perfectly sculpted face, hearing his low voice, smelling his exotic scent. Right. Here was the million-dollar question. Was I going to risk letting him go?

I heard the back door open, and a second later Jock came around the corner, looking like a Greek god in a loose tank top and running shorts. Wonderful. Just the person I wanted to see.

"What are you doing here?" he asked, sweat running down his shiny pecs, dripping off his hardened nipples.

I swallowed thickly. "Cleaning." I held up my wet rag, trying not to show I was flustered by the sight of him, especially since I'd been thinking of him.

"Want help?"

A short hysterical laugh escaped. "No." I lowered my voice. "Almost done."

He raised a disbelieving eyebrow and walked toward me. Slow. Steady. Self-assured. His eyes were so intent on mine I thought he was going to devour me with one blink. "You sure?"

I nodded, biting down on my lip, ignoring the flash of heat tearing through me. "What about you? What are you doing here?"

"I was going for a run. Saw your car." He grabbed a towel and wiped his chest.

Meanwhile, I gawked at the anchor-and-rope tattoo on his left bicep. I knocked back some air, trying to remember over the past few weeks when I'd seen this baby before. Guess I hadn't. His huge biceps had always been covered. But I imagined it was from his navy days.

"Is it fixed?" he asked.

I looked from the tattoo to his face. "Uh, yeah. All pistons chugging." Or whatever it is pistons do.

He grinned and strolled to the shampoo sink. Aiming the hose at his mouth, he chugged water back like any Greek god would. Then he soaked his hair, letting water run down his neck. My throat went bone dry, but I wasn't going anywhere near him *or* the hose.

"You ran here from Cambridge?" I asked.

"I was returning something to a friend's in town. She let me park at her house."

Sure. I widened my stance and crossed my arms, and he shut off the tap like he knew he was headed for a confrontation.

"What happened Saturday night?" I asked.

He towel-dried his hair, blinking at me like he couldn't believe his ears. I almost couldn't believe my own. I took a moment to rethink my attitude. Did I have any right prying into his private life? Damn right I did, when my best friend was about to throw away her marriage.

I carried on with fortitude. "To begin with, you owe me an explanation about your other job. I saw you in Boston. What gives?"

He shrugged. "I do stunt work in my spare time."

"Why didn't you tell me when I hired you?"

"I didn't think you'd employ me if you knew I was here to film a movie."

"You were using me, this job." Candace's ugly voice echoed in my ears.

"No. I enjoy hair." His gaze intensified. "I wanted to settle once I found a salon I liked. Plus, it's been my experience when people know the truth, they act strange around me. Like I'm a movie star. I don't need or want that. I don't even use my real name. I don't want people making a connection."

Admirable. I told my heart to settle down. Star or not, he had enough women falling at his feet. "What name do you go by? J.D.?"

He shook his head. "Think of me as Jock. The other doesn't matter."

Would this guy ever stop being a mystery? "I don't get it. Your main ambition was to become a stylist?"

He tilted his head back, laughing so deep, the room vibrated. "My dream was to be in the U.S. Navy. We lived near the ocean, and the big ships enticed me."

"But you were born in Argentina."

"Yes, but my father was American. Built ships. Went to Argentina and fell in love with my mother. After they married, he traveled back and forth to the States while my mother ran a salon back home. When I was a kid, I helped in her shop. Swept floors, shampooed hair, made a few bucks in tips. Even learned how to cut hair. It wasn't bad, but when I turned twenty, I had an urge to see the world."

"And the stunt work?"

"I was a firefighter as part of a Special Operations unit. My ship provided fifty percent of the air support for the

Afghanistan troops. One day, we got word permission was granted for a Hollywood crew to film a movie scene on board. Half our squad was on land. I was recuperating from a flesh wound on my stomach when one of the actors accidentally went overboard."

I silenced a tremor, recalling the crescent-shaped scar on his ribs, hidden under his tank top.

"I dove in the water and saved the guy's life. Next thing, the director was sizing me up, asking me to jump overboard again. This time for money. I wasn't interested and told him so."

"But you did in the end."

"Yeah, kind of hard to ignore a request when a three-star admiral's breathing down your neck. I did it, found I liked it, got a heap more offers, and had to make a choice."

"You chose the movies."

"It was a hard choice. Then my mother got sick, and I needed to help her out. I couldn't do that on a ship halfway around the world. After my term was up, I came home. Eventually, she got back on her feet. I took in more professional hair training, kept my options open in stunt work, and here I am."

"Pro stylist, movie stuntman, ex-navy fireman."

"Impressed?"

"I know *someone* who is."

"She wouldn't, by any chance, have a good set of lungs."

"You know her? She knows *you* by J.D."

He put up his palms. "And my full name and that I work for you. There was some confusion at first, but I had a feeling Desirée was your friend Twix." He grinned. "You become like family on a movie set. Desirée reminded me of my kid sister." He gestured to the back entrance. "That's where my bike is. She forgot her jacket at the party Saturday."

Relief washed to my toes. "Then you're not involved with Twix?"

His grin got wider. "Would being involved with another woman have bothered you?"

I fidgeted, not sure what the right answer was. But I did know one thing. Jimmy was right. Jock was cryptic. How was I ever going to get used to *that*?

I rolled into my driveway at three-fifteen. Kids hadn't yet trickled home from school, Mrs. Calvino was likely raiding the 7-Eleven for tobacco, and Mr. Brooks had the chainsaw shrieking somewhere in his backyard.

I climbed my porch steps, feeling bloated from the two candy bars under my belt. God gave me a small frame, but gorging chocolates was a no-no. If I gained weight I'd have to lose it, which meant fewer meals at my parents'—which also meant no grilling about boyfriends or blind dates. Could I handle the sacrifice?

I tossed my bag inside the house, then walked to the road for the garbage can. I dragged it back to the garage when something stopped me. I looked around, not sure what was needling me. But I felt spooked. I checked the back door and found it locked. Everything seemed normal in the backyard. Fence. Patio. Lounge chairs. Lawn ornaments. Nothing looked disturbed.

I caught a whiff of mulch and looked across the street where the noisy whine came from. Mr. Brooks and his landscaping. *Relax, Valentine. All that chocolate's made you edgy.* I dusted off my hands and strode back to the front door.

I went inside, took my invitation out of my bag, and set it on the kitchen counter. I stared at it for a moment and considered who I'd ask to be my date for the wedding. The last one I attended didn't end well, and I wasn't sure I wanted to go down the Romero road again. I tapped my fingers on the counter. What about Jock? He'd be respectable, social, and polite. Plus, I'd never seen him in a suit before. I'd seen Romero in a suit, and I could vouch— he looked hot. I was giving it more thought when a fizzing sound caught my attention.

Right. The soda cans. My stomach rumbled unhappily,

and I chided myself again for being such a glutton. Maybe drinking the carbonate would settle my stomach. It couldn't hurt.

I opened one of the cans, and soda spurted up at me. I leaped back and blinked through the sticky mess. *Jeepers.* What a dumb thing to do. I grabbed some paper towels and wiped my face. Then I cleaned the floor for the second time today. While I was down there, I looked for Yitts. Why wasn't she checking the action? I called her name and got nothing. Maybe I failed to notice her nestled on the black beanbag.

I threw the damp rag in the sink and turned the corner into the living room. Nope. Not on the beanbag chair or by the front window. I glanced to my right. Not on top of the piano lid or under the bench. I crept past the piano and got on my hands and knees by the right end of the couch. I looked underneath and found her hiding in the corner. *Huh.* She usually hid when there was unexpected company. Like when Phyllis showed up the other day. Silly cat. I reached for her. "Come on out. Nobody's here."

She growled low in her throat, then I heard movement from my bedroom.

I froze, and Yitts backed up some more. If no one was here, what was that? And how did they get in? I remembered unlocking the front door, going for the garbage can, and then—*Yikes.* Someone must've entered when I was searching the backyard.

Panic skittered to the surface, and suddenly I couldn't breathe. I wanted to crawl under the couch with Yitts, but I was incapable of moving. I gulped some air and peeked under the sofa again. I saw my intruder's shoes at the other end of the couch. Like he'd stepped out from my bedroom. And there was that earthy smell again.

The buzzing saw across the street continued to groan, shutting out my hammering heart.

Run, a voice told me. *Get out of the house.*

I turned to flee but first reached hard under the couch

and grabbed Yitts by the scruff of the neck. Once she was safely in my arms, I darted, head down, for the back door. Halfway there, a sharp prick jabbed me between the shoulders.

I arched my back and yelped, falling to my knees from the sting piercing my skin. Yitts shot out of my arms and scrambled back under the couch.

"Get up and turn around slowly," my intruder said.

I got off my knees, familiar with the voice, worried at what would come next. I took a steady breath, turned around, and faced Virgil. He clutched a paper bag half-filled with something. With his other hand, he shook a pointy, six-inch T-handled garden tool at me. It looked like a spike for poking holes in soil to plant seeds. Now he was going to poke holes in me.

"I couldn't bear to see her suffer anymore." He choked off a sob.

"Her, meaning Sister Madeline?"

He nodded, keeping the tool pointed at me. "She stopped taking her pain meds. Said she deserved the agony after what had happened to her daughter." He rubbed his forehead with the back of his paper-bag hand. "You see, Ms. Beaumont, she knew about Evalene." The bag rattled in his fingers, and his voice quivered. "She'd always had an inkling Evalene was her child, but one day she overheard Evalene complaining to Susan about her past life on Martha's Vineyard, and how Orville was an abusive parent. When Sister Madeline learned about the cancer, she wanted to make amends with Evalene before she died. She wrote letters, explaining the choices she'd made, thinking it'd be easier than saying it in person. But she kept destroying them."

The Pooh phone rang, and we both froze.

A second later, Blair's voice came on the machine. "Romero briefed me on the pathologist's report," she said. "Sister Madeline didn't die solely from arsenic. She would've, given time, but the immediate cause of death was from toxic mushrooms. Amanita Virosa or Death

Angel, which likely sped up the lethal process." She said a few more words and hung up.

Virgil swallowed painfully, his eyes brimming with tears. "She already suspected she was being poisoned. After she ate her meals Evalene delivered every day, there was nausea, fever, and vomiting." His shoulders sagged, and he shook his head. "She was afraid her own flesh and blood was trying to kill her."

It all made sense that this was what Sister Madeline had wanted to share. But I hadn't made it there in time to hear her story. I tried to breathe without guilt over that regret.

"A few days earlier," he said, "I gave her the washed mushrooms. Told her to eat them with her meals." His Adam's apple bobbed. "She didn't know they were poisonous, and I thought it would be in God's hands if she ate them or not." He wiped his tears on his sleeve, then collected himself. "I cared for her. I wanted to help." He met my gaze. "And I want to help you."

This raised the hairs on the back of my neck, since I had a good idea he didn't want to help me grow rhododendrons.

He pulled a handful of white mushrooms from the bag. "I'd like you to eat these. They're from my superior batch."

I gaped at the brown bag. I recalled Jimmy's observation about Virgil sneaking into the cellar with a paper bag days before Sister Madeline's death. Likely, the moment he'd dug up the mushrooms that killed her. Then I visualized the freshly stirred compost pile from earlier.

Fear gripped my chest and sliced down my arms. "No, thank you," I said. "I just ate. Why don't I save them for later?"

"That won't do." He advanced on me. "These are special. They'll take you to the afterlife."

I cringed. Exactly what I was afraid of.

His spike was leveled at my throat, breathing terror into my veins. Blasted Romero. Shredder must've given him my message by now. Hadn't he connected the dots?

"Okay, I'll eat them. But let me get something to wash them down."

This seemed to satisfy him and buy me time. He followed me into the kitchen while I frantically eyeballed for something that could help me.

I edged toward the sink and saw the unopened soda. It wasn't deadly, but if a spray gave him the shock it gave me, it might do. I shook the can, turned around, and flipped it open at Virgil.

Soda spurted all over his face and soaked his clothes. He lost his grip on the spike and fell backside to the floor, mushrooms flying everywhere. I vaulted for the weapon, scooped it up in my hands, and scurried back to my feet. "If you come any closer," I said, pointing it at him, "I'll stab you!"

Right. The only thing I'd ever stabbed was an earring through my pierced ear, but adrenaline was pumping through me at such a fierce rate, brave words flew out of my mouth.

He frowned and wiped his face. "That's not necessary." He snatched a handful of mushrooms off the floor and studied them. "I can't live with it anymore. I never should've given her those mushrooms. She was my only friend." He inhaled like a man taking his last breath. Then he shoved the mushrooms into his mouth.

"*No!*" I tossed away the tool and pounced on him. "You're not going to end your life here." Oh Lord, what would the headlines say? Heaving him into a sitting position, I wrapped my arms around his abdomen, covered my hand over my fist, and thrust up. "You're *not* going to *die!*"

He sputtered and coughed out a mushroom chunk. Then he went limp in my arms.

"No!" I kept my fist tight and repeated the thrusting motion. Sweat rolled down my chest, and my stomach twisted painfully. I didn't think I'd last much longer, but I wasn't about to give up. I gave another push when I heard footsteps on the porch and my name called. Thank God. Romero.

"Hurry," I yelled through the door.

He was at my side in a flash and examined Virgil's airways. Then he pumped his chest. After several tense moments, Virgil came to and spit up.

Romero gave him a few seconds to recognize his surroundings, then spoke to him in a low, professional voice, the one that reminded me why I hungered for him. Minutes later, an EMS truck screeched into the driveway.

"Where are they taking him?" I asked Romero after two medics wheeled Virgil out.

"Hospital. He may have digested some of that mushroom."

The adrenaline rush had ceased, and I was trembling.

Romero pulled me close and smoothed back my waves. "Are you okay? Did he hurt you?"

I relaxed a little and shook my head no. "I'm fine."

"When Shredder gave me your message, I went straight to the retirement home. I ran into Sparks, going through Evalene's office. He said they'd delivered evidence to the station, and when they'd returned, you were gone. Plus, Virgil was nowhere around. One of the residents, Nettie Wisz, said he had a hair appointment. I didn't know if you cut his hair, but I did know you're closed Mondays. I went on a hunch and figured he was heading here."

He paused and looked me in the eye. "From the pathologist's report, we suspected he was our man. I had a feeling you guessed the same thing."

I stared up at him. "Has anyone ever told you you're a smart man?"

This drew a smile that encompassed his eyes.

"This cop, Sparks," I said. "Another Shredder story?"

"No. That's his name."

Oh brother.

Chapter 18

They say love grows, and maybe that's true. I've always been more of a believer in love at first sight, but that's my impulsive nature coming out. No matter how it happens, I *am* a sucker for a happy ending.

I dusted blush under my cheekbones and took a long, satisfying breath. Almost two weeks had gone by since the case ended. The murderers were confined, the retirement home was recovering, and I was at peace knowing Rueland was once again safe. I wished I felt the same about my mother's meddling. Maybe this experience with Harold would teach her to stop interfering with my dating life. One could hope, right?

My hair was in long loose curls and set off my midnight blue dress and audaciously cute spikes. I sprayed a hint of Musk on my neck and posed in the mirror. I wasn't a supermodel, but it's what I had.

I quickly flossed my teeth, since I'd forgotten earlier, and heard a vehicle door slam shut outside. I rushed to the living room and peeked out the window. My heart skipped around nervously. *Stop being so jittery. You asked. This gorgeous man accepted.*

He knocked, and I squeezed my hands tight. *Go for it.*

I opened the door, and my heart leaped to my throat. Romero leaned against the doorframe, one arm behind his back. He was dressed in a tailor-made, Italian-cut black suit, his hair was just-out-of-the-shower wet, and his five-o'clock shadow was already evident, probably since noon. He looked incredibly sexy, and he smelled delicious. Fresh, like Arctic air, but woodsy, like summer.

My thoughts strayed to Jock and *his* tempting scent, and it dawned on me that I cared for both of these men. Maybe more than I wanted to admit. Perhaps time would make things clearer. That was my hope.

Romero's eyes followed the satiny lines of my dress with admiration and longing, and I knew I'd made the right choice in asking him to the wedding today.

With one hand, he spun me around. "God, you have world-class beauty."

Inside, I hugged myself, letting his praise wash over me.

He brought his other arm around and presented me with a red rose. My hairbrush was tied to the stem. "Blair sends her regards," he said. "The rose is from me."

"Thank you. It's beautiful."

He fingered his charcoal and burgundy-flecked tie, pausing to study me. "So is this."

I grinned at the tie I'd purchased at the mall and sent to him by mail. "Well, I couldn't have you walk around out of fashion."

He winked. "And I love the Matchbox tow truck that came with it, and the check—which I tore up." He gave me a reprimanding stare, like I should've known better.

"The tow truck's a reminder that you saved me on that mountain." And captured my heart—even more at this moment.

He smiled at that, stepped closer, and knelt on one knee. He slid a muscular hand down my thigh.

Had I missed something? I froze, too stunned to speak.

He peered up at me, then gently turned me sideways. A second later, he got off his knee and held up a foot-long piece of dental floss. "This was trailing from your derrière."

World-class beauty, all right. "Thanks."

Why were there no bleeps when I was with Harold? No pizza sauce in my hair. No puke on my clothes. Why did these things happen when I was with Romero?

I put the rose in water and told myself to get a grip. Everyone had faux pas. The secret was to keep your head high and act dignified. This wasn't going to ruin my night.

Twinkling lights and pink tulle streamed high over the four corners of the dance floor in Rueland Retirement's recreation room. Chairs for about one hundred were lined in rows. "Moon River" played softly in the background. It wasn't a destination wedding or a wedding on a yacht, but there was something about old-fashioned nuptials that made you feel cozy…reminiscent. Like there was no other place you wanted to be.

Susan MacDonald greeted us at the door and smiled into Romero's eyes like she was in bondage and didn't care if she was ever set free. I knew the feeling. "Nice to see you two under different circumstances," she said.

Romero gave her one of his smiles. Next thing I knew, she was dragging him by the arm, introducing him around while I was left looking for two seats. I grinned, not minding the attention lavished on him. Truthfully, it was flattering.

I found two chairs, then sat down and watched how patiently Romero roamed from senior to senior, shaking hands with one, nodding at another. Yet he didn't forget I was there. He looked over and winked, a faint smile playing at the corner of his lips. Good thing he was thirty yards away. My insides were giddy. If he'd been any closer, I probably would've jumped him.

After a solid ten minutes, Romero joined me. The room filled with guests, some even with good teeth and bones. Hillary smiled and nodded from the front. She looked healthy and well. I smiled back, glad she was here.

Romero's hand softly climbed my spine.

"You're staring at me," I said, without turning my head.

"Get used to it." He took my palm and raised it to his lips.

I was glad I was sitting. At the moment, my legs wouldn't have supported me.

The music faded away, and Reverend Cullen welcomed everyone. A second later, the wedding processional started. Romero held my hand, and everyone waited patiently while Nettie and Wit hobbled down the aisle. They said their "I do's," Nettie chucked her cane, and they smooched. This was probably the first time I'd seen them together without trying to kill each other. Wasn't love grand?

I patted my eyes dry after the ceremony and kissed the bride. "Where's the honeymoon?"

"Disney World," Nettie said. "We're leaving tonight before one of us wakes up dead. If we last through Magic Kingdom, we'll have a safe place to come home to. In fact, the owner is going to run things until they find a replacement for that drill sergeant, Evalene." She wrinkled her nose. "Never could bring myself to trust a woman in army boots."

I had to agree. There was something about Evalene that didn't evoke trust. In the end, I wasn't sure I'd ever understand her reasons for doing what she did, or why she chose to punish Sister Madeline for her horrible upbringing instead of the Hewitts. I guess certain things would remain a mystery. At least it gave me an appreciation for the family I had.

After the catered meal, an aura of stale cigarette smoke drew near, followed by Ruby strutting up to the table.

"Ain't this the cat's meow," she said in her two-pack-a-day voice while pinching Romero's arm. "Do you date all dark-haired beauties?"

Romero looked at her wiry black hair and grinned. "Only the feisty ones."

She hacked out a laugh. "Get in line. Men have always found me feisty." She winked at me. "Seems it's even rubbing off on that daughter of mine."

"Dorothy?" I said. "Is she seeing someone?"

"You could say that. One of them extras from that pirate movie they were filming in Boston brought his dog into the vet's office. Dorothy removed a thorn from its paw. The guy was so taken with her, he asked her out."

I gave a genuine smile. "That's wonderful."

"Yeah. Ends up he's from around here and does bit parts when he's not cooking in his dad's restaurant. Ha. Another thing we have in common. Maybe I should go into business with his dad." She chuckled and looked around. "But I guess I'll stay here. This place needs me."

She rooted around in her tattered evening bag. "I need a smoke." She plucked out a cigarette and whacked Romero's back. "Wanna join me, handsome?"

"You go ahead," Romero said. "We were about to dance."

Joe Cocker croaked "You Are So Beautiful" over the speakers, and everyone piled onto the dance floor. Ruby slipped outside.

Romero secured his arms around my waist, his eyes not leaving my face. Now *this* was a date.

I played with the curls on his collar, his classic looks and virility overpowering me. "When are you going to let me cut your hair?" I asked, gazing into his penetrating blue eyes.

"When you can give me a private appointment."

"Name the time and place."

"You mean we can do this offsite?"

"We can do it anywhere it pleases you."

"Anywhere?" His hands dipped lower, and he squeezed me close. "I love your energy."

The song ended, and he pulled me from the dance floor. "I need to tell you something."

I was all dreamy-eyed from being content. Now he was going to whip me back to reality.

"That night in July at Cynthia's wedding," he said, "when the FBI whisked me away in that helicopter—"

"Yes?" I straightened, remembering the propeller softly

whirring in the distance, adding to what I thought was the romance of the evening. Of course, that was before the helicopter swooped in and took Romero.

"I was needed in an undercover operation. I'd been working with the feds for a year on a case, and we were close to making an arrest." He stared intently into my eyes. "When I left that night, I was taken out of state and holed up in a shack in the woods with two other agents."

He threaded his fingers through my hair, pulled me in, and inhaled. "I couldn't see or touch you. Or let you know I was thinking about you. Hell, there wasn't even time for goodbyes." He leaned back and gave a shrug. "Good thing the neighborhood kid knows to cut the grass and bring in the mail if I'm gone for more than a week."

I smiled sheepishly, thinking about the few times I'd passed by his house while he'd been undercover. I was obviously wrong to jump to conclusions that he was around and avoiding me. And really, I thought playfully, who would want to avoid this face?

"Finally," he said, "everything was in position. Tazotto was at the Red Sox game, and we were ready to move in."

"Wait. Industrialist Levi Tazotto? Killed his mistress? That's the case you were on?"

"Yeah. They just released the full story. Don't you read the papers?"

"Only when I'm in the headlines."

He smirked. "The woman he murdered wasn't his mistress. He was involved in human trafficking. The FBI had been tracking this guy for years. Then I almost screwed things up when I spotted you." He looked deep into my eyes. "You know you stand out in a crowd?"

"*Me.*" I smoothed his cheek. "With that faded ball cap and beard you'd grown, you looked like a mountain man."

He nodded, the humor leaving his eyes. "I caught a glimpse of Max. And the guy on the other side of you."

The omission of Jock's name wasn't lost on me, and for once, I knew when to be quiet.

"I wanted to see if my suspicions were warranted, that

you were involved with him. Then I saw him in your salon and—"

"We just work together."

He considered those four words, then led me back to our table, sitting so close our thighs touched. "I wanted you to know I wasn't letting you go, but I couldn't. I had no choice. That's the consequence of undercover work. But court's done. And I'm back."

I felt a warm glow from his words.

"Two weddings in three months." He glimpsed at the dancing newlyweds. "Think someone's telling us something?"

I smiled at his remark. But my mind wasn't solely on the wedding. "I know the case is done, but I keep thinking of Virgil. He was so distraught."

"His reasons were sincere," he said. "But courts don't like people playing God."

"He didn't know if Sister Madeline would eat the mushrooms. And she wasn't aware they were poisonous."

"Unfortunately, it doesn't change anything. He'll still stand before a judge."

I frowned. "And Evalene? Did she know about the cancer?"

"She said she didn't. We checked with the pharmacy where Sister Madeline got her pills. Their service includes delivery to a shut-in's door, but they hadn't delivered to her in months. It's possible Evalene was telling the truth.

"By the way, we found the item Guido was using to blackmail Evalene. It was a letter the nun wrote to Evalene, explaining why she gave her up. She even forgave Evalene for poisoning her. The letter was locked in Guido's toolbox, which was hidden in Evalene's office. She must've forgotten to search it when she dumped his body in the river."

So, Sister Madeline did complete a letter. But how did Guido find it?

"The story goes, as a young woman, Sister Madeline worked as a maid in the Hamptons for a well-to-do family.

On her way home one night, one of the sons insisted on escorting her. Ended up he wasn't so honorable. He beat and raped her. Told her if she ever said anything, he'd kill her. He was six-five and, according to Sister Madeline, had the body of a warhorse."

Like Evalene.

"She was terrified and didn't doubt his threat. When she realized she was pregnant, she moved away and decided to give up the baby. She pleaded in her letter that Evalene understand she thought she was making the right decision."

I considered this. "In the end, Evalene would've been better off with Sister Madeline."

"Maybe. Sister Madeline was young, had no education, and no family after they learned of her pregnancy. She wanted to spare Evalene the truth and wasn't even sure writing a letter was the right thing to do." He paused. "Sister Madeline had no way of knowing her letter would see the light of day. She'd stuffed it behind the radiator in her apartment."

"How do you know? If Guido was dead, and the letter was in his toolbox…"

He smiled. "Very good, Sherlock. We found another letter with a similar message shoved behind the radiator. Sister Madeline must've made several attempts. Likely, Guido found the first letter when he worked on the heating system after she died. He probably read the letter and slid it in his toolbox, saving it for the right time."

"But why would she have stuffed it behind the radiator?"

"It was near the chair she always sat in. With the heaters not working, she probably stashed letters there when someone was coming into her apartment, unannounced."

I thought of those with easy access. "Susan. Or Evalene."

"Possibly. She also wrote she wanted Evalene to have the locket. We passed it on as requested." His thumb circled the back of my hand while I took this all in.

"At least Phyllis isn't mourning over Guido's death anymore."

He sighed. "The guy was slippery and known to the police. She's better off without him."

"It's still sad. Men don't cluster around Phyllis's feet."

His eyebrows did a subtle lift. "Like they do yours?"

"Who said that?"

"I've seen it for myself."

I gave him a gracious smile and realized the music had stopped, and the crowd had thinned. The newlyweds had been whisked to Logan Airport, and it seemed the night was done.

I bagged my chocolate wedding favor resembling two canes shaped into a heart. Then we strolled to the door.

Reverend Cullen met us on our way out. "Thank you for two weeks ago, Valentine," he said. "Harold hasn't stopped talking about you."

I didn't dare look at Romero. "He's a great guy. I hope his prayers are answered."

"I'm confident they will be," Reverend Cullen said. "We have inside help in that department."

I was conscious of Romero's eyes on my back as we walked away. "Two weeks ago?" he asked. "Harold? Who's Harold?"

A tremor ran through me, but I couldn't see any point in bringing up my catastrophes one might call blind dates. They were what they were, and with any luck I'd see an end to them.

We reached Romero's truck, and he unlocked the doors, then leaned into me, straddling my legs. His breathing was slow and even, his fingers lightly brushing my arms. "If you don't want to enlighten me about Harold, then tell me this. What is it about you that makes me feel so alive?"

My heart soared with anticipation at being kissed by Romero; I couldn't think of an answer.

His eyes turned playful, his voice seductive. "Is it your wit, your sensitive heart, or your stubbornness?"

I was smiling lovingly at the compliments, then jerked my head back at the stubbornness part. "What's that supposed to mean?"

"It means you don't like to listen." He shook his head. "Case in point, the mountain resort. I carried you and your injured foot into the lobby and told you to stay put. When I came back with our bags, I found you hobbling around."

I went to speak, but he put his finger to my lips.

"And when we were stuck in Boston traffic because of that pirate movie, I told you to stay put while I conferred with the cops. When I got back to the car, you were gone."

"That's because—"

"Uh-uh-uh." He pressed his finger against my lips again. "Can we get something straight? Next time I tell you to stay put"—he planted a butterfly kiss on my cheek—"would you listen? I need to know the girl I'm dating is safe."

"The girl you're dating?" A shallow breath escaped.

"That's right."

"Is safe?"

He butterfly-kissed my other cheek. "You heard me."

"I'll do my best."

He grimaced. "Why doesn't that comfort me?"

Other Books in
The Valentine Beaumont Mysteries

Valentine Beaumont is a beautician with a problem. Not only has she got a meddling mother, a wacky staff, and a dying business, but now she's got a dead client who was strangled while awaiting her facial.

With business the way it is, combing through this mystery may be the only way to save her salon. Until a second murder, an explosion, a kidnapping, death threats, and the hard-nosed Detective Romero complicate things. But Valentine will do anything to untangle the crime. That's if she can keep her tools of the trade in her bag, keep herself alive, and avoid falling for the tough detective.

In the end, how hard can that be?

BOOK 3

MURDER, CURLERS, AND CRUISES

In her third fast-paced mystery, Valentine Beaumont leaves Massachusetts's autumn winds behind to board a Caribbean "Beauty" cruise. What could be a fabulous voyage turns desperate when she's joined by her well-meaning family and madcap staff, including hunky stylist Jock de Marco. If things aren't bad enough, Valentine learns dark and sexy Detective Romero is away on a case with his new partner who happens to be a female.

Once the ship sets sail, a feisty passenger is murdered, a drug smuggling operation is afoot, an employee becomes seasick, a family member is kidnapped, events of a hair contest wreak havoc, Jock is irresistible and mysterious, Romero and his partner get too close for comfort, death threats mount, and Valentine is in the middle of it all.

Will this impulsive beautician save the day, or will this cruise turn into another fatal Titanic?

Book Club Discussion Questions

Share these questions with your book club. Enjoy the banter!

1. Who did you feel was the biggest suspect? Why?

2. Who would you rather see Valentine with? Jock or Romero? Which Hollywood star do you see playing their characters?

3. Yitts likes drinking out of Valentine's water cup. What unique rituals does your pet have?

4. How did you feel about Phyllis's return to Beaumont's?

5. Have you ever seen a movie filmed in your town or city? Or know anyone who's had a bit part in a movie?

6. Valentine enjoys wearing cosmetics and is never without some form of makeup. What cosmetic product would you never want to be without?

7. What overriding theme tugged at you the most? *Don't settle for second rate, justice prevails, small people can do big things, or being resourceful with the materials at hand?*

8. What would you like to see happen next in the series?

9. Were there any minor characters you'd like to see brought back in another Valentine Beaumont mystery?

10. What was your favorite scene?

Note To Readers

Thank you for taking the time to read MURDER, CURLERS, AND CANES. If you enjoyed Valentine's story, please consider telling your friends or posting a short review. Word of mouth is an author's best friend and much appreciated. Thank you!

Social Media Links

Website: www.arlenemcfarlane.com

Facebook: facebook.com/ArleneMcFarlaneAuthor/
Newsletter Sign-up can be found on Arlene's Facebook page.

Twitter: @mcfa_arlene

Pinterest: pinterest.com/amcfarlane0990

Arlene McFarlane is the author of the *Murder, Curlers* series. Previously an aesthetician, hairstylist, and owner of a full-service salon, Arlene now writes full time. When she's not making up stories or being a wife, mother, daughter, sister, friend, cat-mom, or makeover artist, you'll find her making music on the piano.

Arlene is a member of Romance Writers of America, Sisters in Crime, Toronto Romance Writers, SOWG, and the Golden Network. She's won and placed in over 30 contests, including twice in the Golden Heart and twice in the Daphne du Maurier.

Arlene lives with her family in Canada.

www.arlenemcfarlane.com

Made in the USA
Coppell, TX
15 October 2020